CW00401094

# OUT ON A LIMB

**Lynne Barrett-Lee**

Published by Accent Press Ltd – 2007
ISBN 1905170068 / 9781905170067
Copyright © Lynne Barrett-Lee 2007

Printed and bound in the UK

Cover Design by Anna Torborg

The publisher acknowledges the financial support
of the Welsh Books Council

This book is dedicated to my beloved nephew, Stephen
Barrett
1987 – 2006

Much loved, cruelly taken, greatly missed.

# Acknowledgements

Spookily, life often imitates art. A few weeks after finishing this novel, for example, I had a bit of major surgery performed on my shoulder, which meant I have spent much of the last year under the exemplary care of a brilliant Orthopaedic Surgeon, Richard Evans, and a lovely physiotherapist, Anne Wilkes.

They were sadly too late to help me with the research for this book, but I'd very much like to thank them both anyway. (Incidentally, I note the timings with particular care; my fictional surgeon, Charlie, being nothing like Mr Evans except in matters of skill and general loveliness, and also a rather naughty boy…)

In the main, though, it's art that's inspired by life, and with that in mind I must also pay homage for inspiration to my children and their friends. In particular to a talented band called The Black Mausoleum, who are, I'm convinced of it, destined for great things. (Just make sure I make the sleeve notes. Okay, boys?)

I'd also, as ever, like to thank my wonderful agent, Jane Judd, and my equally lovely publisher, Hazel Cushion, who continue to support me so well.

Finally, big thanks to my Mum, who, to paraphrase Helen Fielding, is definitely not at all like Abbie's. Except in the matter of telephone events. Sorry, Mum. I couldn't resist it.

# Chapter 1

IT'S NOT EVERY DAY you get given a leg.

'It seemed the perfect parting gift,' my friend Dee explains helpfully, as she presents it to me. 'Kind of symbolic. Losing you is going to be like losing a limb, so we thought we should make it official.'

'I don't know what to say,' I respond, because you tend not to know what to say when someone presents you with a leg, do you? 'Except thank you. This really means a lot. *Such* a lot. I'd have it mounted in the clinic but I'm not sure I should. I might scare away all my patients.'

The leg, which is a prosthetic lower one (complete with ankle and foot, obviously), has been in the orthopaedics outpatient department for as long as anyone can remember, and has always been an object of mystery. Nobody has ever known how it got here or where it came from. It just turned up one day, in pre-history, almost, and no one ever hopped in to claim it. Since then it's been our mascot. Our orthopaedic lucky charm.

And now its mine to take home with me, and everyone's signed it. I'm having to work hard not to burst into tears.

It's pretty grim leaving somewhere when you don't want to go. I don't think I appreciated just how grim it would be until the moment when I took possession of the limb. After all, it was my choice, wasn't it? But it's funny the way parties – such merry occasions – are so good at making people sad. Though understandable, given that it's a leaving party. And given the circumstances of this particular leaving, I guess. Up to now, I've always left what I've left in a state of readiness and expectation. School, university, the PTA, my marriage. With some sadness, of course, the odd regret or two, a trace of apprehension about the future, for certain, but those feelings, up to now, have always been tempered with the thrill of moving on to something new.

We tend not to do grand parties at Highfield Park Hospital. Not unless somebody important's showing up. Like the Queen, or

Prince Charles, or someone famous off the telly. It's said that some time back Bruce Forsyth paid a visit. But it's only a rumour. There's no evidence.

My own leaving party, which has not been graced with any dignitaries bar me, has been taking place in the same outpatient clinic that has been home to the leg all these years. Happening amongst the frayed easy chairs and tired pot plants and coverless copies of *Take a Break* and *My Weekly*, on a floor thinly carpeted with NHS issue carpet tiles, and bound by walls that are similarly, if much more thickly, carpeted, with an aggregate of paperwork that spews from strained push pins in irritable gusts whenever the automatic doors open. Charts of skeletons, charts of muscles, pictures of smiling pensioners, instructions for operating the vending machines, yellowed thank you letters, posters advertising upcoming fundraising activities, children's madly scribbled pictures, and the map of the world with the stuck-on string arrows that lead you to handwritten laminated lists that tell you what vaccinations you need to go where.

And in the bottom right corner of the bottom right cork board, a little yellow rabbit, aged and dusty, which has been attached to the wall by a silver-topped drawing pin, by its ear, for as long as I can remember. Funny to think that the owner of that rabbit is probably in high school by now.

I glance across at it and I wonder if I will miss the sight of that little rabbit as much as that little rabbit must have been missed when it was left here.

'God, God, God,' said Dee, who being my best friend, I knew I would miss a great deal. 'God, how I am going to get through this without blubbing, I really don't know. I just really don't know.'

This was earlier, when we were getting the party food ready, and she was holding a paper plate full of quartered pork pies. We always have pork pies at leaving parties here. I don't know why, but as with much that happens in the outpatient department, it just *is*. Pork pies and Twiglets. Because everyone likes Twiglets. Not much green stuff. Because green stuff almost always gets left. So much for the H in NHS.

'We'll blub together,' I suggested, taking the drum of Twiglets from underneath her arm and picking up a paper cup of breadsticks. 'We'll blub copiously and extravagantly and with absolute abandon.'

She looked stricken. 'Oh, God, Abs, you mustn't!' she replied. 'Once you start I'm done for.'

'Okay, okay! I won't, then!'

It's always difficult to know which tack to take with Dee at present. She put the pork pies down, blew her nose, then picked the plate up again.

'Of course you won't,' she said, almost managing to convince both of us. 'You're so brave,' she added. 'So strong and courageous.'

No, I'm not, I thought. That's piffle. That's what *she* is. Whereas I'm actually being weak-willed and cowardly. If I were strong and courageous I'd be toughing it out. Were I strong and courageous I wouldn't be leaving. But, hey, when you've got to go you've got to go.

And almost everyone came to see me off, which was lovely. My fellow physios, lots of nurses – the whole orthopaedics team, pretty much – the new registrar, Julie, a brace of porters, Will and Phil, Carolyn from the WRVS shop, most of radiology, Karin from reception, Boris from the canteen. And Charles. He came too. We were honoured.

Charles Scott-Downing is a consultant orthopaedic surgeon. He fixes hips and femurs and knees and ankles and shoulders and arms and, well, pretty much any ill-behaved or malfunctioning bone that happens to happen along. He is all those things a consultant surgeon should be. Dashing and handsome, much loved by his patients, respected by his peers, fondly tolerated in his foibles (which are many) by the nursing staff, mothered by the secretaries, swooned over by almost everyone (particularly when in his greens), and a-bit-of-a-babe, all agree. That's the thing about working in a hospital, I think now. It's a whole cross-section of society in miniature. It throws together people from all walks of life.

Throws together *people*. Which isn't always to be wished for. Because that's precisely why I've decided to go.

As well as presenting me with the leg, they've had a bit of a collection. With which they've bought me a beautiful bouquet, an embarrassingly large amount of vouchers to spend in Next, and a 'ME-time' day at EXO, which is a posh spa in the Bay. Two 'treatments' and unlimited use of the facilities, which include all the things a 'me' with some time to kill could want. Which is nice, because I know I'm going to have some. Dee is now sobbing quietly into a paper towel while I attempt to gather enough and suitable words and expressions to make a passable thank you speech.

Julie, the new registrar, makes a speech too. She thanks me for all the help and support I've given her with her research (which makes it sound like I did something clever and important, which I didn't, which makes me go red), thanks me on behalf of everyone present, thanks me on behalf of all the patients who have signed the lovely card she then gives me, and ends on a note of celebration and felicitation, by wishing me luck in my new job at Aches and Pains. Then Mr Scott-Downing, in his greens now, leads the throng in a rousing, if slightly off-key chorus of 'for she's a jolly good fellow'.

Charles Scott-Downing. Who arrived mid-presentation. Who is watching my every move as he sings.

'I hope you don't think you're getting out of here without saying a proper goodbye,' he booms at me from the far side of a table and some chairs, once it's over. Furniture's the thing, I've decided.

He's smiling from over the top of a well piled plate of sandwiches and crisps. Which someone has hastily procured for him. Some men just do that to women, don't they? Mr Scott-Downing is here, therefore it's clearly necessary to procure a plate of sandwiches for him without delay. He is a very busy man and he has come straight from theatre to grace us with his presence. He cannot possibly be expected to procure his own sandwiches. People fight each other for the privilege.

I smile a wan smile and then I shake my head. 'No.'

I wish I was, for certain sure. But no. I don't doubt it. 'I've got a present for you, too,' he adds, in the same loud look-at-me-I'm-absolutely-above-board voice that he has perfected so well these past months. 'It's up in my office. We'll have to go fetch it.' He makes a small gesture with his head.

'Oh, bless him,' says Carolyn, who is a few feet to his left. She doesn't say it to me, but to Dee, who is beside her, and who, despite catching my eye momentarily, still manages to smile and nod her assent.

'He's such a sweetie, isn't he?' comments someone at my side. I turn to see Dorothy, the outpatient administrator. Who is very nearly sixty and in love with him too. They all are, to a greater or lesser extent. Except me.

'Mmm,' I answer. 'Yes.'

'*Such* a lovely man.' She nudges me. 'I wonder what it is?'

I don't. I really don't want any more presents.

It's while I'm thinking just that that I make a fatal technical error. While Carolyn has waylaid him in conversation, I decide to nip off to the loo. Of course, nipping off to deal with three paper cupfuls of orange juice (and just the one of ASDA cava – I'm driving) is the sort of thing one does because one has to, but foresight should have told me that this is one occasion when going to the loo with a friend would have been, as it almost never is, the correct course of action. Not least because the nearest ladies – the one we all tend to use when we're working in outpatients – is tucked along the sort of out of the way corridor that sees little traffic after five.

Which Charlie Scott-Downing knows only too well. Which is something I should have recalled before I went. Which is why I'm an absolute klutz.

I smell him before I see him, so my nose is already braced on the rest of my behalf. The now familiar cocktail of expensive aftershave and Hibiscrub – the industrial strength cleanser the surgeons use to scrub up.

He's loitering outside. And clearly with intent. 'Come with me,' he says. 'I told you, I've got something for you.'

'No,' I say stoutly. 'I'm going back to the party. I'll be missed.'

'Missed!' he rolls his eyes. 'Tell me, Abbie, are you choosing your words specifically to break my heart?' Charlie talks this way to me most of the time right now.

'Don't be silly,' I say. Because I always say that. He takes my hand. Squeezes it. 'Please?'

'Charlie,' I say, holding my ground. 'I *specifically* told you not to get me anything. No parting shots. No tugs at my heart strings. I'm going. I'm *gone*. You've got to stop this.'

He ignores this. And understandably. I've said it – or a version of it – so many times before, and up to now I've always failed to follow through. 'Come on,' he coaxes again. 'Come up and see what I got you.'

There is, as there always is, little room for manoeuvre. I sigh defeat. 'Can't you bring it down here?' I ask him, quite reasonably.

'Absolutely not,' he replies.

So I go with him. Because not to do so would make a mockery of this whole sorry business. Not to do so – to take him on, to fight him, to run away – *anything* – would render the whole purpose, well, purposeless, really. I'm supposed to have taken control here, am I not? So I go with him up the corridor, out through the double doors, along another corridor which is being languidly mopped by a cleaner whose face I thankfully don't recognise, past the montages of photos detailing many a jolly fundraising activity, past the hand drawn six foot picture of a thermometer that marks the progress of that for which we always party and sponsored-walk and duck-race so slavishly, past the fish tank (two fish), the WRVS shop (now shuttered) and round the corner, where he turns around to smile.

It's that smile. Always has been, and suddenly I'm anxious. Anxious that I got it all wrong. That this whole leaving business isn't going to serve any purpose. That I'll leave but in my head I'll still be tethered here anyway. To him. Which I mustn't let happen. So I stop.

There are very few places in a hospital that are truly private, and the east wing corridor, at whose apex he now stands, is by no means one of them, for in its offices live secretaries, technicians, scientists, stray goblins, confused patients, and, in the last room, a store room, often staff involved in clinches or rows. But it is gone six, and all those who are not at the party are not on *this* corridor either.

Charlie –' I say. 'No. Okay? NO. I'm going back to the party. I really can't do this. I'm going back.'

'Please,' he says, closing on me now like a missile. A green surface to air missile on the warpath. And this does feel a little like a war now, for certain. A war of attrition, in every last way. '*Please*?' he says again. 'Just a goodbye hug. Please?' And then his hands are on my face and his lips are meeting mine. So much for doing the right thing.

Grr. Grr. Grr. Right thing, best thing, only thing, whatever. None of them actually fit right. The right thing would be never to have succumbed to his charms in the first place. The best thing, having done so, to have ended it straight away. The only thing? No. Were I a stronger, better, more steely-willed person, I *could*, I suppose, have toughed it out. But that takes two, and as at least one of us was, has been, is *still* not remotely interested in ending it, the odds on it not ending were altogether too great. Which makes me a wimp, and I don't want to be that. From a distance (Aches and Pains, Collin House, 27 Wharton Terrace – which should be just about far enough, I reckon) I can, I am sure enough to feel hopeful I can, be strong.

It was only a kiss, I remind myself crossly as the party begins drawing to a close. Just a farewell kiss. Which prefix makes it seem altogether more benign, more innocent, than it actually was. But it *was* just a kiss. A last kiss. It's *over*.

It's not much to say goodbye to, all things being considered. Now I've done the farewells and the tears and all that. Just grey concrete buildings. Just a workplace. Just a place. Such people that matter – which is most of them, admittedly – will still be there, in some way, shape or form in my life.

Coming out into the car park, Dee at my side, helping with the flowers and tutting about the litter, I take in the low pewter clouds, the sorry state of the paintwork, the superannuated stems of the optimistically planted petunias, the bins, the general air of decay. And I conclude that actually there's not much to miss. Which gladdens my heart and helps re-establish my optimism. I've done it. I really am going.

'That's that, then,' says Dee, who is not and who is sad. 'Another day, another dollar. I can't believe you're not going to be here on Monday.' She waits then, frowning and silent, while I fish around in my handbag for my car keys.

'Nor can I,' I say, frowning right on back at her. It's been wearing on the face, all the smiling. Though, in fact, I *do* feel like smiling now. Just a little bit, anyway. I feel liberated. Decisive. Back in control. I press the remote to open the passenger door, and Dee carefully places the bouquet in the footwell.

'So what was it, then?' she asks finally, as she straightens. 'What did he really give you?'

Charlie, who has an awful lot of letters after his name, is nothing if not intelligent. He announced there was a present, so I must be seen to have got one. Thus as well as the leg, which is under my arm, I am also clutching a second bouquet. Red roses, lots of them, which I know his secretary will have been instructed to ring and have delivered at some point earlier in the day. I put the flowers on the seat and pull a slim box – my proper present – from my handbag.

As proper presents go, it's a stunner. Dee yanks it open and diamonds wink up at her. Roses. Diamonds. Cliché upon cliché. But then, hey, what was our affair if not that? 'Wow!' she says. 'Wow, Abs. It's *stunning.*'

I take it back and lever the lid closed with a snap. 'It is,' I agree, shaking my head sadly. 'Such a waste.'

I watch her scurry back across the car park as I rummage once again in my bag for my phone. We've been such good friends for such a long time, and I know I'm going to spend an inordinate amount of time fretting about her, now I'm all freed up from fretting about myself.

But for now I must shrug off the last threads of memories and fret in the moment – about tea. I have absolutely no doubt in my mind that Jake will have forgotten I told him I'd be home late about fifteen seconds after me having told him this morning, so I open my phone fully expecting to find I've been sent a text saying *where U??????*. But the display, when I switch it back on, shows that voicemail have been trying to contact me, which is the sort of thing Jake would never do. Being male and fifteen, he would no more send me a voicemail message than consider a coat hanger as being related to clothes. Sebastian, then? Now, that *would* be nice.

I connect. It's not Seb. It's my mother.

My mother has just the two main modes of operation. Either slightly dramatic or seriously dramatic. That this is the latter means just the one thing. That my day is about to get worse. 'Oh, darling! she warbles. 'Where are you? I need you! It's Hugo! He's left me! He's gone!'

# Chapter 2

DAMN. I SHOULD HAVE known my mother would muscle in on the day somehow. Should have, but didn't, even so. I sometimes wonder if being someone who should have known things (instead of belatedly remembering I knew them in the first place) is genetically coded somehow. Perhaps it's just the downside of having an optimistic nature. I should know it's going to rain, and yet I don't bring an umbrella. I should know I'm a twelve but I still try on tens. I should have known, in the first minutes, the first seconds of meeting Charlie, that here was dangerous territory in a Hugo Boss suit. But I didn't. I just thought (as we all did) 'gosh, *he's* nice', never thinking where that sort of thinking might lead.

And I should know, because it's obvious, because *everyone* knows it, that bad things always happen in threes. Except in my defence, I *do* actually know that. I just thought I'd had three already.

Sitting in my car with my mobile in my lap, therefore, it occurs to me (as is so often the case where my mum is concerned) that, foresight aside, she really has no business riding roughshod over such a timeless and well established principle. Or maybe, once I consider it a little further, it's *me* that's got the sums wrong. There's Charlie, of course. Disentangling myself from Charlie is definitely the number one bad thing in my life right now. And then Sebastian. Though, when you think about it, your first born flying off to partake of his gap year can't really be classed as a bad thing. Yes, bad for *me* – obviously – because a week in and I'm already tearful at the newly diminutive ironing pile and there not being any need to get Peach Iced Tea from Sainsbury's any more. And sitting on his bed a lot. Sighing. Such is every mother's rite of passage. And there'll be more of that, for sure.

But not bad for *him*. And my own sense of sadness is of course somewhat leavened by my feelings of motherly pride and being able to bang on about his place at Uni and the brilliant A level results that I just know he's going to get, and what a very lovely young man he is and so on. But on balance, on *my* balance sheet, anyhow, bad-*ish*. A thing to have to come to terms with and adjust to.

And then there's leaving here. Unquestionably a bad thing, because I've liked working here very much. Yes, I know it's a cruel-to-be-kind kind of bad thing, and I know that it's a bad thing that will ultimately lead to at least the possibility of other good things, but like giving birth, it hurts just the same.

But maybe because the Charlie bad thing and the leaving bad thing are really just manifestations of the same bad thing, I have made a major miscalculation. Perhaps my mother phoning and wailing at me is, in fact, not the fourth but only the third bad thing after all. Which means I really *should* have seen it coming, shouldn't I?

I try to call her back but the line is engaged. My mother's line being engaged is fairly typical, of course. (Only marginally less typical than her being engaged herself, for she has a whole hand's worth of rings.) If my mother gets it into her head to ring someone then she generally, if that someone is not available and all-ears, finds someone else to telephone instead. She is probably on the phone wailing at someone else now. My sister, perhaps. But there's no one at her house. So I get on and ring Jake instead.

'Where are you, Mum?' he asks me.' I'm starving.'

'I told you,' I tell him. 'I've been at my leaving do.'

He grunts. 'Are you coming home now, then?'

'I'm not sure. I might have to pop round to Nana's. Make yourself some toast or something. I'll try not to be too long.'

'What's wrong with Nana?'

'Oh, don't worry. I'm sure it'll be something and nothing. You know Nana.'

How could he not? 'Can I go down the shop and get a microwave pizza, then?'

'If you must. Oh, and Jake, take Spike with you, can you?'

He groans. 'Do I have to?'

Poor Spike is missing Seb. Seb always used to walk him. Whereas Jake doesn't like to because he's such a small dog. We called him Spike largely for self-esteem reasons. But Jake's self esteem is a fragile beast also. He'll stress in case he's spotted with a mop on a lead. 'Please?' I add. 'Pleeeeze? I'll be back as soon as I can, promise.'

'Can Ben have a microwave pizza as well?'

Ben is Jake's friend. He plays bass and has these quite astounding blond dreadlocks. Not a million miles away from having spike on his head, come to think of it. 'Yes,' I say. 'He can as long as you promise you'll take Spike to the shop with you. I'll call you again once I'm there.'

Once I'm *there*. At my mother's. Which was absolutely not where I'd intended to be at this point, and the irritation rises with the aftertaste of Twiglets. My first thought, listening again to my mother's message is, somewhat uncharitably, 'rats'. All I wanted was a metaphorical five minutes to myself, and I have been stymied not ten seconds into the exercise by my mother, who everyone who knows my mother knows has needs so much greater than most.

I try her again but the line's still engaged, so I'll just have to go round there, which galls me. My actual plan for this evening was to go straight home, eat something trashy with Jake, open a bottle of wine and feel sorry for myself. I had already figured that I was allowed to feel sorry for myself on this occasion. Indeed, I'd decided that feeling sorry for myself, as long as it was in carefully metered doses and didn't encroach much beyond Sunday, would be good for me. They say that for every action there is an equal and opposite reaction, so I figure that having felt bad about myself for so long (which territory also means I have been denied the luxury of feeling sorry for myself thus far, having made and lain on my own bed etc.), I must now be due at least a little bit of self-indulgence. Not that I want to pig-out on self-pity or anything. I did make my bed. And, yes, I – *we* – did lie on it. And, as it happens, I'm not feeling sorry for myself right now. But that's not the point. There's a principle at stake here. I'm quite sure I'm going to be feeling sorry for myself later. And I'd like to do it on my own. With some candles. In the bath.

But, hey-ho, as I am in no way as experienced and naturally competent in feeling sorry for myself as my mother is (though there's a fifty percent chance it's in my genes, which is a worry) I am not going to be allowed to in any case. Not yet.

12

Not for the first time, I find myself wishing my mother was a bit more like other people's mothers. It's a truism, I know, but that's only because it's true. Most of us covet the things we don't have, and my sister and I were probably no different from anyone else in that respect. What we wanted was a proper mother. Who wore an apron, who sewed costumes, who rationed squash and biscuits. Free rein at her ginger ale and carte blanche with the Quality Street soon palled as treats when they were all there was for breakfast. She was exotic, bohemian, beautiful and difficult. Which is not necessarily what you want your mum to be.

And our mum was not necessarily what *she* wanted to be. She had lots of other, more important, things to do. My mother, first and foremost was – still is – Diana Garland. That's Diana, take note, with a lingering middle 'a'; Di-*a*-na. Di-*a*-na *Gar*-land. All a long time ago now, of course, but there was a period when Pru and I couldn't even walk to the laundrette without someone stopping us (us two embarrassed and diminutive envoys) to tell us what a wonder she was. Such was the marvel of television exposure at a time when television had just the three channels and almost all the population tuned in.

When I was a gaunt fourteen-year-old and Pru was still in the juniors, my mother became 'Dance-with-Diana' Diana, having landed, after several glittering years in musical theatre, the then much coveted role of being the new television face of fitness, cementing her position as an exercise icon and ensuring that wall-to-wall shame and embarrassment would be our constant companions for several excruciating years. She wore an all in one purple body stocking, stripy legwarmers and a pink headband, and had a regular slot on the new Wake Up! TV channel, during which, having been spirited away before dawn Mondays to Fridays, she would energise the nation's sleepy thirty-somethings through the medium of stretching and dance. It was a kind of sexed-up music, movement and mime, for people too old to pretend to be trees.

I'm not remotely surprised Hugo's left her. Though I'm absolutely sure he will be back, or at least on his way back, by the time I get there, the business of him leaving her (having left her, being about to leave her again, being left *by* her – there have been many permutations) has become very much the theme *du jour* just lately. She blames her knee, of course, and, by extension, me, That-Wretched-Hospital, (though, typically, not Charlie, who was the one who replaced it) and, of course, the Friday Tea Dance Club, which among other things boasts a male:female ratio of about one to twenty, which means competition is *hot*.

God, don't most people get too *old* for this stuff? I put the key into the ignition and allow myself a little sigh. My mother, regrettably, is *still* not most people. I switch on the engine, almost cheered up to note that I'm feeling sorry for myself now in any case.

Mum and Hugo (who is her fourth husband – my dad was her second) live in a three bedroom semi on the other side of Cardiff, six or so miles from my own. She used to live closer, in a little flat in Heath, but she moved in with Hugo just before they got married, and they spent much of what she got from the sale of her flat on a seven week cruise around some fiords.

My mother's marital history reads rather like *Hello!* Magazine. Not quite the same celebrity head count, admittedly, but pretty much the same emphasis on weddings. A little wistful pang flutters down onto my shoulder at this thought. But, one day, one degree of separation at a time.

When I pull into my mother's close, however, what I see straight away replaces the rumblings of regret with very different ones. Ones of alarm. As well they might be, because what my eyes first alight on is an ambulance. It's parked, admittedly, at least three houses down, but some powerful sense alerts me immediately that it is here, without a doubt, because of her. And the feeling is endorsed when I see my sister's car parked across the road as well, which means she's already driven here from Bristol. Oh, God. Is something *really* the matter? Has the shock of Hugo's departure caused her to collapse in a swoon? I park quickly and untidily in the first gap I can find, and hurry back towards the house, pulling out my door keys as I run.

There's no need to let myself in, however, because the front door is already open. The kitchen door is pulled almost shut, though, and I can hear a muted voice from behind it. The kind of voice I hear all the time when I'm at work. A solicitous voice. A gentle, caring voice. And then my mother's, which sounds neither. I push open the door.

'Darling!' she shrieks at me. 'You got here! Oh, darling…oh, oh, oh…' And more stuff along the same lines.

I take in what at first seems a highly improbable scene. My mother is sitting at the little bistro table-for-two she has in her kitchen, one leg up on the remaining bistro chair, and a large glass of dry sherry in her hand. Beside her stands a paramedic. A cheery-looking guy in his mid thirties. Or at least a guy who has the sort of face that would be cheery looking, if he wasn't so steadfastly in role. But there is no sign of a medical emergency in action, and I am at a loss to know what's going on.

'Mum, what's happened? Why the ambulance?' I take note of her seated position and frown. Then I squat down beside her. 'Where does it hurt? God, you haven't fallen and broken your knee again, have you?

My mother is now on her second knee replacement, having snapped the first one into two perfect pieces, a mere four months since Charlie put the thing in.

The paramedic shakes his head and starts telling me not to worry, but as I don't know what it is I should be worrying about exactly, it falls to my mother to fill me in, just as soon as she's flapped a dismissive arm at me, and paused to swig another mouthful of sherry.

'Of course not!' she says.

'Then why the ambulance, Mum?'

'Why the *ambulance*?' she parrots at me, as if I'm really thick.

I get up again and plonk my bag down on the worktop. 'Yes, Mum,' I say levelly. 'Why the am-bu-lance?'

She blinks. 'What else would they take the poor man away in? A horse and cart? A Sainsbury's To You van?'

I gape at her. '*Hugo?*'

'Of course Hugo! Who else?' Unusually, she now looks as lost as I am.

'But you said…' I trail off as it suddenly hits me. 'Hugo? You mean Hugo's been *hurt*?' Is this the ultimate solution to his philandering ways? Has she hit him with her NHS crutches? What?

15

The paramedic looks at me as if I'm quite, quite mad. As does my mother. She shakes her head and lifts a delicate hand to her mouth.

The man clears his throat before addressing me, frowning. 'I'm so sorry. He's dead,' he says gravely.

I look from one to the other. Clear my own throat as well. 'But you said he'd left you. You said he'd *gone*.'

'But darling, he *has*. Oh, oh, oh…'

'Cup of tea?' suggests the paramedic, patting her absently. 'I did make a fresh pot. It's still warm.'

It's about now that I become aware of noises coming from the ceiling above us.

'Pru's up there, is she?' I ask, essentially to my mother, but as she is too busy pouring herself more sherry to respond, it's the paramedic who answers me again.

'That'll be your sister? Yes, she's just sorting out a few bits and pieces. My colleague's up there –' He nods his head slightly towards my mother, 'doing, you know, the usuals.'

I realise he has probably spotted my uniform under my jacket. I nod absently at him, still taking it in while I'm taking it off. My mother's house is, as ever, like a sauna.

'What does it look like?'

'His heart, we imagine. GP's en route, but it certainly looks that way.'

'Oh, dear,' I say, because there doesn't seem to be anything else to say. I bend now to where my mother is sitting, feeling all at once terribly guilty.

'What happened, Mum? Were you with him?'

She sniffs back a fresh wave of tears. I am, albeit ever so slowly, beginning to absorb the weight of her shock. Whatever he was, whatever their differences, whatever the shambolic state of their short marriage, a moribund relationship is really no competition for one that's now dead by default. She shakes her head. 'No. I was in here. I was doing my crossword. He was upstairs getting ready to go out.' I see though, even now, a wave of exasperation infiltrate her grief-stricken features. It's a Friday, I remember. It's a dance day. Whatever else happens, a part of her will always hold a certain someone responsible. A certain someone called Hester, who now dances – *danced* – with Hugo,

16

and who has been Mum's nemesis since the beginning of this year. It won't be long, I imagine, before her name's on Mum's lips. Along with two other ones; 'just' and 'desserts'. But for now she seems genuinely traumatised and shaky.

As there's nowhere to sit, I take her hand and kneel beside her, on the floor. 'I just heard this noise,' she goes on. 'This dreadful noise. Not a shout or a scream or anything. Just this horrible gurgling sound. And then a really loud bang. No. Not one. It was two. So of course I called out, but he didn't answer, so then I got myself up the stairs to see what had happened. Which took for ever, of course, what with this wretched knee of mine. And when I got into the bedroom there he was, sprawled on the floor. Still in his underpants, God rest him, and with his bedside table on top of him.' She laces her fingers on the tabletop and swallows. 'So I got down as best I could to feel for a pulse, and then I called for an ambulance. The phone was right by his head. But I already knew he was dead. Even then. You just do, don't you? You just do.'

She's right. You just do. I've seen it often enough. And though she's not medical herself, so has she. 'Tea,' says the paramedic, passing me a mugful.

'Thanks,' I say. 'Good God. Poor Hugo.'

Then, as if on some sort of celestial cue, there is another loud bang overhead and for a moment I consider resurrection. But no. It's obviously just the other paramedic, doing what he has to upstairs. The one in the kitchen with us calls out. 'You need me up there, Daniel?' Then he heads off up the hall to do what needs to be done, closing the kitchen door behind him.

There is a look, a distinct and unequivocal look that becomes standard between sisters over time. My own sister, who joins us in the kitchen moments later, catches my eye and it passes between us, just as it has done for decades. It's a look with one meaning, and that meaning is clear. 'Damn,' it says. 'Now we've got trouble.'

# Chapter 3

MY FIRST POSTCARD – HURRAH!

Frontside: Eiffel Tower by night.

Backside: *Dear Mum, just to let you know we're still alive. Though only just, as Jonathan spent most of last night throwing up. He blames the snails. Yeah, right. On to Madrid manyana. (Not sure I spelt that right!) xxx Seb.*

It was Sebastian who made my mind up. Not consciously, naturally, for he didn't and still doesn't know that his mother is – no, *was*, and only briefly at that – a mistress and a harlot and a fallen woman. Some things are best left unsaid. But it was Sebastian's plan – to take time out from the daily grind of exams and revision, to see a bit of the world, to get drunk on weeknights, to meet interesting people, to sleep on a beach under the stars, to ponder the fundamental questions about being, to exist on pizza and beer, to just *exist,* period – that put the idea in my head.

Not that much of that sort of thing hadn't been in my head already. There must have been umpteen rainy Monday mornings when, like any other sane person, I would dream of escape too. Going somewhere else. Being someone else. Getting on a bus. Climbing aboard a train. And like any other person, when a plane flew overhead I often wished I was on it too.

But in my head as in right *in* my head; as in a cohesive, realisable, actual resolution to my problems – that came only when planning Sebastian's gap year made me realise that herein lay a solution of sorts for me too.

I couldn't go off inter-railing round Europe with a backpack, of course. Couldn't afford to, and wouldn't want to, in any case. There was – is – still my lovely Jake to consider, but as I had recently made the final payment on my mortgage (a spur on its own – how could I be that OLD?), there was a small chunk of cash I could usefully re-route. And as Sebastian and Jake's dad, who among his many virtues, had the foresight to have been born into a family that included at least one elderly, indulgent and maiden aunt, and therefore the wherewithal to fund at least a part of both his sons' ventures into academia, I could, if I could just pluck up the impetus to do it, re-route it mainly to me. And so organise a kind of mini gap-year of my own, and extricate myself from Charlie's clutches.

In a manner of speaking, at any rate. Like most of the population who were once beguiled by notions of fulfilment as promised in NHS recruitment ads, I worked in the health sector and thus I wasn't rich. So I would still have to work. And I would still *want* to work. But, for once, for the first time, for a little time at least, I could do it on *my* terms; i.e. not quite as much and not quite as hard, and with a day off each week to do just what I pleased. And if what I pleased was still a matter for some thought, the sheer relief at having actually made the decision was enough to make it *feel* like a gap year. A gap, at least, and all I had to do was leap into it. All very straightforward. *Not*.

Because it wasn't just me that was involved. One of the most difficult aspects (in a circumstance positively awash with difficult aspects) of finding yourself romantically involved with someone who turns out to be not actually available to be romantically involved with you, is that often – all too often – the relationship is based on a marked inequality of need. There are straightforward cases, of course. He's unhappily married, she's unhappily married and they go off, as one, To Be Together. But lots of cases are not like that at all. In lots of cases, he's unhappily married, yes, but not so unhappily he's about to do anything about it bar have his wounds licked by someone pleasing and solicitous, with a helping of sex on the side. And she's single. Or divorced. Oh, yes. Almost invariably.

There are many other permutations, naturally. But it seems to me that if you winnowed all unhappily-but-not-quite-enough men out of date-based society, you'd deal with a huge chunk of affairs at a stroke.

Oh, Why did I – *how* did I – get involved with Charlie? How could I have been so naïve?

*    *    *

Because naïve I most certainly was. Naïve to the point of imbecility. For many months I laboured under the misapprehension that Charlie – poor Charlie – was separated from his wife. Not that I didn't have good reason to, because although it was generally (and, of course, politely) accepted that he was just away from home because of his job, that was precisely what he told me. And it did all figure. He lived here, in a flat, and his family (his GP wife, two sons and one stepdaughter) lived elsewhere. I thought – and it's laughable, with the benefit of hindsight – that *I* was the only one who knew the real story. The only one close enough to know the stark truth. And I accordingly felt for him. Felt moved. Felt *sorry*; poor, poor Mr Scott-Downing (or so my early thinking rattled), pretending all was well, keeping up the pretence, when in reality his marriage was in meltdown. I'd been there. I empathised. I knew how these things went.

Of course, not being a complete simpleton, I didn't live under that misapprehension for very long – just a couple of infatuated, intoxicating months. But that was easily enough time for it to matter. Long enough to ensure there would be damage to undo. He was lonely, unhappy, disorientated and regretful. And very much in need of a friend. And I, in the grip of the mother of all adolescent crushes, was not at all adverse to providing that friendship. I was flattered, beguiled and not a little overwhelmed. When you are five years divorced and a little light on the love front, the attentions of an attentive and charming alpha male can be pathetically difficult to resist. Thus we fell into smiling, then we fell into chatting, then we fell into both sitting in his office for whole stretches. And then we fell into meeting, and then the meetings became dinners, and then, finally, *finally*, we fell into bed.

A very long, very tentative, very hesitant courtship. But a short sharp shock of a *dénouement*. Which happened when, one sunny Monday, I saw the light. Well, saw *by* the light, at any rate. His fridge light, to be precise. Which illuminated a large dish of chilli within it. And also my terrible folly.

I recall the moment well. I was in Charlie's little kitchen making us a cup of tea. And there was this casserole dish – this very large, hefty, family-sized casserole dish – sitting on the shelf in his fridge. I opened it – the smell was pungent, intense – and it was about a third full of the sort of rich dark aromatic chilli that had been many hours in the making. I put the lid back on the casserole. I got the milk out. I fished the tea bags from the mugs. And I thought 'hang on. Who made that chilli, exactly?' And then, having rejected the very first (and most obvious) thing that came to mind, I cast frantically about for other plausible reasons why Charlie, living alone in a flat, and being someone I already knew to be not particularly enthusiastic on the home-cuisine front, would have such a large vat of left-over chilli in his fridge. A proper, home-made chilli. A home-made chilli following a weekend in which he mostly spent his time not *at* home – travelling to Oxford to see his kids. A weekend in which he had precious little time to go and buy the myriad ingredients he would have needed to make such a thing. It didn't figure. I added milk to the mugs, and I pondered. I would just have to *make* it figure, wouldn't I?

Perhaps his mother? No. She was in a nursing home, wasn't she? A friend, then? His step-daughter? A neighbour, maybe? Perhaps I was wrong. Perhaps he *did* make it himself. Or, okay then, perhaps *sh*e – perhaps his almost-ex-wife did? Perhaps the impression I'd been given by Charlie (that she wouldn't make a chilli for him if he was the very last man on earth and hadn't eaten for a month) was wrong. Perhaps they were actually on fairly good terms; post-modern, co-operative, friendly even. Perhaps they were going to have an-amicable-divorce. Perhaps she made him this chilli to illustrate the fact.

I put the milk back in the fridge, and locked the chilli smell away again.

Or perhaps not, I thought. And my stomach endorsed it. Perhaps, in reality, there was to *be* no divorce. So I stopped casting about for reasons to be cheerful and, expecting the worst, I took the mugs into the living room. I smiled. He smiled back. I said 'Who made the chilli? Come on, own up. Can you cook after all?'

And Charlie stopped smiling. He frowned and said 'ah.' Though he didn't really need to, because right between 'own up' and 'can you cook after all?' his expression had already answered my question. It looked stricken for an instant and then it look relieved. Thank God, his expression said. Because I've had enough of lying. Now I can tell you the truth.

And seeing that expression made me all at once realise that deep down, some clear-thinking, unconscious part of me actually already knew. So I was, in a way, though mostly mortified, obviously, just a bit relieved as well.

I'm going to be just fine, of course. I was happy before I met him, I am happy again now it's over. He, on the other hand, went into this unhappy, is coming out of this unhappy, and there's absolutely nothing I can do about it. I *can't* make him happy. The logistics won't allow it. So all that's to be done is to move on.

But it does make me realise that the crucial thing (for the purposes of a thorough analysis of why Charlie, who I no longer love, is still ever present in my mind, like a persistent cold sore) is that if you slip into an affair born out of any sort of problem, then woe betide you. Because you are merely the symptom, and when you are removed, the problem, of course, still persists.

As does the problem with my mother.

'Your turn,' says Pru, without pre-amble or explanation, less than five days after Hugo's lifeless body has been relocated to the hospital morgue. Explanations are unnecessary. I have been allocated the technical duties of dealing with the undertaker, sorting out some clothes for them to dress him in, ringing and advising such people as I can get hold of, drafting a short notice to put in the local paper, and taking care of the tropical fish. Light work, in comparison to looking after Mum. 'I'm sorry,' Pru adds. 'But she's driving me nuts.'

I had, being essentially a good and dutiful daughter, offered to take Mum home with me on the day Hugo died. My sister, however, had insisted. I had initially been somewhat taken aback at her uncharacteristic readiness to cart Mum back to Bristol with her (my brother-in-law, among other things, not being noted for his selfless devotion to his mother-in-law at the best of times, for which absolutely no one could blame him), but, given the longer term implications of the situation – that, given her recent op, Mum wouldn't be able to manage on her own for a good few weeks yet – it wasn't long before it (admittedly rather uncharitably) dawned on me that getting in first, and for a finite duration, was a very clever way of lessening the likelihood of being stuck with her for terribly long. A sort of biting the bullet now in the hopes of relief later. As in passing the bullet on to me.

'What a surprise,' I say, perfectly equably. Because I'm really not surprised, and I really don't mind. And I must do my bit, after all. 'Has Mum spoken to his daughter yet?' I ask her.

Hugo has a daughter, who is called Corinne, who neither of us have ever met. Mum has seen her a few times, though only by accident, because though the last Mrs Hugo long pre-dated *our* Mrs Hugo, Mum and Hugo as an item – Mum and Hugo as in *married* – did not, it seems, go down very well. I don't think it was Mum, particularly – I think it would have been the same with anyone. None of us were really sure why that should be, but families are complex and not always to be fathomed, and as Mum didn't seem to care much either way, we didn't have reason to either.

Anyway, Corinne (plus her family) has apparently been away on holiday for a fortnight. Between them, Mum and Pru have been calling her home twice daily, and yesterday they connected. With a woman – the next door neighbour, apparently – who'd popped round to check on her gerbils. I don't know Corinne any more than Corinne knows me, but I really do feel for her now. This will all be such a terrible shock. There's no love lost, for sure – she even boycotted the wedding – but whatever the differences between her and her father, it seems a shame she has to find out like this.

'I did. This morning,' Pru tells me. 'And she says she's okay with the date.'

'Poor thing.'

'Yes. Poor thing. She sounded pretty pole-axed. I've given her your number so you can run the arrangements by her. She said she'd call you this evening. That okay?'

'That okay.'

'And I'll drive Mum over once Doug's in from work. About seven? We'll stop at hers on the way to get some clothes. And her address book, of course. She's got a guest list she's working through. You know, friends she's inviting –'

'Guest list? You make it sound like a party.'

Pru tuts. 'Not *me*. But, hey. You know Mum.'

I do, and yet I don't. We are still all observing the proprieties at the moment. And in fairness to her, when she and Pru arrive (plus my eleven-year-old niece, Chloe, who has come along in the hopes Jake will be here for her to dote on), Mum does look very much the newly bereaved widow. Pale. A tad distracted. A mite shaky. A little quiet. And though I know much of her current demeanour probably has as much to do with having been present at my nephews' eighth birthday party as her recent bereavement, there is still an air of quiet grief about her. Which is novel. Mum doesn't do quiet as a rule. Or, indeed, going to bed at ten.

This, however, is exactly what she does.

'I've made Sebastian's bed up for you,' I tell her, on our way up the stairs. 'With two quilts. And I've plugged in the fan heater, too.' I know it's June but my mother can't be doing with draughts. Or plants in the bedroom, for that matter. Or semi-skimmed milk. Or Ainsley Harriott. Or frozen peas. Or Gordon Brown's mouth. Already compiling a things-she-can't-be-doing-with memo in my head, I leave her to orient herself.

Twenty minutes later, I'm sitting in the kitchen, when the silence is shattered by a bone-shaking scream. I climb the stairs, breathlessly, three at a time.

She's sitting up in bed, with a hand clutched to her nightie. 'What on earth's *happened*, Mum? Are you okay?'

She's still a little shaky. She's had a nightmare, I imagine. But she's certainly wide awake now.

'It's understandable you're having bad dreams,' I tell her gently. 'What with everything that's happened. Your mind's probably teeming with horrible thoughts.'

'It's not *that*!' she snaps. 'It wasn't a *dream*! It was opening my eyes and seeing *THAT*!'

I fetch the ladder, move the bed out, climb the treads, get my balance. And then I carefully remove Jordan from the ceiling.

# Chapter 4

Hi M . Hi J . Hi S. Got yr txt. Sorry bout Hugo. Wot a shock! Poor nana. Hope she bearing up. Give her hug 4 me. Madrid 36 degrees 2day!!! Hope Barcelona cooler. XXX.

It was a terrible day for a funeral. And not just because it was also the day I should have been starting my new job and now couldn't (irksome though that was). It's because funerals, to my mind, demand a bit of meteorological gravitas. Roiling black cloudscapes. Squally rain. Hail. None such on this day however. All elbowed out of the way by the sun. You never did see such a big blue sky (except perhaps in Madrid, of course). There wasn't so much as a cobweb of a cloud, and the heat was so fierce they had to keep spraying all the wreaths. My mother was fanning her face with her order of service – a hastily compiled pamphlet with a cross on the front that had been printed on paper in that washed-out shade of green that made it look like an old take-away menu.

'I told you I should have worn my lilac,' she hissed at me. 'I'm melting in this wretched thing.'

'Shh. We'll be inside soon,' I hissed right on back at her. Why is it that, however much you don't think you ever will, there always seems to comes a time when you start speaking to your parents as if they were your children?

To be fair, it's not that you can't wear lilac to a funeral if you want to. Some people even make a point of stipulating that they're sent off by mourners in colourful clothes. It's just that the 'lilac' to which my mother referred – she'd shown me – was a boat-necked affair with a slit up the thigh and an explosion of lace at the way too high hem. The last time she wore it, as far as I can remember, was to her friend Celeste's seventieth bash. But though the evidence from the photos made it clear it wasn't remotely out of place on that occasion – there were as many pastel wash-n-wear crystal pleats as there were bottles of Cristal –

here she'd just look like she'd mistaken St David's crematorium for a branch of Castle Bingo.

'Well, I just hope they've got air-conditioning in there,' she muttered crossly. 'Or, believe you me, I shall be dropping dead as well.'

In order to make the most of what little breeze there was, I took the wheelchair for another quick turn around the guests. Because of her knee replacement-replacement her right leg shot out in front of her horizontally, like a ladder on a window cleaner's van. I perhaps should have tied a bit of rag around her ankle, because it preceded her at crotch height and kept jabbing people's bottoms. She looked a bit like a short prow maiden minus the prow. Which was fitting, at least, because she met Hugo on a boat.

Oh, I so didn't want to be at a funeral. I particularly didn't want to be at this funeral. I knew I had to support my Poor Dear Mother, of course, but already it was beginning to look like there was going to be trouble, because everyone DNA-related to Hugo seemed alien, hostile, from an entirely different clan. And none of them seemed to want to talk to us. Which was odd. His daughter Corinne, who I had now spoken to on the phone and who I also recognised from various photos, was shooting us looks of such naked hostility that even the peonies between us were wincing.

So it was with a powerful sense of things being not quite right that I picked up the sounds of raised voices in the distance, and noted the vicar, who must have been roasting in his funeral frock too, hurrying across the lawn at the behest of the undertaker, who seemed to be in a very un-undertakerly state of flap.

Pru, who had been in a state of flap herself all morning because Chloe and the boys (my niece and nephews) had been rollicking around on the garden of remembrance ever since we got here, rushed across now, eyebrows raised.

'What on earth is going on?' she panted, pointing at the entrance. There was some sort of to-do happening over near the crematorium gates, partly obscured by the planting. Members of the other clan were beginning to peel off towards it. From what we could see the vicar was involved in some sort of minor altercation.

'Wheel me over there,' my mother commanded, her view of events clearly not commanding enough. But my grip remained steadfast on the chair.

'Good Lord,' Pru said. 'Do people really *do* that?'

'Do what?'

'Take photos at funerals.'

My mother harrumphed. 'Nothing would surprise me. He did have some fearfully common friends.' But then she started in the chair. 'Good Lord! Pru! Abbie! *Look*! Good grief! You know who that is, don't you?' We followed her gaze. She's sharp-eyed, our mother. All those years of scanning dimly lit audiences for scouts. And two seconds ahead of us, for sure. We both saw what she saw simultaneously.

'God!' said Pru (though he probably wasn't listening). 'That's Lucy Whittall! What on earth can Lucy Whittall be doing here?'

None of us knew, of course, but Lucy Whittall's being here did explain the hoo-hah in the entrance. Lucy Whittall being one of the most famous of our famous TV stars right now. On screen she plays one of the leading characters – a nurse, funnily enough – in the long running soap-drama *A & E*, and off screen she fills more column inches of glossy than just about anyone else you'd care to name. From the contents of her handbags to the labels on her thongs, to her protracted and much documented battle-with-drink-and-drugs. No wonder the paparazzi followed her here. They follow her pretty much everywhere.

'And him,' my mother added. 'I know his face as well.'

'Whose face?' I asked.

'Him! That man with his arm round her. *Him*.'

I didn't know who the him was. Tall, broad-shouldered, wavy goldy-blond hair, and – yes, I was right – a slight limp. I always spot limbs that aren't working on message. Another knee was my guess. Though I suspected that this one was a real one. They moved on then. Were walking arm in arm towards Hugo's daughter.

'I know who that is,' said Mum's friend, Celeste, who'd come to join us, swishing festively across in a strawberry two-piece. 'He's that new weatherman off the telly. Always wears such lovely ties. They're an item, they are. I read it in *Depth*.'

'*That's* it!' said my mother, whose state of animation by this time was beginning to border on the unseemly. 'I knew I knew the face,' she said, fanning her own. 'Goodness! How exciting this all is!'

But the excitement was soon over. Once the photographer had been ejected, and the celebrity contingent ushered into the crematorium (without reference to us at any point – we were beginning to feel like a bunch of local peasants who just showed up at a hanging on the off chance), the service itself went pretty much as services at funerals do. We sang a bit, the vicar spoke a bit, and someone (in this case a someone called George) told a couple of anecdotes that were in somewhat bad taste. But it was a gathering that lacked any real sense of gravity, because so many heads kept swivelling around to try and clock the stars in our midst. To her credit, my mother did weep copiously as the casket rolled off stage, but even then I detected a slight touch of the theatricals, which should have alerted me, though it didn't, that all was not quite as it seemed.

And it seemed I wasn't wrong. We filed back out into the sunshine. We filed past all the flowers. We stopped to read the notes. We were just moving off to get back into the car when a tell-tale plume of smoke started spouting from the chimney. My mother glanced up at it and stabbed a finger in the air. 'Good riddance to bad rubbish!' she said firmly.

'Honestly,' said Pru, as we hastily wheeled her back to the car and bundled her inside. 'What a thing to say! Supposing someone had heard you?'

'No one heard me,' my mother replied testily.

'God did, Nana,' observed Chloe.

'God will understand,' Mum told her, patting her knee. 'God sees and hears *everything*. God *knows*.'

Unless you're God, and I'm not, it's never a good idea to think you've seen and heard everything. Mainly because God moves in mysterious ways, and we're fools if we think we can predict them.

But the many mysteries of the universe are the last thing on my mind when we get back to Mum and Hugo's, occupied, as it is, with that most delicate of delicate social occasions, the post-funeral gathering over tea. As is often the case (unless you're Irish, of course) nobody seems to know quite how to be.

And this gathering – this non-party – is even worse than most. Peopled, as it is, by two factions of mourners who were it not for certain parties' late forays into matrimony (and the presence of celebrity, of course), wouldn't have anything to do with one another, let alone engage in tea and Battenburg.

I'm not sure quite why it is that the atmosphere feels so uncomfortable; whatever our private thoughts about our respective parents' spouses, we have, as far as I can tell, no reason to feel any antagonism towards each other, yet Corinne, who was perfectly civil during our phone calls, still seems decidedly disinclined to engage with either Pru or I.

'Her father did just die, I guess,' comments Pru, ever the sage.

'I know,' I say. 'But even so… Don't you think she's being a bit, I don't know, offish?'

'Offish?'

'Well not offish so much, as just a bit anxious to avoid us, you know?'

She shrugs. 'I guess she's just not that bothered about speaking to us. Chances are, after this, she'll never clap eyes on us again.'

Which thought seems to sum up just how arbitrary some relationships can be. We're just connected by circumstance and now the circumstance has changed. I wonder who'll end up with the sideboard.

Of course, sideboard aside, I'm not remotely aware of just how very much the circumstances *have* changed at this point. Not a bit of it. I am too preoccupied with the circumstance in hand; the one where I'm stuck in a house with a bunch of people I don't know, who I don't particularly want to know, who certainly don't seem to want to know me – which is fine – and wishing the whole tedious business was over, so l can get back to the much cheerier and also necessary business of taking up residence in *my* life again. But for now I must cut cake and make tea.

Thus it is that I'm holed up in the kitchen waiting for the kettle to boil so I can make a pot. Jake's mooching round the garden, trailed by his cousins, and chatting to someone on his mobile. Likewise, I'm chatting to Dee on mine. She's called to update me on Charlie (I keep telling her not to, but she takes absolutely no notice) and to make arrangements for badminton next week. Can I make Tuesday okay? Yes, I can. Post-Charlie, Tuesday badminton has become my new black. I'm not very good at it. I'm actually quite bad at it. But it's one hundred percent better than *being* bad, for sure. Plus it's very efficacious on the bingo wings front, which, looking at my mother when she's in her triangle stand, is clearly a matter about which to be concerned. 'You won't believe what Mum said,' I'm telling Dee as I empty out the teapot. She says oh yes she will. So I tell her.

'Come to think of it,' I'm saying. 'It's exactly the sort of thing she would say. God, but my mother is incorrigible.'

The kettle boils then, so I ring off and reach for tea bags. Humming to myself and with my back to the kitchen door. So it's no surprise that I don't know someone else is in the kitchen. Not until it speaks to me, at any rate.

'I suppose,' the voice says, 'that she did have a point.'

As the voice says this at least five seconds after I last spoke, I assume for a moment that it must be engaged in conversation with someone else. But when I wheel around, it's to find myself face to face with the face of the weatherman – who, now I think about it, does look vaguely familiar – and I realise there's no one else in here. So he must have been talking to me. He sort of smiles but not quite, as one tends to at a funeral. 'Gabriel Ash,' he says equably, proffering a hand.

I wipe my own hands on a tea towel and then extend one to shake his. He's still looking sort of smiley, in a faintly self-reproving way. He's got that kind of face. Animated. Changeable. A bit like the weather. Adjustable according to the season.

'Oh, God,' I say, flustered, realising that he's probably – no, definitely – referring to my mother. 'How embarrassing. You didn't hear her, did you?'

'I didn't need to,' he says, equally equably. 'I just heard *you*, didn't I? But I can't say it was any sort of shock.'

As I'm still not sure who he is (well, apart from a television weatherman with a celebrity girlfriend), I'm not really sure how to respond.

'You knew Hugo, then?' I plump for, because I guess he must have – or *she* must. He may be showbiz – he certainly has the usual smooth patina – but he's nothing to do with my mother. He nods.

'In a manner of speaking. I'm his son.'

Now I'm really embarrassed. 'His *son*? Hugo's? I didn't know he *had* a son.' Didn't know much about him at all, when it comes down to it. And the same might be said of my mother. Has she ever mentioned a son at any point? No, she most definitely hasn't. How *excruciating*. But then I have a thought. 'And why d'you say "in a manner of speaking"?'

'In the sense that we hadn't actually spoken in twenty years. Shall I rinse out some of these for you?'

He moves purposefully towards the sinkful of crockery and I move aside to let him. 'Er, yes. Yes, thanks.' I'm not used to television people offering to wash things up. It almost doesn't seem seemly. But then perhaps things have changed since my mum's day. Though I still can't imagine Lucy Whittall with a tea towel. But then I imagine she's doing what she probably does best. Standing in the living room being quietly adored. And why not? It's made half the guests' day, that's for sure. But now I know what I know, why are they here at all? Specifically, why him? Twenty years is a very long time. And would explain why we were all unaware of his existence. I don't know quite what to say to him, so 'Oh dear,' is what comes out. 'Oh, dear. That's so sad.' But he's shaking his head.

'Not really,' he says, filling the washing-up bowl with water. 'Washing-up liquid in here?' He opens the undersink cupboard.

I nod and then shrug. 'If you say so,' I answer. What a curious turn of events. I start to fill the tea pot. 'It seems pretty sad to me.'

He says nothing for a moment. Just swooshes mugs in the water. Then he glances up. 'You're one of his wife's daughters then? Abbie, isn't it?'

I grimace. 'Is it that obvious?'

He looks at me carefully. 'No,' he says, 'it's not. My sister pointed you out.'

He doesn't say it pointedly, but there exists, between the words he's just spoken and the ones I might be tempted to

31

respond with, a certain mutual but unspoken acknowledgement of relations not being quite as they might be in that department.

'It's all been very difficult,' I say carefully. 'Well, not difficult so much as uncomfortable, really. Here we all are at the same funeral and we none of us really know each other. Not properly. It's not been –'

'I know. Corinne told me.' He finishes rinsing out the mugs and cups and now he reaches across me to pick up the tea towel. He smells of coconut.

'Parents, eh?' I say.

And then I wish I hadn't, because the sort of person who has not had a relationship with at least one of his parents for two whole decades (two, even – how would I know?) is probably someone with a whole different take on the concept of parents and their foibles than someone like me, who is all foibled out.

'Your mother's disabled, then?' he asks me politely.

My mother's disabled many things in her time. Stage sets, hearts, marriages, cars, at least one washing machine, a mobile phone. I shake my head. 'Only temporarily, we hope. She's had a knee replacement. And then she broke it, so she's had another one.'

'Oh, dear,' he says. 'I didn't even know you could break knee replacements.'

'Most people can't.' I point then, his comment having made me remember. 'What's the matter with *your* knee? If you don't mind me asking. Anterior cruciate ligament?'

'You already worked that out?'

'An educated guess. And a fairly safe bet. I'm a physiotherapist.'

'I know.' He nods. 'Your mother told me. She said you were – '

'Ah, *there* you are, Gabriel!'

We turn, as one, to see Lucy Whittall framed in the kitchen doorway, clutching a bottle of something with a corkscrew in the top. 'Be an angel and get this open for me, will you?' She winks conspiratorially, and it's mainly at me. Then she tosses her head back. 'None of those old codgers in there have got the strength, bless 'em. Though, fair play, they all had a damn good try.'

I'll bet. Close up, she is jaw-droppingly beautiful, with hair that really does have the colour and form of a field of wheat in a breeze. And whatever ravages her lurid past have writ on her features, the pen has been gently, even lovingly applied. She's about thirty, I imagine – younger than me and him, certainly – with intelligent, sparkling, been there-done that eyes. And she glows – in that way that beautiful women do, in that way that can't help but immediately alert me to my great age, my lacklustre, not-quite-any-colour hair, my insignificant bosom, my lack of lipstick, my pinny (no – my mother's pinny), my chronic inability to get noticed in bar queues and the fact that the polish on my fingernails and toenails (the former hastily applied to go with the funeral get-up), don't just not match, but positively clash. Oh, and that I wish I hadn't taken my shoes off in the first place, because not only do I look like the Hispanic housemaid, but I am also a good foot smaller than them both. Yes, yes, yes, I *know* people get paid for grooming the likes of Lucy Whittall, and to the *n*th degree, clearly, but it still makes me feel like a wizened old hag.

Which is a shame, because immediately I like her.

Gabriel Ash takes the bottle and does the job in seconds, and there follows a wordless but still obvious exchange, involving his eyebrows (raised), her eyebrows (furrowed) then an expression on her part that seems to say 'I *won't*!' and one on his that seems to answer 'make sure you *don't!*' I could be wrong, obviously, but I don't think I am. It's related to the contents of the bottle.

She sashays back out and we get on with the drying, while her aura lingers fragrantly in the air. I wonder again quite why they're here. Why *he* is. Why now? After two whole decades of non-contact? What a day this is turning out to be. 'She seems very nice,' I say, because I have to say something. He grins. 'And beautiful,' I add. 'You know, in the flesh, as it were.' That the grin becomes a smile is, I assume, because he much enjoys hearing that said.

And then it occurs to me that I'm silly feeling inadequate, because Charlie thinks *I'm* beautiful, too. But it's a dozy kind of thought, and I've no business thinking it, because however grateful I am to have been briefly thus adored, what Charlie thinks no longer matters.

33

*     *     *

By the time we're ready to leave the house, having dispatched the last of the guests, cleared everything away, assembled yet another cache of maternal essentials (this is beginning to feel like moving house by correspondence course), checked the doors and windows, fed the fish and the parlour palm and waved off Pru and the children, my mother has become really quite jolly.

Outrageously and highly inappropriately jolly. I'm only grateful she's kept it buttoned up thus far. 'Fancy that!' she trills gaily, as we get into the car. 'I was flabbergasted! Absolutely flabbergasted! Who'd have thought we had such a celebrity in the family?'

I note the 'we'. And her somewhat loose interpretation of the word 'family'. They are certainly no longer a part of ours. 'Who indeed?' I reply.

'Oh, it seems such a terrible shame!' she twitters on.

'What does, Nana?' asks Jake, who hasn't up till now been listening, on account of having been plugged into his iPod for as much of the duration as possible.

'That I never even knew about him! Such a terrible waste.'

Unlike my mother, who is patently not brooding on the loss of a potential stepson, but rather on the perceived lost Career Enhancement Opportunity (it was ever thus), Jake, naturally, is wholly unimpressed. Unsurprisingly, he's never even heard of the weatherman, and though by now hormonally awakened to the charms of girls' squashy bits, he doesn't know who Lucy Whittall is either. Mainly on account of a television diet of twenty-four / seven MTV and *Kerrang*. And to him she must seem fairly aged, I guess.

Indeed, he even seems a little pre-occupied. When we get home, he goes straight upstairs to his room, and doesn't emerge for an hour. When he does finally reappear downstairs he still looks lost in thought, and I wonder if the funeral's upset him. But no. He's got something in his hand, which he thrusts at me.

'What d'you think,' he asks me, 'of this as a plan? I thought I could put it up in Pearson's.'

It's a postcard. On it is written *'Vocalist/rhythm guitarist (must be <u>committed</u>!) to join established band 'One Black Lung'. Pontcanna area. Our musical influence's are Metallica, Metallica and Metallica.'*

One Black Lung are called One Black Lung because Ben had pneumonia last Christmas. Neither of his lungs went black as far as I know, but it's a catchy kind of name, even so.

'What d'you think?' Jake asks me again. 'Will that do?'

I'm glad he's okay. This funeral's a first for him. But he's clearly more pre-occupied with more important matters – like replacing One Black Lung's feckless ex-member, David, who was always failing to show up for band practice, and who therefore committed that most heinous of musical crimes – lack of commitment. They've since been trying, and failing, to find someone else. Because they're really very picky, and quite right too. Yes, I think, and then say. It will do very nicely. I ruffle his hair, which he hates, but I can't help it. 'But there's no apostrophe in influences,' I tell him.

# Chapter 5

Hɪ ᴍᴜᴍ

Thanks for your text – the longest in recorded history? – sounds like everything went okay with the funeral. J says did you get Lucy Whittall's autograph? No he didn't say that (ho ho) but I'd better not tell you what he did say. We are sitting in an internet cafe in Monte Carlo – how cool is that? Is so posh here we almost didn't spot the McDonalds – it's done out like tea room and everything's green and gold instead of red and yellow. Bizarre! Burgers just same tho' – phew! You can see where the F1 route goes, and there's rubber all over the roads. Yachts like you wouldn't believe!

Cheers. Sxx

They're certainly not letting the grass grow. Though mine sure is. Memo to self, of last Monday. 'Day off. Cut grass. Sunbathe.' Some hope.

Mr F W Gladstone, solicitor of this parish, and whose short letter summoned us here on this bright sunny morning, ushers us to seats and then sits down himself. His office, the walls of which are comprehensively covered with pen and ink studies of fat men bearing golf clubs, is gloomy to the point that miners' headlamps would not feel whatsoever ridiculous, and his desk, which is as properly big and old and dusty as you'd expect it to be, is almost completely covered in piles of paperwork and files, and as he is a short man, he appears to lurk, rather than sit, behind it, in the manner of a Dickensian villain. He looks bored. But then it's another nice day and I'm sure he'd rather be playing golf. My mother leans her crutches against the arm of her chair, and they immediately clatter to the floor.

We're a party of five. Myself (for I am chauffeur), Pru, my mother, Corinne (in suit and killer court shoes) and the weatherman again. Who is, I assume, making like a Cardiff

Council bus fleet. Not a sniff for ages, then an *embarras de richesse*. Both are looking very like they've recently swallowed wasps. He does smile a brief hello at us – TV type standard issue – but no pleasantries are proffered or returned.

'He did make a will, then, did he?' I asked my mother some days earlier. 'Do you know what's going to be in it?'

She nodded and flapped her hand at me (such it is with dancers). 'Of course I know what's in it. He's left me everything, of course.'

It seemed to me that there was no 'of course' about it. They had, after all, been married a scant three and a half years. And she was 100% out on the offspring count, wasn't she? Not a terribly auspicious start. 'Bet that'll go down well,' I said. 'No wonder his daughter was so frosty at the funeral.'

No wonder she's so frosty now. Because it seems Mum was right. He *has* left her everything. Well, pretty much. Mr Gladstone rattles through the formalities at a surprising lick for one so sluggish of demeanour, and then reads from what looks like an impressively long list. Long, but as it turns out, not terrifically impressive; the watercolour by... (some artist I haven't ever heard of) I leave to George Bathhurst, the gold cufflinks and matching tie pin I leave to Edward Noble. My bowls (eh? Ah – bowling ones) I leave to Mrs Moira Bugle, and so on and so forth till we get to the last bit; the residue of my estate I leave to Diana Mary Imogen Patterson-Garland, my beloved wife.

So this was written before the tea-dance club debacle, we must assume. Or perhaps the tea-dance club debacle was in fact not a debacle at all, just one of my mother's many flights of fancy. I watch her dab at her eyes out of the corner of mine. And as we're seated in a kind of horseshoe I can make out Corinne's expression too. I wonder how she feels about all this. I doubt the long-lost son was expecting anything, of course, but little though it seems Corinne saw him, she *was* his daughter, but for her all I've totted up is a few bits of jewellery, a Welsh quilted bedspread and a clock. She looks utterly impassive and I wonder what she's thinking. But she's clearly thinking thoughts that fail to register on her face.

The solicitor straightens finally. Concludes the short meeting. Thanks us for coming, gets Mum to sign something, then he turns to Corinne.

'There are,' he says to her, 'a few formalities for us to deal with in relation to the property, of course, Mrs Smith. I'll be writing to you to that effect sometime later this week.'

Corinne nods her head and leans down to pick up her handbag. It is Louis Vuitton and looks new.

A silence falls, while we digest what he's said. Or try to. Why is he talking just to *her*? 'I beg your pardon?' squeaks my mother.

The solicitor turns his rheumy eyes upon her. 'I'm sorry?' he says.

'What formalities?' she adds. 'What property are you talking about anyway?'

He blinks and looks confused. As if having been unexpectedly addressed by a pot plant or a hole punch. 'Er…' he says.

'*Er*?' says my mother, brows aloft.

The solicitor looks doubly confused, and now uncomfortable too. He looks at Corinne. Then back at my mother. Then he frowns.

'Mrs Patterson –'

'It's Ms Garland, actually.'

'I'm sorry. *Ms* Garland. But the question of the property…er…'

'*What* question precisely?'

He looks over at Corinne again and clears his throat. 'Forgive me, Mrs Smith, but has the matter of the house not been discussed yet between you?'

Uh-oh, I think to myself. *Now* I get it. She's planning to contest the will. Of course she is. It all fits. No wonder she's been so reluctant to talk to us. And I can't say I'm surprised. Though what little I know of the family suggests theirs is/was not the closest of father/daughter relationships, he is/was still her father. And no matter how much anyone protests otherwise, it must be pretty damn galling to have your father take up with some stranger in his twilight years and promptly re-direct your inheritance. Blood has been shed for far less.

But why *was* he talking just to her, in that case? And my mother, quite clearly, is on the same track as me.

'Excuse me,' she says sharply. She is not used to being ignored. 'What d'you mean, discuss? There is nothing *to* discuss. The house has – quite rightly – been left to me. The will said so. It –'

'No, it didn't,' Corinne says, and her gaze is unflinching. 'And it didn't because it hasn't. And it hasn't because it wasn't his to leave you.'

Now I *am* surprised. How can *that* be? Oh dear, oh dear, oh dear. This really does not look very good.

'Hang on,' says Pru, who has also clocked the eye stuff and is now looking straight at Corinne. 'Are you telling me your father didn't actually *own* his house?'

Corinne shakes her head then picks a speck of something from her jacket sleeve. 'No,' she says levelly, glancing at her brother. 'We do.'

'*You* do?' Pru and I say, almost exactly as one.

'Yes, *we* do,' she says again. 'And I'm afraid we need it back.'


It's as clear as mud, as these things so often are, but we eventually manage to winnow out the most salient point, which is that the house – which was originally, it turns out, the marital home of the earlier (*an* earlier, at any rate) Mr and Mrs Hugo – does indeed belong to his children, it having been bequeathed to them by their late mother. Who apparently owned it outright. Not both of them. Just her. Which has one somewhat stupefying implication, obviously, which is why we're probably all too stupefied to speak.

No one seems particularly inclined to tell us more, either, and the temperature in the room, already somewhat chilly, plunges a few degrees lower.

The Smith and the Ash component leave shortly after (the Smith component sweeping out as if leaving an arena having felled fifteen Christians and a goat, which seems excessive), it having been not in the least amicably agreed that they, I and Pru would communicate the next week, to discuss the 'disposal' arrangements. Or rather, in proper words, the sale of the house – the sale of my mother's home from under her. Though I imagine neither of them have the tiniest interest in discussing what they think we're going to do with our mother next. That they don't much care seems understatement indeed. It's almost too much to take in. So much for the idea of her contesting the will. Her/*them*, come to think of it. Bloody *hell*.

'Can we contest the will ourselves?' I ask the solicitor afterwards.

'Not really,' he says kindly, 'you don't have any grounds. The house wasn't *part* of the will.'

'Jesus, Mum! Jesus! You are absolutely bloody unbelievable!' snaps Pru. 'Christ, this really takes the biscuit! First some long-lost son crawls out of the woodwork, and now we find out Hugo didn't even own his house! How on *earth* could you have failed to know something like that?'

We're back in reception now and my mother, it has to be said, is looking somewhat flustered. Her own fault entirely. She did produce us after all. And in her own image. So it's no less than she should expect.

'Because I didn't!' she snaps. 'How would I? Why would I? He told me he *did*! Why wouldn't I believe him? Forgive me, Prudence, but you of all people should know a marriage is based upon trust!'

But not me, of all people? Though I don't pause to ponder it. 'God, but what *now*?' I lament roundly instead. Because 'God, but what now?' is really all I can think. Can they really just evict her? Just like that? Legally? Surely not. I pull open the glass door and scowl at the sunshine. There must be some law to protect people like my mother, though regrettably none springs to mind.

When we emerge on to the street, it's to find that the long-lost son, now very much found, appears anxious to press his presence home. He's outside still and obviously waiting for us. Hovering on the pavement like he's early for a date. Of the sister, though, there is not a sign.

'Look,' he says, speaking as he jerks to attention and strides (no – limps) purposefully across the pavement towards us. 'I just wanted to say how sorry I am about all this.'

We're both pretty quick off the mark, Pru and I, but today she's marginally quicker.

'*Sorry*?' she rails at him. 'I beg your pardon, but 'sorry'? Well, forgive me, but don't you think that's just a teensy bit inadequate under the circumstances?'

He has the good grace to lower his head slightly at this.

'Yes,' he admits, 'it probably is.' Two women walk past us at this point and I can hear the 'Is that the man off...' and 'Jeepers, it is too!' conversation swell and ebb as they pass. It must happen all the time. It must be quite distracting. But then he probably deserves it. 'But,' he adds, 'you know, if there's anything I can do...'

'And just what is it you think you might be able to do exactly?' I ask him now. 'Build my mother a shed in your garden?'

I don't know if he has a garden, of course, but I'm quite sure he must do. A big one. With a weather vane in it. And one of those things that measure rainfall, most probably. And now he has half of another one, to boot. Humph. 'I had no idea until this morning,' he goes on, ignoring me.

'Oh, come on...' I retort. 'You expect us to believe that? Isn't that precisely why you showed up at the funeral?'

To get his hands on the spoils? Oh, yes, it's all becoming horribly clear now. But he ignores that too. Just frowns and turns to Mum. Who responds in the usual Garland fashion when being addressed by a member of the opposite sex who isn't too old to escape the radar. In the blink of an eye, she's whipped off the scowl and is suddenly all teeth and eyelashes. 'What I *mean*,' he explains to her, 'is that I really had no idea you didn't *know* about the house. I'd assumed you were already aware.' Which I grudgingly suppose I do believe. I mean, the solicitor didn't, did he? But even so.

'What the hell difference does that make?' Pru rounds on him angrily, voicing my very thought. 'The net result is the same. My mother is now effectively homeless!'

The mother in question rounds on her now. 'Oh, Prudence!' she twitters. 'Goodness gracious me! Will you desist from airing my business all over the street!'

Pru ignores Mum. This seems to be the day for it. 'But don't imagine for a moment that we're going to take this lying down.

41

That you can just throw an elderly woman on to the street willy-nilly, because believe me –'

'Prudence!' my mother tinkles faux-smilingly again. 'I am *not* elderly!'

Gabriel Ash looks pained. 'I don't –' he begins.

'Don't *what*?' retorts Pru. 'Hmm? Well? Don't *care*?'

'Oh, for goodness' sake, girls,' my mother snaps, finally. And in doing so, reverting seamlessly to the sort of tone that can still stir exit door curtains in the very back of the stalls. 'Leave the poor man alone, for goodness' sake! It's not *his* fault.' I'm not sure how she worked that out exactly. I would have said the opposite was true. But, no. He's a man so he's forgiven by default. She pats his arm and beams at him. 'I do apologise for my daughters,' she coos. 'It's been a stressful time for them. I'm sure we can all do this without undue hostility. I'm quite sure we can sort something out.'

'Mother,' Pru snarls as we drag her away. 'Stop bloody simpering, for God's sake!'

'I wasn't simpering, young lady. I was simply –'

'You were *flirting* with him, mother.'

'No. Being *civil*. No situation is ever made better by shouting.'

'Mum. You are homeless. This is not a time for civility.'

*Or* flirting, for that matter. Good point. 'And very *much* a time for shouting, in my book,' I add.

But my mother, being my mother and therefore not like other people, goes 'Goodness. All this *fuss*! Girls, calm yourselves, will you?'

'*Calm* ourselves?' Pru barks. I bark nothing. I'm speechless. Just how can she be so relaxed about all this?

'Yes, darlings, *calm* yourselves. All will be well. Remember. *Que sera,* girls. *Que sera.*'

I'll give her *Que* bloody *sera.* Mum, there's no milk… Oh, dear. *Que sera!* Mum, my boyfriend's just dumped me… Oh, bless. But, chin up! *Que sera*! Mum, I think I cocked up my Geography O level… Darling, don't panic . Remember – *Que Sera*. I've really come to hate Doris Day.

Trouble is, it is my mother's philosophy of life perfectly captured in three cheesy syllables of Spanish. The mantra with which she has wafted through, let me see, three careers, four husbands (two dead, two divorced, none beheaded at the last count), and at least two stray fiancés that I know of. But while it may have served *her* well – and it has, up to now – it's certainly not serving Pru and I well now. And I did fail my Geography O level, as it happens. And what if I'd passed it? Things could have been so different. I could be working as a cartographer in Brisbane or Nairobi. And could send my commiserations on a postcard from there. Still. At least she's going back to Pru's again tonight. For that we must be grateful. *Que* hurrah.

'Gawd, gawd, gawd!' says Dee, with some feeling. 'That is some bombshell! But surely they can't just throw her out. Doesn't she have any rights?'

Taking your worries out on a shuttlecock doesn't have quite the anger-quenching properties of a session with a punchbag, but in the absence of one, it will just have to do. 'Apparently not. Well, she has all the usual ones – if she barricades the door and refuses them entry they'll have to get a court order to evict her. But she's not even there, is she? She's at my sister's.'

And will soon be back at mine. And then at Pru's. And then mine again. We're passing her back and forth as if engaged in an intense bout of correspondence chess. Is this how the next few weeks – God, *months* – are going to be? And if that's not indigestible enough a thought to be going on with, the next one – the nagging one – the one that can't seem to help propagating in my head, is the thought that we all know whose house *she'd* rather be billeted at; the one with a vacant room (but it's not vacant! It *isn't*! It's just temporarily unoccupied!), the one without two eight-year-olds, but mainly the one without an irritable husband already installed as head of state.

Dee opens her water bottle and takes a long swig from it. 'Well, she should hot-foot it back there and stake her claim, if you ask me. It's disgraceful.'

It's impossible. She can't function on her own yet, and even if she could, she doesn't want to. When did she ever? 'We were thinking of launching a counter-attack over the matter of the conservatory, as it happens,' I say. 'That cost them close on fifteen thousand. And I know for a fact where the money for it came from. Her flat. *God* – sorry, excuse me for a second – but what a low life bastard scoundrel that man has turned out to be! I mean, he knew, Dee! He knew all along! Yet he happily helped her spend *her* money! It's all gone, you know. All spent on bloody cruises!'

Dee thinks for a moment. She always thinks about things. In her position (which is one of being married to an alcoholic, and thus having undergone months – no, *years* – of sitting in therapists', mediators' and counsellors' offices), I guess looking at angles and weighing up least-worst options and trying to calmly fathom motivations and solutions becomes pretty standard after a while. 'I'm sure it wasn't *quite* like that. I mean, they were getting on, weren't they? And it's kind of what you do when you're old, isn't it? Go on cruises and that. I mean, to be fair, why wouldn't they? If they could afford it, why not? You can't take it with you, after all. And what would they want to save up for at their age?'

I pick up my own bottle, rather wishing it contained gin instead of water. 'Oh, I know, I know. That's what *she* keeps telling me. But that was based on the fact – no, the fiction – that she was financially secure! That her home was her home *whatever* happened. Jeez. I can't believe she could have been so dumb. I mean how do people not know things like that? How could she have been so naïve?'

I can see from Dee's expression that she is considering pointing out that my mother certainly doesn't have the family monopoly on naïvety. That it's pretty rich of me even to suggest it. But she is too much the good friend to voice it. Anyway, it's different. My heart might be a soft touch, but my head has never failed me. Oh, damn. Now I'm fretting about Charlie again. *Damn*.

'And you forget,' she says instead, 'she's from a different generation. Women didn't concern themselves with that sort of stuff back in her day.'

My mother in particular didn't concern herself with 'that sort of stuff'. Any stuff, if she could get away with it, frankly. There was always someone else to do it for her. 'Anyway,' Dee continues, 'I'd hang right in there and get everything you can. If you can prove she paid for the conservatory, then they'll have to pay her back for it, won't they? That's something, at least, isn't it?'

Something but not much. 'I think Doug's going to look into it. Mind you, that Corinne doesn't strike me as the sort of woman who'd roll over without putting up a fight. I wouldn't mind, but, you know, she looks pretty well-heeled to me. So why all this haste to get Mum out and sell up? It's so heartless.'

Dee sighs. 'I guess she's just thinking 'why *not*?'. It's not as if she's got any reason not to, is it? And you know what families can be like, especially with later marriages. Sounds like they weren't terribly thrilled about it in the first place.'

I nod. 'You're certainly right there.'

'Oh, but your poor mum. It's pretty mean, isn't it? They could at least have given her a few months to get herself sorted.' She shakes her head. 'Life takes such horrible turns sometimes, doesn't it?' She looks reflective for a moment, and I think 'Yup, she'd know'. Then she pats me. 'Anyway, you just hang in there. I'm sure if you fight it she'll get what she deserves.'

I don't like to think too hard about what, to my mind, constitutes what my mother most 'deserves'. A good ticking off is the very least of it. 'Well,' I say, 'whatever she gets – assuming she gets anything – it's not going to amount to very much. Certainly not enough to buy somewhere.'

'So where will she live, then? A council place?'

I almost choke on my water. My *mother*? Diana G*aaaa*rland? In a council flat? She'd rather squat in a tuareg's tent. I pick my racquet up again. 'That's exactly the problem. That's the worst of it, frankly. It's not actually been said in so many words, but you know, she's unnaturally un-fazed by all this. If you saw her you'd see. She's really not that bothered at *all*. Even for an inveterate nomad. No tears. No hysterics – either actual or acted. No fuss at all. Almost the opposite in fact. '

'Well, hats off to her for taking it so bravely, I say. That's got to be a good thing, hasn't it?'

'It's the worst thing imaginable! Dee, don't you realise? I think the reason she's taking it all on the chin is that she thinks she can come and live with *me*!'

45

'Oh, I *see*.' But she doesn't. She thinks she does but she doesn't. And if I thought I could explain, then I would readily do so. But how *can* I explain to someone like Dee? Her home life is so grim she'd probably consider living with my mother as a veritable stroll in the park.

Yeah. As in Jurassic. We get back to our game.

Is there some sort of game going on in other departments too, I wonder? Because when I get back from badminton, mottled pink, sweaty and looking like I just went ten rounds with a wardrobe, the man himself is waiting outside my house, in his car.

The man I am no longer seeing. The *married* man I am no longer seeing. The man who promised he wouldn't do this. And he's parked in my parking space, to boot. Which means I have to slot myself into Mr Davidson's one, which will inflame an already inflamed situation unless I make sure I unslot myself pretty damned quick. I park across the road hastily and irritably and have already jumped out of my car by the time Charlie's meandering languidly to meet me.

The first thing I register is that he looks very tired.

And the second is that I've no business registering such things. How Charlie looks is no longer my business.

I spread my arms, palms up, as he approaches.

'Charlie, for God's sake. What d'you think you're doing?'

He holds his own hands aloft. 'It's Tuesday,' he says. And then, noting my expression, 'It's *okay*. I already watched him go.'

Which would be absolutely fair comment were we still together, because Tuesdays (7 till 10 pm at any rate) were when Seb went to five-a-side and Jake went to youth club – still does – and thus became one of those pockets of time that bad people with bad things on their mind tend to fix on. I first had sex with Charlie on a Tuesday. I last had sex with Charlie on a Tuesday. Oh, oh, oh. It's all so *seedy*. Tuesdays leave *such* a bad taste in my mouth. Though it's no longer relevant and I really mustn't dwell. Tuesdays, from now on, are Badminton Night. An altogether more wholesome form of exercise. I reach back into the car and get my racquet and towel out.

46

'Charlie, this is not about it being Tuesday or otherwise. It's about the fact that we are *over*.' I start marching towards the house.

'Half an hour. A cup of tea. Where's the harm in that? Look –' he's caught up now. 'You were the one who said we could be friends.'

'I lied,' I retort. He ignores this. Utterly. 'And if we're friends, where's the harm in you acting like one and letting me come in for a cup of tea?'

Charlie always drinks tea because coffee gives him heartburn. Camomile. Blackcurrant. Spiced apple. Green. I have an awful lot of packets of tea bags in my house. And nobody to drink them any more. (Memo to self. Abbie, just throw them *away*.) '*Because*, Charlie, okay? *Because*.' I've got my door key out now. He's showing no signs of going. 'How many more times am I going to have to say it? Anyway, what about my mother?'

'Your mother's not here.'

Rats. 'How do you know that?'

'Because Dee told me yesterday. She's gone back to your sister's.' I scowl at him. He smiles at me. I scowl some more. He strokes my arm. 'Come on. How's it been? You look seriously stressed out –'

'I *am* seriously stressed out.'

And I'm not sleeping either. I just lie there and fret. He strokes my arm a second time. 'Then let me in and you can tell me all about it.'

'I don't want to tell you all about it.'

'Yes, you do. You know you do.'

I don't, but I let him in anyway.

# Chapter 6

ANOTHER EMAIL. AM MOST impressed. Or, oh dear. There's a thought. Is he bored? Lonely? Missing home? Missing Jake? Missing *me*?

Howdy mum,

Venice. Done; St Mark's square, St Mark's basilica, Bridge of Sighs, Rialto, Peggy Guggenheim collection... NOT. Actually, we got train to Padua and had v good time. Venice very smelly. Would have got you some glass but would no doubt smash it. So didn't. Tell J it's okay about the X Box. S xx

Aw, aw, aw. It's not *fair. I* want to go to Venice. *I* want to be there. And what *about* the X-box, exactly?

Okay, okay, okay. I know I shouldn't have let him in. But it *was* okay. We didn't *do* anything. I made him a cup of tea (green tea, with mango), I told him all about it – the gist of things, anyway – and then he insisted on giving me a shoulder massage, because of course, as ever, he was absolutely right. Mine were up to my earlobes – though it didn't escape my notice that that was thanks in no small part to him. But I let him massage my shoulders anyway. Let him massage my shoulders for a good ten minutes, almost drifting off, because I was tired and he's good at it. He didn't speak. He never does. So much of what felt good and right in our relationship didn't involve any words. Damning, indicative, but nevertheless true. So, ten minutes, give or take. Though it could have been longer. In any event, right up until the moment when he intruded on the comfort of the silence and said 'D'you remember that scene in *The Fabulous Baker Boys*?'

'No,' I said. 'I don't'. Because I didn't right off. I'd seen the film years ago. So it hadn't been with him. I was still semi-drifting. Still floating in a place that said 'It's actually okay, this.

Perhaps it's all right. Perhaps we can go back to being, you know, close but not that close. For now. For a short while. Till he's properly over it...' Stupid mare.

'Yes, you do,' he said, pressing his thumbs into the back of my neck. 'You know. The one at the end of the New Year's Eve gig, when Jeff Bridges and Michelle Pfeiffer are sitting at the side of the stage and she comments that her shoulders are stiff.'

And then I did remember, because Jeff Bridges reminded me. We'd discussed, at some point, our favourite film stars, as you do. And I'd mentioned Jeff Bridges and he'd mentioned Michelle Pfeiffer and we'd both of us commented how good they were on screen together, and...uh-oh...uh-*oh*...suddenly I felt myself stiffen too. 'Charlie –'

'And Jeff Bridges says 'come over here'. Something like that. And he starts to massage her neck.' Charlie starts to massage mine. 'Remember it now? And she's got that red dress on, and he undoes the zip –'

And that's when I bundled him out. Stupid mare.

The A and the P of the A and P Physiotherapy Clinic don't really stand for Aches and Pains. They stand for Ashford and Pierce. Those being the surnames of Ken and Brendan, who own it. I don't recall now who it was that first coined its pet name. Only that it was considered as an alternative for a time, until they decided that given that at least half their patients suffer from the sort of chronic aches and pains that make their lives enough of a misery to render them somewhat snappy in the matter of making jokes about it, it was axed in favour of the former. But everyone who knows them still calls it Aches and Pains. It's how I've always thought of it, too.

The clinic, which has been open about a decade now, is thriving. It's based on the first floor of a rather grand building, the downstairs of which is occupied by a similarly posh estate agent's, staffed by glossy young lovelies and aggressively groomed men.

To get to us, however, you have to eschew the deep pile of the estate agency doormat, go round to the side door and press the entry buzzer on the wall. At which point, Candice, the receptionist, will bellow a rousing '*Hi*yah!' at you, and then, if you're lucky, also remember to let you in. Inside the door is a small hallway in which an optimistic umbrella plant is making a bid for the canopy, and a decrepit-looking stair lift (and, yes, I'll admit I've had a ride on it) for those patients reluctant and/or unable to negotiate the somewhat precipitous stairs.

I've known Ken and Brendan for a very long time. Ken was in the same year as me at college, and Brendan used to work at Highfield Park too. Early on they were an item, and then they weren't an item, but though their romantic partnership was short-lived, they've remained business partners and friends.

And friends of mine too, for which I am very, very grateful. They've actually been after me to go and work at A and P for years, which is obviously very flattering, and which also made it easy for me to decide to do so now. Yep, I'm going to like working here.

And on this, only my first full week at the practice, there is a note of celebration in the air. Candice, who has only the two volume settings (one and eleven), falls upon me with delight as I enter.

'Ah, Abbie!' she cries, even before I'm fully inside, 'Have I got exciting news for you!'

As I'm a little light on the exciting news front right now, and feeling a touch over-burdened with the other kind, I am indeed excited to hear this. Even though I've no idea what the news could be. Candice seems to find almost everything exciting, so it could be just that someone's found the teaspoon (am I the only female person left on the planet who takes sugar in their tea?), but that will do fine. I slip my jacket from my shoulders and go to hang it on the coat stand by the door. Yep, I'm really going to like working here. Because everyone's always so *happy*. Perhaps I will absorb it by osmosis. 'Great,' I say, smiling. 'What is it?'

She removes her pen from between her teeth and beams. 'You have your very first new patient,' she tells me.

'Great!' I say again. Because it is.

It's a bit of a novelty to be working somewhere where a new patient is a cause for celebration. Up to now I've always been working in a system where volumes of new patients were not so much a cause for celebration as a cause for people shaking their heads and tutting and scowling and moaning on about shortages of staff and New Bloody Labour. But having one's own patients in this situation is important – one's own specific referrals are of course something to be pleased about. So I am. They made me up some natty business cards before I started work, which I have been brandishing at almost every available opportunity. They say Abigail McFadden MCSP on them, beneath the little leaping stick man that is A and P's logo. I'm really rather proud of them. I've never had my own business cards before. But it's still early days, and up to now (and for much of the immediate future I suspect), I have mainly been seeing such patients who have called for appointments, but have not specifically requested that they see anyone else. Or June's. Who I've replaced. And they're sometimes disappointed. But they get me whether they like it or not.

I hope they *do* like, once they get to know me. 'Specifically asked for me?' I ask her, chuffed.

'Yup.' She's still beaming. 'Coming in Thursday week.'

'That's great,' I say again.

'Go on,' she goes on. 'Say "and" then.'

'And what?'

'Don't you even want to know who it is?'

'I assumed you were about to tell me.'

She claps her hands together at this. 'You are so, so lucky. Oh, I'm *so* excited. Come on. Have a guess.'

'I can't.' A lot of cards. A lot of guesses.

'Have a try.'

'No, really, I can't.'

'Tall, blond and handsome?'

'Well, that's an encouraging start, certainly.' Though none springs to mind. But *Charlie* – of course. He's been putting the word out for me too, bless him. So now I'm thinking rugby player. Athlete. Footballer, maybe. Sports person, obviously. Hmm. Tall, blond and handsome... or perhaps an unusually well developed afghan hound? 'Go on, then,' I say. '*Who*?'

'Ta ra!' she trills. 'Wait for it! It's the BBC weatherman! You *know*. Gabriel Ash!'

'Gabriel *Ash*? Coming to see *me*?'

'Yes, to see *you!* Do you know him?' she asks eagerly.

51

How utterly perplexing. How very *odd*. I must be frowning, I realise, because she then says 'What's the matter? Aren't you pleased?'

I'm mainly quite shocked. 'Well, I…are you *sure*? I mean, he actually asked for *me*?'

She nods happily. 'Your reputation has obviously preceded you. I mean, he obviously knows who you are, doesn't he? *Do* you know him?'

'Er, well, no. Not really. I mean, I've met him, but –'

'Met him? Wow-ee. What's he like?'

Hmm. I think. First impression; personable enough. Second impression. Heartless, money-grabbing toe-rag.

'I didn't say *that*, obviously,' I tell Dee when I ring her later. 'I made all the right noises. It's obviously all to the good to get high-profile patients in. But, good Lord. Why me? *How* me, more to the point? How did he know where I worked?'

'Well, you did tell him you were a physio, didn't you? He must have looked you up or something. Anyway, why worry? It's good publicity for you, isn't it? And, hey, I wouldn't kick him out of bed.'

I snort. 'You and Candice both.'

'Who's Candice?'

'Our receptionist. I think she's already booked her bikini wax and pedicure.'

'Well, you've got to admit, he is rather gorgeous.'

They're both mad, clearly. He is *so* not that. 'Gorgeous? Gorgeous nothing. All I know is that he's responsible for chucking my mother out on the street. Which is hardly going to enamour me of him, is it?'

'I thought that was his sister.'

'Oh, come *on*. It's still half his house. And why else would he just fetch up out of the blue like that? And don't you think it's just a little bit rich that he should think it okay to blithely make an appointment for me to look at his knee after all that's happened? Like he'd even think I'd *want* to. I was pretty off with him at the solicitors, I can tell you. Does he think he's doing me a favour or something?'

'Perhaps he does.'

'Well I certainly don't want any favours from *that* lot. I've a good mind to tell him to take his bloody ligaments elsewhere.'

'Perhaps that's what *he* thought. And he's obviously made the effort to track you down, so perhaps it's by way of a conciliatory gesture,' she suggests.

'Oh, yeah, right. We make your mother homeless but have a thirty pound consultation fee to make up for it. Great.'

'Or perhaps he wants a chance to talk to you. He probably feels bad about it. Or perhaps he –'

'Oh, yeah, right. Like you really thinks he gives a monkey's? Forget Mum. He hasn't even spoken to his own *father* for twenty years. And then, all of a sudden, up he pops for his inheritance. I think it's an absolute disgrace.'

'Actually, I *was* going to say that perhaps he fancies you. Have you thought of that?'

'Oh, don't talk such piffle. He's engaged to Lucy Whittall, don't forget.'

'Good Lord! *Is* he?'

'They're getting married at Christmas by all accounts. It was all in *Depth* magazine. Candice showed me.' I hear myself tutting. 'It's sickening, it really is. The whole lot of them are obviously loaded – that Corinne drives a Jag, you know – yet they don't seem to have the slightest compunction about throwing a defenceless little old lady out of her home.'

Pru laughs. 'You know,' she says. 'I can think of lots of words to describe your mother, but those are the last I'd have thought of.'

More's the pity, I think. More's the bloody pity.

# Chapter 7

POSTCARD: FRONTSIDE – OLIVE GROVE, wizened person, flagon, donkey. Backside – *Hi all! Hic! xxx*

Oh, oh, *oh*. What I wouldn't give to be sitting in an olive grove right now. What I wouldn't give to be sitting in *any* sort of grove right now. What I wouldn't give to be sitting, period.

Memo to self: Friday: a.m.
    If not raining, cut grass, bath dog. p.m. DO NOTHING.
    If raining, a.m. brush dog, Go shopping. Lunch with Dee. p.m. DO NOTHING.

Things I do NOT wish to be doing on my day off: driving to my mother's house, hoovering her carpets, scraping – indeed, even *touching* – any part of Hugo's rancid tropical fish ensemble complete with nodding Victorian novelty diving person, collecting up post, putting rubbish out for dustmen, watering pot plants (with exception of the cactus in the downstairs loo, which is not to be watered at any point *ever*), locating and removing Hugo's car keys (they'll not be getting their hands on *that*), gathering up black jacket, beige skirt, peep-toed lemon sandals, eau de nil cardigan, dressing table mirror, bottle of Opium, all knickers in top right dressing table drawer, all slips in bottom left dressing table drawer, other reading glasses, thing in bathroom for sandpapering hard skin on feet (eeewww), library books (3 only – Corinne can take *his* back) and taking said spoils (bar the books – another errand) over to Pru's house. In Bristol. Oh, and bringing my mother back to my house.

Things I am doing on my day off. See above.

The cul de sac my mother lives in is one of a kind rarely seen in suburban Britain for many a year. It is in a little pocket that time recently forgot. Every house, without exception, has net curtains at the windows. I wonder, as I drive along it, how this can be. Do potential purchasers, having made the cultural leap into a non-net curtain hanging lifestyle, simply throw their hands up in horror, do a three-point turn in the bit of road reserved (and *always* available) for the purpose, then drive off again shaking their heads? Similarly, do potential purchasers that are still very much net-aware fall upon The Myrtles (for that is the name of the cul de sac), in raptures of net-fuelled delight? Sad to say that were I to take a turn around The Myrtles with a house move in mind, I would definitely be one of the former. Not because I hold net curtain owners to be a lesser kind of life form, but simply because people with net curtains, in the main, are more mature, in the main, and more quiet, in the main, and are therefore likely, in the main, to be more than averagely horrified if Jake and his drum kit and his skateboard moved in. And outside almost every house sits a sensible car, all of them sparkling like extremely smug pins. Always a reliable clinical sign.

My mother's house (which, strangely, is how I have come to refer to it now that it isn't any more) has a big For Sale board outside. This is as of last Wednesday, and is the principal reason I am here today. On principle, I tabled the motion that it ought to be Corinne (and her smarmy long-lost brother, for that matter) who was earmarked for the scrub up before people came-a-viewing, but my mother was quick to point out that a) she has not the least intention of having that woman rummaging through her personals, and b) neither does she want some 'trumped up' estate agent, who's no better than they should be, passing judgement on the state of her carpets and surfaces unless she's one hundred percent sure they are all up to scratch. Which is fair comment, I suppose, because neither would I. Anyway, once the necessary complement of trips have been made to divest said house of all her belongings (which will be many, and many of them Doug-based – bet he's pleased), Corinne can clean her bloody house herself. No decision has yet been arrived at re the fish.

Yet for all this fighting talk my mother is still so damn *jolly*. Preternaturally jolly, disgustingly jolly, and the only reason I haven't yet passed comment about it is that I'm almost sure I know exactly why that is, and can't face the conversation I know will ensue. I need time to adjust. To gird what needs girding. And to prepare a watertight case for the defence.

I pull up and park my (dirty and dented) car across the drive – Hugo's Nissan Sunny is going nowhere, after all – gather rubber gloves and bin bags and squirty stuff and Spike, then I march grimly up the path and let us both in.

Already it smells different. For one thing it no longer smells of my mother, or, rather, of the pot pourri refresher oils for which she has long had a fetish. Or of Hugo's 'occasional' (where the word 'occasional' equals daily) cigars. Now the house is infused with that distinct but unmistakeable fragrance of being somewhere where nobody's living. Dust, perhaps. Even though there's no one to make it. Still air, marking time. Growing stale.

I pull my key out of the open door and step into the hallway. Such post that has been delivered is not on the doormat, but in a neat pile on the little semi-circular table by the stairs. I flip through it, wondering as I do so which bits of it I should take away. Just Mum's? Hugo's too? What's the protocol for these things? I realise there probably isn't one. I take Mum's, plus the couple of letters addressed to them both, and make a mental note to ask her about the others.

The kitchen is grim. Not grim as in teenage under-bed-world grim. Just grim as in the way kitchens get to be grim when occupied by people who don't feel any pressing need to make-over, de-clutter or otherwise tart up their lives. There is just stuff *every*where. Biscuit barrels, Tupperware containers, empty sherry bottles, egg-timers, expired airplants on amusingly shaped pebbles, ramekins full of used tea bags, spoon rests with stains on, tea towels stuffed randomly through the handles of cupboard doors. And all of it dominated by a pre-historic spider plant that's wedged on a high shelf in the corner by the cooker, and from which a waterfall of dozens of little spider plants hang. And on almost every available square inch of the window sill, further baby spider plants burgeon from plastic flower pots on tide-marked saucers, trailing on the draining board, crawling into the sink, sidling along the by-ways of the worktop.

Spike, having sidled and found nothing to amuse him, is now clamouring for action by the back door. I find the correct key, then let him out into the garden, with instructions to go poo at will. And then I make a start on the fridge.

As I have had painful cause to acquaint myself with recently, there's nothing as revealing about a person (or persons), as a careful examination of the contents of their fridge. I bend down and gingerly acquaint myself with Mum and Hugo's. No one has much been here since the day of the funeral, and though both Pru and I have made sorties with Mum to pick stuff up, we've none of us lingered here long enough to make forays into its sepulchrally lit interior.

It's chock full, as expected. Though not remotely in the sense that you'd go 'yeehah! Let's eat!'. On the top shelf there are two dusty eggs, a small plastic bowl with seven wizened baked beans in, three almost empty jars of jam with rust accruing on the lids, a jar of pickled onions (one onion left), a folded butter wrapper and half an apple wrapped in cling film. I attempt to pick it up. Correction: apple puree.

On the lower shelf there is a similarly cling-filmed casserole dish (remaining contents taupe and unidentifiable), an empty Branston Pickle jar, a tea plate with half a dried-up lemon and a teaspoon on it, a third of a packet of supermarket own brand block margarine, about a sixth of a cucumber (now essentially slurry), another plastic bowl with two grey boiled potatoes in it, another folded butter wrapper (?), an open packet of streaky bacon (one streak remaining), a mug full of what I presume must be dripping and a fruits of the forest yoghurt with a violently stressed lid.

The door (in a nod towards health and fitness, I presume) contains four little bottles of bacterially beneficial yoghurt drink (way out of date), a small tub of eye gel, some interesting looking plastic eyewear called a Gunk Wonder Mask, the remains of a small bar of diabetic chocolate, a half full bottle of red wine with a kitchen roll stopper, and a carton of the dairy product formerly known as milk.

In the salad drawer there is nothing bar one cherry tomato, for which I am really most grateful.

I'm just pouring the curds and whey into the sink when I'm suddenly startled by a loud bang from upstairs. I turn the tap off and listen harder, but the silence is once again total and I wonder if I'm imagining things. I peer into the garden. Perhaps it was coming from outside. But then I hear it again. Accompanied this time by a sort of scraping noise. Definite. Actual. Real. And upstairs. And not a million miles removed from that bit at the beginning of *The Exorcist* when the mother thinks they have rats in the attic... Except she's wrong and it turns out to be something much worse. I put down the milk carton and tiptoe to the kitchen door. If they're rats, I decide, then they're big ones. No. *Human* ones. There's definitely somebody up there. Oh, God, I think. Burglars! But it surely can't be burglars, can it? Who would be so brazen? It's a sunny Friday lunchtime. We're in net curtain land. There are Neighbourhood Watch plates on every other lamppost. Nothing bad can happen in The Myrtles, can it? But there's something – no, some*one* – upstairs, that's for certain. I feel a shiver of alarm. Hugo's ghost? I hover some more in the kitchen doorway, anxious, a bit frightened, and not at all sure what to do.

But then I mentally shake myself. What sort of wimp *am* I? I decide upon action as opposed to evacuation and take four determined steps to the newel post.

'Er...hello?' I call up. No one responds. But then the scrapes become thunks. 'Er...hello-oo?' I say again.

But it/they can obviously not hear me calling, so now I take a tentative four or five steps up the stairs. Looking up now, I can just see the corner of the loft hatch, and the edge of a step ladder spread underneath. So I wasn't imagining it. There *is* someone up there (rats – even giant rats – don't set up ladders), but the question is, who can it be?

It's not terribly long before I find out.

'Hel-LOOO!!!' I say again, albeit ready and braced. I can still be at the front door in seconds, if needs be, though something tells me a daylight-hours burglar at large would have altogether more finely honed hearing. Even so, my heart isn't exactly on message. It's chuntering away like a train now. After all, why wouldn't a burglar burgle here? It's unoccupied, inviting, full of silverware...cripes – they might well have even staked the place out. Oh, God! And what about Spike in the garden? I'm just dithering about whether to fetch him and then make a getaway via the side gate, when there's a bump, then another, then some shuffling and banging. Then a new voice – a male one – shouts down 'er…hello?'

And then says it again. I grip the stair rail tighter and try to keep calm. Would a house-breaker ever say 'er…hello?' when confronted? But then I realise I'm sure I've heard the voice before. And I'm just at the point of remembering where it was that I heard it when Gabriel Ash – well, his startled face, anyway – suddenly appears in what I can see of the hatch.

I start as well, and for a moment we're both speechless. Then he grins at me. *Grins*! The cheek of the man! 'What the *hell* do you think you're doing here?' I bark up at him.

'Er…' His face disappears back into the blackness for a moment, then his lower legs swing down through the hole. They hover, somewhat precariously, about a foot above the ladder, but though good sense would dictate that I go up and hold it, I decide that as he got himself up there unaided, he can bloody well get down by himself too. Which he does. And he's got cobwebs in his hair. Possibly a family of migrant spiders as well, though he doesn't seem to notice, in that way that men don't. He pauses on the second to top step of the ladder and reaches back into the hatch to take hold of a box. Now I stomp up to the top of the stairs.

'Well?' I say again, 'just what do you think you're doing?'

He looks sheepish, but not that sheepish. And even a bit jovial. 'Oh, I'm sorry,' he says nicely. 'Did I scare you? I'm sorting some stuff out. In the attic. I'm sorry. I didn't know you were here.'

'More to the point,' I point out crossly, 'is that I didn't know *you* were here. You frightened the life out of me!' Which is somewhat overdoing it, as I'm patently alive still, but he deserves it anyway. He *could* have.

'I'm sorry,' he says again, and I concede that he looks as if he is. Well, quite right too, frankly. 'I didn't hear you,' he explains. 'I've been down at the far end.' He indicates the general direction. 'Phew, but it's dusty up there.' He makes a few sweeps across his jeans, as if to illustrate, showering the carpet with bits of loft insulation. Then he follows my gaze. 'Er, sorry,' he says again.

'Sorting *what* stuff exactly?' I ask him pointedly, because the more I think about it, the crosser I find I am becoming. It's one thing to find out that Mum's home actually *isn't* that, quite another to find Hugo's prodigal son fetching up and breezing, bold as you like, through the contents of her loft. A bloody cheek, in fact.

'Things of my father's. My sister said –'

'Oh, so that's all right, then, is it?' I snap. 'God, I really can't believe you people!' I park my knuckles on my hips and glower up at him. 'Not only have you turfed my mother out of her home before the crematorium cooker's even gone cold, now you're invading it as well! Look, it may well be that you own the house – though NOT the conservatory, so you can expect to hear a bit more about *that*, believe me – but tenants do have certain rights, you know. To privacy, at the very least. So neither of you has any right whatsoever to enter this property without prior permission from my mother.'

'But –'

'Yes, I *know* the estate agent has a key. Of course he does. He has to. And he at least does us the courtesy of telephoning first to see when it's convenient to show people round. But it's absolutely *not* okay for you to think you can just –'

'But she said it was.'

'But it's not *up* to her! It's up to my mother! And I'm quite sure the last – the *very* last – thing she'd want is to find some stranger here riffling though her things!'

He winces a little – well, I guess I am being stroppy – and then he shakes his head. 'No, no. Look, if you'd just let me *finish*... You don't understand. I *meant* your mother. I *did* telephone. And –'

'*What?*'

'I said I *did* speak to your mother!'

I'm open-mouthed now. 'When?'

'Earlier this week. And she said it would be fine.' He spreads his hands. Which are filthy. 'Didn't she mention that to you?'

No. Curse her. She most definitely *didn't* mention. Thanks, Mum. Thanks a *lot*. 'Oh,' I say, feeling stupid now, and therefore even crosser. 'In that case –'

'Come *on*,' he says, smiling again. 'I wouldn't do that. What on earth do you take me for?'

What indeed? I mainly take him (as I must) as what I already know him to be. The estranged son of the man my mother was most recently married to, who (though he could never hold a candle to my father) I thought was okay at best, a bit tedious at worst, but who has turned out to be something of a rat. And though I really must try not to judge his son by association (after all, before we found out what we found out, I thought he seemed perfectly pleasant) he's still come swanning into our lives and pulled the plug on my mother's life, and, by implication and extension and bloody biology, also *mine*.

Though I dare say he hasn't thought about *that*. He climbs two-thirds of the way up the ladder again, and pulls another box from its depths. Then he pulls the little light cord, slides back the loft hatch, descends the ladder once again (this time I do grudgingly hold it – I'm not *that* mean), puts the box with the other one and then takes the ladder down.

'So,' he says cheerfully (for he has everything to be cheerful about, doesn't he? He has leached all the good cheer from my life, for sure), 'Have you come to pick some bits up for your mother or something?' He leans the ladder carefully against the landing wall. 'I can give you a hand if you like.'

His change of tack and tone don't impress me in the least. I am not in the mood to be mollified. 'Yes, *and* 'or something'' I say testily. 'And feed the fish, and water the plants, and clean the fridge out, and hoover the carpets...'

He glances at his watch. 'Fine,' he says. 'I'll help you.'

'No, really –'

'I'd be happy to. Least I can do. But first I'll put the kettle on, shall I?'

'I'm sorry, but I've got to get on,' I say crisply. 'Besides, there's no milk. I just got rid of the last of it.'

'I'm sure we'll find something.'

Get the 'we', I think. Hark at him! Twerbling away at me as if he owned the place. I think some more. Er. Which, in fact, he does. Half of it, anyway... I think still further. The consequence

61

of which is that my mother is *homeless*. Lovely. Thanks very much.

I shake my head. 'I don't want a drink, if it's all the same to you. As I said, I've got to get on. I don't want to be stuck in here all day.'

'Oh,' he says, looking a bit abashed. 'Right. Well, er...if you're sure, then. I suppose I might as well get off.'

I turn to descend the stairs again. 'Whatever,' I throw over my shoulder. 'It is your house, after all.'

Which barb is quite unnecessary, I realise. Though I realise too late to stop it from having escaped from my lips. God, what's got *into* me today? He follows me back down the stairs. 'Look,' he says, and his tone has become somewhat pointed. 'I really am sorry this is all causing you so much hassle. But there isn't a great deal I can do about it, is there? If it was just up to me your mother could stay here as long as she needs to. But it *isn't* just up to me, and I'm afraid there's nothing I can do.'

Because Corinne 'needs' her out. And he's obviously not about to try and dissuade her. But he doesn't elaborate further. 'Well, whatever,' I say again, blinking at the dust motes that a shaft of summer sunshine is idly fondling in the hallway. Tomorrow is mine and it will be raining, for sure. I have half a mind to ask him if it will. No, in fact, to *blame* him if it does. Everyone else probably does. 'You really don't have to explain yourself to me, you know,' I answer. Then I turn my back on him and stride off back into the kitchen.

Again, he follows. 'So,' he asks conversationally, while I pull my rubber gloves back on. 'What *is* going to happen with your mum, then?'

Like he even cares. 'Well, isn't that just the sixty-four thousand dollar question?' I respond, with a definite edge to my voice. I catch my reflection in one of my mother's many, many mirrors. And I wish I hadn't. My hair, hastily scraped into the worst kind of ratty, uncombed, chaotic sort of ponytail, is sprouting in mad clumps in every direction, and my eyes, squinting in the harsh glare of the midsummer sun, are weighed down by sooty-smeared coalbags. I look a fright. There's no other word for it. Memo to self: being tired and bad-tempered is *so* not a good look. Put head in ice bucket soonest, and *chill*. Get some sleep, at the very least. You look the absolute pits. 'We don't know yet,' I tell him, as he's clearly not in any sort of rush. He's busy washing his hands now. 'She's staying at my sister's at the moment.'

'She doesn't want to come back here? You know. For the time being at least? While she sorts something else out?'

'Not remotely,' I assure him, wondering exactly what 'something else' he assumes she is going to sort out. 'I mean, would *you*? With estate agents tramping strangers all around the place while you pack your whole life up in boxes?' I shove the milk carton into the bin bag with the rest of the sludge. 'No,' I say tightly. 'She doesn't. She can't manage on her own while she's using crutches, obviously, and the rate your sister is pushing things along here, I don't doubt that by the time she can you'll have sold the place from under her anyway.'

All of which, frankly, is quite beside the point. This is my mother and she's not like most people. Where Pru and I see a crisis and a bad situation, all she seems to see is her latest adventure. Were she hauled off the Titanic into a row boat in the ocean, she'd be barely in her seat before she started up a conversation that began 'Well, now. Isn't *this* exciting? Wonder where we'll be shipwrecked?' and then start up a chorus of *Wandering Star*. Except she wouldn't, of course, because it hadn't been written then. But still. That's the gist of it. That's what she's *like*. For all her maternal failings (and I don't doubt the two things are connected), I've always admired her pluck, her optimism, her pioneer mentality. I'm just not so keen on the ever-looming possibility that she now wants to pioneer a new settlement at mine.

'Oh, dear,' he says, because he doesn't know her, of course. 'Is she terribly upset?'

I think 'No. Not a bit of it. No, that's just Pru and I.' But I'm not going to tell *him* that. That's none of his business. So I say 'Y*es*. Of *course* she is! She's seventy-four and disabled, for God's sakc! If you were in her shoes, wouldn't *you* be?'

I know I'm ranting, but I can't seem to help it. I have lost Sebastian, Charlie, my day off, my weekend, and in exchange I have inherited my mother. Only intermittently, I know, but that's plenty bad enough. I do *try* to think positive thoughts about the

63

future, but there just doesn't seem to be anything to look forward to any more. And his solicitous platitudes really don't help. Him saying how sorry he is doesn't change anything, does it? He looks at me carefully while he dries his hands on a tea towel. 'Yes,' he says, nodding. 'I imagine I would.'

Then he's back at the sink again (does he do it on autopilot?) filling the bowl, gathering up the plastic dishes and the tea plate and the casserole dish I've just emptied, and peering under the sink, presumably for a scourer. I pick up the bin bag and relocate it to the back door, by which time he's delved into a drawer for a clean dishcloth and is busy wetting it under the tap. Does he have some sort of fetish, or what? And, frankly, why doesn't he stop all this trying to jolly me along? Why doesn't he just go away and leave me to get on with my sulking?

'Look,' I say, picking up my cleaner and mop. 'You don't have to do this, you know.'

He smiles over at me as he wrings out the cloth. 'I know I don't,' he says mildly, and carries on doing it anyway. It's probably that, more than anything, that makes me see red. The way he looks – and has made himself – so very much at home here, while my mother sets her merry sights on doing just the same at mine. Childish, unreasonable, petulant and mean-spirited. Yup. Today, sadly, that would seem to be me.

Because I then say, 'I mean, I'd rather you *didn't*.' Which, once I've uttered it, shocks me almost as much as I imagine it does him. He looks over and starts to smile (television person's default expression), but then, seeing *my* expression, which I'm sure is fairly shrewish, his brow furrows instead. And it suddenly – belatedly – enters my head that perhaps I'm not the only one in this kitchen who's feeling a bit testy and vulnerable and emotional today. Sure, I know why *I* am. I could write a bloody essay on the subject. But what thoughts, what regrets, what conflicting emotions are running through *his* mind right here right now? Twenty years is a great deal of time to have lost. I almost feel chastened. But I suspect I'm too late. Because his frown has morphed into a glower.

'There's no need,' he says stiffly, 'to bite my head off, okay? I'm only trying to be friendly.'

And though I don't mean to I feel even testier. 'Believe me, there's no need for you to do *that*,' I reply.

There's a very long silence while our eyes square up to each other. Measuring the odds while we stare each other out. Except he's just got a dishcloth to my trigger pack of *Mr Muscle*. 'Fine,' he says, eventually, slapping down the cloth. 'Message received and understood. I'll be off.'

Ooh-er. Abbie, too much. *Too* much. 'Look,' I start to say. 'I'm sorry, but –'

He lifts a hand to stop me speaking. 'You know what?' he says coolly. 'Please don't waste your breath. Because I actually don't think you are.'

'But I –'

'No, no. That's absolutely *fine*. Suit yourself.'

And then he leaves the kitchen.

And then he leaves.

In a huff.

Humph, I think, watching as he bangs out through the front door with his boxes. Okay, so that was a bit over the top, but, well, humph anyway. He's right. I'm sorry but not *that* sorry. It's really been that kind of day.

And then I realise that our encounter has been so short, sharp and entirely to the point that I haven't even had a chance to ask him how he came to make the physio appointment with me. So be it, I decide. Presumably now he'll cancel. And if he doesn't, I *will*. He can take his bloody ligament and shove it up his nose.

# Chapter 8

I RING ON PRU'S doorbell a full seven times before managing to attract any attention. Once inside, and then outside – and now in the back garden – it's clear why. My niece and nephews (plus assorted other small children – there's always an assortment of other small children at Pru's, much like there's always an assortment of other big ones at mine) are galumphing around the garden, while my mother, reclining gracefully with her skirt pulled up in one of a pair of garden recliners, is sipping tea and flicking through a copy of Sainsbury's Magazine. Childish, I know, but it makes me feel even more ratty. How come I didn't get to spend any part of today – my day off – reclining in a garden in the sunshine?

Spike, to whom all of life is suddenly becoming just one big glorious garden idyll, launches himself enthusiastically into the fray.

'Thanks a lot, Mum,' I say, flopping onto Pru's recliner while she goes back inside to make me a cup of tea.

'For what, darling?' she replies, not looking up.

'You might have warned me Hugo's son was going to be there as well.'

'Oh,' she says, turning now. 'Was he?'

'Yes, he was. He was ferreting about in the attic. I thought there'd been a break-in. No, worse, I thought someone was breaking in right then. Fancy not mentioning it, Mum. He frightened the life out of me. ' Okay, I know he didn't. But why should she be the only drama queen around here?

'I'm sorry, dear. I thought he was popping round earlier in the week. And to be honest it completely slipped my mind.'

'Well, I wish it hadn't, Mother. Because I really, really wasn't in the mood. God, and I was foul to him, too.'

I feel myself slump in the recliner. I know Gabriel Ash's opinion of me is of absolutely no consequence either way, but even so, that thought has been depressing me the whole of the way here. It's so not *like* me to be like that. To be so scratchy and

66

crotchety and peevish. So now I feel bad about myself as well as miserable. Memo to self: get some *sleep*.

'Foul to him? Why ever were you foul to him, Abigail? He seems like such a nice man to me.'

Yes, rub it in, why don't you? 'Mum,' I hear myself snap. 'He may be the nicest man in Niceville, for all I know, but that doesn't mean he's not also one of my least favourite people right now.'

'But it's not –'

'*His* fault. So you keep telling me! So does he! But what on earth were you thinking anyway? Giving him carte blanche to go into your home? You know, Mum, you don't actually know the first thing about him. None of us do, do we? Yes, he's clearly Hugo's son, I'll grant you. But we're talking about someone who's just turned up out of the blue, here. Don't you think that's just a little odd? Where's he come from? Where's he *been* all these years? What's his angle? And what's with all the snooping in the loft? And why did Hugo never mention him? Hmm? Don't you find *that* odd as well? I mean, how do we know he hasn't spent the last twenty years in prison for some terrible crime?'

'Oh, don't be so melodramatic, darling. Anyway, he hasn't. He was an officer in the navy. That's where he trained in meteorology. Then he spent some time working in Germany and Italy, I understand. And he's certainly not been in prison. Don't be so ridiculous. You honestly think they'd put a convict on the television news?'

My mouth's hanging open. 'How d'you know all of *that*?'

'From chatting to him, of course.'

'When?'

'Oh, here and there.' She glances pointedly at me. 'I thought *someone* ought to build some bridges.' Yeah, right. For 'bridges' read 'useful celebrity contacts'. Some things never change. She puts her magazine down and looks reflective. 'Such a pity, isn't it?'

'What's a pity?'

'Oh, don't play dense, dear. I mean about him and his father, of course. I do wish I'd known.'

'Oh, you chatted about that too, did you?'

There's clearly something in my tone that irritates her. She looks at me sharply. 'You know, getting yourself into such a state about things is really not going to *help* anything, Abigail. We have to work with and accept things as they *are*, not hanker after what we would wish them to be. It's the only way to –'

'Did you just read that in that magazine of yours?'

'Tsk,' she says. 'Honestly, the way you go on, anyone would think it wasn't me but *you* that had lost their home!'

I absolutely cannot answer that.


Pru comes back out then, with a mug of tea for me, but almost immediately asks me if I'd mind coming back in, so I can help her dish up the kids' tea.

I follow her back in gladly – I'm not in the mood for any more Garland homilies today – and once we're in the kitchen she wastes no time in coming to the point.

'Listen,' she says, as she hands me a tea towel. 'Do you want another weekend to yourself?'

My mood lightens considerably. I know a lot of my scratchiness all day has been the thought of Mum coming home with me again this evening. And feeling guilty about thinking unseemly thoughts like that has, of course, made me more irritable still. 'I'd love one,' I say, feeling better. 'What's the catch?'

'Ah,' she says, pulling two pizzas from the oven. 'Hit the nail on the head, there, Sis.' She puts them down on the hob and pulls off her oven gloves. 'There is a catch. And it's a big one.'

'Which is?'

She pulls a drawer open and ferrets around in it. 'Which is…well, things are – how shall I put it? – getting somewhat strained around here.'

'Oh, dear,' I say. 'No surprises there, then.'

'Doug is getting dangerously close to meltdown, to be honest. You know how things are between them.'

'Don't worry. I do.'

As they ever were, is my guess. In that Mum and Doug were never about to pal up and audition for the Generation Game. (Though I wouldn't be in the least surprised if the thought hadn't

68

occurred to her at some point. Exposure is never terribly far from her mind.)

She pulls out a little metal wheel on a stick. A gadget, I realise, for cutting up pizzas. 'Well, think 'bad' and then treble it,' she says.

'Oh, dear. *That* bad, eh?'

'More than that bad. The atmosphere couldn't get much worse if they built a sewage plant next door.' She starts whizzing the pizza cutter across the first of the pizzas. A gob of onion flies off and hits the floor. I pick it up and throw it in the bin. Pru's generally fairly unflappable, but the strain's clearly showing. 'She's just so…so…bloody *there* all the time, you know? With her opinions, her pronouncements, her bloody Lactulose bottles. She's up before us every morning, doing her bloody yoga with the television blaring. I mean since when did you do yoga to breakfast TV? And she never goes to bed! Never!'

'Tell me about it.'

'I *know*. And, you know, yesterday, she just waltzed into our bedroom at one in the morning! While we were…well …' She grimaces.

I feel sorry for Pru. She's the most easy-going person imaginable. But it clearly *isn't* easy when the going's down a path that's in the middle of a mother/husband war zone. 'Look, you clearly need a break, so I *will* take her back with me tonight. And don't worry, I know what you're going to say, and it's fine. I'll keep her for as long as you need me to, okay? Hey, at least we can drown her out with drumming. Even Mum can't compete with Metallica.'

She doesn't smile. 'But that's just it, Abbie –' She puts down the pizza cutter and goes across to shut the back door. 'That's the whole point. That's the catch. Doug's said she can't come back here. Not next week. Not next month. Just '*not*'.'

'Ah,' I say, as comprehension fully dawns. 'I see.'

'God, I mean, you know if it was just up to me –'

Comprehension as in a one-way ticket to my place. 'No, no. Don't worry,' I hear myself saying, in my best big-sister, unstressy voice. 'I *understand*. I do know how things are.'

'I mean it's not like she can't come and stay for the weekend from time to time. It's just that, well, things really aren't so hot around here right now. Doug's stressed out with work like you wouldn't believe, and what with the kids, and…well, the main problem is that we always said we wouldn't, that's all. We'd *agreed*. I mean, even when Doug's dad had his stroke and everything…even *then*. You know, I did offer. I mean, you *do*, don't you? You make all these rules but when it comes to it, when something like this actually *happens*, everything changes, doesn't it? You re-think, don't you? But Doug was pretty firm about it. He wasn't going to put us – *me* – through it with his father, so I can hardly dump all this on him now, can I? I mean you do understand, don't you? He's just not prepared to…'

I start gathering plates and cutlery. 'Pru, it's okay. I *do* understand. I'll have her.'

'Either that, or we think about finding somewhere for her to rent. I don't know. What do you think?'

I shake my head, much as I'd like not to have to. 'She can't rent. Not yet, at least. Not till she's walking unaided. It's okay. I'll *have* her, Pru. Stop looking so anguished.'

'Oh, you're such an angel. I knew you'd be okay about it. I don't know why I've been getting myself in such a state about asking. I don't even know why I feel so guilty about it in the first place. It's not like she's ever really…well… you know…'

I put my arm around her, and try to feel angelic. Up to now I hadn't realised how close to tears she's been. 'You just *do*. Doesn't matter what sort of mother she's been, does it? There's no balance sheet, is there? You just do.'

'But are you absolutely sure? I mean really? I just thought that with Seb being away right now, it wouldn't be *so* awful, would it? I mean, you'll be at work most of the time anyway, won't you? So at least you can escape from her a bit. And it's not like it's going to be for ever, is it? And she's much better off there than here, isn't she? It's not sensible for her to be stuck out here, away from all her friends. At least with you she could still have some sort of a social life. Get out from under your feet a bit. And we could start looking at options, couldn't we? Doug spoke to the solicitor this morning, and he apparently sounded quite confident about Mum getting something out of them for the conservatory – I mean, it's added to the asking price quite considerably, after all.

So there's nothing to stop us at least starting to look at places, is there?'

'You've talked about this to Mum?' I say. She nods. 'So how does she sound?'

'Well, she's not champing at the bit about it, obviously. But we talked about maybe going to see one of these retirement developments – not sheltered, or anything – God, she'd have a fit! – but something *like* that, at any rate.'

'But even if she does get a few thousand out of them, that's a drop in the ocean in terms of buying somewhere.'

She looks suddenly brighter. 'Actually, it's not as bleak as we thought. Doug's been looking into it. Apparently, some of these places have shared equity set-ups. You pay a proportion of the current market value and they retain the rest. And then when she dies they take an equivalent proportion at market rates then. It's quite a clever system. And he's quite keen – well, he hasn't said no, at any rate. I mean it would be an investment of sorts, wouldn't it?'

I don't have much use for the word investment in my life, but suddenly I can see that this might just be a solution.

Pru reaches into the fridge and pulls out a bowl of salad. 'And you know, if we crack on, we could have her sorted and settled in a matter of – well, not more than a couple of months or so. Don't you think? And then, God willing, we can get back to *our* lives. And in the meantime, well, as I said, we'd obviously have her here from time to time to help you out and so on... We wouldn't expect you to take *all* the responsibility. It's just that she really, really can't stay here for much longer, Abbie.'

A couple of months. I try on the idea of a couple of months and find myself re-writing time. It will be the absolute longest couple of months in history, I don't doubt, but then again, what can I say? Pru's right. It *isn't* just her she has to consider. Whereas right now I only have Jake to consider. And Jake won't give a fig. Jake will think it's fun. Jake thinks his nana is a hoot.

I put my arm around her shoulder again and give her a hug. 'Pru, I told you. It's *fine*.'

'You absolutely sure? I feel awful about it. I mean she's every bit as much my responsibility as she is yours – more so, in many ways –'

'How d'you work that out?'

'Well, she's been there so much more for me, hasn't she? Still doesn't amount to much, admittedly, but, well, you know... What with the children and everything...'

Which is, I guess, true. Though I'm not about to say so. It wasn't actually planned that way. Just the happy conjunction of Pru having had her children when Mum was between husbands and cruises and having one of her sporadic I'm-an-uber-granny periods. If I'd fared less well (husband three – her *Viva Espana* decade) then so be it. It had never occurred to me that she would or even *should* be around much. We – latterly I – were just fine as we were. But that's not how it works anyway. You do what you do because that's what you *do*. *Que Se* – oh, bugger. (Memo to self: must watch that.)

But Pru clearly feels it. 'Don't talk daft,' I say.

'Oh, I know, I know. I just feel dreadful having to land her on you like this, just when you've got a bit of time to yourself. Just when there's a chance you might...well...' She stops speaking and looks at me hard, but she doesn't say the next bit she's thinking. She's long since stopped enquiring about my love life. She doesn't know about Charlie, naturally. And, tempted though I've been at times, because I know she wouldn't judge me half so much as I do myself, I'd never ever tell her. But then again, I don't know. I sometimes think perhaps she does. In any event, she knows *something* has changed.

'Pru, I told you. It's absolutely fine. Hey, give it a few weeks and she'll be lining up husband number five.' Pru laughs and rolls her eyes, but neither of us think so. Not really. Not now. 'Look, okay, then. I *will* have my weekend. Give me a chance to get Seb's room straight for her, then, well... Let me see. Monday evening? Actually, no. You won't want to drag over late, will you? So perhaps you'd better make it Sunday.'

'You're sure?'

'I'm sure.' I hug her. Now my worst case scenario is actually happening, I feel an unexpected sense of relief. At least I won't have to waste time fretting about it any more. 'As long as it's p.m., okay?' I say, smiling. 'Come on. Let's go feed these kids, eh?'

*　　*　　*

That's it, then. The deed's done. Sunday. I've committed. Now all I have to do is get used to the idea.

'But I mean, what *could* I say?' I ask Spike as we rattle back across the Severn toward a uniformly blue sky and my last forty-eight hours of freedom. My last forty-eight hours before morphing from newly single reasonably optimistic forty-something-on-a-gap-year (GSOH, all her own teeth, no baggage to speak of, interested in gd times, gd conversation, travel, married men need not apply) to middle-aged scratchy singleton with elderly dependent relative (up for most things but must be in by eleven at all times – and absolutely no sleep-overs, ever). Spike doesn't comment, but I can tell he's sympathetic. 'What *can* I say?' I ask him. 'She's my mother, after all. This is the sort of thing you just have to *do*, isn't it? Lots of people do it. *Loads* of people have their parents to live with them, don't they? And it's not like it's going to be for ever, after all. I mean it's not even as if she's going to *want* to be there for ever, is it? It's hardly ideal, is it? I know she thinks it's going to be more congenial at our place: no Doug, no kids, no military manoeuvres. But we shall see. She's never actually lived with us before, has she? And what with Jake and his band, and Mr Davidson next door, and me out at work so not available for taxiing, and you know how much she hates noise and muddle and mess and – yes, I'm sorry, mate, but your dog hairs as well. No. It'll be all right. It is just going to be temporary. She'll be desperate to leave in no time at all.'

Spike goes 'woof!'. And I know just what he means. What he means is 'come *on* – didn't you clock her expression? You're talking absolute bollocks and you know it. She's cock-a-bloody-hoop, is your mother.'

Oh, dear. And now Mr Davidson is here, to seal this lovely day with a very loving kiss. Mr Davidson, who lives next door, is a postman, which means he is quite possibly the person least circadian-rhythmically suited to living next door to a house in which an internationally famous pop star lives. Thus at no point, I suspect, will relations ever be loving. Even grudgingly polite to vaguely cordial would be nice.

To be fair to Mr Davidson (for being fair to Mr Davidson is an ever present factor in my life), living next door to someone for whom drumming is the recreational pursuit of choice is not exactly ideal. To be scrupulously fair to Mr Davidson, of course, Jake is not as yet an internationally renowned pop star, so I can fully appreciate that his commitment to his craft carries not quite the same weight as, say, Phil Collins's might, but if he can't drum how will he ever BE an internationally renowned pop star?

To be fair to everyone else who does not have a pop star in waiting in the family, I wouldn't much like living next door to us either. Indeed, before having children (having sons, specifically, as they are both much more noisy than girls and much more hated than girls by society generally – particularly if they wear sweatshirts with hoods on – as any mother of sons knows already), I probably would have agreed that it's just, come on, *not on*, to have persons drumming and plugging amps in and singing badly into microphones in a residential area.

But once I became a parent to someone who does all those things, my attitude, of necessity, changed greatly. Having established a bullet-pointed plan of times when drumming/playing/rehearsing was *un*acceptable i.e. most of the daytime and all hours of darkness unless certain noise-minimisation principles were observed, and thus whittled practice down to a few scant hours a week, not to mention doling out draconian punishments for episodes of transgression, then it became – *still* becomes – a little galling to note that other noisy activities (about which I paid never-no-mind at one time), such as lawnmowing, strimming, hedge trimming, drill manoeuvres involved in the putting up of patios/conservatories and water features, leaf blowing and jet washing, tend to be done, in such areas, at pretty much any old damn time without reference to anyone, and without the expectation of any sort of come-back at all. Scrub something, lop something, erect something out of breeze blocks and no one seems to mind at all. But pick out a tune, add a paradiddle and a flourish, and you're everyone's least best friend. So drumming, band practice and all related pursuits happen mainly, in our house, from four till six weekdays, between ten and four Saturdays, and never, never, never on a Sunday.

And then Mr Davidson moved in next door. Mr Davidson who is a postman.

As well as being a postman, Mr Davidson is divorced, in his late fifties, short of stature and short of temper. I'm not sure which of the first three can lay first claim to being the reason for the last of these, but suffice to say, when he moved into the house, no one warned him of the many-cymballed beast that lived next door, therefore second claim, obviously, has to be that.

'Ah, Abbie,' he says, ambushing me as I get out of my car, while effecting to have been simply fortuitously in the location of it – something which he has perfected over many years.

'Mr Davidson,' I say back.

It's a cause of some irritation to me that while I have always, unfailingly, called him Mr Davidson, he has equally unfailingly always called me Abbie. As if I wasn't a forty-four year old mother of two sons but a little girl next door he gives sweets to.

'I'm glad I caught you,' he says, bending down to stroke Spike, who is already belly up at his feet. Irritatingly, Spike is a bit of a turncoat in the matter of Mr Davidson. Spike, who, being a dog, has absolutely no business toadying up to a postman in the first place, actively *likes* Mr Davidson .

But *I'm* not glad he caught me. Not at all. I'd quite like to tell him to bog off, like Jake always does under his breath. Except I'd quite like to say it in a very loud voice. 'Bog off, Mr Davidson!' It could slip out so easily. Would roll so sweetly off my tongue. But instead I affect my empathetic face, while he maintains his 'I've got a bone to pick' one. What the man really needs is some joy in his life. Just to *get* one would be a start. Can't he go out now and again, perhaps? Take up a hobby? But then I remember. He already has a hobby. Sitting in his house making endless tetchy lists about the noises that emanate from mine. 'Is there a problem, Mr Davidson?' I ask him, because even though there clearly is, I'm not about to encourage him.

'I've had an hour and a bloody half of it this afternoon…really not good enough…something must be done…making that infernal racket with the windows open…trying to have five minutes peace in my own garden…' And so on and so forth and yadda yadda yadda…

75

Still. There's always a silver lining in the blackest of clouds. Next week my mother will be coming to stay. I shall set her on him instead.

When I finally get inside and upstairs, Jake and his pals have finished band practice and are sitting in a little fairy ring on the carpet in the drum room, eating toast. I'm aware I should be cross – and I will be so once his friends have left, of course – but one of the paradoxes about my relationship with Mr Davidson is that the more he rants about 'Your son and his racket', the more childishly 'yah-boo-sucks-you-old-haddock' I become. So, for now at least, I look upon this assemblage of hair and hormones and I feel that most pleasing of parental sensations: a glow of pride at my son's talent and, yes, commitment, and a great love for every similarly dedicated young man in the land. After all, they're not out mugging old ladies, are they? I am, I also feel, the custodian of their futures. It is my job – no, my *duty* to fend off Mr Davidson and to nurture their blossoming careers.

That said, I do catch my breath as I enter. The room smells of Lynx and sweat and the sort of universal non-specific aroma of putrefaction that seems to accompany all teenage boys' gatherings the minute any of them take off their trainers. I climb over an amp and go and open a window. Four almost empty chocolate mousse pots are lined up on the sill, their gooey remnants quietly liquefying in the sun.

Three, then, are now four again. So the ad obviously worked. 'Hello!' I say brightly to the one I don't recognise, who, having finished his toast, is now twiddling with his strings.

'Er, hello,' he says back, blushing furiously under his fringe, and looking shocked and appalled at having being spoken to at all, in the way boys of their age always seem to be. Bless him.

'This is Hamish,' says Jake. 'He's joined the band.'

'Lovely!' I trill. 'Well, it's very nice to meet you, Hamish. I do like the colour of your guitar.'

'Ignore my mum,' Jake then adds to Hamish. 'She's mad.'

'So,' I say, because I must at least make a token stab at being stern. 'Truth now. Have you been practicing with the window open again?'

Jake finishes his last mouthful of toast. 'Come *on*, Mum. You can see how hot it is in here, can't you? And it wasn't for long, honest. Just half an hour or so. And it's not like it's late or anything. It's not like –'

'Even so,' I cut in. 'You know the rules.' I look around me. 'Anyway, where's the fan gone?'

The fan which I purchased from B and Q not four weeks back. The fan which is nowhere to be seen. Jake frowns.

'Er…'

'I'm sorry, Mrs McFadden,' pipes up Ben. 'I…er…broke it. Um…I'm going to replace it…I'm saving up, and –'

'It wasn't his fault, Mum,' Jake is quick to point out. 'It was David's fault.' David who is no longer a quarter of a Black Lung. Which is pretty convenient for David, I guess. No loss. He didn't have enough commitment anyway. 'It was him that put the can of Coke there. You weren't to know, were you?'

'Yes, but…'

'Well,' I say, because at this precise moment my largesse is at its zenith. (It will ebb away, I know, the nearer Sunday gets, but for now, I'm just glad to have come home alone.) 'Not to worry, Ben, okay? It wasn't expensive.' £16.99, to be precise, which is not a lot of money, except to someone whose only income stream consists of a paper round and a bit of babysitting. Besides, I could never be cross with Ben anyway. His mother has Parkinson's and the father is long absent. He has to leave his amp here because he can't get it home. At times, I've even thought I'd be happy to adopt him. I'd rather have Ben than my mother, for sure.

'But I will,' he says. 'I –'

'Absolutely not. I won't hear of it. Accidents happen. But in future, boys, don't bring your drinks up here, eh? Not with all this electrical equipment plugged in. I don't want to come home one day and find the house has exploded, do I?'

They laugh politely, because they are all well brought-up boys. And Mr Davidson is just an old goat.

I pick up the overflowing bin as I exit, as I don't doubt it's probably contributing to the smell. It's only when I get it downstairs and start trying, and failing, to offload the fetid contents into a bin liner, that I see that what's causing the blockage is a very large wodge of roughly crumpled sheets of paper, that have been recently wedged into the top. Vaguely interested (as with fridges, the contents of boys' bins are invariably instructive) I tug it out. The first of them has the letter 'K' written on it, in thick black marker pen, and a piece of sticky tape stuck at the top. Properly curious now, I pull out another – and on this one is written an 'E'. And then another, and another, till I have six in all. Appropriately arranged they appear to make a banner, for the purpose, I surmise, of sticking in the window. RENKAW? KENWAR? WRAENK, perhaps?

Silly me. It spells WANKER. God. *Boys.*

I'm just clearing away the tea things and thinking about how best to spend my penultimate evening sans mother (God, and for how *long*?), when my mobile and the doorbell clamour for attention at almost precisely the same moment. As it is my practice to attend to all mobile phone calls as a matter of priority right now (though it could well *be* my mother, it could equally well be Sebastian, in extremis, which is reason enough to be alert at all times), and as it is more often than not someone for Jake on the doorstep, I attend to the former, while bellowing 'JAAAAKE!!! DOOOORRRR!!!' up the stairs.

But it isn't Seb or Mum. It's Charlie who's calling. My thumb hovers for a few seconds while I decide what to do. Not to press green would be the sensible option, but my thumb steps straight in and overrules me.

'It's me,' he says.

I know that already, but my heart leaps in any case. I do wish it would stop doing that. 'I *know*.'

'Can I come over?'

'God, Charlie. NO. You most certainly cannot.'

'Okay, okay. Keep your hair on. Just thought I'd see if any cracks were showing yet.'

'Charlie, this is not some sort of game! Stop doing this, will you?'

'Okay, okay, *okay*. Point taken.'

'Good! And good*bye*!'

'Hang on! Don't hang up! This is a legitimate phone call!'

I don't hang up because even though I know I should I'm too cross now. 'Yeah,' I say, 'right.'

'No, it *is*. I do actually have a bona fide reason for calling you.'

My heart's stopped leaping about now, at least a little. Which is encouraging. It must just be an autonomic reflex. 'Which is?'

'I've been having a sort out.'

'Oh.'

'You know. Of the flat. And I seem to have accrued quite a lot of your stuff.'

'What stuff?'

'Two jackets, some CDs, a bunch of potions, a pile of paperbacks…'

'Oh.'

'So I wondered when would be best time to bring them round. I don't want to appear on your doorstep at an inopportune moment, do I?'

'Charlie, *every* moment would be an inopportune moment.'

'Don't be like that.'

'Just give them to Dee.'

Charlie doesn't like the fact that Dee knows – or, rather, knew – about us.

'I'd rather not,' he replies.

'So just take them into work with you and leave them in your office. I can pick them up from there.'

'When?'

'God, *whenever*! I don't know, do I?'

'Wouldn't it be simpler if you just picked them up from me at home?'

Which home does he mean? And how on earth did this conversation fetch up at this juncture? 'No, Charlie. It wouldn't. Please. Just take them to work.'

I hear him inhale. Then there's a pause while he exhales. 'You okay?' he says finally.

'No, I'm not.'

Another long, long pause. 'Me neither.'

'Charlie, I've got to go.'

'No, I mean it. I feel dreadful. I'm not sleeping, I'm not eating, I feel like –'

'Charlie, *really*. I've got to *go*.'

'Okay, *okay*. I'll take your things in, then. Tomorrow.'

'Great. Thank you. I'll collect them when I can.'

He starts saying something else, but I have to cut him off because my throat hurts so much. Bloody, bloody hell. This is just so much harder than I thought it would be.

I'm just wondering when, precisely, I will stop worrying about Charlie (this week? Next week? Sometime? Never?) when Jake shuffles into the kitchen. 'Er,' he says. 'Mum,' he says. 'Er,' he says again. He tips his head back a little and makes a very funny face. 'Dee's here,' he adds, nodding towards the hall.

'Really?' I say. I'd completely forgotten about the door. So it wasn't for him after all.

I sniff back a snuffle and snap my phone shut. 'Oh!' I say. 'Right! Hi, Dee!' I call out.

Jake's face is still doing stuff, I notice. Odd stuff. Eyebrow stuff mainly. 'She's still on the doorstep,' he hisses at me. 'She's a bit…well…you know…'

'*What?*' I nudge him aside and move past him into the hallway, to find, just as he says, that Dee *is* still on the doorstep. And indeed, as Jake said, a good bit '…well…you know…' Spike trots up and sniffs at her. I stand there and gape at her. Jake's wrong. I *don't* know. 'What the hell happened to you?' I gasp. 'Jesus. Get inside, will you?'

She does so, bringing with her the evocative odour of a Tuscan trattoria on a warm summer's night. She glances behind me. Jake's still in the kitchen doorway.

'Perhaps I ought to stand on some newspaper,' she ventures.

There's really no need. She's not so much dripping as evaporating. But perhaps I need to stop Jake from gawping at her anyway. 'Jake, go get a newspaper for me, please, will you, hon?' He shuffles off with the perplexed air of a boy who thought he'd seen most things, but is suddenly having to have a major rethink.

I touch a finger to her hair, her face, her shoulders. 'My God, you need a shower and then some,' I observe. 'And I wouldn't bother undressing. Look upon it as a pre-wash. What the hell is this anyway? Worcestershire sauce?'

She manages a wan smile. 'Nothing so common. A bottle of Oak Aged Balsamic vinegar.'

*     *     *

By the time I hear the shower pump shut off upstairs I've decided to dispense with the tea and break out a bottle of wine instead. It is Friday night, after all. And I deserve one. I'm just prising out the cork when she returns to the kitchen, wearing my dressing gown and with her hair in a clip, looking (and smelling) much, much better.

'Just as well you're dark-haired already,' I tell her.

'Just as well I have good reflexes,' she responds. 'It must have missed my head by this much.' She parts finger and thumb a scant inch or so.

'Well, thank God for that, at least.'

'Thank God nothing. I think it's high time He took a bit of notice of me, frankly.'

As God may or may not have witnessed, they were – as in her and her husband Malcolm – in an Italian restaurant called Spiro's, in Cardiff Bay. About to have dinner. About to Have A Serious Talk. They do this all the time. Well, Dee does, at any rate. Keeps at it. Keeps trying. And had it not been for one tiny, all-important detail, perhaps she would have managed to do so this time as well. The detail being that Dee was going to Al-Anon after work, and Malcolm was going to his AA meeting, and that after said meetings they'd meet up in the Bay, and discuss how both meetings went. This is what they do. Well, in theory, at least. Because on this day, and it was nowhere near the first time he'd done it, Malcolm had not been to his. He'd been running late at work (at least he still manages to do *that* okay) and he'd decided he couldn't be bothered. This despite them having agreed that his going to his meetings was the one non-negotiable part of the deal. The deal being that all deals were off until such time as he could be relied upon to turn up to the meetings. And he hadn't. Hadn't because, excuses aside, he no longer thought that he needed to. So he went off and had a beer instead.

'I could even smell it on his breath! And I just flipped, Abs. I just completely lost it. I just *snapped*. I mean, the front of him! It's like this whole business is just one big joke to him –'

'Oh, Dee. Surely not –'

81

'Well, okay, if not a joke, still not something he takes remotely seriously. He seems to think – no, no, he even *admits* – that it's something he's doing for *me*!' She shakes her head. 'I mean just what's it going to take for it to sink in that it's not about me. It's about *him*!' I wish I knew the answer to that one, but I don't. 'Anyway, I'm still not sure what got into me, but, you know, I just couldn't stop laying into him.'

Which is not the sort of thing Dee does, ever. 'So he threw a bottle of balsamic vinegar over you?'

'God, no.'

'You mean you tried to throw it over *him*?'

'God, no! That was the waiter.'

'The *waiter*? Blimey, were you really ranting that *much*?'

She shakes her head. 'He didn't *mean* to. He was just coming up to pour some oil and vinegar into a dish – you know, like they do – and he was behind me, and I didn't see him, of course – I was too busy ranting at Malcolm – and just as he was about to pour it into the dish, I flung out my arm and it knocked the carafe out of his hand. It just –' she flings her arm out again now, to illustrate – 'just launched right up into the air, hit the wall behind me, and then just exploded all over my head. You never saw anything like it. Just, literally, shattered into a million pieces and the whole lot rained straight down on me.'

She takes a big gulp of wine, and I wonder, would the oil have been better or worse? There are a couple of tiny cuts, I notice, on the backs of her fingers. She's trying to smile now, but comic though it sounds in the telling, it could have been oh so much worse.

Though it was bad enough, clearly. She drinks some more wine. 'I don't think I've ever been so embarrassed in my entire life. It was just excruciating. There couldn't have been a single person in the place who wasn't staring at me. Absolutely *everyone*. And you could have heard a pin drop. It was *awful*.'

'I can imagine.'

'And you know what Malcolm said?'

'I can't begin to think.'

'You won't believe it. He said "You stupid fucking cow". Like, really *really* loudly. Just "You stupid *fucking* cow". Can you believe that?'

Regrettably, I can. 'Oh, God, Dee. The ba –'

'Exactly. Bastard! The *bastard*!'

Two expletives in one utterance. This is *so* not like Dee. 'And then what happened?'

'I left. I stood up, I shook my skirt out... God, I was *so* embarrassed... and I was out of that place like a rocket. Bits of glass flying everywhere, Malcolm shouting at me, the waiter shouting at Malcolm, the...oh, *God*, Abs.' She puts her head in her hands. 'It was just *awful*.'

I gesture to her hands. 'You've cut yourself too.'

She turns them over. There's an angry looking weal in her left palm as well. She looks at it distractedly. 'I did that in the car, I think. I was trying to pick the last of the glass off of my lap. I didn't even realise till I saw I'd smeared blood on the steering wheel.'

'Oh, you poor, poor thing.'

She shakes her head then. 'Not me. No more. Oh, no. No more 'poor Dee'. Not a *bit* of it. No, as last straws go this has been a particularly effective one. You know, I think I've finally had the kick up the backside I need.' She empties her glass then sets it down on the table. 'Well, blow on the head, then.' She smiles wanly. 'Whatever. That's it. I've had enough. I've done my best, I really have. But I really can't do it any more.' She picks up her glass again and drains the contents in one swallow. 'Can I have another glass of wine?'

I pour her one, and top up my own while I'm at it. 'So. D'you want to stay here?'

She nods. 'Do you mind? Just for tonight? I really don't think I can face him.' We've been here before, often. Poor Dee. *Too* often . 'Oh, but that's a point.' She glances around her. 'What about your mum? Isn't *she* here?'

'Not yet.' My face pulls a face. It can't help it. 'She's moving in properly on Sunday.'

'Moving *in*? That sounds ominous.'

'Well, for now, anyway. Till she's got herself sorted. Pru really can't cope with her any more.'

'And you can?'

I shrug. I consider Dee. I consider being married to Malcolm. I consider what it must be like to be Charlie's wife. I consider dead Hugo. Which puts the lid on it, really. There are so much worse situations I could be in, after all. So I smile. 'I guess I'll just have to, won't I?'

# Chapter 9

TXT MSG; DON'T WORRY. Is FINE about Nana, mum. No sweat. But tell her no toy boys in there, OK? ☺. And no riffling through my Nuts either... ☺ ☺ actually, don't tell her that. Hope u all well. Xxxxx

Dee was sick, now let me see, five times in all. Once on Friday night, three times on Saturday morning, and then once more, rather violently, on Saturday lunchtime, just after I suggested she try a bit of toast. Dee – oh, the irony! – is not built for drinking, that's for sure.

Ah, but now it's Monday morning. Lovely, lovely Monday morning. Tra-lee tra-lay, what a very happy day. Spike, extra choc drops for you!

I think it was Mark Twain that said that the happiest and most successful person works all year long at what he would otherwise choose to do on his summer vacation. Regrettably, it's hard to imagine a career that would involve the twenty-four / seven wine books nachos sleeping sea sand sex scenario most of us aspire to during our two weeks in the Med or whatever, so most of us don't sing on Mondays. But on the whole I do quite enjoy what I do, and on this particular Monday I also have the benefit of perspective. All things considered, a little singing feels right. For I am much looking forward to going to work.

Extra happy to be leaving the *house*. No matter that my list for today includes at least one odious old letch (Mr Potter – who also smells), I am *happy* to be going to work.

Even Candice, who is generally semi-comatose till ten, notices the spring in my step. Candice, for a time, had her mother-in-law living with her, and her mother-in-law was by all accounts a witch, so she absolutely understands why.

'Funny, isn't it?' I tell her over coffee. 'My own mother drives me mad, but my mother-in-law was actually very lovely. I didn't see much of her, of course, because she still lived – still does live – in Dublin.'

'That's probably why you got on, then,' she observes dryly. 'Mothers-in-law should be made to reside on other continents, in my book.'

'No, no. She really was. Very sweet lady. She made my wedding dress, you know.'

My own mother is no seamstress, but even if she had been, she was way too preoccupied on the run-up to my wedding fretting about what *she'd* be wearing.

But, truth be told, I feel a little bad moaning on to Candice about my mum. She has after all, offered to do my ironing while I'm at work. An occurrence that is so spectacularly out of character that I am still in a state of shock, and trying to work out what the angle is. But then I conclude that she is simply trying to make herself indispensable, having been deposited at my place along with a large sheaf of pamphlets about retirement developments and their many and varied advantages. Pru has been hard at work, bless her.

'I didn't have a wedding dress,' Candice says wistfully. 'I had a turquoise two-piece from Debenhams. Registry Office do. We decided to save the money and buy a leather sofa.' She sighs extravagantly. ''Course, *he* got that. Bastard. You live and learn, eh?'

'I've still got my dress. Though I don't know why I've kept it, to be honest. It's not like I'm going to use it again, is it?'

She's leafing through *Hello!* and now she stabs it with her finger. 'That's me,' she says. 'If and when I get married again, I'm going to have the whole bloody shebang. Horse and carriage, six bridesmaids, five-star reception, honeymoon in St Lucia, hair extensions, the works. I'm going to make sure of it... Ah, good morning, Mr Dobson!'

I note she's bellowing now, suddenly, and I turn around to see an elderly gentleman shuffling in. A deaf one, I presume. She closes up the magazine and directs him to a chair. He sits slowly and gingerly, wheezing and puffing as he does so. He obviously didn't want to risk the stairlift. Candice beams her best beam. 'And how are we today?'

'Oh, tickety boo,' he says brightly, through his panting. 'Tickety boo.'

'Well, that's good.'

He nods and smiles. 'And how are *you*?'

'I'm just *fine*, Mr Dobson. Oh, and this is Abbie,' she trills at him. 'Abbie McFadden. She'll be looking after your back today for you.'

'Oh?' he remarks, but not in the least bit unpleasantly. 'No June?'

'She's retired now. Remember?'

He nods. 'Of course.' Then he looks at me carefully. Now he's recovered his breath, I can see that he's absolutely the sort of man who'd eschew the convenience of even a shiny new stairlift. He's ramrod straight, proud-looking. Sharp-eyed and intelligent. Stoical. Ex-forces is my guess.

'Hello, Mr Dobson,' I say, proffering a hand.

He almost breaks all of my fingers.

Mr Dobson, it turns out, *is* ex-forces. Very ex, by now, of course, because he is eighty-seven, but he still has that bearing, that robustness. He was a tail-end Charlie in a Lancaster bomber and was the sole survivor when the plane got shot down in the Bay of Biscay. He then spent three years in a prisoner of war camp and came home to find his young wife had met someone else and run off with him, taking their two and a half-year-old with her. He married again, in the fifties, but his wife has had a stroke now, and he looks after her all by himself. Which is how he came to have the fall that resulted in his disability. He has, in short, lived a bit and suffered a *lot*. Though you'd never know it to hear him talk. He pooh-poohs all my commiserations. As far as he's concerned, every single day after the day he hit the ocean is one day more than the rest of the crew had. He considers himself very, very blessed. We spend an amiable half-hour getting to know one another. I could use lots of patients like him. Always good to be reminded that, however tedious one's own life, there are others whose lives are so much poorer. Or perhaps, when I think of it, they're actually richer. Less centred on self. Much more focussed on others. Memo to self: keep Mr Dobson in mind at all times. Especially in the matter of mother.

Just as I'm closing the cubicle curtains so he can dress, I get a sharp rap on the bottom with a rolled-up magazine. It's Candice and she's clutching a stray *My Weekly* and grinning. Proper ear-to-ear grinning. 'Just to let you know,' she says, as if imparting some terrifically important secret. 'Your next patient is here.' Then she nudges my arm. And she winks. 'Wow-*eeee*.'

'Wow-*eee* what?'

'*D'oh*,' she says, clapping me on the arm this time. 'You'll see! Cor, you are one lucky cow.'

'But who *is* it?' I persist. 'I thought I had a gap now.' A gap between patients, in which Brendan and I were going to go through some protocols for a research project he's currently involved in.

She shakes her head. 'No longer. I slotted someone in.'

'But *who*?'

'Da da!' she sings. 'Gabriel *Ash*!'

I am somewhat shocked, to say the least, by this news. I didn't cancel his appointment, of course, because whatever truculent thoughts I might have had about doing so, it was not my business (or, indeed, in my interest) to be taking it upon myself to turn away new patients. I am A Professional Person, even if there is the odd occasion when being so can be a little trying. And besides, I thought he'd cancel it anyway. But, as is evidenced now by Candice's breathless announcement, he didn't. I haven't liked to ask Candice because I don't want to start her off on any investigative forays, and it would be altogether unseemly to start furtively scrabbling through the appointments book to check. And, in any case, I thought his appointment was on Thursday.

'He's here? Now? *Today*?' I hiss.

She nods happily. 'Called just after Mr Dobson got here. He wanted to see if he could change the time of his appointment on Thursday because he's got some recording thing or other he's got to go to but I couldn't do that, of course, because you're fully booked up all Thursday now so I said we'd have to go into next week but then it occurred to me that you had a slot today and he said fine, because he wasn't far away anyway, and – hey, why the face on? I thought you'd be pleased!'

The curtains part. Mr Dobson is back in his trousers, so I make my farewells, and follow him back out to reception. Where

Gabriel Ash is indeed now sitting, filling out an Aches and Pains form. He stands up as I enter.

'Good morning,' he says brightly.

What an ache and what a pain. 'Oh!' I say, pasting on my professional smile in the vain hope that it might draw attention away from my oh-so-fast reddening cheeks. 'Goodness!' Which is a stupid thing to say. This is a physiotherapy clinic and he is a man with a limp. And an appointment, for that matter. With me.

My machinations are clearly not uppermost in Candice's mind, however. When he stands up and hands her little clipboard back to her, it's all her lower lip can do not to slide straight down into her cleavage.

Though he seems completely unaware of this. I presume he's used to women looking doe-eyed in his presence. Probably thinks it's a default expression. Except on old harpies like me.

She takes the form from the clipboard. 'All yours, then, Abbie!' she says brightly. 'Tell you what, though,' she whispers as she follows us back through. 'I am *so* in the wrong sort of job.'

Still somewhat in a state of shock and mortification, I take Gabriel Ash into a cubicle and direct him to the couch. He's wearing a navy linen suit and an open-necked shirt and there isn't a dishcloth in sight.

'So,' I say stiffly, feeling acutely self-conscious (not least because I'm in my practical but style-free A and P polo shirt and track suit bottoms), embarrassed about him being here, and like absolutely everyone's listening. And I'm sure that they probably are. 'What can I do for you, then?'

'Um, give me some physiotherapy, please,' he says nicely. 'That is, if it's not too much trouble.'

I feel thoroughly flustered and not at all sure what to say to him. The last time I saw him it was tea towels at ten paces. Him being here today feels all wrong.

'But why *me*, of all people?' I find I can't help but blurt out.

He looks surprised that I should even ask the question. Then he shrugs. 'Erm…because I like you?' he says.

Which though disarming, is an entirely reasonable assertion, in itself, I suppose. There are worse ways of choosing a physiotherapist, after all. But under the circumstances (i.e. that this is *me* we're talking about here) it is more than a little unexpected. But perhaps Dee was right. Perhaps he *is* keen to make amends. Though to what end, I know not. And he's certainly not going to get round me like *that*.

I say 'oh,' and I blush.

'And also because your mother tells me you're very good at what you do. She gave me your card at my father's funeral. She said you were looking for new patients.'

My God, but she doesn't miss a trick, and that's for sure. I guess I really should be pleased at her PR skills. Even hire her at ten percent commission, perhaps. But mainly I'm perplexed. So much has happened since then. So much has *changed*. Why on earth would he still want to come to me? I have been thoroughly horrible to him every time we've met.

Perhaps he likes a challenge. Or perhaps he just has a penchant for old bags. 'So here I am,' he says cheerfully. Or he must have no memory. 'Can I be one, please?'

'Well, yes,' I say, regaining my composure. 'Of course you can...but aren't you under someone already?'

He shakes his head. 'Well, I was at the beginning of the year. I had a few sessions straight after the operation. But you know. This and that. Things started improving, so it kind of tailed off. But then I had a fall a few weeks back –'

'Oh?'

'Playing football.' He looks sheepish as he says this. They always do. 'And I seem to have done something deleterious to it. It feels like I'm back to square one.'

I reach for the nearby chair, then sit on it and take a bit of a history. (Normally – for that is the patient-friendly way at A and P – I would perch on the end of couch with him, but in this case it feels way too personal). It's the usual story. Years and years of sport, a nasty on-field injury. Operation. Recuperation. Physio. Rehab. And then too soon back in spikes because that's what men always do.

Men with their addiction to contact sports. Of which Candice, I know, has a different one in mind. You can't knock on curtains, obviously, so she doesn't. She coughs just outside. 'Tea? Coffee? Soft drink? Magazine? Just give me a shout if you need me!'

Gabriel Ash smiles at this. And despite his earlier apparent insouciance, it seems a rather knowing sort of smile. 'Your fan club,' I say dryly.

Now he winces. And I realise that it's not that at all. He's actually just plain old embarrassed.

'Well then, you'd best get your trousers off,' I tell him, handing him a robe. 'Give me a shout when you're ready.'

Candice is still lurking with intent as I emerge from behind the curtains.

'Tell me, just how well *do* you know him, exactly?' she hisses. So she's obviously been earwigging, as I thought.

I cross the room so we're at least half out of earshot. She follows along eagerly. 'Not well at all,' I say. She looks disappointed. 'He's just my mother's dead fourth husband's son.'

She takes a moment or two to compute this. '*He* is? Cripes – why didn't you *say*? That means you're almost related to him! Wow! Not *related* related, obviously. But, you know, near enough.' She grabs my arm and computes a bit more. 'Hey, there's a thought. Do you get to see him socially at all?'

Much as I have grown fond of Candice (and I have), her relentless pursuit of her next capital R Romance gets a touch wearing at times. I shake my head. 'No. I don't see him socially. Honestly, I barely know him.' I don't elaborate, because I am hardly intending to, either, except in the matter of Conservatory-gate, after which our paths will probably never cross again. Except perhaps in here, of course. But I doubt that would be for long. Candice looks crestfallen. Then she elbows me. 'He's ready.'

I wheel the TENS machine in and start untangling the leads. Back behind the curtain, Gabriel Ash is looking altogether less the shiny-happy-media-type now divested of his jacket and trousers. He has a fuzz of golden hair on his forearms, and a similarly downy thatch on his shins. He looks fit, athletic, toned, robust. As he would do, I guess. What with having been in the navy. Striding about the deck looking for typhoons on the horizon. Or whatever it is that they do.

I bend down to fish around on the trolley for the gel, and wonder what he looks like in uniform. Way better than I do in mine, I suspect.

'I owe you an apology,' he says, as he watches me.

I straighten. I'm blushing again. 'What on earth for?'

He looks at me hard. 'Not for the sins of my father, on this occasion. I think we've done that bit to death, haven't we?'

'Well, that's a relief.' Though there's always his sister's, of course. 'But what, then?'

'For being so short with you last week.'

I was right. He is clearly amnesic or something. I find myself smiling. And then all at once feeling humbled. And suddenly, and perhaps because of that, anxious to put things straight. Well, straight-ish. Straight as they can be, under the circumstances. Now he's sitting before me, I realise I've been brooding about our unpleasant exchange of last Friday pretty much ever since it happened. I'm not an unpleasant person. Not normally, I'm not. And it's played on my mind that he must think I am.

'You? Short with *me*! I'd have said the opposite was true.' I squeeze a little gel onto my fingertip and apply it to the first of the pads. 'So it's me who should be apologising to *you*,' I say, sticking the pad onto his leg and now fervently wishing I'd already done so. 'I'm not normally so ratty.' He grins at this and raises one eyebrow. A very neat trick if you can master it. 'No, *really,*' I say. 'I'm *not*. I'd just had a really bad week, and I'd been looking forward to my day off, and the last place I wanted to be was round at my mother's house...sorry, *your* house...doing the wretched cleaning, and, well, I suspect you already realised that, didn't you?' He nods. 'Anyway, there we are. I didn't mean to be so off with you. I do know it's not your fault. It was just you being there, and...well, it all just sort of boiled over. It's just that the implications of everything that's happened are...well, you know where it's left us, mother-wise, of course. It's been getting us *all* down, to be honest. But we'll get her sorted. In the end.' I find I'm frowning now. Memo to self: Don't! You will become wrinkled and furrowed and prematurely wizened. I turn it back into a smile, 'Well, one can but hope, anyway, eh?'

'Phew,' he says, grinning again. And then he looks thoughtful. Or is perhaps just still digesting my speech. 'Were they happy, d'you think, at some point?' he says. 'You know, your mother and my father?'

'Er…' I say. 'Pass.' I stick another pad on his leg and shake my head. 'No, that's not right. I *think* they were. On the whole. Initially, anyway. It's just that things weren't so good in the last year or so. Not since her first operation, really. But that's what happens, isn't it? It's the sort of thing that puts a strain on the best of relationships, isn't it? And she's not the easiest of patients. Not the easiest woman to live with, period. She's quite demanding.'

He seems to find this amusing. 'I imagine that the same could probably be said of my father, come to that.'

And was. By my mother. At his funeral, of all occasions. And I just know from his expression that he's remembering that too. He must think we're a family of acerbic old piranhas. I lower my gaze from his. 'I really didn't know him well enough to comment,' I tell him hurriedly. 'Hardly at all, in fact.'

'Ditto,' he says.

It's such a leading comment that I can't possibly pass up the opportunity to respond to it. 'Why didn't you see him for twenty years?' I find myself asking. 'I mean, twenty whole *years*. That's such a long time. What on earth *happened*? If…er…you don't mind me asking, that is.'

He looks as if he doesn't. 'Nothing that dramatic. I just ceased to consider him my father, that's all.'

'But why? What did he do?'

'He left us. My mum and my sister and I. I was fourteen. And I came home from school one day to find out he'd gone. Just like that. Well, not just like that, as it turned out. There'd been some problems with his business, and he just, well…' he shrugs, '…ran away. Just upped and went. We didn't hear a word from him for over a year. Didn't see him for another four after that.'

Despite his light tone it's a very bleak statement. 'What, *nothing*?'

'I know he got in touch with my mother a couple of times. But she was always very loath to discuss it. I think she thought it would be better all round if we just carried on as if he didn't exist. I don't think it was the first time he'd let her down. She probably just wanted to protect us.'

'And that's the last time you saw him?' It all sounds very confusing to me. This is the same man who was living in his son and daughter's house. Most odd.

'Oh, no,' he says. 'Then he came back.'

'And?'

He shrugs again. I suspect he has embraced the shrug as his metaphorical defence against being abandoned so cruelly. It seems such an automatic 'yeah, whatever' type of gesture. A form of denial in fact. 'And I assume the deal was that we were supposed to forgive him. And Mum did, to an extent. Never had him back, of course. Nothing like that. And Corinne did too, in time, of course. I think women are better at that sort of thing, don't you? Where men are concerned, anyway.'

Which makes me think of Charlie. And of all the little accommodations and justifications that were so much a part of my relationship with him. Thank God that's no more. Yes, I think. He's probably right. 'And what about you?'

'Ah,' he says. And this time he doesn't shrug. 'I didn't.'

I look at him. His face is impassive. His tone matter-of-fact. Which feels all wrong to me. I think of my own father, who died when I was twelve, and I can't imagine anything ever being so bad between us that I'd ever give him up if I'd still had him. Ever give up *on* him. But that's me. That's not him. I'm not in his shoes.

'And still haven't?' I ask.

'No,' he says levelly. 'Not yet.'

'I think that's terribly sad,' I say, even as I think it, because that 'yet' is a very big word. A word that assumes there's room for hope. But there's no 'yet' about it in this case now, is there? It's too late. He knows that. He must know that. But he doesn't seem to mind in the least.

Just gets back to his shrugging. 'If you say so,' he says.

Ken's not in denial. He's just dead impressed, and more than a little bit smitten. Ken, who must have treated the rogue limbs of just about every famous footballer and rugby player hereabouts over the years, is rather taken with our latest new patient. 'I didn't realise you were going to be attracting such high profile patients here, lovely. Got any more up that sleeve of yours?'

'Gawd, Ken. Don't tell me you fancy him too.' Candice says. 'I'll fight you for him, you know. I saw him first. Anyway, he's not available, more's the pity. He's engaged.'

'To Lucy Whittall,' I add. 'They're getting married at Christmas.'

'And you're married anyway,' she reminds him. 'Well, whatever your men's version of it is, anyway. Whereas I'm free as a bird and badly in need of a … Ah! Mrs Threpple! How are you today? Any improvement with your groin?'

When I get home from work, buoyed by the restoration of good relations with the weatherman (who I have provisionally forgiven on the house front on account of him having, like me, a tortured soul on the parent front, even if he isn't admitting it – *yet*), and also armed with yet more information about retirement developments, it is to find that my mother has executed a double whammy. No – I miscalculate – a triple whammy, in fact. Not only has she done all my ironing, she's also made a pile of fairy cakes (Mother? Cakes? *Eh*?), and thirdly – and this is the biggest of them, frankly – she's cosied up with Jake at the kitchen table, and they are having a bit of a chat. It is all very sweet. It is all rather scary. It is all too easy to see, as I'm sure she does, that her being kutched up in the kitchen with Jake presents just the sort of picture a disinterested observer would respond to with something like an 'ahhhh…'. Granny and her grandson. Bonding over tea. A happy moment for the child in a day (as in most of them) where his poor single mother must be out earning crusts, and said grandson is forced to stay home alone with nowt but his latchkey for company. Eeewww!

'Trojan,' Jake's saying, licking off pink icing, 'means, like, hard. As in difficult.'

'Oh, I *see*. And what's a mosher?'

'Well, a mosher is like…' he considers. 'Well, you know, as in mosh pits –'

'What on earth is a mosh pit?'

'You know, Nana. The bit in front of the stage where the moshers all go.'

'What stage?'

'*The* stage. You know, when you're at a gig.'

'And it's a *pit*?'

'Well, it's not *really* a pit, obviously. But it still gets pretty minging…'

'I'm entirely at sea now. What's "minging" when it's at home?'

'Minging is not good. Minging is, well, minging. Kind of gross.'

'*Ah*, now. As in the state of your bedroom?'

'No. As in Louise Petworth.'

'Who's Louise Petwoth?'

'Ex-girlfriend,' I mouth from behind him.

To the uninitiated, of course, all very unremarkable. Because she is, in short, behaving like a normal granny-type person. Jesus, this is getting seriously worrying. She'll be trying to darn his socks before I know it.

# Chapter 10

BECAUSE IT *IS* MAINLY the Jake effect. I can see that. Of her five grandchildren, Jake's always been the one she's had the closest relationship with. Not that she ever really did 'close' when any of them were little, any more than she did with us. There's possibly more maternal instinct in an amoeba than that which resides in my mother's breast.

But despite her lack of input on a practical level, Mum and Jake have always seemed to share a certain harmony of spirit. Whatever she's got in the get-up-and-go genes department, she's undoubtedly passed on to my number two son. Added to which, they are physically alike too, which I'm sure makes a difference as well. Where Sebastian inherited his father's dark looks and muscular frame, Jake has his grandmother's sprung form and long legs, not to mention her good looks and her downy blonde locks. In short, all the bits Pru and I would have liked to inherit but which, like twins, seemed to have skipped a generation. And he's always loved her stories. The places she's been, the people she's met, the outrageous bits of gossip that trip so salaciously from her tongue. Oh, yes. Jake and his nana are like two peas in a pod.

Which is fine. As long as they're not both in *my* pod, that is.

To which end, at the end of the following week, I have arranged for us to go and look at a retirement development, to which, hopefully, she will very soon retire.

Abercorn Gate is a brand new development not far from Mum's old place. It has gold-tipped wrought iron gates, new pea green turf, a glossy young shrubbery, a rank of box clipped to within an inch of its phloem, and an awful lot of heavy wooden benches. Though fortunately – I check – none of them have little bronze plaques affixed to them detailing which dead person they're dedicated to.

*Yet*. And just to remind us of such delicate matters, the frontage is dominated by a ten foot high hoarding from which a pair of silver haired persons beam indulgently out.

'This is nice,' I say nicely.

My mother looks up at their smiling faces in disgust. 'God's waiting room,' she mutters. 'That's what this sort of place is. God's waiting room. It even smells of death.'

'It doesn't smell of death, it smells of grass clippings,' I snap irritably. 'Stop being so negative, will you?'

But negative seems to be her chosen role for the day. Much as 'too bloody bad, Mum' is mine. Things don't improve much as we're shown around either, despite the best attempts of the agent.

'I don't doubt you've already seen a little of the nice communal garden,' he enthuses as he leads us inside. 'It was landscaped by Peter Mapplethorpe, you know.'

About which, I presume, we are supposed to be impressed. This man clearly doesn't know my mother.

He's called Mr Preston, and is not at all like the ones that reside downstairs from A and P. For though still routinely urbane and professional, he is closer to my mother's age than my own, which is not something you tend to see much in estate agency, them all being burned out or millionaires by thirty. He is also in a brass-buttoned blazer and beige slacks. I wonder if he's been hand-picked for wooing ladies of a certain age. He certainly seems to be wooing my mother.

Trying to, at any rate. He's not necessarily succeeding. 'Communal? Won't I have my own one?' she asks incredulously. 'How will I be able to sunbathe topless?'

Though (oh, yuk!) it's true, I know she is saying this partly for impact, so it's to his credit (and her chagrin) that he responds to this question as if it were the sort of thing they get asked about almost every day at Abercorn Gate. 'If you opt for the second floor,' he answers smoothly, wafting his brochure upwards, 'you do get a balcony –'

'Mum, get a grip,' I hiss. 'You're seventy-four, for goodness' sake!'

She fixes me on the end of one of her famed Garland scowls. The one that used to have chorus girls weeping.

'Yes, Abigail. *Seventy*-four. Not ninety-four. Which hardly makes me Methuselah. Just you wait till you're seventy-four, young lady. You'll change your tune then, mark my words.'

Though I doubt I'll be flashing my bosoms. I try to imagine myself as a seventy-four-year-old, and, depressingly, I can do it all too clearly. I'll be wrinkled and worn-out and hunch-backed and exhausted, because I'll still be looking after a one hundred and eight-year-old witch.

'Well, I think it's very nice,' I persist. 'It's handy for the shops, and not too far from your friends at the theatre club. And you'll be able to make lots of new friends here as well.'

She looks at me as if I had just suggested she join EXIT.

'Theatre club?' says the agent politely. 'Would that be the one in Cyncoed?'

Mum lifts her chin and strikes a pose for him. It's so automatic I don't think she even realises she does it any more.

'Why, yes!' she simpers, changing tack on a sixpence. 'Fancy! Do you know it?' He nods enthusiastically. 'I've been a member for oh, *umpteen* years. I've always tried to keep my hand in. Ah...' She sighs wistfully. 'These things are in one's blood, aren't they? (I don't know why she'd think he'd know about that, but perhaps fellow am-drammers have some sort of secret code.) She does a delicate little frown and lifts her walking stick. 'Though sadly, not so much lately, of course. What with my knee and so on.' She sighs again. 'I sometimes fear my days in the spotlight are finally behind me...'

'Garland!' he says, slapping his brochure against his thigh, eyes alight with excitement (God, don't these people have *lives?*). 'Of course! Dance with Diana!' He la-la-las the music, with all the right hand movements too. 'I knew it! I *knew* your face was familiar! Well, I never. How about that?!'

Mum bats her lashes happily, having discovered a new groupie. 'Well, now, that *was* a long time ago, Mr Preston. Goodness, I'm very flattered that you even remember it! Gracious, how amazing you knew who I was! Oh, look. Now I'm blushing...'

She does the same speech at everyone. And there's more.

'*She Stoops To Conquer*!' declares the agent, clicking his fingers together and beaming at her. 'Ninety-six? Ninety-seven? In the Community Hall?'

'Gracious,' Mum says again. 'You saw me in *that*?'

'Absolutely!' says the agent, hugging his brochure to his chest now and smiling warmly at my mother. He's thrilled, I don't doubt, at having seen her in person. Inflamed also, just possibly, at the thought of her breasts. But mainly, I judge, he is hopeful. Because there's something in the very effusive nature of his manner that smacks of a man with a sale on his mind.

I wish him luck. By the lorry-load. I must live in hope.

# Chapter 11


A POSTCARD. FRONTSIDE: LEANING Tower of Pisa (by night). Backside: *Dear Mum, Jake, Spike and Nana, we're not actually here. We're in some bar in a place called Collesalvetti, (we camped here last night) having a drink while waiting to catch the train down to Florence. Nothing much to report. Big news here is that J thinks he was standing behind Jeremy Beadle in the bread shop this morning. I say not. I think he is hallucinating due to too much grappa. Tho' the barman here has a sign up saying 'Tony Blairs and family most welcome!' We're keeping our eyes peeled ... LOL S xxxxx*


'Absolutely not,' my mother says firmly. Despite the enthusiastic patter of her new number one fan, my mother doesn't want to live at Abercorn Gate, and she doesn't want the sideboard either.

Another weekend, another trip to the Myrtles, another sunny Saturday lost to Project Mum. 'Oh, I don't *know*,' she sighs. She's spent much of the morning wafting in skittish bursts about the living room like a wraith on a moped. 'Do I want *any* of it, frankly?' She lifts the hand without the sherry in it up to her brow and looks at herself in the living room mirror. She'll want to take that, at least. Take all of them, no doubt. She smoothes her brow with a finger and pouts at herself. 'Oh, this is all such a *chore*...'

'Mother, you'll need furniture,' Pru says irritably.

'The nest of tables?' I suggest to Doug, who, along with Jake (who's been a sweetheart), has been humping stuff since he got here and has by now adopted the sort of defeated and slightly desperate expression he usually reserves for Bristol City FC. I point. 'And that armchair at the very least. And how about that bookcase, Mum? You might as well have a bookcase.'

But my mother is not to be jollied along. 'Abigail, what's the point? I've read every single book in the house already. And I certainly can't afford to buy new ones.'

We all sigh in unison as soon as her back's turned. 'Let's take the bookcase anyway,' Pru whispers. 'She can fill it with her bloody trophies instead.'

Which are currently parked in a box in the hall, along with all the theatre posters and programmes and framed reviews, and her 'Best Legs on Telly' award. It occurs to me that, no, she probably doesn't need much else. She could live on thin air if it clapped her.

The house looks very different now. Denuded of its detritus and what things of Hugo's Corinne decided to take away, it has the feel of a park the day after a funfair's been through. Faded patches on the walls, dents and troughs in the carpets, assemblages of disparate items of bric-a-brac in untidy, no-place-to-go piles on the floor. On Monday, after we've taken what's left on the want list (correction – the 'oh, if I *must*' list), it will go through its final stage of dismemberment, when the clearance firm Corinne's organised come and clear out what remains.

'I feel disinclined,' my mother says, sitting down heavily on the sofa she doesn't want either, 'to take *any* of it, frankly. And what's the point, *really*? It's all *far* too big. Given that I'm likely to be living in a shoebox.'

Shoebox notwithstanding, the day chunters on, and by mid-afternoon we wave off Pru and Doug, who have shoehorned such items as we've deemed worth taking into the hired van, which they are now going to drive back to Bristol. And there, in storage, will the said items stay until such time as another Abercorn Gate-type development elicits sufficient enthusiasm from her to allow us all the luxury of hope.

Having spent a decade and a half being married to a man who left items of apparel in just about every hotel room he ever stayed in, I'm just on my final check round of backs-of-drawers and corners-of-cupboards upstairs when I realise the hatch to the loft has been left open, and that the loft light is still on as well.

Thinking even as I'm doing so that their electricity bill really isn't my worry, I nevertheless erect the step ladder and climb up to pull the light cord. The loft now is empty bar a couple of rolled offcuts of carpet, but as I reach for the light cord, I notice a familiar-looking object half hidden behind two of the struts. Not a shoe box, but still a box. One of my mother's old hat boxes, in fact. I'm about to turn to leave it when I have a change of mind. Whatever else she really can't be bothered with taking, my mother almost never ever parts with her hats. Perhaps this is an old one that got shoved up here when she moved in. I'd at least better check, so I climb to the top rung to reach it out.

Straight away I can see that the top isn't dusty, so I imagine this has probably been overlooked only due to being buried under another box of some sort. I reach for the cord carrying handle and slide it back across the boards. It's also much weightier than I'm anticipating, and as the other carrying handle is missing, as I pull it towards me to get hold of it properly, I almost send the thing clattering to the floor, and myself tumbling headlong down the stairs.

And I'm right to be surprised, because once I've manhandled it down the step ladder and onto the landing, I see that there isn't a hat in there. It's stuffed with a large carrier bag, which, when I open it, I see is itself stuffed full: of papers and photos and cuttings. At first I think it's simply more of my mother's theatre memorabilia, but a quick riffle through straight away makes me realise it isn't. These papers must all belong to Hugo. I pick up the first of them and start reading with interest.

It's a copy of the local newspaper, obviously read, and folded so the middle pages are now on the outside. There's a headline 'Cardiff Weatherman Gabriel to marry his very own Angel', beneath which is a photograph of Lucy Whittall and Gabriel Ash, emerging from the doorway of what looks like a restaurant, smiling happily for the cameras, arm in arm, heads close, her left hand held out to show the photographer her ring. I skim through the piece, which is reporting their engagement – I check the date; last Christmas – in the sort of relentlessly upbeat and sycophantic manner that local papers are often wont to do. I look further. Beneath it, there's an almost identical photo, but this time it's on a page torn from a magazine, and the headline this time reads slightly differently: Fair Weather for TV's Fallen Angel?' and the copy beneath it is altogether more cynical; wisecracking, sneering and determinedly mean-spirited. No forecasts of fair weather in this one, for sure. They predict, with much glee, stormy weather.

I look back in the box. Most of it, it seems, consists of similar things. Newspaper snippets, dating back years. From his appointment as a TV weatherman just over a year back, through various pieces, and correspondence, including some in Italian, going right back to a faded newspaper photo of a young team – football, I guess, because someone is holding one – beneath which his name is underlined.

I put it back with the others and close up the carrier, a small flame of excitement alight at what I've found. About twenty years' worth of memorabilia, is my guess.

I put the lid back on the box and take the box down to my car, where Jake's already installed and plugged in to his iPod. Mum's two doors up, chatting with a neighbour in her front garden, while Spike, via a cocked leg and a 'who, me?' expression, attempts to claim ownership of her beds.

I stash the hat box carefully in the boot. If it's left behind, the clearance firm will probably end up with it, and it seems to me it might be something Gabriel Ash would want. Perhaps this is the sort of thing he was hoping to find last time. Or, no, perhaps it isn't. He's not ever struck me as particularly interested in his father. Though not *un*interested, surely. How could anyone be? So perhaps this will be a pleasant surprise. Feeling mildly cheered about being the bearer of glad tidings instead of the harridan harbinger of doom, I insert a proper memo in my telephone reminder. I can check when he's next due in at the clinic for his physio and present my box of booty to him then.

We have to leave Hugo's car on the drive, of course, as there's no one available to drive it.

'Be best if we do bring it here, though, I suppose,' I'm telling my mother, once we're home and Jake and I have unpacked the car. 'That way, I can put an ad in the paper and be on hand if anyone wants to see it. I'll have to speak to Pru. See if we can sort something out.'

'I've been thinking about that,' she replies, while Jake nudges her. 'In fact, Jakey and I have been having a little chat.'

Jake and my mother chatting is not always, clearly, something about which to feel encouraged. From where I stand, at any rate. 'Oh, yes?' I ask.

'Yes,' she says. 'I've told him he can have it.'

'*Jake*? Have Hugo's *car*? Mother, that's ridiculous. It may have escaped your notice, but he's only fifteen!'

'Nearly sixteen, Mum,' he is quick to point out.

'Yes, nearly sixteen, but that's not seventeen, is it? What on earth do you suppose we would do with it for the next fifteen months?'

He shrugs. 'Park it somewhere, I guess.'

'Jake, you can't just 'park it somewhere'. Not for over a year. It would have to be taxed. And besides, you can't just leave a car parked for that length of time anyway. The engine would seize up.'

'So you drive it in the meantime,' my mother suggests, quite reasonably. 'It's a lot better than that smelly old crate you rattle around in at the moment.'

I'd quite like to point out that it's the very same car that I rattle *her* around in. To Yoga, to Bridge, to Celeste's, to the tea-dance club (where she doubtless sits and seethes), to her bloody am-dram…, and that she should, perhaps, be bloody grateful. But she's right; from almost any perspective, it is a sensible, rational, reasonable point. My car is an all but knackered, ancient heap, and has been around several hundred blocks. And yes it does smell. But only of Spike. So that's fine. My mother's fur coat smells of mothballs and cigar smoke, but I don't imagine she'll be putting it on eBay and replacing it with an anorak any time soon.

But she's right as in yes, in the fullness of time (and full-er-ness of bank account, obviously) I'm going to have to trade it in for a new one. Well, new-ish, anyway. But not now. And not for Hugo's. Not in a million years. Hugo's car is, well, an old person's car. An old person's car which is the colour of a rich tea biscuit. Or Complan. Or a pair of surgical stockings. An old person's car with a sensibly small engine. A car unfettered by delusions of being built for a driver. A car that glories in being just like every other car that's parked in the day centre or bingo hall car park. Which means I could never drive it, ever. I'm sorry, but I can't. Jake will/would be able to, of course, because when you're seventeen you can drive an old person's car with humour and irony and a 'needs must' expression, add go-faster stripes and put a sub-woofer in the boot. But I can't. I know it's the most shallow thing imaginable, but driving in my heap – with all its memories and prangs and battle-scarred poppy red paintwork – at least helps maintain the fiction that I am young and up for it and still a bit of a gal. It has character. Personality. A sense of humour. A sense of fun. But if I swap my little Peugeot for my elderly mother's dead husband's hearing-aid-coloured car, people will assume that I have exercised choice and in doing so chosen, well, *that* one. And thus another little flame of youth will be extinguished and I will age fifteen years in a second. I will become the sort of person who has a 'mum's taxi' sticker in the back (oh, how they'll laugh) and calls her transport 'my run-around'. Someone – *mon dieu*! – who wears drip-dry elasticated skirts.

And who lives with her elderly mother.

I know it's only a metaphor for the way I'm feeling right now, but just thinking about it is depressing.

'Yeah, Mum!' Jake says. 'That's an idea. Then I could have your car!'

Oh, yes. He can do irony if needs be, my son. But given the choice, *he'd* rather drive my car as well.

I shake my head and pat his shoulder. 'It's not an idea, Jake, and it's not going to happen anyway. Nana needs to sell Hugo's car to put towards her new flat. You know that. I'm sorry, hon, but let's talk about cars when you *are* seventeen, shall we?'

He doesn't look too crestfallen. After all, it was a pie in the sky idea in the first place. But then he delivers his *coup de grace*, straight out of left-field.

'Why does Nana have to go and get a flat anyway?' he asks, and I'm quite sure he asks it quite innocently too. We both turn. Two lots of breath are now bated. 'Why doesn't she just stay living here?' he asks me. 'You know. Like, permanently. With *us*.'

# Chapter 12

TEXT; LUV U 2. No. Florence bit dull (no REALLY). On nite train 2 Rome now. Oh – also plz put some credit on J's fone! Also ask him got my txt? If not, £30 resrve min. Ta mum S xxx

Ah, the innocence of youth. What a precious thing it is.

And, sometimes, from where I stand, what a *pain*. There were about three seconds during which nobody breathed. Jake because his brain was already occupied in trying to interpret the doubtless confusing array of expressions that my face was conveying to him from over his grandmother's shoulder, myself and said grandmother because our sharp intakes of breath were so very sharp that they'd sucked almost every last molecule of air from the room.

My mother cracked first. 'Gracious, me, Jakey!' she twittered. 'I'm quite sure your mother doesn't want an old lady like me rattling around cluttering up the place.'

Jake glanced up at me for corroboration. '*Well?*' his face intimated, '*is that right?*'. 'You don't clutter up the place,' he then said, with commendable sincerity. 'It's nice having you living with us. *Isn't* it, Mum?'

Jake, of course, would say something like that, for he is (happily) not daily flagellated by the countless irritations of living with her. He doesn't shop for her, cook for her, do her handwashing-in-Dreft for her, drive for her, or put up with her tantrums and gripes. Mainly, though, he doesn't have *issues* with my mother, because she's not *his* mother, is she? He's her most favourite grandson and he loves her to bits. I know that. I applaud that. I think it's rather special. I'd just enjoy it so much more if she lived somewhere else.

'Of course it is,' I said anyway, because it would take a much doughtier person than me to make any other sort of response to that question in these circumstances. 'But Nana needs peace and quiet – she needs her own routine, her own space, Jake. And there's precious little of that around here, is there?' I added a laugh. For levity. But it didn't leaven much. Just hung in the air, like a smell.

'And so does your mother,' mine added, smiling nicely. 'Oh, and speaking of which, I'll be out from under your feet tonight, dear. Bridge Club's at Mary's. Can you drop me there at seven?'

I breathed out. First round over. 'No problem,' I told her.

'And I imagine I'll need you to pick me up at ten-ish. But naturally I'll phone and let you know.'

And thus we roll around to yet another Sabbath, which is why I only swear under my breath.

In The Beginning, as is documented in the Bible, God was a pretty busy Deity. What with heaven and earth to get made, day, night, moon, clouds, sun, rain and so on to get organised (not to mention preparing the foundations for a later-date flood), plus with all those fig trees, asps, wanton women etc. to fashion, he must have been pretty darn knackered. God, however, being the Supreme Being (or so I imagine) didn't have to concern himself with kip.

Sadly, supremacy is not my main forte. Thus sleep (shut-eye, rest, slumber, repose, any form of unconsciousness will do, frankly) is now very much my major concern. Much as I thought I empathised with Pru's bleats on the noise front, the reality that is living with my mother is so very much worse than I'd ever imagined.

Which may sound rich coming from someone whose existence happens to a background of decibels in three figures, but the noise my mother generates is just *horrible*. Fingernails down a blackboard horrible. From the dawn chorus (show songs, phlegm removal, chanting, Darth Vader breathing) right through to the small hours night watch (channel five, tea cup banging, phlegm removal, gargling) there is a constant backdrop of insidious, irritating noise.

I know, I know. It's probably just because it's *her*. Though I hold fast on anyone's phlegm removal, frankly, I dare say I'd have no issue with most of the rest of it were it emanating from Jude Law or Ewan McGregor. But there are times in every relationship where one person's endearing trait becomes another person's incitement to murder most foul. This is very nearly that time.

Worse than that, being woken in the small hours is one thing. Being woken in the small hours when your brain is actively looking for things to be awake *about*, is quite another. My brain goes 'yeehah, gal! Let's fire up those neurones!', so, once conscious, I simply cannot get back to sleep. I fret about Charlie being unhappy, I fret about Sebastian getting mugged, I fret that I should re-locate Jake to stage school (how? why?), I fret about Spike being ten and a half. Memos to self (urgent) Monday thru Friday: Get over yourself, will you? Just STOP IT.

Because *everything* seems worse at three in the morning. Everyone knows that. I certainly know that. But at three in the morning I always forget.

And I'm always wide awake at three in the morning. Thus by Thursday night, seven-ish, when Charlie calls my mobile, I am almost asleep on my feet.

Charlie calling, moreover, *again*. Two weeks, three days and seven hours. That's exactly how long it's been since I've spoken to him. I know I shouldn't be counting (I'm way too busy to be counting), but, like a prisoner in Alcatraz, I find the notches on the calendar are soothing somehow. Will take me steadily, week by week, towards freedom. In that time, he's phoned me five times. He's left voicemail messages. Sent texts. Made enquiries via Dee. He's even sent a postcard of the hospital (where'd you get *them* from? And who would want one anyway? 'Hi all! It's me! I'm feeling dreadful!') on which he wrote, rather unimaginatively, 'wish you were here'. But I have been strong. I have resisted. I have failed to respond. And I certainly don't intend responding now.

Five minutes later, he calls me again. I don't respond.

When he calls me a third time in as many more minutes, I do, I am the first to admit, teeter on the brink of doing so. But then he rings off in any case. And then I get a text.

'Okay,' the text says. 'Ignore me if you must. On your own head be it. Okay?'

And that's it.

*     *     *

Which wakes me up and then sends me into a panic. What does he mean by 'On your own head be it'? What's happened? What's *that* all about? I put my phone on the kitchen table while I fashion a few frames of a slash movie, most of which feature his wife coming at me with a meat cleaver, yelling 'Adultress! Temptress! Jezebel! Trollop!', and cleaving said cleaver to cleave off my head. On my own head be it. Oh, damn him. Should I ring? Or should I not ring? Is this just another ploy to engage my sympathies? And why is he after my sympathy anyhow? Sympathy is *nothing* like sex.

And not sexy either, which is fine from where I stand. If only he could see that as well and move on.

'Are you all right, dear?' says my mother, entering the kitchen. She sees me trying to stare out my mobile, and leans across me to inspect it. 'Who was that?'

I snap it shut. 'Oh, no one,' I say breezily, as I have managed to do a thousand times and in a thousand similar situations before this one.

'I'm going to get myself a sherry,' she announces. 'Can I pour you one, dear?'

'No thanks.' Not for at least another twenty-five years hopefully. I'm sure drinking sherry will do things to my brain. Perhaps I *should* send a text. Just to check he's okay. I fashion another few frames. Soft focus ones this time, in which Charlie has become a sort of Nelson-come-Russell Crowe in *Master and Commander* fusion, and is sprawled on the deck of his clipper, shot to buggery, and telling his first mate that he needs...groan ...to get ...gasp... a message...wheeze, death rattle etc...to his beloved Lady Hamilton (or whoever that woman is Russell Crowe married in the end) and he can die a happy(ish) man... Except the ship's sinking fast and Morse Code hasn't been invented yet, and the boy who's supposed to do the flag signalling thing is holed up in the rum store saying prayers...

And then the doorbell rings.

'Door!' chirrups my mother, causing Russell's anguished features to dissolve into the cannon smoke. She always does this. The doorbell goes (which I, of course, hear) and she goes 'door!'. The phone rings (which I also, of course, hear) and she goes 'phone!'. All this despite the fact that, for the past twenty-four-odd years of my life, I have been responding to doorbells and phone bells quite successfully without any vocal contribution from her. In a domestic situation full of major irritations, this is, admittedly, only a minor irritation, but it's a sad fact of life that irritations, like radiation, are cumulative beasties. Give it six months and it will become major. Give it twelve and I might need therapy.

'I know. I heard it,' I say (preternaturally nicely), walking across the kitchen. 'It'll doubtless be someone for Jake. JAAAKKE! DOOORRRR!!!' I then bellow up the stairs. Because that's different. He *doesn't* hear, obviously.

My mother winces, as she always does, at my unmaidenly pitch and volume. All this shouty stuff visibly pains her. But then she's never done boys, has she? Perhaps it will remind her just how very much she *does* value her peace and quiet. One can but hope (and – memo to self – be very noisy). She takes her sherry back off to the living room and whatever soap opera it is that she's currently perched in front of. She watches them all, and it doesn't escape my notice that we're all busy starring in one of our own.

Jake clatters down the stairs. 'Probably Hamish's mum come to pick him up,' he says, loping past me to yank open the front door. But it isn't Hamish's mum. It's not anyone's mum. It is Charlie who is standing on the doorstep.

'Good evening,' he says pleasantly, while eyeing my tonsils. 'I've come to collect my...er... son.'

One thing that immediately becomes apparent is that as neither Jake nor Charlie seems in the least aghast at this state of affairs, I am the only person in the environs of my hallway who is mute and in a state of utter shock. I lean against the kitchen door in the hopes that it will absorb some.

'For Hamish, right?' says Jake. He yanks the door open wider. 'Come in,' he says brightly. 'We're just getting his stuff.' Charlie wipes his feet then does as instructed. 'Righty-ho,' he says. This has got to be a dream. 'Righty-ho.'

Another thing that almost as immediately becomes apparent as well is that things are clearly not as they might seem. Hamish, then, (for there is only Hamish left residing in Jake's bedroom right now, the other two having been picked up by Tom's mother half an hour back) is – *must* be – Charlie's son. But Charlie doesn't have a son called Hamish. Charlie has a son called Oliver, who lives just outside Oxford, with his mother and his half-sister and his brother. And a cat.

Except he obviously does. He just said so, didn't he? He said 'I've come for my son' and Jake said 'for Hamish, right?'. What the hell is going *on* here?

In the five seconds it has taken me to reach the conclusion that I have failed to reach any sort of conclusion, Charlie has shut the front door behind him and engaged me in the sort of wordless conversation that goes 'See? You silly mare. I did try to tell you. But would you listen? Not a bit of it.' (I, of course, am still going '*whhaaaattt????*') And now he's grimacing a bit too. I close my mouth and let go of the door jamb.

'*Hamish*?' I mouth.

He nods. He looks sheepish. 'Oliver,' he says. 'Hamish to his friends. It's the Scott bit, of course.'

Of course. I should have realised. *No*. There's no 'of course' about it. How would I disseminate that from that? Gawd, and of all the bands in all the world, how come he walked into Jake's one? I'm stupefied. 'But he lives in Oxford.'

Charlie shakes his head. 'Not any more. They're here now.'

As in Cardiff. They're all *here* now. 'And he's joined Jake's band. Good God.'

Charlie frowns. 'It would seem so. I believe he answered an advert.' We've been keeping our voices low, but a series of bumps and bangs and guffaws overhead seem to indicate that the getting of stuff is still in mid-operation. We both look upwards. He takes a step towards me and speaks normally again. 'I had absolutely no idea, Abbie,' he says. 'No idea whatsoever. Not until Claire rang me and asked me to fetch him. I couldn't believe it when she gave me the address.'

Claire. *Claire*. I try to recall the last time Hamish was collected after band practice, and more specifically if I saw whoever it was that collected him. I can't. But then I often can't. I'm often out, or in the kitchen, or just simply not involved. They come, they practice, they get collected at some point. I sometimes have a chat with Tom's mum (they've been pals for some years now), and I used to see David's dad from time to time. But not much. Their parents usually wait in the car. We don't engage much. That's the way it works once they're older. Which means – and I start at this thought – that Charlie's *wife* has probably been here at some point. Collecting Hamish – well Hamish/Oliver – and I never even *knew*.

And neither did she. 'Oh, God. This is awful,' I say. And I mean it. It doesn't take a genius to collate the implications, from the jolly doorstep encounters with Charlie's wife over amp leads, all the way up to One Black Lung's 'best of' farewell gig at the Royal Albert Hall, in fact. Will I ever be free of him? *Them*?

'You're looking good,' observes Charlie.

'You're not,' I respond. And I mean that as well. 'You've lost weight.'

'I know.'

'Are you ill?'

'No. Well, not as in –' He stops and glances upwards. 'Look, Abbie, can't we do dinner one night? Just dinner. That's all. No games. I just need to –'

'No, Charlie! God, please don't go there. Not now.' Oh, this is too, too dreadful. And what's most dreadful about it is not that he won't stop asking such things, but the realisation that what I would most like to do at this moment is to take three steps across the hall and gather him into my arms for a cuddle. To make him feel better. To stop him hurting so much. But, no. I'm wrong. *Most* dreadful is making eye contact with him, and the realisation in doing so that that is precisely what he'd like me to do too.

We spend a moment in silent contemplation of each other, because neither of us knows what to say. 'Are they good?' he ventures eventually, while the bangs and bumps resolve themselves into the unmistakeable sound – and then vision – of an amp being lugged down the stairs.

'They're very good,' I tell him. 'Hamish – sorry, Oliver – has a beautiful voice.' Hamish, halfway down now, hears this, and blushes. 'But you know that already, I guess.'

'Not really,' he says. He smiles at his son, and I'm beginning to get all choked up at the wonder that the sweet, polite boy who has been coming here just lately – has become my own son's

113

*friend* – is the actual, physical, flesh and blood child of the man who I've been so horribly infatuated with. It's a strange and unsettling web of relationships, and a strange and unsettling feeling. A feeling I don't know quite what to do with. The boys hit the hall and we move out of the way to let them out through the front door to put Hamish's amp in Charlie's car. He hands his son his car keys as he passes, then watches them both go down the front path. He is visibly proud and it makes me catch my breath. I've never seen him in his role as a father. 'He's very reticent about his singing at home,' he says. 'Doesn't warble in the bath or anything.'

'They've got their first gig planned, you know,' I find myself saying without thinking. 'Tom's sister works at Club One. You know? In town? Actually, perhaps you don't. But anyway, she arranged it. October, I think. They have these teen nights. They're very excited.' And then a thought pops into my head. 'God, Charlie, how did we never talk about this?'

'What?'

'*This*. The fact that you have a son who sings. And plays the guitar – no, I lie, you did mention that once, I think – but, you know, *them*. Our children. Just the fact of who they are, *what* they are. You know?'

He shrugs. And it all suddenly seems like such a terrible shame. But it's a shame with a point to it. A shame with a reason. Our lives were never, *could* never be, connected like that. We were just each other's guilty secret, and so we didn't want to dwell. Which thought makes me want to hug him even more. I wish he looked better. Looked happier. Looked more just, well, *okay*.

'Well I never did! Mr Scott-Downing!'

My mother, with timing that could outdo an atomic clock, appears in the hall at this point. Actually, I'm rather glad of it. I'm beginning to feel terribly tearful. And if Charlie were to spot it, repercussions would ensue. Grave repercussions. Giving in and moaning *Que Sera* into his neck kind of repercussions, most probably.

'Diana!' He feigns a comparable look of wonder. 'What a night for surprises this is turning out to be! How's that knee doing? Still managing to keep it in one piece?'

She nods and she tinkles. 'Gracious, doctor. Is this a house call?' Then she tinkles some more. Because she's never learned you really shouldn't laugh at your own jokes.

'In a manner of speaking,' he says. 'I've – we've – just found out that my son has joined your grandson's band. How about that?'

Mum looks from him to me. 'Well, what are the chances of *that*? How delightful!'

And she means it. She always did have a thing about doctors. The only man to break her heart (which apparently happened between husband number one and my father) was a Consultant Cardiologist. Cruel irony, that. And he didn't even offer to fix it.

And, well, like mother like daughter, perhaps? Except it's not my heart that's broken. It's his.

Jake comes back in now, while Hamish hovers on the doorstep. 'All set, Dad,' he says. Then he turns to me. 'Thanks for having me,' he says shyly. He's so sweet.

'Best be off, then,' says Charlie. 'Nice to see you again, Diana. And er…Abbie.' He turns to Jake and holds out his hand. 'And you too, mate.' Jake shakes it self-consciously. And then they're back off down the path.

Charlie turns to wave before getting into the driver's seat. I wave back. So does Jake. 'He's pretty safe, isn't he?' he says.

'Safe? That's a new one,' says Mum. 'What does 'safe' mean?'

'Cool. A good bloke. Okay. That sort of thing.'

Yes, he's probably all those. But not safe. Not Charlie. Not to *be* around anyway. Not for me.

115

# Chapter 13

HURRAH, HURRAH! A TEXT at last!

Yep ok u can open them. Txt me back l8r... Sxx

I don't of course. I'm way too excited. Though I know he only sent the text to stop his mobile from warbling at him (and in fairness, he does sound as if he's sitting at the bottom of a pond with caddis fly larvae up each nostril) I am way too euphoric for w8ing till l8r. I need 2 spk 2 him NOW.

'Maths – A! – Yessss!!!! D.T. – A! – Yessss!!!! History – B – well, no worries, B is *fine*, darling, *fine*. General Studies – A! – A *again!!!*. Hurrah, hurrah, hurrah! Oh, darling, this is brilliant!'

Sebastian says, 'bleurrgh.'

'Oh, I am *so* proud of you, darling!'

Sebastian says, 'bleurrgh.'

'You see? I *knew* you could do it. I just knew!'

'Bleurrrgh,' says Sebastian again.

A few more bleurrrghs into the conversation and I am persuaded that though he is indeed thrilled with his A level results he has insufficient brain capacity to express very much more than bleurrrghs in response until such time that his hangover has receded sufficiently that he is capable of sentient thought.

'I'll ring you back later, then, shall I?' I ask him. 'But in the meantime, can I tell everyone else? Can I? And what about dad? Shall I call him as well for you? Oh, this is fantastic, Seb! Oh, I'm so *happy*!'

And I am, too. Three As and a B. Three As and a B! THREE As and a B! THREE As!!!!!!!!!

'Actually, mainly, I'm just so relieved,' I am telling Dee fifteen minutes later, after I've woken Jake up and told him, ditto Mum, ditto Spike, ditto the lady on the corner when I walked him, plus called Pru, Seb's father in Marseilles, his nana in

Dublin, my auntie Phyllis and my cousin Sarah. Plus advised the man who came to drop off a pack of council black bags. 'Thrilled, yes, of *course*. But it's mainly just *such* a relief. Funny isn't it? You sometimes don't realise just how much you've been fretting about something until the moment you don't have to fret about it any more. Poof! All gone! It was like the first time I'd breathed out in months. Anyway, sorry to prattle. I'm just a bit hyper this morning. And you're busy, of course, so I won't keep you.'

'No problems. I'm absolutely thrilled for you. Of course I am. Send him my congratulations too, won't you?'

'Anyway, *anyway*, enough of me, frankly. Much more to the point, how are YOU?'

I haven't seen much of Dee since the vinegar debacle. Not even for badminton, because she's been ill. 'Oh, I'm fine,' she says brightly, so she's obviously better. 'I'm...er...actually, Abs, I'm glad you called. Are you doing anything later?'

'God, you must have read my mind! I've got to take Mum's wheelchair back to the hospital as it happens, and pick up some stuff, so I was thinking, as it's such a lovely day, why don't I scoop you up while I'm at it, and we can go off and have some lunch and a proper chat, yes? I promise I won't drone at you.'

'Don't be daft. You can drone all you like. But I can't do lunch because I have an appointment. At one. At the solicitors. To, well, get things moving, as it were. I was going to ring and ask you. Would you, you know, come with me and hold my hand?'

My God. So she's actually going to do it then, is she? I'm shocked. I know there was lots of fighting talk last time I saw her. But I never actually thought she'd go through with it. Seems I thought wrong. 'Oh, Dee, of *course* I will. God, I feel awful. Here am I prattling on about Seb, and you've got all this to deal with. I'm so sorry.'

'Don't be, Abs. Really. Nothing to be sorry about, believe me. Making that appointment was the best thing I've done in years.'

Except it's not really. How can it be? That much I do know. I've done a divorce. The only thing, maybe, the right thing, admittedly, but the best thing. Noooo. It's not that. It's painful

117

and dispiriting and tragic and sad. Still, at least there are no children involved.

Which is ironic. Had there been children, I think, perhaps she wouldn't even be here. Perhaps Malcolm wouldn't either. Who knows?

But what else can she do? She really couldn't have tried harder. I resolve that no, I *won't* drone. What she needs is a friend. Not a klaxon.

I'm actually quite shocked, therefore, when I find her in outpatients. She's not only looking healthy, she's positively glowing. Clearly the decision she's made has been the making of her. In the short term at least, and for that we must be thankful. She shrugs on her jacket and picks up her bag.

'You probably think I'm such a wuss,' she says, not sounding it in the least. 'But I just felt I needed a bit of moral support.'

Moral support is perhaps the last thing she needs. Support, yes, but no one could accuse Dee of ever trying to do anything but the right thing. The moral thing. Dee's morals have always been architecturally sound. 'You've got it,' I say anyway. She squeezes my arm. She's had her hair cut and straightened, and the look really suits her. And she's wearing mascara, which is an uncommon occurrence. And a sure sign she's not planning on doing any crying, because that's why she generally doesn't bother.

Once we're in my car, she pulls an envelope from her handbag, and pops it in the tray above the glove compartment.

'Card for Seb,' she explains. 'Though as soon as I went and got it, it occurred to me that he's not here to open it, is he? Still, no matter, eh? Be something for when he gets back.'

'You are *so* thoughtful,' I tell her, touched by her kindness. 'That's really sweet of you. And I can get it to him. Not right away, obviously. But I'm sending stuff on to his Dad for him, so he'll get it in October, at least.'

Seb's going to stay with his Father in Marseilles in October. He's got him a work experience placement at his engineering firm, where he's going to stay and work till early spring. Which feels like a very long time at the best of times, but a particularly long time today.

'Of course,' Dee answers. 'I'd forgotten about that. There we are, then. All sorted.' She turns towards me. 'You must be missing him right now, eh?' she adds.

I nod. 'I am.' I will continue to do so. And worse than that, and something that's never far from my thoughts, is that Jake's going there for Christmas, as well. Which will make this only the second Christmas I've not had them with me. Which will be strange. Just Spike and I. Oh, God. And most likely my mother as well, now. I wonder if I can go too?

I say so to Dee.

'Or you could come and spend Christmas with me!' she says. 'That would be fun, wouldn't it?'

But the words, so lightly spoken, hang heavy in the air space between us, and the weight of the ensuing silence brings me up short. I'm sure that, like me, she is contemplating her life becoming suddenly so very different to the way it has been up to now.

Which is scary. I've been here before. And exactly the sort of anxious ruminating about the future that is the last thing she needs to be doing right now. 'I must say,' I observe brightly, as we round the last bend on the approach to the car park. 'You're looking great. Absolutely great.'

'Am I?' she says, fiddling with the strap of the handbag in her lap. 'Well, I thought I better make an effort.'

In contrast to her earlier jaunty tone, now we're almost there, she's become tense and preoccupied. As she would, I guess. It's not the easiest of appointments to be showing up for. As with the dentist, the closer you get, the harder it is to keep calm. I reach over and squeeze her right hand. 'You sure you're okay?'

She exhales. 'My stomach's in knots about the whole thing, to be honest. It's such a big step to take. I mean I know I'm doing the right thing, but even so, I can't help but feel churned up about it all. Doesn't matter how many times I tell myself I mustn't, I can't help but worry about him, Abs. I mean, what's going to happen to him now?'

'I know,' I say. 'And I absolutely understand. But you have to move on. And so does he, for that matter. All the while you take

119

responsibility for him, he's not taking responsibility for himself. You know what the doctor said. And you've been so close to this so many times already. And not going through with it's not got either of you anywhere, has it?'

She almost seems to squirm in her seat. 'No,' she says, and then I see her chin jut. 'But this time I *am* going through with it. I *am*.'

'Good for you,' I reassure her. 'And you know, this really is the worst bit. Once you've crossed this hurdle, you'll feel so much stronger, believe me.'

'I hope you're right,' she says.

'I am.'

'Because I'm sure going to need to be.'

'And you will –'

'Abs?' she says suddenly, turning in her seat and looking straight at me.

I swivel my head round. '*What*? What is it?'

'There's something really important I have to tell you. I…'

'What?'

She fiddles some more with her bag strap. 'Abs…oh, dear… it's, well… Abs, I'm pregnant.'

I'm so stunned I almost crash the car into the barrier. 'You're *pregnant*? Good God!' And then I almost drop the ticket I've just pulled out of the machine too, because trying to assimilate this new news with this morning's news and make any sense of the one in relation to the other is nigh on impossible. Being pregnant is all she's ever wanted, all she's longed for. The one thing that's kept her going over years of unhappiness and Malcolm's various infidelities. The one thing that's kept her married to him, in fact. Hope. That if they had a child everything would be okay again. That's about the size of it. Just sheer hope.

And now she *is* pregnant and she's about to divorce him. God, could there ever be a worse time to find out something like this? What on earth is she going to do now?

'How pregnant?' I ask her.

'Eleven weeks.'

No wonder she's been ill. And sick. Of *course*. Eleven weeks pregnant! 'God, Dee. Have I lost the thread here? I thought you and he were no longer…well. But, look, I mean, we're going to the solicitors, right?'

Her hands are still in her lap. She's looking straight ahead, impassive, but even out of the corner of my eye I can see – no, more kind of sense – something odd in her expression. 'Right.'

'To see about a divorce, right?'

Still she's motionless. 'Right.'

'But what about the baby, Dee? I mean, are you *sure* about this? And what's Malcolm said about it? Does he know where you're off to today?'

'No.'

'But he knows about the baby, right?'

'Wrong.'

I pull into a space then kill the engine and twist around to look at her properly. 'You haven't *told* him?' She shakes her head. But *why* hasn't she told him? Then I have a horrible thought. 'Dee, you're not planning to…you know…'

She's one step ahead of me. 'Have an abortion? God, no!'

'So why haven't you told Malcolm? It's not like he's not going to find out before long, and –'

She takes a long slow breath before answering. 'I haven't told him about it for a very good reason. Abs, I haven't told him because it isn't *his*.'

I remove the key from the ignition and gawp at her. 'You're kidding!' Then I shake my head. No, that's stupid. Of *course* she's not kidding. Who'd kid about something like that? 'God, Dee,' I say. 'Whose is it, then?'

It occurs to me then that it needn't be anyone's. Well, it must be someone's, obviously, but is this a real person or a virtual one? Has she been down to a sperm bank? Gone off and had IVF? What? Or just paid someone to… My brain whirrs. The problem was Malcolm's, after all. Not hers. They had every kind of test. In the early days they did, anyway. In the last couple of years it's been academic anyway. She and he haven't even been sleeping in the same bedroom… So what *has* she done? It's all too much to take in. But she's smiling now and shaking her head. Reading my thoughts. 'He's not someone you know.'

I can tell by her voice anyway; there is clearly very much a 'him' in this equation. And if that's so, how did I not know about it? How didn't I *guess*? It's suddenly so blindingly *obvious*. The face I see is animated in ways I haven't seen it move in for years. As if she's got muscles in it she's only just discovered. Cat who's got the cream ones. 'I don't know what to say,' I say, because I really don't.

Much of the tension has drained from her now, and I realise it wasn't about seeing the solicitor. It was mostly about telling me her news. 'I'm so sorry I haven't told you before,' she says earnestly, as if not having told me is her greatest crime in all this. As if I have any right to know.

'Dee, you don't have to –'

'It's just, well, *you* know, don't you? What it's like, and all that. I've felt so *awful* about it. So guilty. So grubby. So *bad*. I've been wanting to tell you, but somehow I've never seemed to be able to –'

I'm about to point out that it was Malcolm and not her who broke their marriage vows first, when a sudden chilling thought occurs to me. 'God, Dee. He's not married, is he? Please, please, *please* don't tell me he's married.'

She smiles again. Shakes her head. 'He's not married.'

'Are you absolutcly sure?'

'He's not married. He's been divorced for five years. He's thirty-eight. He has a daughter of ten who lives in Swansea with her mother.'

'But where did you meet him? At work?'

'No. At Al-anon, actually. Crazy, isn't it? That I should meet him there, of all places.'

'But you said he –'

She shakes her head again. 'His brother. He goes with his sister-in-law. You know, to support her.'

'Oh, I see.'

'And, well…we got talking, and…well, here we are.'

'How long have you been seeing him?'

'Oh, off and on, about…well, about five months all told.'

Five whole months. And she's slept with him, too. And I never even twigged. Mind you, I have been somewhat preoccupied, I suppose. 'And it's serious?'

'I think so,' she pats her stomach. 'I *hope* so!'

'Does *he* know you're pregnant?'

122

She nods. Smiles again. 'Oh, *God*, yes.'

'And?'

'And he couldn't be happier.' She touches my arm gently. 'Oh, Abs, and neither could I.'

And his name is Tim and he's a software consultant, and they weren't planning on Dee getting pregnant, obviously, but now she is and she's going to be a mother at last and though she's as hopeful as anyone could be that this is the start of a new and better and happier time in her life, she's not getting carried away on any romantic flights of fancy. One day at a time is good enough for her.

But God obviously did hear, after all.

By the time I have dropped Dee off and taken back the wheelchair, it's getting on for three and I'm getting tight for time, having planned to pick up my things from Charlie's office, and having also promised my mother I'd get home in time to ferry her over for tea at Celeste's. So I'm half walking, half running as I round the corridor corner, and almost cannon into Charlie himself, whom I haven't seen for another whole week now, and who's busy rushing somewhere in his greens. There's a microsecond when we're just two people about to dance a polite jig to get around one another, but then we see who we are and our faces fall as one. Then he takes a step back and scrutinises me carefully.

'Hmm,' he says finally.' I take it you're not here to see me, then?'

'I was bringing back Mum's wheelchair. So I thought I'd come up and pick up my stuff.'

'Oh, right.' He turns as if to pass me then, which brings me up short. I'm already braced for an entreaty to meet him, and its failure to happen leaves me entirely unprepared.

I touch his arm, automatically. 'Hey, you okay?'

'You know I'm not, so why do you bother to keep asking?'

And he says it really irritably, childishly, *hurtfully*, and with a hostile and unforgiving light in his eyes. And I'm shocked. Truly shocked. Because it seems so out of character. But once I think about it, (and I do, as I watch his retreating back), perhaps this brush off is actually a positive sign.

I turn around and head back to the hospital entrance. I can pick up my things some other day. Yes, positive, I decide. Hey, this is what I want, isn't it? I want him out of my hair, don't I? I *want* him to move on. Maybe I should heed the advice I gave Dee. I really must not consider myself responsible for his wellbeing any more. I really must try to move on myself.

# Chapter 14

AN EMAIL;

Hi mum, am typing this from an internet café just off the Via Condotti. Is raining right now so no inclination to go yomping round the collosseum. Reading the Da Vinci Code so have done Vatican etc. Wow. (Tell Nana the Spanish Steps were very underwhelming. Tho' can see why she likes it here – is all frocks and handbags.) We're going to head up towards Rimini tomorrow and chill for a couple days – gonna meet up with Owen and Mike, hopefully.

I want a scooter!!! LOL S xxx

I absolutely never read *Depth* magazine. Really, I don't. Yes, I pick it up in the hairdressers occasionally, just the same as everyone else does, but only if there's nothing else to look at. I'd never, ever buy it. Of course I wouldn't. I have far better things to do with my time and much more edifying things to read about. *Depth* is not depth as in intellectual rigour. *Depth* is depth as in scouring the bottoms of ponds.

The following Thursday morning, and I am reading *Depth*.

'Thought you'd be interested,' says Candice, who has already read it. 'He looks good, doesn't he? Did you clock the boots? Don't think much of that frock though. Mind you –' she pauses to emit a loud gale of laughter. '– she doesn't look like she'd know a Versace from a bin bag, state she's in.'

I'm not really listening. I'm too busy reading. Well, gawping, mainly. There's not much actual stuff to read. The photo takes up almost all of the page, the headline '*Uh-oh!* Is *TV's Luce back on the juice?*' much of the rest. Such copy as there is confined to the sort of faux-moralistic carping *Depth* excels in, and the usual hackneyed references to the weather.

Mainly I'm looking at Gabriel Ash, who is making a manful stab at pretending everything's just fine and that his fiancée is perfectly capable of remaining vertical of her own accord despite the fact that one leg is buckling underneath her. Heavy squalls expected indeed.

'Oh, dear, this is awful,' I say.

'Hardly a shock, though, is it? Tsk. What a waste. I mean I know she's got a boob job and a St Tropez tan and perfect teeth and long legs and wealth and fame and beauty and so on, but I mean, I *ask* you. What can he *see* in her?'

You want to ask Dee that one, I think but don't say. 'That's such a shame,' is what I do say. Because that's what it is. Ordinary people don't have to put up with this stuff. Oh, poor, poor them. How excruciating.

It also takes some of the gloss off the little surprise I have been looking forward to imparting. And I have been looking forward to it, I realise, very much. Though none of it has anything to do with me, obviously, I can't help but find myself feeling a little sorry for Gabriel Ash. My first impression, as first impressions so often are, was probably right after all.

I shouldn't have, of course. But I did. When Jake was out with his mates and Mum was out at whatever soirée I'd dropped her off at (I lose track) I sat down and went through the contents of Hugo's box. I felt very guilty about it, because it really was – is – none of my business, which is partly, I realise, why I didn't show it to my mother. Partly, but not wholly. It also struck me that if he didn't see fit to discuss it with her, then it perhaps wasn't my place to either. And, well, it was snooping. I really had no right. So best that I kept it to myself.

The contents of the box made for very poignant reading. As little as I knew about Hugo already, it seemed that here was someone who had a whole other side to him, and I wondered again why he'd never told my mother about Gabriel. Was it guilt? Was it shame? Perhaps it was both. It would hardly have shown him in a very good light. Or perhaps, less charitably, it was born out of just the same sort of secretive nature that meant she didn't know about the house. And I had to remember that this largely innocuous retired gent was at one time the worst kind of bad guy. No moral backbone, as my father was wont to say. A bit of a rotter, all told.

Yet here, laid before me, was evidence of someone who clearly wished he'd been better. Who, though he had (for whatever reason) failed to be reconciled with his son, obviously cared for him. Cared very much. Enough to record his whole life. Well, the last twenty years of his life, at any rate. Almost every one of them had its moment, all much thumbed and doubtless read and re-read. From a piece about him graduating from university right up to the pictures I had seen the other week.

And there were also lots of photos. Mostly of Gabriel himself, over a span of many years, several in uniform, some formal, others less so. But also some of a pretty dark-haired girl, whose name was Maria. From babyhood right up to what I presumed was fairly recently. I knew this because the backs of the photos were all marked. *Maria, aged four. Maria aged 7.* And then I found another, this time of a group; Corinne, Maria, and two other children (hers presumably), all larking about in a summertime garden, while Gabriel, in surfing shorts, soaked them with a hose. It was marked on the back '*Job clearly going to his head, eh, Dad?*' in the same writing as many of the others.

So I presumed it was Corinne who kept Hugo posted.

And that Maria was Gabriel's daughter.

And now he's here in the clinic, and the life I have eavesdropped on so comprehensively has another chapter, another documented snippet, to its name. Though one that obviously isn't going in any box. Which is probably no bad thing.

I get him set up with the TENS machine and a cup of coffee, and go off to write up my last patient's notes. It's been raining heavily and steadily and unremittingly all morning, the window panes thrumming out a mournful wall of sound.

When I go back to unplug him, he's reading the *Guardian*, but the copy of *Depth* is also by his side, on top of a pile of magazines. I glance at it, and he straight away glances at me glancing at it.

'Oh, rats,' I say, peeling the contacts off his leg and cursing whatever lack of rigour caused that particular magazine to find its way on to that particular pile and that pile into this particular cubicle. And then it occurs to me that it might not be accidental. Perhaps Candice is busy planning some sort of coup. And using

Lord Haw Haw tactics to help expedite things. 'Dear me,' I add, picking it up and pushing it to the bottom of the pile. Pointless, but I feel I need to do it even so. 'You weren't supposed to see that.'

He looks bemused – no, even *amused* – by what I've done. 'Don't worry,' he says equably. 'I already have.'

There doesn't seem much to say to that. Well, not unless he says something else, which he doesn't, so I busy myself with the rest of the contacts while he sits there and watches me do so.

And what's to be said, after all? This sort of public scrutiny is presumably something he's used to. Something he has to put up with as part of the job. And it's certainly not for me to pass comment. I take the heat pad from the trolley to go and put in the microwave. The air is sweet and exotic. Coconut again.

'And what I don't see myself I always hear about eventually,' he goes on, when I return. 'My sister always keeps me informed.'

There's something in his tone as he says this that suggests he's not a hundred percent impressed with that particular state of affairs. I wonder how he'll feel about the fact that she's spent two decades doing similarly with his father, about him. Angry? Dismayed? Or will he find it a comfort? I don't buy into his insouciance, his I-don't-care manner. His father's just died, and if I know anything about anything, it's that, whatever he says, it must hurt. Perhaps hurt all the more because of the unfinished business. Because his father is no longer there for him to forgive. But it's none of *my* business, so I don't comment on that either. 'Speaking of which,' I say, instead, because I'm keen not to dwell on any *Depth* related topics. 'Any news on the sale of the house?'

He shakes his head. 'Not as far as I know,' he says. 'I think there've been some viewings. I'm not really that involved, to be honest.'

Which would figure. 'Tell me,' I ask him, because I've been wondering. 'How did that come about? I mean, how did it turn out that your father lived in the house that was left to you by your mother? From what you've told me, I'd have thought that would be the last thing she'd want.'

'She didn't know. That all happened much later. After she died.'

'Oh. I see.'

'Though I dare say she turned in her grave.' His smile turns into a wince as I begin to massage his leg. 'But, well, he needed somewhere to live, and the house was there. She'd been renting it out for several years, and they were thinking about selling it. And, well, I guess it made sense.'

I note the 'they'. So he didn't have anything much to do with it, clearly.

'And you were happy about that?'

He shrugs. 'Made no odds to me where he lived. Anyway, I was in Italy at the time.'

I think about his dark-haired daughter called Maria, and I wonder who her mother is – or was. And it occurs to me that I've no business wondering. It really *is* none of my business. Not at all.

'My son is in Italy at the moment,' I say instead.

'Oh?' he says. 'Whereabouts?'

'Rome, when I last heard. But he could be almost anywhere by now. He's inter-railing round Europe with a friend. He's on a gap year.'

He looks so genuinely surprised that I'm almost tempted to let myself believe what he says next, which is 'You have a son old enough to be on a gap year?' But then I remember he's a television person, and smooth enough to know that I'm a woman of an age where such comments hit every sort of right spot every time.

Though I don't hold it against him. It's sweet of him to say it, even so. 'I had him very young,' I say. Which is, in fact, true. Anxious to build a proper home and family of my own, I did everything very young, when I come to think about it. Or so I imagine a psychologist would say. It wasn't conscious, not at all. But it's certainly true that I wasted no time in getting married, having children, paying a mortgage, growing frown lines. And now I have a resident mother to add to the list. And to the frown lines, no doubt. I smile widely and purposefully to smooth them all out. 'And I don't know where the time's gone. I certainly don't *feel* old enough to have a son on a gap year.'

He doesn't gild the lily by repeating his compliment. Which makes me believe it even more. 'My daughter's in Italy,' he says. 'Just outside Siena.' Which makes me start, but then I realise she's probably no big secret anyway. Just something – someone – that simply hasn't come up. Why would it? I barely know him, after all.

Just things *about* him. Which is different. 'Oh,' I say. 'On holiday?'

He shakes his head. 'No, she lives there. Her mother's Italian. I was out there for several years.'

Though not now. Is he divorced too, I wonder? I nod. 'Oh, yes. My mum mentioned that.'

I hear a ping then, so I go to fetch the heat pad from the micro. 'How's she doing?' he asks when I return. 'Your mother. Or shouldn't I risk asking without donning a tin hat?'

I pull the sort of face that his amused expression seems to warrant. 'Hmm,' I say. 'What's that word? Begins with an 'H'. Habituation, that's it. We are becoming 'habituated' to one another. Though I suspect she's becoming more habituated than I am, so I'm trying to keep her on her toes. Touch of ground glass in her porridge, the odd trip wire. Spiders in her bed at night. That sort of thing.'

He laughs. 'Seriously though, it must have been one hell of an upheaval for you. All this. I'm not sure I'd maintain my sense of humour quite so well if I had to have my mother live with me.'

I reach under the trolley for a towel. 'Who said I was?'

'You seem to be to me.'

I smile at this. 'She's not the only actress in the family, you know.'

'Quite a woman, though, isn't she? I had no idea she was so famous. Not till I saw all the trophies and so on. By the way, turns out that Lucy's aunt was in a show with her once. I meant to tell you.'

I fold the towel and place it over his knee, then put the heat pad on top. 'Really?'

'A musical? In the early seventies or thereabouts.'

I nod. 'That would be about right. She was in several. Which one?'

'I forget the name of it. She's going to dig out a photo for me. I'll have to bring it in. Small world, eh? Ouch. Is that supposed to be so hot?'

'Yes it is. Can you bear it? It'll start cooling down soon. Actually, now you remind me,' I rattle on, because this seems the perfect time to do it, 'I have something at home for you too.'

'You do? What?'

'Some things I found when we were clearing Mum's stuff out the other weekend. Some papers of your father's. I thought you might want them.'

'Oh?' he says. 'What sort of papers?'

'Erm...I'm not really sure. Mementoes, mainly. Things to do with you, I think.'

'Really?'

I study his expression. Aha! So I was right. He *is* interested. It's as plain as the rather fine nose on his face. 'I think so. You know, photographs and so on...'

'Really?' he says again. 'What of?'

'Well, you, in the main. I was going to bring them in today,' I hurry on. 'But then what with one thing and another it went straight out of my head and I forgot to put them in the car... But I can bring them in next time you come, if you like.'

'Be easier if I pick them up from you after work one day, wouldn't it? Save you the trouble.'

'It's no trouble,' I start to say, but then I realise he's probably suggesting that because he doesn't want to wait another fortnight. He wants them *now*. Which is nice. And I'm glad for him. 'But if you want to, then fine. I'm fairly central. Only in Pontcanna. Tell you what, I'll go and get some paper and write down my address for you.'

Candice stops by the cubicle at that point, as is getting to be her wont. 'Another coffee, Mr Ash?'

He shakes his head. 'No, thanks.'

'Gawd, will you look at that!' she adds, looking past us out of the window. 'Hammering down. You'd never think it was August, would you?'

We both turn to look. 'Actually,' Gabriel Ash says, 'this is perfectly normal. People often don't realise, but August is one of the wettest months of the year.'

'Never!' says Candice enthusiastically, clearly flushed with the thrill of having engaged him in conversation, and newly enamoured of precipitation generally.

'But it's going to be a lovely weekend,' he adds.

'Honest?'

He winks at her. 'Starting this very afternoon, as it happens. Remember. You heard it here first.'

I see him out soon after and I think, yes. It *is* going to be a lovely weekend. I shall make sure of it. I don't know why, but seeing Gabriel Ash has put me in a good mood. Yes, I do. It's because I can tell seeing me has put *him* in a good mood. That my news about his father has brightened his day. And on a day that probably needed some brightening too. I'll bet he'll be on the phone before I know it. I'll bet he'll be round to collect the box tonight. I know it's not my business, and I know it's not my family, but it's made me feel that at least *something* positive has come out of all this. Perhaps some of it will rub off on me too.

'God,' Candice sighs, as he heads off down the stairs. 'Why are all the good guys already taken?'

I smile at her naivety, even though I know it really isn't. It's simply rhetoric, and I often think the same thing myself. 'But Candice, that's just the point,' I remind her. 'They're taken precisely *because* they're good guys. That's the way it works.'

'I know,' she says. 'Ain't life a bitch?'

No! Well, yes it is *sometimes*, I guess, but thinking such depressing and dispiriting thoughts is the absolute worst way to carry on. And not how I intend to, so, when I leave the clinic at five, it is with the firmest of firm intentions that I will start this upcoming lovely weekend a day early. Tomorrow's my day off, after all. And true to Gabriel's words, the rain has stopped, the clouds have all dispersed, and the puddles on the road are shrinking even as I watch. Yes, I think, I will sit in the garden and read a book. Better still, I will buy a bottle of wine on the way home. Or some Pimms. What the hell. Yes. And I might even buy a lime. I have nothing to do and nowhere to be. And Jake's sleeping at Tom's tonight, so I don't even have to cook. I can prepare a feast of tortilla chips and salsa and cornichons, and mother will just have to lump it. And there's a thought. Perhaps I will ring Dee and see if she'd like to come over. Perhaps I will even get-the-barbecue-out.

It's with such pleasing thoughts uppermost in my mind that I pull my phone from my bag and switch it on.

It starts tootling and squeaking at me almost immediately. Two text messages, voicemail, the whole kit and caboodle. And an incoming call now, as well. Dee herself, in fact, I see. How very handy. Yes, we'll have a barbecue, maybe. That is, if she's not already got a prior date with Tim. Strange to think she's been living exactly the same double life I have. Strange to adjust to the possibility that she might already have something else on. Thrilled as I am for her, tonight I hope she hasn't. We can sit and talk babies while the sun sets.

'It's official,' I tell her happily, as soon as I connect. 'Straight from the weatherman's lips, in fact. High pressure system moving in over the Atlantic. Hot dry and sunny in all parts all weekend.'

She doesn't respond entirely as expected.

'*There* you are,' she says breathlessly. 'I've been trying you for ages. I thought you'd want to know about Charlie.'

'Charlie? What *about* Charlie?' I ask her.

'Abs, he's had a heart attack,' she says.

# Chapter 15

WHEN I GET TO my car I spend a number of minutes just sitting in it, listening to the blood pounding in my ears. Charlie's forty-six years old. Forty-five to fifty-five is heart attack territory. Charlie looking ill. Charlie looking pale. Charlie looking too thin, too drawn, too listless, too *not like Charlie,* and my ignorance and arrogance and sheer bloody stupidity had me thinking it was something I could put down to me.

Then I drive straight to the hospital, where I sit a few minutes more, berating myself. Hating myself. Perhaps I'm not so way off beam. Perhaps it *is* something to do with me. But then I berate myself further. I am – no, I *was* – just a symptom of his problems. But I feel culpable – guilty as charged – even so.

None of which has any bearing on the matter in hand, however, which is that I absolutely have to see him and make sure he's okay. Though it doesn't escape my notice that it's now a little after six on a Thursday night, and the chances are that he already has a visitor or two, I have driven to the hospital to do exactly that and, try as I might to convince myself I shouldn't, I don't intend leaving until I've done so.

I think. I'm still in my A and P uniform, of course, so I'm at least reasonably well attired for the one woman covert SWAT Team exercise that I realise might have to form the basis of my getting to see Charlie without arousing suspicion. If anyone – okay, his family – wonders at my being in the hospital, they might reasonably suppose I still work here. I get out of the car and lock it, and make my way across the car park. Or if not, at least that I could be here in relation to work. Better, much better, than if he'd been down at the BUPA hospital. But then he always did say that, if he was a patient, right here, amongst friends, is where he'd want to be.

And doctors, on the whole, don't tend to go private. Not for things like this. Not for big things. They don't need to. They look after one another. There are precious few perks to an NHS career, but this, at least, thank God, is one of them.

All I know from Dee is that he was admitted to the Coronary Care Unit at some point yesterday evening. I know nothing more because she doesn't either, apart from the fact – oh, thank *God* – that he's still of this earth. She's been off work today for an antenatal appointment, and only knows what she knows because Carolyn mentioned it when she happened to call her earlier today.

When I finally fetch up on CCU, however, it's to find, to my surprise, that he's no longer there. The two nurses at the nurse station, busy with their current charges, direct me without fuss or questions to the relevant ward. Once there, however, my initial reconnaissance through the window in the door tells me nothing, as all the eight bed bays are curtained. No choice, then, but to go in and see for myself. The very worst that can happen is that the family will all be there, and if so, I can slink right back out again and wait.

Whatever. I go in. The Ward Sister, a young woman I'm only on nodding terms with (it's a big hospital), doesn't seem remotely fazed that I'm here to see Charlie, and it occurs to me that she probably doesn't even know I no longer work here. And doubtless many of the orthopaedics team have been up here today already. She confirms he's on his own, and then points me towards him.

He's been put in a side room just off the main ward. A sunny nook, west facing, with a whole wall width of window, beneath which he's sitting, not in bed, but in an armchair, reading the *Telegraph*. I mentally breathe out. Not in bed. Not on a monitor. Not wired up to anything. Bar the dressing gown and slippers, he could be a visitor himself.

The dressing gown, the slippers, the holdall in the corner. The newspaper. The box of tissues. The two paperbacks. The wash bag. The china mug. The box of fruit teabags on the table. Most of all, the box of fruit tea bags on the table. She's been here already. Getting him sorted. Getting stuff in. *Looking after him*. The door's open, but even so, I knock.

He turns around, and then looks surprised, and then smiles.

And then shakes his head. 'See?' he says. 'Told you it would come to this, didn't I?'

He says it so matter-of-factly, so calmly, so dispassionately, that I immediately find myself bursting into tears. Well, not

135

bursting, exactly, because one tries not to burst, exclaim, squeak, wail, or otherwise make a spectacle of oneself in the presence of a sick person, but the net result is the same. I am suddenly a muddle of spouty tears, tight throat and facial contortions and in trying to tourniquet any impolite floods I am rendered incapable of speech. So instead, I gently push the door almost closed behind me and sit heavily down on the bed, snivelling.

Charlie puts down the paper and considers me. 'It's all right,' he says gently. 'I'm not going to die on you.'

Which completely undermines my first attempt at hysteria-management, and necessitates a hasty re-grouping. He reaches across to his bedside table and plucks a tissue from the box. Which I take from him. 'I doe,' I say. 'I doe.'

He looks a little disappointed about that. '*How* d'you know?' he says, narrowing his eyes.

I lower the tissue from my face and let good sense kick in automatically. 'Because you're *here*. They'd hardly let you leave CCU if you were critical, would they? Oh, but Charlie, I should have realised. I should have –' And then I'm off on one again.

He plucks another tissue from the box and hands it to me. 'I didn't even have a heart attack, if that's what you've been thinking.'

'But Carolyn said –'

He shakes his head. 'Just a nasty little bout of viral pericarditis. I'll be off home tomorrow as long as my temperature's down.'

I lower the tissue from my face again and exhale heavily. 'Oh, thank *God*.'

'Oh, I've done a fair bit of that, believe me,' he says wryly. 'I might even consider re-engaging with the Church. Anyway,' he says briskly, 'dry your face and come over here and give me a hug. I think I'm entitled, don't you?'

So I step over the holdall and round the over-bed table on wheels, then bend down to let him wind his arms around my back. It's an awkward sort of clinch, with him seated and me standing, but we're long past the point where I might sit on his lap, and in some ways that makes it much nicer. He eventually lets me go, and once freed up and straightened, I lean down again and plant a kiss on the top of his head. His hair smells all hospitally and is warm against my lips.

That done, I go back and sit on the bed, not knowing quite what to say or do next.

'So,' he says, as if addressing a nervous patient. 'How are you?'

'I shouldn't be here.'

'You bloody should. I've been waiting and waiting. What kept you, anyway?'

'I didn't *know*.'

He touches my knee with a fingertip. 'Hey, now, you. I'm only winding you up.'

'Well, don't. This isn't funny, Charlie.'

'No,' he says. 'It isn't, is it?' He lifts his arms and laces his fingers in the air above his head, then turns them palms upwards and stretches. 'No,' he says again. 'But instructive, for all that.'

'How do you mean?'

He unlaces his hands again and sits forward, re-lacing them loosely between his knees. I realise I've never seen the dressing gown before. Never seen him in a dressing gown at all. Never seen this dressing-gowned version of the man I thought I knew. The one I knew always strode around naked as the day. I wonder if he's left the flat now. I wonder if they're all settled back living together again. I wonder, mainly, how he *really* feels about the future of his marriage, which is something I've never allowed myself to wonder about before. Not properly. Not truthfully. Not in the sense which that packet of fruit teabags has forced me to wonder about it. 'God, I'm going to miss you,' he says suddenly.

Like he hasn't up to now. Like we haven't already parted. Like, most of all, that he's making a point. And then I have a thought. 'Why? Are you going somewhere or something?'

He shakes his head. Then his eyes leave mine and he turns to scan the dark sky. It's a clear night. And a bright one. With an almost full moon.

'No,' he says. 'Just back, that's all.'

'You haven't been anywhere.'

'I've been with *you*, Abbie.'

'Yes, I know that, but –'

He taps his temple. 'But now it's time to go back.'

'Charlie, we already split up,' I remind him.

'No,' he says. 'There was no 'we' about it, Abbie. You left me.'

'I never had you.'

'But that's just it. You did.'

'No, Charlie. That's not true. I had a bit of you. That's all.'

'And yet I had every last bit of you, didn't I?' I say nothing. 'Which I should never have pursued and certainly didn't deserve.'

There seems no answer to that, other than a knowing affirmative. Yes, he did. For a short while. And looking at him now, I realise, with relief, that I have no regrets about any of it. So I stand then, and join him in gazing out at the sky. Growing ultramarine now above the blackening buildings. I feel his hand reach for and clasp mine.

I turn. 'Is anyone likely to –'

He squeezes it. 'Don't panic, Mr Mainwaring. She's not long left. To get some things. Pick up the kids and bring them down. We have at least twenty minutes.'

I almost laugh. 'To do what, exactly?'

'To give thanks and to reflect.'

I let my hand remain in his. 'You've gone all strange,' I say. 'All philosophical. All, well, I don't know… *funny*. '

'It's probably the virus. Infected my hard drive.' He turns then, to look at me. 'Abbie,' he says.

'What?'

'I'm very, very sorry,' he says.

My eyes fill with tears again because though he's said those words to me many, many times, this time I know he really means it.

'For what?' I ask him anyway.

'For involving you in my mid-life crisis, I suppose.'

'*Your* mid-life crisis? Tell me about it.'

'What a pair we are,' he says softly. 'Eh?'

My turn to squeeze *his* hand now. '*Were*.'


I leave Charlie feeling lighter of heart than I have done in a long time. It's the stupidest thing. Which is odd, not to mention pretty damn ironic. I'm all cried out, of course – long since all cried out about Charlie – but I thought when I came here that something terrible would happen. That I'd see him and, well, I don't know, that I'd get sucked back in all over again. That I'd be all overcome and infatuated again. Compassion doesn't mix well with sexual attraction. It's too volatile a cocktail to be stable. But it hasn't happened, and shocked as I am, I feel free.

Free, and also – perversely – as if this whole sorry shambles has actually been good for me. As if Charlie's attentions, inappropriate as they may have been, have been a shot in the arm when I needed it most. An escape from my way-too-long post divorce purdah. Which is enough for me to begin to feel optimistic about the future, at any rate. And having been an optimist since birth, of course, also means that it doesn't feel in the least unreasonable to suppose that my exit will be as uneventful as my entry, and free of any further Scott-Downing sightings. But that, in itself, is unreasonable. There is only one main corridor that links the wards with the main entrance, and as I know the family are en route back at some point, there is, of course, every likelihood that we'll meet up.

Thus it's no surprise really that we do. And with spectacularly bad timing, to boot. Thirty seconds sooner and I could have slunk off down the byway to X-ray. Twenty seconds later and I could have dived into the sluice room. As it was, I have made just sufficient progress down the corridor that I'm marooned in the bit of it that offers up no alternatives. The bit where all the admin offices are. Admin, of course, as I have had previous cause to consider, being that thing hospitals do only between nine and five.

They're headed straight towards me. All of them. *En masse.* Charlie's wife, Hamish, a smaller version of Hamish, and a tall young woman who is clearly her daughter. And as the distance between us shortens, I can see that Hamish – Hamish/Oliver? Oliver/Hamish – which? – who has obviously recognised me, is telling his mother who I am. No chance, therefore, to slide past without contact. I hope it's not obvious I've been crying.

We draw level, mid-corridor. I take a deep breath. I smile.

It's so obvious *she* has. 'Hello,' I say, straight at her, with a nod towards Hamish. 'I'm Abbie McFadden. You must be Oliver's mother.' She nods but doesn't speak. We don't shake either. We're two women, and women don't shake hands. I don't know why I know that but I suspect it's something my mother drummed into me at a very early age. It's an anachronism these days – why wouldn't we? Why *shouldn't* we? I idly wonder if the same drill has been passed on to her.

Charlie's wife Claire is much taller than me, with artfully – and no doubt expensively – mussed hair. I force myself to meet her gaze, which is intelligent and focussed and quizzical. She has perfectly tweezered eyebrows. She is wearing a grey suit. I feel shabby and insignificant beside her. 'I heard about –' God – what do I say? Charlie? Mr Scott-Downing? Your husband? What?

'…Charlie,' is what I plump for, and there's something in her answering expression that seems a little disapproving. And momentarily, much as I don't want to, much less have the right to, I find it instinctively makes me disapproving of her. Because, really, it *is* the right form of address. We were colleagues. Okay, so he's a lofty consultant and I'm a lowly physio, but that's how *he* asked me – asked all of us – to address him. From day one. And so we all did.

But perhaps, were I her, I'd want to puff him up too. Want people like me to know their place around him. Around *them*? Keep their distance, at any rate. By some instinct? Or intuition? The benefit of experience? This woman is clearly not stupid. She must know how attractive a man Charlie is. How charismatic a man he is. How very *lucky* she is. And I decide, in an instant, recalling his words, that it's *she* who's undeserving. Of *him*. And also that I doubt she's ever hugged him enough. That she doesn't look *after* him properly. Outrageous, I know, and probably way off the mark, given that I know she's a busy GP with enough problems of her own – least of all her straying husband, but even so, the thoughts tumble out regardless, thumbing their noses at propriety. I indicate behind me. 'So I just popped by to see him.'

'Jake's mum used to work here with Dad,' Oliver explains to her. For which I'm grateful, as it spares me from having to do so myself.

'Oh, I see,' she says. 'Small world.'

'I'm a physiotherapist,' I add, as if it actually matters. 'I was working here,' I bolt on, 'till a couple of months back.'

I note the way her daughter's arm is linked so tightly in the crook of hers. Like they're shoring each other up. 'Oh,' she says again, politely. I am, I realise with mixed feelings, not even on her radar. Just some instantly forgettable ex-member of the staff. 'Right,' she says. 'Well, nice to meet you, anyway.'

I nod. And never now, God willing, will be. When next we meet, *if* next we meet, it will be as fellow mothers. Which is an interesting thought. 'Yes, you too,' I say. Then to Hamish. 'See you soon.'

I pause a moment to watch their progress as we part, and wonder if this brush with her husband's mortality will make her appreciate him more.

And then I wonder if he has any right to expect that. Any knowledge (or lack) of his infidelity is irrelevant; it is he who reneged on the deal. And whatever she does or doesn't know about Charlie, she must surely know the one thing – the *only* thing – that matters. That he's a keeper of secrets that he doesn't share with her.

And there's something about her that tells me she *does* know. Not specifics, not names, I don't think, just the fact of it. That she knows but can do little about it except hope. Her shoulders are slightly uneven, I notice, under the weight of the basket she has in the crook of her other arm. More things for Charlie. Some fruit? Another book? Certainly another newspaper. And Hamish is even, I think, carrying his laptop. His family are all looking after him.

I brought nothing. As it should be. *All* is now as it should be. For the moment, at least. But their future's not my problem. Now it's time for me to go home.

# Chapter 16

WHEN I GET IN, the house is silent, and from the hallway I can see that my mother is sitting at the kitchen table doing my *Times* Su Doku puzzle. I presume she thinks she has the right, given that I've come in so late. Probably in a huff about sorting her own dinner. Well tough, frankly. Too bad. I'm not the bloody maid. It's only when I'm taking my jacket off that I notice that, though she's sitting in the kitchen, she's dressed for an altogether grander location. She's all dolled up in her pink floaty top and skirt thing, and has her triple string of pearls around her neck. All dressed up but with nowhere to go. *Is* she supposed to be going somewhere this evening? Is she going somewhere right now?

'Oh, *there* you are,' she says sourly, as I enter the kitchen and put my keys down on the table. And her expression makes clear that no, she ain't not goin' not nowhere not now. But she should have been. Oh, yes. No doubt about that. Then the penny drops. Rehearsals. No. Actually, a casting. Cyncoed Theatre Club. *Tonight*. Oh, dear, oh dear. She puts down my pencil-with-a-rubber-on and glares at me.

'Oh, God, Mum. I'm sorry,' I say.

Which history should tell me (but chronically forgets to) is the absolute last thing one should ever say to my mother. For she has only the one stock response.

'And so you should be!' she snaps. Which makes something snap in me. Why not vary things a little? Why not something along the lines of perhaps asking for an explanation? Why not some startlingly innovative cognitive reasoning process that culminates in her wondering – even if for just the tiniest instant – if there might just be a very good reason why I, this daughter who runs around for her pretty seamlessly pretty much whenever instructed to do so and has been doing so, like, *forever*, might have – no patently *has* – forgotten to come home on time and deliver her to her club? Why not just a straightforward 'has something bad happened?' Why not any and all of above? Huh?

I check the time. Eight-forty. I snatch the keys up again.

'Right,' I say. 'Come on. We'll go now.'

She wafts a hand in the air. I am clearly not going to get off that easily. 'Oh, it's much too late now. They'll be almost done.'

'I'm sure they won't. It's only –'

'Abigail, they started at seven.'

'So you'll be a bit late. It's not the end of the world.'

'And they've already cast the principals anyway.'

'How do you know?'

'Because I just spoke to Wilfred.'

'Wilfred who?' She picks the pencil up again. Pointedly. 'Wilfred *who*?'

'Wilfred who could have come and picked me up!' she barks. 'Only I told him not to because I thought *you'd* be back!'

'Look, come on. Let's go now. We can be there in ten minutes.'

'No, no. Please don't you worry yourself about *me*. I don't want to go now, anyway.' She turns her attention back to the puzzle. Well, *fine*. If she'd rather sit there and sulk she can go right ahead. I know full well that she's expecting more appeasement and cajoling, but she'll be waiting a bloody long time.

I put the car keys down again and go over to the fridge, but the scant glassful of wine I had left in the bottle in the door isn't there any more. I turn around. It's standing empty on the windowsill above the sink, along with a similarly empty Tio Pepe bottle. I shut the fridge again and slap on the kettle. My puzzle. My wine. My solitude, most of all. Perhaps I should persist. Perhaps I should just manhandle her from her chair and bundle her into the car and deposit her at theatre club after all. Perhaps not. I don't have the energy for it. Or for making tea. I switch the kettle off again and pour myself a glass of milk instead, aware from the dusky reflection in the kitchen window, that her eyes are now boring into my back. I turn around.

'Mum, don't look at me like that, please.'

'Like what?'

'Like *that*. Look, I'm sorry I'm home so late, but something important came up, okay?'

'What?'

'Just something.'

143

'Too important for you to phone me?'

'Look, I didn't phone you because I forgot all about your meeting, okay? I didn't know I *needed* to phone you, did I?'

Down goes the pencil again. 'But you should have phoned me *anyway*. Meeting or no meeting. Would that have been such a chore? I'm well aware that your comings and goings are entirely your own affair, but if you'd at least extended me the courtesy of bothering to phone me I could have asked Wilfred to come and pick me up on his way, couldn't I?'

It occurs to me that it would be deeply satisfying to point out that if Wilfred was available to pick her up, then he could have picked her up in the first place. But I don't point it out, because that would be childish, and I strenuously don't wish to do any single thing that might inspire her to treat me like one.

And she's quite right. It *did* occur to me to call home. Had Jake been at home I'd have definitely called. But she's not my child. So I didn't feel the need. No, more than that. I even *resented* the obligation to inform her of my movements; were she not in my house, it simply wouldn't apply. And I know all too well that what I mainly resented was that if I had rung my mother I would have had to explain, which might necessitate me telling her a lie. Childish again. Mean and selfish and discourteous. But I *do* resent it. I resent it all the time. I can't help it. 'I'm sorry,' I say instead. '*Really*. I'm sorry. I was at the hospital, all right?'

'At the hospital?'

'Yes, at the hospital.'

'Why?'

'A had to go and visit a sick friend.'

'What, at this time?'

I drink some milk. It's disgusting. Because someone left it out. 'Yes, Mum. At this time.'

She says nothing more, and goes back to her – *my* – puzzle, while I clatter about putting things away. It's some time before I realise she's now stopped doing the puzzle again and is silently following my progress around the kitchen.

I close a cupboard. '*What*?'

'Who is he?' she then asks. And her tone's entirely different.

I open another one and force in the cake rack. Then I realise it's still dirty and pull it out again.

'Well?' she says.

I feel cornered. 'Well what?'

'Who *is* he?'

I put the dirty cake rack in the sink and turn on the tap. Oh, please. Please, not now. I'm too tired.

'Who said it was a he?'

'Well, isn't it?'

I sigh heavily. 'Yes, it's a he.'

'I thought so.'

I say nothing. I look at the clock on the kitchen wall. Would it be so ridiculous to go to bed at this time? Yes. I won't sleep anyway. No. I shall have a bath. A long one. Decided, I tip the remainder of the milk down the sink. Perhaps there's a beer knocking about at the back of the fridge. I return to it and rummage. The silence is clamouring in my ears.

And then she breaks it.

'So you weren't at the hospital at all, then.' *Whhhaaat?* 'Hmm,' she says, before I can answer her. 'Thought not.'

Which feels like such an outrageous thing to say under the circumstances, that it's all I can do not to rush across the room and club her with the cucumber I currently have in my hand. Is that what she's thinking? That I've been off on a tryst and am making up stories to try and mollify her? That I'd *do* something like that? And then a second thought rides up and elbows the first one out of the way. That I'm a fully grown woman, with a grown up child of my own, and that I do not – do *not* – have to answer to her. I put the cucumber back in the fridge with great deliberation.

'Yes, of course I was at the hospital!' I say.

'Well,' she says, tartly, rising now from the table. 'Whether you were or whether you weren't is really neither here nor there, Abigail, is it?' She shakes her head as she shuffles round to get her stick. Fires off her "found *you* out, young lady" expression. 'No wonder you were so reluctant to have me staying here,' she mutters.

I have to let that go. I can't put her straight on that tonight. I can't trust myself not to be toxic and hateful. I return my attention to my quest for a beer.

But before I've even had time to see it coming, the contents of the fridge begin to shimmer and mist. Behind a veritable Niagara

145

of hot fresh tears. Which is the last thing I want at this moment, in this company, so I slam the fridge shut and push past her out of the room. Fast.

I hear her huffing her way up the stairs long before she's tapping at my bedroom door. I feel sixteen again. All puffed up with hormonal upheaval. Traumatised. Braced for her inevitable disapproval. A little scared. A lot defiant. But not at all In Charge.

She taps again. 'Can I come in?' she says softly. I don't need to answer, because straight away, of course, she does.

I sit up on the bed and swing my legs over the side.

'Do you want to tell me about it?' she says. She's still in the doorway at this point, but she soon relocates to the dressing table stool. 'Well?'

It's funny seeing her there. I'm used to Jake sitting there. Coming in to impart some terrifically important piece of musical intelligence, late at night, or to run through some Saturday itinerary with me. Which invariably includes some tortuous bus or train journey somewhere, and me offering to take him because he never ever asks. Wouldn't dream of doing so. I wish he was home.

And I wish my mother felt more a proper part of my life and less like a stranger at the foot of my bed. I can't remember the last time she was in here, before she moved here. We'd shop, sometimes, lunch sometimes, I'd go there for tea sometimes. Sometimes – though rarely – she and Hugo would come for dinner. But mainly I drove her. I'd go there and get her. We'd do what we'd do and then I'd take her back home. And Jake went there weekly. For his tea. On a Thursday. Now he has tea with her most days each week.

But I always went to where *she* was. And here she is, in my bedroom, in my personal space, looking worried – looking worried about *me*, moreover, which feels suddenly, intensely, uncomfortable. This is not what we do. We do *her* problems, not mine. I haven't gone to my mother with a problem since I was twelve. And hardly before that. I always had my father. And after he'd gone, when we might have grown closer, she hardly ever seemed to be there.

And she's looking at me from the stool where Charlie always tended to sit too – I can see him sitting on it now, while putting on his socks. I play with that thought for a moment, then let it go. Used to. No longer does. I feel no sudden twang of my heartstrings, and it soothes me. 'There's nothing to tell,' I tell Mum flatly. 'Yes, he's a he, and yes, he's in hospital.'

'Is he very sick?'

'No, he's okay. Well, he's going to be. Just a heart scare.'

'*Just*?'

'It was just a virus. Of the surface of the heart. It's not life-threatening.'

She nods. 'What's his name?'

Oh, ye Gods. 'You don't know him.' The lie feels acid on my tongue. I pull out my bedside drawer to rootle for some tissues.

'And neither am I supposed to, I imagine.' Not a question, but a statement. I attend to my nose.

'It's academic anyway. We're…well, he's –'

'Married. Yes, I think I gathered that much.' I look over at her, astonished. Now she's shaking her head. 'Abigail, you must think I came down in the last shower of rain.' She says this pointedly, but not in the least bit unpleasantly. I say nothing, and then she looks at me in an almost motherly way. Almost, but not quite. 'But I didn't, I promise you. How long's it been going on?'

'How long's wha–'

'Come on, Abbie,' she says immediately, though gently. 'There's no need to pretend. I'm not stupid, you know.' She lifts a finger towards me. 'That expensive watch on your wrist, for example. Not the sort of thing one tends to buy on an NHS salary. And the perfume on your dressing table. That necklace.'

We both turn, in unison, to where it sits, behind her. Still in its box. As it has been since I put it there. For an instant I feel a surge of outrage that she's been in here. That she's looked at it. But it dissipates again, because it hasn't any substance. Of course she's been in here and looked at it. Why wouldn't she have looked at it? I hadn't hidden it or anything. I hadn't barred her from the room. And, after all, she's my mother.

And she *lives* here. I ball the tissue in my hand. 'Too long. Not that long. But too long.' I stand up. 'A few months, that's all. But now it's over.'

147

'That's not how it looks from where I'm standing.'

'You're sitting.'

She narrows her eyes. 'Even so.'

I go around to the other side of the bed and open the window. 'Well, you're wrong. It's long over. It was just a bit of a shock, that's all.'

She inclines her head and makes a 'tsk' sort of sound. 'I take it he wouldn't leave his wife, then?'

As if he *should* have. As if he had no business *not* to. 'Mum, I didn't *want* him to leave his wife. *He* didn't want to leave his wife. He has three children, for God's sake.'

She dismisses this trifle with a waft of her hand. 'Oh, yes. Don't they all?' she says tartly. 'And I dare say the arrangement suited him very nicely. But what about *you,* Abigail?'

'What *about* me?'

'You just accepted that, did you?'

'No! I didn't *know*, Mum.'

She goes 'tsk!' for a second time, and I find myself close to crying all over again. I don't think I can bear it if she's going to start on Charlie. I think I might feel inclined to lamp her. With the copy of *Memoirs of an Unfit Mother*, which is close at hand and beckoning from the floor beside the bed. What does she know about it anyway, huh? What does she know about *him*? I can stand a lot of things, but I can't stand her standing in judgement over Charlie. Me, I can deal with, but not him. But perhaps she's already figured that one out anyway. Because her sour expression softens. 'Do you love him?' she asks.

I shake my head. 'I thought I did,' I answer truthfully, my anger now abating. 'I thought I might. But I was wrong. I was just a bit swept off my feet by him, that's all.'

And saying so no longer feels like a pep talk. I can say it and mean it. Because I realise it's true. They're now very much back on the ground.

# Chapter 17

WHEN I WAKE THE next morning, it's to the almost molten sensation of the sun seeping into my bedclothes, and I realise I've just awakened from the longest period of uninterrupted slumber I've had in months. My glass of water sits untouched on the bedside table and the last LCD time that burned on my retina read 22.29, not 02.30, or 04.10. It now reads 08.11. Almost ten hours asleep.

I push the duvet from my chest and draw my legs up to stamp it down to the end of the bed. I can hear street sounds, a dust cart, crows calling, traffic. The murmur of the television wafting up from downstairs. And something else. My mother's voice. She's obviously talking to someone on the phone.

I pull on my dressing gown and head down the stairs. I'm still not fully used to the business of being in my house on a weekday, any more than I'm used to finding someone else in it every single time I turn around. She's in the hall, replacing the receiver.

'Ah, you're up.'

'Who was that?'

'It was your friend Dee,' she says. 'About booking badminton for Tuesday?'

I nod. 'Okay.' She'll also want to know about Charlie. Still, no rush. No panic. I inspect my synapses as I think this. No pings. No jolts. I really am free.

'Anyway,' continues my mother. 'I told her you'd call her back. So,' she says then, inspecting me properly. 'Feeling better for your lie-in?'

I also forget that to my mother 8.11 *is* a lie-in. Still, she's right. It does feel like I've had one. I nod. 'And hungry. I didn't eat last night. You had breakfast?' Silly question. 8.11. She'll already be thinking about what to have for lunch.

Spike's bouncing at my heels, so I pick him up and take him into the kitchen with me. Mum follows.

'Shall I make you something? A boiled egg? Some porridge?'

I almost say an automatic 'no, I can do it,' but then I realise that in her cack-handed, unapologetic way, she is actually trying to make amends of some sort. At the very least, to make some sort of connection back to last night. And it makes me feel awkward around her all over again. I don't actually much want to re-visit last night. I don't want to talk to her about Charlie, for one thing, and for another, and more importantly (for I think I can see where we're headed) about her and me. About her being *here*. In short, I don't want to confront it. I'm more comfortable dancing the dance, observing the usual rules…i.e. strenuously *not* being honest and upfront. Where would that get us, after all?

I put Spike down. 'I'll just have some toast, thanks,' I say instead.

She crosses the kitchen – she's managing indoors sometimes without her stick now, I notice – and gets the bread out of the bread bin. 'So,' she says. 'Do you have plans for today?'

I pull out a chair and let her attend to my toast. Spike puts his front paws on my knees and I scoop him up again into my lap for a cuddle, burying my nose into the fur on his neck.

I sometimes wonder quite what I'd do without Spike. Perhaps take to hugging cushions. Or trees. One of the starkest of stark realities about being on your own is the terrible dearth of physical contact. If you're a huggy kissy touchy sort of person, like I am, that sort of thing really matters. And though my sons will hug me, and frequently do, there's a subtle shift once the testosterone kicks in. There are times when they can but many more when they can't. And all too soon, giving their mother a cuddle will be something they do just on greetings and partings and birthdays.

I look at my mother and remember my father. He did. She didn't. It just wasn't her style. We air-kiss on parting and we air-kiss on greeting. And that's it. And it's sobering, to me, if not her. It's not as it should be, but where do you start?

And where will we end? Two grumpy old women co-existing without contact and shuffling around together with our force fields intact?

She puts a plate and knife and the butter in front of me and refrains from commenting about dogs at tables, which is a first. I put spike down again anyway, because much as I love him, his breath smells of dog food. Which means she's fed him as well.

'Erm…' Plans. I consider. My brain's been so hijacked, I can barely recall that it's Friday. Plans. Plans for Friday. Did I have any plans? I try to think what plans I might have had. To cut the grass. Yes. But then I always have a plan to cut the grass. Cutting the grass never seems to be far from my mind between April and October. It's one of those things I constantly plan to do and then don't. Because it's raining. Because it's windy. Because something else comes up. Because all sorts. Latterly Because Mother. Because trailing round estate agents. Because never seeming to find a single moment for myself.

Hmm. Memo to self. When next moment to self happens, is lawnmowing number one priority? Gadzooks – you must seize it, woman! Get life and soonest!

But right now I can't seem to think of anything better to do. 'I thought I might cut the grass,' I respond.

She brings two slices of toast to my plate. Carefully props them in an upside down 'V'. 'Only Celeste and I thought we might go through our lines, and –'

'No probs. I'll take you over there. What time?'

She still looks apologetic. 'Will about ten be okay?'

Order restored. And some moments to myself. 'Sure.' I pick up the knife. But there's a thought. *Lines?* 'Lines?' I ask. 'What lines?'

'Our lines for the play.'

'*Your* lines? I thought you said you'd missed the auditions.'

She folds the tea towel in her hand and slides it carefully over the handle on the oven door. 'Wilfred called me back last night,' she says sheepishly. 'He'd been pulling my leg, bless him. They'd already put me down for Medea.'

*God.* And after all that bloody *fuss*.

Still, I think. What's new? But then I think some more. And I blink at her. 'Medea? *You*? Playing *Medea*? Correct me if I'm wrong, but wasn't Medea, well, *young*?'

And a bit of a babe, by all accounts. I'm not as clued up on Euripides as I might be, but as far as I can remember she was a vampy young Greek sorceress who duped someone into cutting up their father and boiling up his bones, before knocking off both her kids after a hissy fit with Jason. Hmm. Bar the age, I *can* see it.

151

My mother tuts. She has no concept of the world 'old'. None at all. 'Not *this* Medea. This is Wilfred's contemporary re-working of the play. It's a sort of allegory, set in an old people's home.'

The mind boggles. That sure will take some re-working. And I was wrong. She does seem to have the word 'old' in her vocabulary. Just doesn't tend to apply it to herself. 'That sounds bizarre,' I say, buttering my toast. 'What's your contemporary Medea about, then? Is she the new kid on the block, come to stir up the residents and woo a retired colonel called Gerald?'

'Hmm,' she says sniffily. 'I can see you *are* feeling better, then. And yes, as it happens, something like that. And the killing's an accident. We don't want too much gore. It's for a Cyncoed audience, after all.'

'Any bones boiled?'

'I believe there's a scene with a symbolic leg of lamb.'

'You mean mutton.'

'I beg your pardon?'

'You mean leg of mutton, don't you?'

'Now you're just being silly.'

And feeling all the better for it. Order most definitely restored.


And so it came to pass that I took Medea to Celeste's house, took Spike for a long walk and took a parcel to the post office for Jake. Seb's X-Box, as it turned out, which he'd agreed to Jake selling on eBay, to put towards a double bass pedal for his birthday next month. Which made me feel all warm and woolly and proud. And then I came home to cut the grass.

For all the time I spend thinking about cutting the grass and then forgetting I thought it, deciding I will cut the grass but then not getting around to cutting the grass, definitely scheduling grass cutting on the calendar, and then double booking other stuff instead, it would be easy to suppose that I don't actually like cutting the grass very much.

This, however, is not true.

One of the more enduring legacies of my marriage is an aged red petrol-powered lawn mower. Though one might assume such a thing to be more usually something that ends up in the 'his' pile, Sebastian and Jake's dad was going to live abroad, and so many things normally testosterone-related ended up with me by default.

I wasn't, it has to be said, the grass-cutting half of the marital partnership at that time, any more than he was the clothes-washing one. I did, however, learn, as a woman on her own must. I even once stripped it down and cleaned the filter.

But on this particular morning, its filter is academic, as (as is always the way with these things) it's almost entirely out of petrol. And the few drops I had left in my red plastic petrol can have clearly, in the absence of applying themselves to lawn mowing, decided to become vapour instead.

So I have to pop down to the petrol station in order to get some more. Which turns out to be no sort of pop, but a marathon chore. As I wait at the back of one of eight separate queues of four cars each, all of whom seem to be off on some holiday, or away day or theme park or beach, I wistfully wonder quite why it is that I'm not doing something similarly edifying. And then, having wondered, I reach the sort of conclusions that I decide I really mustn't wonder any more. I must Get Out More, that's what I must do. Go and re-engage with the world.

The sad truth, of course, is that I have been in self-imposed purdah. Such it is with mistresses. Thank God I'm not one of those any more.

I'm just coming back into the house, all petrolled up, when I become aware of some warbling from the depths of my handbag.

A mobile phone warbling, and once I get it out and check it, I see it's a text message from my good friends at Vodafone, who are telling me I have two missed calls. I also notice, belatedly, that the answerphone light's winking in the hall, so I poke the play button on that while I scroll through to see.

'Gabriel Ash,' the deep voice says without any preamble. 'I'll try your mobile instead. Bye-ee.'

I like the 'bye-ee'. It's so sunny day jolly. I bring the call register screen up. He has.

When I connect I think I've dialled the wrong number at first, because it's not Gabriel Ash who answers. But then I realise I can't have, because I didn't dial the number, but pressed the return call button. So it has to be right.

'Hiyah!' says Lucy Whittall's pretty, sing-song voice. 'How are *you*?'

She talks as if I'm her long-lost sister in Halkidiki, but I find I don't mind in the least. 'Oh!' I say. 'Hi. Um, fine thanks. You?'

'Fabulous! *Fab*ulous!'

'Good. Er…I think Gabriel was trying to get hold of me?'

'Yep,' she says. 'Indeed he was. He's driving at the moment, but it was about some stuff you have for him? He wanted to stop by and pick it up?'

'Yes,' I say. 'That's right. I'm sorry – I was out. When did he want to call in?'

'Hang on. When d'you want to do it, Gabe?' I only half hear his reply. 'You still there?' she says.

'Yup.'

'We were wondering if we could stop by sometime today if that's okay with you?'

'Sure. What sort of time?'

'Hang on.' A second exchange follows. 'Are you home now?'

'I am.'

'Then, let me see. An hour or so? An hour or so, you think, Gabe? An hour or so suit you okay?'

Only the silliest and most insecure of persons could possibly do what I decide to do next. But in my defence I am intermittently both of those things, particularly at this juncture in my life, and it's not every day you have local – nay, *national* – celebrities turning up at your house at short notice, and one must be prepared. Yes, I think, as I motor around the lawn with teeth rattling velocity. I must achieve two things above any other. I must cut the grass and then I must put on my wafty skirt and flip flops and some mascara and lip gloss. I must, above all, above *everything* in fact, not look like a fright when I answer the door.

'Oh, oh, oh!!!' exclaims Lucy Whittall, thrusting her face alarmingly at my bosom an hour and a half later. 'Aren't you just the sweetest, sweetest, *sweetest* little dog?'

Spike, who's in my arms, speaks several languages, of course, but none quite so fluently as Adoring Female Person With Long Fingernails. His tail's going so fast it could power a faerie wind farm. I hope he doesn't crack up and wee all down my front.

'He's called Spike,' I tell her.

'Spike!' she cries. 'Oh, you little *cutie,* you! You absolute *cutie*! Oh, Gabe, we just must *so* get a dog!' She fans at her face with her teeny tiny clutch bag. 'God, but isn't it just *boiling* today?'

Lucy Whittall, who belies this incontrovertible fact by looking as though she is cocooned inside her own invisible air-conditioning system, is wearing a wispy gauzy scrap of something in peach. The sort of dress that you could twizzle up and stuff into a very small matchbox, but which probably cost many hundreds of pounds.

And worth every last penny of anyone's money. Except perhaps mine, because I'm not Lucy Whittall. And it just wouldn't look like that on me. She, of course, looks every bit as fabulous as she feels. And I feel even stupider for having changed for the occasion. Who did I think I was kidding, getting all tarted up for a five minute encounter on a doorstep?

'Yes, it is,' I agree. As does Spike, who's dripping spittle down me now. 'I'll, er, just go and fetch the bag for you. Won't be a tick.'

'Actually,' she confides, 'I know it's very cheeky, but d'you mind if I skip in and use your loo? We've just driven back all the way from Monmouth, and I'm absolutely busting for a wee.'

'Oh, of course!' I pull the door wider. 'Come in, then. Come in. I point. 'That door there. Help yourself.'

I hope she's not going to have to help herself to fifteen sheets of loo paper to mop wee from the toilet seat as well. With the amount of young males coming and, well, *going* in my house, I could really do with having one of those hourly check procedures that they have in motorway service stations by operatives called Janet. When did I last check it? Oh, fret fret fret fret.

'All go here, then,' observes Gabriel Ash, glancing heavenward as he steps over the threshold to wait, while the boys twang and bang enthusiastically upstairs.

'Oh, that's my son and his friends. Practising.'

'Ah,' he says. 'Practising. I see.'

I don't know quite what they were doing in Monmouth, exactly, but he has the slightly reticent air of a man for whom one's fiancé's toilet stops are just one more inconvenience in a

155

day that has already been overburdened by them. I wonder where they've been. I wonder when he manages to fit work in. When does she, come to that? Or perhaps, like me, they are having a day off as well. A day off *à deux*. Or perhaps he still has work to get to. Who knows? I'm just wondering whether to offer him a drink or something, when an unfamiliar mobile ring tone starts up and he delves into a jeans pocket, stepping back onto the doorstep and making a gesture which I presume means he'll stay out there till he's done.

Which is exactly what he does. Which means I either have to shut the front door in his face, or leave it open and risk Spike making a bid for the heady freedom of the street. I take Spike back out into the garden and shut him safely out there, and am just returning to the hall when Lucy Whittall emerges from the downstairs cloakroom, blowing her nose delicately on some loo roll. Which I hope isn't indicative of anything too noisome and swampy, but rather fear probably is.

'That's better!' she exclaims. 'God, that was close. I really thought I was going to wet my pants! Hey, I couldn't trouble you for a glass of water as well, could I?'

Gabriel joins us in the kitchen just as I'm pouring Lucy Whittall a glass of orange squash, and heaping rebukes on myself for not having anything more stylish on offer. Had they only come tomorrow, I'd have had Ribena as well. Oh, it's life in the fast lane at my place.

I nod towards the table, where the carrier bag full of his father's things sits. 'That's it, there,' I tell him, and he approaches it. I pour him a squash too.

'Who was on the phone, angel?' Lucy Whittall asks him.

He frowns then. 'Maria.'

'And?'

'And *manco morto*, in essence.'

Lucy Whittall pulls a face. 'Come again, ange?'

'Over my dead body,' he says, frowning. 'I'm telling you, she's not going to budge on this one, Luce.'

She turns to me. 'Tsk,' she goes. 'All this nonsense over a few scraps of fur. I mean, I ask you, Abbie. Is it really such a heinous crime? We're only talking a bit of trim on the facings and hoods.'

As I don't have the first clue what it is she's asking me, let alone what he was telling her, I am at a loss to know how to respond.

'Her bridesmaid's dress,' Gabriel Ash explains as I pass him a glass. 'For the wedding. Lucy has her heart set on an ivory fur trimming. Maria – my daughter – is *not* happy about it –'

'Which is ridiculous,' Lucy interjects swiftly, though quite jovially. 'When you consider Italy must be one of the leather goods capitals of the world! I mean, what's the difference? It's all *skin*, for God's sake!'

'Except fur is *farmed*,' says Gabriel, evenly. And involves lots of dead bodies as well. I get the impression they've had this discussion several times before.

'Oh, and like cattle *aren't*? Like we don't stuff down zillions of burgers each year?' She wafts a hand towards him. 'Anyway, she'll come round. You know what teenagers are like. It's all principles this and principles that, but once she sees it –' She turns to me again. 'Abbie, they're to die for. To *die* for! – she'll change her mind quick as you like.'

Which unfortunate choice of words – conjuring, as it does, visions of butchered bunnies and blood-spattered wedding trains – is not lost on any of us. Least of all, Lucy, who throws back her head and laughs the sort of hearty laugh that you might normally associate with, well…a jolly mink farmer, I suppose.

It's at this point that One Black Lung all shuffle into the kitchen. Jake looks me up and down a bit, obviously bewildered. 'Blimey,' he says, removing his baseball cap to scratch his head. 'You going off to a party or something, Mum?'

As the kitchen is now playing host to enough sweat-soaked armpits to make breathing an extreme sport, I suggest we drink our squash in the garden. I had not planned on a garden party, obviously, but Lucy Whittall is showing absolutely no impetus as far as going anywhere is concerned, and every intention of sitting on my patio and entertaining her new quartet of fans.

Which is actually quite nice, I decide, once I'm over my sartorial blushes. I can't remember the time I last had anyone out here. That is, if you don't include Charlie. And my mother doing her downward facing dog on the lawn and terrifying Mr Davidson next door.

Though initially looking reluctant, Gabriel Ash, who has perched himself on one of my B and Q special offer of last year garden set chairs, starts to make a cursory inspection of the contents of the carrier bag, while Lucy fires questions at the boys about their band.

'Wow,' she says, at length. 'Can you play something for me? I *so* love Metallica. I went to see them when I was your age, you know.'

This intelligence fills them with almost as much joy and awe as if Lars Ulrich himself had fetched up in the garden and asked them if they'd like to come round and try out his drums. Questions are fired at her. Mouths hang open in quiet reverence. Suddenly her all-right-for-an-oldish-bird status has morphed into the sort of cool to which, in teen land at least, very few can aspire. She's seen them. She's been there. She *was* there. Which is *all*. Before you can say *hold my breath as I wish for death*, they've scooted her off for a quick blast upstairs.

Uncertain what to do while the impromptu concert takes place, and mindful that Gabriel Ash is now delving deep into his carrier bag, I collect up their tumblers and head back inside.

But clearly not delving that deep, for he follows me in soon after.

'Thanks for that,' he says, placing the carrier back on the table, and heading purposefully towards the sink with his own glass.

'Oh, no. Give me that,' I tell him. 'You are not washing up in *my* kitchen. No way.'

He doesn't seem to find this funny, but he does hand it over.

'You get used to this, do you?' he comments, indicating towards the ceiling with an eyebrow, and pushing his now redundant hands into his jeans pockets.

I nod. 'I barely hear it. Well, I do *hear* it, obviously. But not in the sense that it bothers me to hear it. I enjoy it.'

'They certainly sound accomplished.'

'I have great hopes.'

He stops and listens. 'You're absolutely right to. They're good. And speaking of great hopes, did your mother tell you about the offer on the house?'

'No, she most certainly didn't,' I answer. 'When was that?'

'Only this week. So perhaps she doesn't know yet. I only found out this morning myself. I think Corinne was going to speak to your brother-in-law about it. Perhaps she hasn't called him yet.'

Yeah, I think. Whatever. It's all academic anyway. Till such time as mother can be cranked out of her persistent meditative state and back into flat-hunting gear.

He takes his hands out of his pockets and folds his arms across his chest. 'Anyway, assuming everything goes through okay, I think we've settled on twelve thousand for the conservatory.'

He seems self-conscious standing in my kitchen, which is odd. Perhaps he should whip his leg out and I could pummel it for a bit. Perhaps then he'd look a little less stiff. 'Well,' I say, because I don't doubt he's had a hand in it. 'That's very generous of you. Thank you.'

'You're welcome.'

Which conversational avenue putters to a halt, on account of his unexpected lack of seeming to have anything further he can think of to say. Most curious. Perhaps I should have let him fill the sink up after all. Perhaps he feels more comfortable with his hands in some suds.

'Well,' I say brightly, because I'm a well brought-up girl and know my manners. 'You were certainly right about the weather.'

He nods. 'We do our best,' he says. 'That's what they pay us for, after all. Though we certainly don't always get it right.'

'Mainly you do,' I say, because he looks like he's brooding heavily on this failing. 'I mean, I know everyone likes to moan on about weather forecasters getting it wrong all the time and everything. But you actually don't much these days, not when you sit and analyse it, do you?'

'Even so, it's still an inexact science. You can predict all you like, but weather systems are essentially pretty unpredictable things. No, you're right. We do pretty well. Better than we're given credit for, that's for sure. But blaming weather forecasters

159

is a national sport. Be a shame to spoil the fun, wouldn't it?' He looks like he's having absolutely no fun whatsoever at this moment, and I wish I knew why. 'Anyway, it would get pretty boring if you knew exactly what the weather was going to do every single day, wouldn't it?'

'I suppose. But it must be a very satisfying sort of a job, though,' I say. 'You know, being in a position to predict the future.'

He seems to want to ponder that concept. I wait. 'Except you're not actually doing that,' he says eventually. 'Not really. What we mostly do is just collect and analyse all the data we get from all the observation points and the satellites. Plus we do have a very, very big computer. Can make billions of calculations per second. It's really all about maths and not at all about checking if the cows are sitting down.'

'But you must need to be pretty clever, though. To take all that information and work out what it means for the future.'

I open the dishwasher door and start putting the glasses in, while he looks out of the kitchen window. 'Oh, I'm definitely not that,' he says, almost to himself. 'Much as I wish I was, I'm no better at predicting the future than anyone else is, believe me.' I notice that 'we' has changed to 'I', and that his tone of voice has altered as he says this. And I realise, glancing up from the dishwasher, that he's no longer looking out of the kitchen window either. He's turned around and is looking at *me* now. And in a way that I can only describe as pretty damned earnest. So much so that I almost feel I'm going to have to look away. How odd. 'Actually,' he says, and he lowers his voice now. 'In some departments, let me tell you, Abbie, I am *woefully* inept.'

He's still looking at me oddly, and I think he's about to say something else. But he doesn't. Instead he splays his fingers and pushes both his hands ever so slowly through his thicketty gold hair, and then he tips his head back and sighs.

Sighs heavily. And watching him, suddenly, I twig. Suddenly I realise what this is all about.

D'oh. I'm so *dense*. 'Your father,' I say, nodding towards the carrier bag on the kitchen table. Of *course*. Why didn't I *think*? No wonder he's so agitated. This is evidence that changes everything, isn't it? It's one thing to harbour hatred for a father you think abandoned you, quite another to square it with the demands of your conscience when faced with the fact that you got it all wrong. That he actually loved you very much. And that perhaps, after all, you should try to forgive him. Or, rather, *should* have. And now can't. The poor man. I hold his gaze, and he flops his hands down to his sides again then considers me silently for several moments. Then, just as I think he's about to speak, he shakes his head.

It's actually a sort of head shake-come-sigh combination. God, there was me thinking he'd be so pleased with what I found, but of course it's just so much more complicated than that. It has shocked him. It doesn't fit with how he feels about his father. Has, in fact, blown all that away. 'I know,' I say, closing the dishwasher door and straightening. He's looking at the bag now himself. 'But there's no point in beating yourself up about it, is there?' I tell him briskly. 'No point in regrets. No one could have predicted that he'd die so suddenly, could they?' He's looking at me again now, but I'm not sure he's listening. He seems lost in thought. Somewhere else altogether. 'But I do understand how seeing all this must make you feel,' I go on anyway. 'I *do* know what you mean.'

The music has stopped, and there are voices closing in now. Lucy's voice. Jake and his pals. Laughter. Feet on the stairs. They're coming back down. Gabriel Ash scoops up the carrier from the table, then he lifts one hand and places it lightly on my shoulder.

'Hmm,' he says, and now there's a ghost of a smile forming at the corners of his mouth. 'You want to know something, Abbie McFadden?'

'What?'

'I wish I thought you did.'

It takes me a moment to digest what he's saying. Except I fail to because I don't understand what he means. 'But –'

'Hey, no worries,' he says quickly. 'Maybe I don't, as it happens. Forget I even said that, okay?' He lowers his hand and then glances at the wall clock. 'In fact, I think it's time we left you in peace.'

*   *   *

It's really far too hot for the boys to continue their practice without the windows open, but as Mr Davidson is now back from his round and pottering in his own garden, they have no choice but to either abandon it, or to slope back off upstairs and be fried. And I don't doubt they will be because they're half fried already, on account of the Lucy Loves Metallica effect.

They choose the latter regardless. Thumping up the stair treads two at a time, still joshing each other about who said what and when. At a loose end now until I have to pick Mum up at five, I go back out into the garden, intending to read the paper (and do my fiendish Friday puzzle before she gets her hands on it) but am unable to concentrate on it, as I'm still too preoccupied by what Gabriel Ash said to me just before he left. Brooding on it, in fact. What did he mean by suggesting I forget he even said that? Is there more to the situation with Hugo than I first supposed? Some dark and terrible secret that I've missed? There's certainly something he's not letting on, and I try to think if there was anything I saw in Hugo's collection of bits and pieces that might give me a clue as to what. I can't think of a single thing, but there's obviously something on his mind. Something bothering him. First he's wishing I knew what he was saying and then he's telling me to forget it. I have a hunch that had we had a few more moments to ourselves he might have been about to impart a little more. A confession? It certainly had all the hallmarks of one. But a confession about what? About whom?

# Chapter 18

'AND THEN I HAD another thought,' I tell Dee while we change into our swimming gear the following Tuesday evening. Badminton, and now swimming as well. What next? Between the fall out after Charlie and Dee's ante-natal zeal, I shall be a gym rat before the year's out.

'What?'

'I thought 'Hang on a minute. When I mentioned his father, he shook his head'. Of course, I thought that was just, well, a sort of acknowledgement about how he was feeling, you know? But then once I got to thinking about it a bit more, it occurred to me that it might have meant he was referring to something else altogether.'

'Which was?'

I pull the strap up on my swimsuit and start folding my clothes. 'Lucy Whittall, of course!'

'Lucy Whittall? What about her?'

'That's just the very thing I've been pondering. The way she *was.*'

'What way was she?'

'Well, hyped up, excitable. A bit manic. Well, sort of. I didn't really think anything of it at the time – she's that sort of person anyway, isn't she?'

'Is she? She always looks pretty hatchet-faced on A and E.'

'Well, she's in role then, of course. And it's all blood and guts. But that *is* what she's like. Well, would seem to be from what *I've* seen of her, anyway. And it *was* a lovely afternoon, and they'd just been out for lunch, and I thought she was, just, well, jolly. Couple of glasses of wine on board. That sort of thing.'

'But?'

'Well, it was something Ben said afterwards. You know, Jake's friend. Not to me, of course. They were just chatting about her, generally. And he used the word 'wired'. He said she looked like she was wired.'

'Which means what, exactly?'

I stuff my socks in my trainers and shove them in a locker. 'Well, I don't know for sure, of course. But isn't it the sort of thing they say about people on drugs?'

'What, you think she was *on* something? Stoned?'

'I don't know about stoned. Pretty much the opposite, I'd say. And it reminded me of something Candice said a while back. About how she'd been busted for cocaine a couple of years ago.'

'Cocaine? Blimey. Lucy Whittall? You really think so?'

I shake my head. 'I don't know. And I'm not about to bandy the idea around, obviously. But when you sit down and think about it, it doesn't sound that far-fetched, does it? It's not like that sort of thing isn't in the tabloids all the time.'

Dee's now in her bikini. Pink with lime polka-dots. Though small still, her stomach's already taut and smooth-skinned. I had two dreadful, much ruffled pregnancy costumes. How times have changed. And how nice. She looks great.

'So you think it's actually about that?' she says, gathering up her own clothes. 'You know, with him? That he's stressed out because she's taking drugs again?'

'Well, it could be, couldn't it? Given the history. Given all the stuff there's been in the press about her.'

'Oh, that's dreadful. What a waste. I mean, if you're right, that is. Are you going to say anything to him?'

'*God*, no. It's none of my business, is it? And it may not even be that, after all.'

'But it does sound like he's looking for a shoulder to cry on.'

'Hmm,' I say. 'You might be right about that. But he's not having mine. I've already been there, remember. With Charlie. And look where *that* got me.'

In bed with an already married man. In hot water. Which can be efficacious in the case of frozen shoulder, say, or chronic arthritis, or a collar bone injury, but is not something I'd like to find myself falling into any more. And I'm not sure, in any case, that it *is* as I've conjectured. I still favour the notion that Gabriel Ash is just coming to terms with how things were between him and his father. Affairs of the heart are too depressing to contemplate. And I contemplate more than enough depressing things already, what with living with Medea and all.

'Hmm,' says Dee now, as we exit the changing room. 'You say that, but it's hard to resist your basic personality type. You're like me, you are. A Nurturer. You can't help but want to help people.'

Dee is doing a part-time course in Applied Psychology at the moment. Ostensibly part of her Grand Career Plan, but in reality the degree she's been slaving over for the past four years has been mainly a reason to get out of the house. But psychology is certainly pertinent to her situation, I guess. And useful. Perhaps I should study it too. 'I hope I can,' I say. 'I'm fed up with nurturing people. You know what I'd like? *I'd* like to be nurtured. *I'd* like to be looked after for a change. It's not even as if I'm even very good at it, am I? And it's certainly not good for me.'

Which makes me think of my mother, who is, at this moment, with any luck, leafing through the details of Winding House Close, the latest retirement development on the list. Except that's probably not what she's doing. Far from it. She's probably watching *Eastenders*, knocking back the sherry and practising her bumble bee breathing.

Dee tuts at me. 'Er, what about Sebastian and Jake?'

'I wasn't exactly thinking of them.'

'Hmm,' she says. 'Things getting on top of you at home *chez maman*?'

I slosh through the foot bath. 'Oh, no more than usual. We're just terminally incompatible as housemates, that's all.'

'As you would be. She's your mother. And you're so different too.'

'You can certainly say that again. What's her category, d'you think? Imperious matriarch come despot?'

'Hmm,' she says again. 'I think she's probably a Performer.'

I laugh. 'You really needed to read that in a *book*?'

'Actually, no. Thinking about it, she's more a Go-Getter. Yes, that's more your mum, I think.'

'Is it? Well, fingers crossed then.'

'About what?'

'That she'll hurry up and go-get a new place to live.'

But perhaps I'm wrong about the efficacy of my shoulder anyway, because when I come out from seeing my first patient on

Wednesday morning, it's to find that Gabriel Ash has cancelled his Thursday appointment, due, or so Candice says, to something coming up at work. What sort of something? A whirlwind? An earthquake? An untimely monsoon? Despite what I told Dee, I'm a little disappointed. It's one thing to not want to get involved in someone else's travails, quite another not to want to *know*. Or perhaps I'm just reverting to type, like Dee says. In which case, I must really try not to. He…she…them…it…*all* of it, frankly, is absolutely none of my business, after all.

What *is* my business, though I fervently wish it wasn't – not this decade, anyhow – is the fact that I still have my mother in residence and not the teeniest inkling that that state of affairs is about to change any time soon. And the reason it won't change is because *I'm* the one not changing it. Left to its own devices, it is a situation that could rumble on for ever, much like I'm inclined to suspect she will.

But harbouring such mutinous and unsavoury thoughts is no way for a grown woman to behave. What I *should* do, of course, is talk to her about it, *tell* her, except every time I gear myself up to do just that, I find I'm paralysed with anxiety about just what to say. It should be the easiest thing in the world, shouldn't it? Talking? I can talk the hind legs off the most sturdily built donkey most of the time, so why this pathetic inability to communicate, when communication is the only sure way to resolve things?

Why does it make me feel scared?

'Because you've always let her bully you, that's why.' So says Pru, with some feeling, when she calls me the following Monday. She's taken to calling me lots since Mum moved here. We've always talked often, but never *this* often. And I know it's because she feels guilty as well.

But what have we to feel guilty *about*, exactly? I keep asking myself that question, over and over, and have reached no sort of rational answer. And worse than my inability to get a handle on the guilt trip, is the fact that such musing is becoming dangerously counter-productive. Because despite all the doughty sentiments I so recently expressed to my sister, every time I open the box marked 'reasons not to feel guilty about Mum', out they keep popping, ever growing in number, like scarves or white rabbits or sausages or doves. Shame there's no magician to wave a magic wand and – poof! – make them all disappear.

'Well, that's going to stop,' I say firmly. I can always be firm when I'm talking to Pru. Just can't seem to replicate it where my mother's concerned. 'As of now. I'm a grown woman, for God's sake!'

'Yes, *exactly*,' she says. Then she makes a little sound that's almost a 'tut'. 'Abs, you know, you've just got to be honest with her. What else can you do?'

Not 'we', I note. *You*. As in me, and not her. She – or rather Doug – has already made her position clear. For the first time since this began I feel a sense of real resentment that this burden has become mainly mine to shoulder. I know I shouldn't – I did put myself in this position, after all – but I can't help but think how unfair it all feels. I wish *I* had a husband to put his foot down about it. A Doug of my own to stand up for me. Which is not something I've found myself thinking in many a year. Often I've been glad that I haven't any more. Mainly I've not been in a position where it's mattered – not in the way it matters now. About *this*. But I mustn't resent Pru. It's not her fault we're here. 'I know I have to,' I say. 'But I just can't bring myself to. Because it's a conversation I just know is going to end in tears. Because she'll want to know why. And I'm frightened I'll lose it and I'll tell her. In detail.'

'Just tell her you need your own space.'

'Just like that, eh?'

'*Yes*. Just be firm. Abs, you *have* to.'

Just as she is being firm with me now. I sigh. 'I know, I know. But it's so much easier said than done, isn't it?'

'No, it *isn't*. You just sit her down and explain that it's not an option. You don't have to get involved in reasons and reproaches and justifications about it. You don't have to make it personal or dredge up the past. Look, I know she'll turn it on big time to try and make you feel bad, but you've got to be tough. Believe me, you'll feel so much worse a year down the line if she *is* still there. Just be firm. Tell her straight. All the while you don't she'll keep working away at you. Keep thinking it *is* an option. Which will make it all the harder when you *do* put her straight.'

I take this all on board and the more I do so, the more I realise that it's just not the same for Pru as it's always been for me. Where emotional blackmail enters into the equation I'm an absolute, category one, out-there-on-my-own wuss. Always have been. 'I wish I was you,' I say. 'You're so much better at standing up to her than I am.'

Pru laughs a little laugh. It's both loving and knowing. 'Of *course* I am,' she explains gently. 'Because I was the lucky one. I've always had *you* to look after me!'

And as she says so, I realise she's absolutely on the button. She did, and she has, and it makes her so much stronger. But it also works both ways. 'You're very welcome,' I say.

'And you're going to do it, yes? Just keep in mind that you're an adult *and* a mother, and that you're simply not prepared to let her have Seb's room. Okay?'

'Ok*ay*!'

'How's he getting on, anyway?' she then says, obviously as anxious not to dwell on my problems any longer than I am. 'Still having a good time, is he?

'D'you know, I don't actually know. I've heard nothing from him for a week.'

She laughs. 'I think I'd take that as a yes, then.'

I laugh too, now. 'Yes. You're probably right.'

Friday. No, Abbie. You're probably wrong.

Txt msg; Sorry 2 bother u – bin trying 2 call – has Seb been in touch at all? Jonx

168

# Chapter 19

NO. HE HASN'T BEEN in touch.

No Text message, no email, no postcard, no *nothing*.

Being both a law-abiding person, and also someone who pummels damaged limbs for a living, I try not to use my mobile while driving. Thus I ignored the two incoming calls that preceded this message, as I was on my way back from dropping Mum at Celeste's house. Though when the text came – heralded by some nonsense noise programmed in by Jake – I decided to attend to it while I was held at the lights.

I read it again now.

Sorry 2 bother u – bin trying 2 call – has Seb been in touch at all? Jonx

As reading text messages of the kind Jonathan has just sent me are not generally conducive to driving with due care and attention, I then attend, as soon as is practical, to stopping the car. I pull up outside the hire shop on Caerphilly Road, where ranks of mini cement mixers and floor sanders and rotavators are always ranked neatly outside, gaily orange. Coaxing people of an entirely different species to my own to an excitable frenzy of lifestyle improvements and the notion that happiness is all about having a DIY project on-the-go at all times.

Oh, that it was. Jonathan connects almost immediately. 'Mrs McFadden!' he gasps at me, breathlessly. 'Is that you?'

His voice is so loud in my ears that for a fraction of a second I think he's not in Italy, but speaking to me from just inside the shop.

'Jon? Yes, it's me! I just got your text. What on earth's going on?'

'Oh,' he says, sounding crestfallen. 'I take it that's a no, then.'

I am not liking the sound of this one little bit. 'No, Jon. I haven't heard from Seb. Should I have done? What's happened?' A thought occurs to me suddenly. 'Have you two fallen out?'

'No,' he says swiftly. 'No, no. Nothing like that. I've just, well, I've just sort of mislaid him.'

Even now I can feel stealthy tendrils of cold fear begin to tighten around my stomach. 'What d'you mean – mislaid him? How? Where? Jonathan, what's happened?'

'Erm...' he says. And I can almost see him scratching his head. 'Well, we were at this disco –'

'Where?'

I hear shuffling. 'Um, I forget the name of the place. What's the name of this place?' He obviously has someone else with him. 'Cervia. That's it.'

Which means nothing to me. 'And?'

'And, well, we kind of got split up. We, er, met these girls and, like, I was with, er, Fulvia... and Seb was with this other one...'

'And?'

'And I assumed he'd gone off somewhere with her.'

'Gone off? Gone off *where*?'

'I don't *know*. They're staying at this campsite and they thought they had some free pitches, and, well, I just assumed he'd turn up there with her later. Assumed that's what he *had* done. Except he never showed. And when I called him this morning, his phone was on divert, and I haven't been able to get hold of him since.'

All morning, then. All *morning*. What's *happened*? Remain calm, I think, thinking this. Remain calm. Remain rational. It's only lunchtime. He'll be asleep still. That's all. 'And he hasn't called *you*?' Stupid question. Of course he hasn't.

'No,' he says. 'It's like, really odd. We were supposed to be getting a train at ten.'

No, it's not odd, I think. He's just sleeping off a hangover or something. Or is still...well...well, ensconced. With whatever her name is... No, Abbie. *Don't* think about that. 'What about this girl he was with?' I ask Jonathan. 'Did these two girls know each other?'

'Yeah, they do. Well, sort of. They're all with different firms. But –'

'Firms?'

'You know, camping firms.'

'Oh, I see. You mean they work there. Well, doesn't *she* know anything? Doesn't she know where this other girl might be?'

'Yeah, course she does. We went round to her tent this morning. But she hasn't seen him either.'

'So he didn't go off with her, then.' Oh no. Sex I can cope with. Sex I can manage. But that's not what happened, clearly. Unless he met someone else. God, what has my son been getting up to, exactly? Is he on some sort of pan Europe seed-spreading mission? This is getting less and less palatable by the second.

'No. Well, he did,' says Jonathan. 'Well, sort of. There was a whole bunch of them. They were going to go down to the beach and –'

'So what happened? What did she say?'

'Nothing. She said he told her he wasn't feeling too great, and he was going to head back to the campsite and get the tent sorted –'

'Except he never got there.'

'Not as far as I can tell.'

'So where did you sleep?'

'Um…'

You dozy mare, Abbie. Where d'you *think* he slept? 'No matter, no matter, no matter,' I say quickly. 'But you're sure he's not on the site anywhere, are you?'

'Definitely. We've been all over trying to find him. I'm getting a bit worried.'

*He's* getting worried. 'And you've kept trying his phone.'

'Yeah, all morning.'

Okay, okay. Think Abbie. *Think*. 'Right,' I say, having thought. 'I'm going to hang up now in case he's trying to get through to you. And I'll keep trying him too. What's the name of this place you're at again?'

'Cervia.'

'Okay. Is that with a 'C'?' He says yes. I write it down. 'And do they have a police station or anything?'

'Um, I guess so. Fulvia, er… carabinieri?' I hear a girl's voice. Then Jonathan's again. 'Yeah, they do.'

'Right. I want you to head straight there, okay? See if they know anything. I'll keep on trying him in the meantime. Yes, that's best. You find the police station and see if you can find anything out. Ring me the minute you hear anything, okay? I'll do likewise.'

'Okay.'

Calm, Abbie. Keep calm. 'And Jonathan?'

'Yes?'

'Don't panic. Don't *worry*. It'll be something and nothing, I'm sure.'

I wish I thought it was. Oh my God. My son is a missing person. Oh my God. Oh my God. Oh my *God*.

I drive home with all the due care and attention I can muster – which still probably leaves it hovering at around a barely legal level – then spend about five minutes in a wall to wall button-pushing frenzy. Contacts list – S – Sebastian – Call Contact? – Nothing – Retry? – Retry – Nothing – Retry? – Retry – Nothing – Retry?

I stop retrying then, as it is patently pointless. So, all out of options, I burst into tears.

Bursting into tears is, of course, equally pointless. Bursting into tears will achieve nothing whatsoever, but is the main unavoidable side-effect of thinking all the things a mother simply cannot help but think at times like these. He is lying in a ditch somewhere, of course. Sick, mugged, damaged, unconscious, having been divested of both his rucksack and tent, and the phone with which I am trying to make a connection is lying in a ditch with him, silenced and discarded, while its Sim card has been purloined, and – even as I think it – is now safely installed in the phone of some teenage Mafioso gangster, who is running up Seb's Vodafone bill making calls to other gangsters, who are engaged in putting contracts on people or gun-running or extortion, or smuggling eastern bloc young peasant girls into the west for a life of prostitution and drugs.

I carry on in this vein, with commendable focus, until, some fifteen minutes later, my phone rings again.

'It's me again.' Jonathan.

'Jonathan! Any news?'

''Fraid not. Look, I'm just calling to say my battery's going and I'm going to have to charge it, so if Seb gets in touch with you, can you tell him I'm heading back to the campsite to wait for him there?'

Like Seb, Jonathan has a wind up phone charger, for those occasions where they can't get to power points. Which I presume he can't now, what with being on the road to some campsite in the middle of nowhere. So now he'll have to spend thirty minutes winding the bloody thing, during which time anything could happen. Oh, God. But then I have a thought. And my heart leaps to grab it. That's it! That must be it! Seb's battery is flat too! 'There's a thought!' I say to Jonathan, and suggest it.

'Then he would have used a payphone to call me instead, wouldn't he? If he was in a position to, that is.'

In-a-*position*-to. Ah, but what would constitute *not* being in a position to? No payphone? No money? No *digits*? Aaarrrgh. 'And what did the police say?'

'Not a lot. He didn't speak much English. But he's taken my number. And I gave him yours too.'

'And have you got one for the station?'

He tells me it. I note it down. I reassure him again. I ring off. I wait. And I wait. And I wait. And I wait. I really don't know what else *to* do.

I'm still waiting when Jake appears. He's back in school on Monday, so has been eking out his last hours of freedom with his friends at the skate park, doing twiddles and twirls on his skateboard. At least, twiddles and twirls is how *I* like to think of them. Potentially neck-breaking, skull-splitting stunts doesn't have quite the same ring to a mother. But to think the very pinnacle of my maternal worries once was that one of my offspring would fracture a small bone.

'Something up, Mum?' he asks. He's drinking from a two-litre bottle of Sprite, which is how he gets most of his nutrition at such times, augmenting with occasional Mars Bars.

My phone rings again, just as I'm filling him in. And this time – hurrah! – at long last, the display says – 'Incoming call. Seb.'

'Oh, thank the Lord. Thank the *Lord*!' is what I'm already saying as I flip it open and put it to my ear.

What comes out of the earpiece isn't the voice of my missing first born, however, but an incomprehensible stream of something indecipherable and foreign – and I hazard a guess at Italian. Yes, definitely Italian, I decide. It has that pizza restaurant menu kind of ring.

What I also establish, because I have been spending most of the afternoon engaged in the business of terrified conjecture, is that the man speaking to me now (for it is a man, and a mature one) is – thank heavens – probably not a member of the Corleone family. Because it takes mere nanoseconds to compute that no criminal, having stolen a mobile phone Sim card, is likely to make his number one priority to scroll through the victim's address book and phone up a contact marked 'mum'. I exhale shortly after. He's still gabbling at me.

'I'm sorry. I don't speak Italian,' I say slowly. 'Do you speak Any English? Er, Inglese?'

'Inglese,' he says back. Or something quite like it. Then. ''Ello. But no.'

Ello, but damn. *Damn*. 'Se-*bas*-ti-*an*?'

This elicits a 'Si', which is certainly encouraging. But then he's back to being incomprehensible again.

Jake's jiggling my forearm, slopping Sprite on the carpet. 'Mum! What they *saying*?'

'I don't know!' I hiss. 'Signor?' Is signor the right parlance? Signore? 'Seg-nor-e,' I plump for. 'Me non-com-prend-ez vous!'

'That's *French*, Mum,' says Jake. 'That's no good.' And he's quite right. It isn't. 'Ask if there's anyone else there who speaks English.' I do. Seems there's not. Though I wouldn't know either way, would I? I make an executive decision.

'Signor,' I say firmly. 'I speak no Italian. Have you, um, a telephono in, er, casa that I can call you back on? A Land Line?' I'm beginning to feel Like Julie Walters in that Victoria Wood sketch. Speak Very Slowly And Loudly to Foreigners and With Any Luck You Will Be Understood.

And, by God, I am! 'Si,' he says. 'Telephono. Si si. Nombre. Si.' He reels it off to me, and I carefully note it down. I write it out in words, phonetically, just to be on the safe side. Though I'm not altogether sure about 'settee'.

'I will ring you back in ten minutes,' I tell him. 'Er. Grazi.'

'Si, Senhora. Ciao,' he says, enunciating similarly carefully. He has obviously seen Wood and Walters as well.

'Right,' I say to Jake as I end the call. 'We've got a number. Which means we've got *something,* at least. Go and find the Italian phrase book, will you? If we can cobble together a few sentences, we might be able to make some progress.'

'*Durr*, Mum. We don't *have* an Italian phrase book. Not any more. Seb took it with him, didn't he?'

Rats. Of *course*. But then I have a better idea anyway. 'Go and switch the computer on, then. We can use Google or something. Or BBC education, or whatever. I'm sure there's some website where you can translate stuff online. God, Jake,' I say, as we troop through the hall. 'What on earth is going *on*?'

We decamp to the dining room in which we don't do any dining and boot up the computer without delay.

'Right,' says Jake, who has found a likely looking website. 'What shall I type in, then?'

'Erm... how about "can you tell me what has happened to my son, please". Yes?'

He types it in. 'Er...here we are,' he says. 'Um... "*Puoi dirmi che ha succedere verso mio figlio, pregare*?".'

'Okay. Hang on. Let me get that written down. Puoi... how on earth do you pronounce that when it's at home?'

'Pooh-oy, I guess.'

'Okay. Pooh-oy derr me chey (chee? Cheh?) has suss ay deary verso me-oh fig-leo, pre-gare (or pre-gar-ray? Pre-gar-ee?).' I read it back. 'That sounds okay. You think that sounds okay?'

'I s'pose so. Go on, then. What next?'

I suggest 'do you know where he is now?', which produces another bunch of words. But six or so carefully annotated utterances down the line, and I am fast beginning to realise that we're on a twenty-four carat hiding to nothing. 'God, this is hopeless, Jake,' I say, putting my pen down in despair. 'Because we've forgotten one crucial thing.'

He glances across at me. 'What?'

'That if I can barely read this lot back in the first place, then how am I going to have the first clue what he might be saying back to me? Damn, but I wish I spoke Italian!'

And in saying so something wonderful suddenly occurs to me.

'Yes!' I say. '*Yes*! Jake, I've just had a thought. I know someone who can speak Italian!'

'Who, Mum?'

'Well, at least I presume he can, anyway. Some at least. He must do. He lived there, didn't he?'

'*Who*, Mum?'

'Gabriel Ash!'

'What, that weather guy who came here? Hugo's son?'

'Exactly!'

Gabriel Ash is doing the tea-time weather forecast. Live. On air. On TV. Right at that very moment. Wearing a pink and purple tie. Which is why I can't reach him on his mobile, I presume. I leave a message on his voicemail and a text message too, and try to desist from making any more random conjectures about why an old Italian man might have my missing son's phone. But they come at me anyway, like runaway scuds. He's caught Seb with his daughter. He's locked him in a cowshed... no, no. It can't be. He left the girl didn't he? Another girl then... No! Why a girl, anyway? Perhaps he ran him down? Or perhaps he was out cruising for vulnerable young men... Perhaps... Oh, God. Too many perhapses for a mother.

'And for all those of you hoping to make the most of the weekend,' Gabriel Ash is saying brightly, 'Make your plans for the Saturday if you can, because this current round of weather is likely to break by early Sunday, when this low pressure system –' he wafts a hand towards his map '– will see rain in most areas by noon.'

Yes, yes, yes. I think. Get on with it! *Ring* me!

Exactly ten minutes after Wales Tonight has started, he does.

Which is impressive. 'This is an unexpected pleasure,' he says politely. 'Is there something I can do for you, Abbie?'

'Oh, thanks so much for calling back, Gabriel! Um, yes. At least, I hope you can. I was wondering how your Italian was?'

'My what?'

'Your Italian. As in the language. As in speaking it, I mean. *Do* you speak it? Only I presumed you probably did, and I was wondering if I could ask you a really big favour. There's this Italian man, and I need to be able to understand what he's saying, and it's really important, and...'

I have to pause here, for oxygen. 'What man?' he asks, taking advantage of the gap. 'Where?'

'In *Italy*. Only he's got my son's phone, and my son's gone missing, and he obviously knows all about it – well, at least, I *hope* he does – he could have just found the phone, of course, and be trying to trace its owner, but...'

'Your son is *missing*?'

'*Yes*. His friend has lost track of him, and this man has his phone, but without being able to understand what he's saying, I don't even know where he is, let alone what he has to do with anything, and I thought if *you* could call him, you could find out for me, and then I could put him in touch with Jonathan and then he could...'

'Okay, okay,' he says, soothingly. 'First things first. You have a number?'

'I have two. I have my son's mobile number, and I have a land line number. I thought I ought to get one in case Seb's battery dies.'

'Good thinking,' he says. 'Hang on. Let me grab a pen. Right. Give me both.' I reel off both numbers, the latter just as I wrote it. Amazingly, all my chink-ways and settees make sense to him. 'Right, then,' he says, in a businesslike fashion. 'Did you manage to get this man's name?'

'God, I didn't think of that.'

'No matter,' he says swiftly. 'But your son's called Sebastian, right?'

'Sebastian McFadden.'

'Okay. Leave it with me. I'll see what I can find out and call you straight back.'

'Oh, thank you, thank you, *thank* you. I'm so sorry to bother you.'

'You're very welcome. Hey. And keep *calm*.'

\*       \*       \*

Keep calm. Yes. I know I must keep calm. But it's so hard. All I can think of are the myriad ways in which trauma and disaster might have visited my son. 'Oh, God,' I say to Jake. 'What can have *happened* to him?'

'Probably nothing,' Jake says with his reliable lack of panic. 'He's probably just dropped his phone somewhere and this guy has picked it up.'

'But he wasn't feeling well. Jonathan said he wasn't feeling well, didn't he?'

Jake shrugs. 'Probably just had too much to drink. Left his phone somewhere. Something like that.'

Oh, I wish I had your confidence, Jakey.

The house phone rings less than ten minutes later, but already it feels like ten hours have sped by.

'I'm sorry to have taken so long,' says Gabriel Ash. 'I had to make a couple of calls.' And he says it in such a serious voice that all thoughts of hangovers and phones being mislaid now implode. I'm immediately scared absolutely witless.

'What's happened?'

'Don't worry. He's all right.'

'Oh, thank God. Oh thank God.'

'But he's in hospital.'

'In *hospital*? Oh, God. Oh, my baby! What's *happened*?'

'Well, by all accounts, he's had his appendix removed.'

I gasp at this, floored. 'His *appendix*?'

'His *appendix*?' echoes Jake.

'Yes. His appendix,' confirms Gabriel Ash. 'And he's okay. He's fine. Look, are you at home?'

'Yes. Yes, we're here. We're at home.'

'Right,' he says. 'Stay there. I'm on my way over. I'll be there in ten minutes.'

'But –'

'Sit tight,' he says. 'Don't worry. Keep *calm*.'

As soon as I see Gabriel Ash's car pull up, I'm out of the front door, Spike tucked under armpit, Jake close on my heels. He's still wearing the jacket and tie he did the weather in. He could be someone who's come round to sell me an ISA.

In any other circumstance I would find his arrival somewhat amazing. I know full well that Broadcasting House is only a couple of miles away, but even so, it seems to go against the laws of physics that he could be smiling out from the middle of my TV screen at one point, and then walking up my front garden path minutes later. It almost doesn't seem possible. But he's here, even so.

For which I am terrifically grateful. He locks his car and strides across the street to the house. His limp, I notice, is already markedly improved. Is now barely noticeable, in fact.

'Right then,' he says, finally, sitting down at the kitchen table and unfolding a couple of sheets of A4 paper. There are lots of scribbles on them, some in English and some in Italian. He passes one of them to me. A name and an address. 'Here's the man's details. Thought you'd want to have them. So. I think I've pretty much got all the facts. The guy I spoke to –' He nods towards the paper, '– well, he found your son on his way home last night. He was doubled up in the lane, apparently, and when the guy stopped, he thought maybe he'd been hit by a car or something, but when he got out to see if he was okay he couldn't get any sense out of him, so he got him into his truck and drove him to the hospital – 'he checks his notes. 'In a place called Ravenna, where they took him in. He obviously didn't know anything about him at that point – but he did leave his name with the hospital receptionist. He'd dropped your son's rucksack off with him, of course, but when he went to use his truck at lunchtime today he realised his jacket was still in his truck, and that it had his phone and wallet in it. And of course he realised the phone was beeping at him, and saw all the missed calls. Which was when he thought he'd better try and return the last six.' He smiles. 'The word 'mum', I think, is pretty universal, don't you?'

'Oh, bless him. *Bless* him. And thank heavens for that!'

'Anyway, he told me he's going to drive back up to the hospital later and drop it all off for him.'

'I should phone them, pronto, shouldn't I? Find out how he is.'

'It's okay,' he says. 'I've already done that.'

'And what did they say?'

'That they operated last night. And that he's doing just fine. I've got the number of the hospital so you can call them yourself though. The nurse I spoke to –' he indicates a name and a number '– speaks pretty good English, and she'll be able to fill you in.'

'God, I must ring Jonathan too,' I say. '*Now*. I must tell him where Seb is so he can he can get there. Is it far, this Ravenna, do you know?'

'About fifteen, twenty kilometres north, apparently. Not too far.'

'Right. I'd better get to it, then. And I should ring his father too, shouldn't I? Yes. He's only in Marseilles. He can get down there too. He can probably get down there tonight, even. And I must get back on the internet and try and book a flight. Oh, God. What a thing to happen! Oh, my poor boy!'

Gabriel Ash slides the pieces of paper across the table at me. 'Quite a shock, eh? Look, do you want me to make you guys a cup of tea or something?' He rises from the table in a purposeful manner.

'Oh, God, I'm sorry,' I say, doing likewise. 'Where are my manners? No, no. really. We're fine. But what about you? You've come rushing all the way over here, and –'

He rolls his eyes. 'It's only a ten minute drive.'

'I know. But it's so kind of you to do this. I'm so sorry to have bothered you. I just didn't know what else to do.'

'You did absolutely the right thing,' he says firmly. 'I'm happy I could help.' He glances at the wall clock. 'Look, I'd better be getting get back to work. But if there's anything else I can do, just give me a shout, okay?'

We reach the front door and I open it for him. There's a chillish breeze in the street, coaxing the first lemony leaves from their billets in the birch trees, and causing my upper arms to goose-pimple. I rub them.

'Hey, good timing,' he says, 'for an Italian mini-break. Don't forget what I said. If you need me, just call.' He looks hard at me. 'Really,' he says. 'I mean it.'

On impulse I reach up and peck him on the cheek. He looks embarrassed. 'I know you do,' I say.

And then, also on impulse, I hear myself adding, 'Look, you know that time when you told me you were just trying to be friendly and I told you not to bother?'

He lifts a brow minutely. 'How could I forget?'

'Well, I can't tell you how sorry I am that I said that.'

'Please don't be,' he says, shaking his head. 'I know you didn't mean it.'

'I hope so,' I say. 'Because I'm very glad you did.'

'Hey, all part of the service,' he says.

I bought a set of three matching Jane Shilton suitcases on wheels at a sale of seconds at McArthur Glen three years back. In an organised household, they would, naturally, be carefully stowed, all tucked up inside one another like a set of Russian dolls, and thus available and ready at all times. Not so in this house, however. Things get stowed in our loft on a shove-it-up-there basis, and generally only after their presence on the landing has begun to invoke health and safety concerns. Typically, then, the one I want on this occasion (i.e. the one that is just the right size for the sort of woman who goes off on impromptu weekend breaks, which, sadly, I'm not) is gathering colonies of spiders in a far distant corner of the loft. Which is where I am when the phone rings again an hour later. I've spent much of the preceding one in phone conversations; with Jonathan, with Sebastian's father, Rob, and, lastly, with a number of airline reservations clerks, the upshot of which is that I'll be en route tomorrow morning, to Bristol airport and thence on to Venice. Bologna is a bit nearer (or so Seb's dad tells me) but there wasn't a seat on a flight until Sunday, and I need to be there, like, *now*.

'Who on earth have you been on the phone to?' demands my mother crossly, just as soon as I clamber down and pick up the receiver in my bedroom. 'I've been trying and trying and trying and trying. Didn't it *occur* to you that I'd be trying to ring?'

My mother, who has been with Celeste to see a special showing of one of those turgid French films with sub-titles that she's always claimed to be so fond of, sounds three sherries in – she's pretty turgid herself. Well, of course she is. What else would she do? She is sitting, she informs me, in waspish tones, in a bar on St Mary Street. Waiting.

For *me*. For me, as-was-not-at-any-point-arranged, to pick them up. Just assumed. As with everything, always. Just *assumed*. So it is, it must be said, with just the tiniest bit of entirely inappropriate pleasure that I am able to cut short her bleating. Only short-lived, obviously, because first and foremost I am in a state of chronic maternal agitation about the fact that my sick son is almost a thousand miles away from me just when he needs me most, but it is nevertheless a small oasis of joy in a veritable Sahara of stress.

'No,' I say crisply. 'It *didn't* occur to me, I'm afraid. I have had much more pressing things to worry about, Mum.'

'Such as?'

'Such as your grandson is in hospital.'

'What, *Jake*?'

'No, Mum. Sebastian.'

'*Sebastian*?'

'Yes, Sebastian. He's had to have an operation to remove his appendix.'

'His appendix?'

'His appendix.'

'Oh,' she says. 'Gracious me. Is he all right?'

'Yes, yes, he's fine. Well, so his father says, at any rate. He's going to set off for Italy tonight. I've got a flight booked for tomorrow.'

'A *flight*?'

'Well, how else am I going to get there? In a row boat?'

I hear her sharp intake of breath. Her naked surprise. 'What,' she says. '*You're* going to Italy?'

She gathers herself then, of course. Oh, of *course* I must go. Absolutely. And no problem. She and Celeste will find a taxi. And so on. So it's only after I've put the phone down that a sense of utter incredulity descends upon me. What on earth does she think I'm going to do? Just sit here? I'm his *mother*! But then I remember, with a jolt of sadness that takes me quite unawares, that *my* mother's definition of the word 'mother' is entirely dissimilar to mine.

## Chapter 20

THE PEGGY GUGGENHEIM COLLECTION, or so the in-flight magazine tells me, boasts paintings by all sorts of famous artists; particularly by Jackson Pollock, for whom I've always had a bit of a fondness. In my early twenties, in fact (during that brief adult period when I was childless and time-rich and prone to such fancies), I even attempted to emulate one of his splatter pictures, using a selection of emulsion paint leftovers from one of my ex-husband's then projects. However, the resultant Great Work, rich in every aspect of artistic creativity, not least of which was paint (which I had applied by the trowel-load), was so heavy that we were unable to hang it anywhere on our then flat's paper thin walls, leaving me little alternative but to prop it against the wall of the living room out of sight behind the sofa, as there was no other bit of wall big enough to accommodate it. I'd rather like to see a Jackson Pollock for myself, but, on this trip, anyway, despite my tantalising proximity, it doesn't look as though I'm about to.

No sooner have I had an all too brief glimpse of Venice itself – a shimmer of spires rising from the teal blue water – than we land, in no time at all, at Marco Polo airport. It's a very new looking place – clearly dedicated to the needs and desires of the discerning middle-class, culture-seeking holiday-maker. Glass cabinets on plinths sprout like randomly placed religious icons, promising myriad ways to divest tourists of their money, and elegant slim women carrying briefcases and coffees criss-cross me in click-clacking shoals.

Rob, is, as promised, there to meet me. I was actually all off and angsty and resistant about the idea of him driving all the way up here to fetch me today, not only because he's already driven so far already, but also because old habits and hard-won independence die hard. I intended, and expected, to hire my own car. But in fact, now I am here, I find I don't mind in the least. I never thought it would be possible, because people always tell you it isn't, but as I spot him in the arrivals hall I no longer think 'hateful ex alert, adopt face-on and keep guard up' but instead I think, with a rush of something almost approaching affection, 'that's my sons' father, that is.' I can see them both in him. It feels rather fine. If more grown up than I fancy I really should be, pre-bus pass.

He waves, smiling cheerily. He looks lean, and is tanned. 'Abbie!' he calls brightly at me. 'Long time no see!'

And it has been a long time. The last time I saw him was at Heathrow, two and a half years back, where we executed a change-over to dovetail with some conference, before he whisked the boys off for a week's skiing in the Alps. 'Hmm,' I say, though not in at all a hmm-ish sort of manner. 'If not in the best circumstances, eh?'

He takes my case from me, even though I'm quite capable of pulling it, but once again, I don't mind. It would feel churlish to refuse. 'He's doing absolutely fine,' he says, reassuringly. 'You'd hardly know he's had surgery, honestly you wouldn't. They're going to discharge him tomorrow as long as his temperature's normal and his bowel is working okay.'

'That *quick*?'

He nods. 'I know. I was shocked too. But apparently that's standard procedure these days. Anyway, how are *you*? I hear you've got your mother living with you. Bet that's a blast.'

I give him a potted history on the way out to the car, which has him chuckling intermittently and rolling his eyes. And in the telling, I think, the whole thing does sound comedic. It's just the reality that's so short on laughs. But then he knows this already. Knows *her*. Indeed, in one of the few angry moments that preceded our final parting, he even ventured to suggest that her removal from his life would be almost more thrilling an event than would mine.

But that's history now. Over and long since forgiven and forgotten. Or if not completely forgotten – bad words do tend to linger, like snatches of pop songs – at least consigned to a box marked 'recriminations various. Of no practical worth. Store below 5 degrees C'.

His car – a Mercedes – is roomy and air-conditioned and expensive. As it would be. He's an architect. He earns lots of money. And he's booked me a room, too. Same place as he's staying. Nothing pricey, he tells me, for which I am most grateful. Sanguine though I am about case-pulling chivalry, I would baulk at the idea of him paying for my room.

Ravenna, according not to the in-flight magazine but to the enthusiastic large lady in the seat next to me, is apparently a largely overlooked Byzantine Jewel. And is also very famous for its world-beating mosaics. A veritable Mecca for tesserae enthusiasts. An absolute, absolute must-see. She even wrote me a list of all the places I could go. San Vitale, so she tells me, knocks St Mark's Basilica into a cocked hat any day. But it's all academic. They can keep their mosaics. The only sight I want to see right now is my son.

'So,' Rob says as we wend our way out of the airport environs and then on to the motorway south. 'You got everything sorted back home, then?'

The backs of his hands are the colour of almonds, and the first suggestions of grey stripe through his black hair. 'Just about. Mum's gone off to Pru's, Jake's gone to his friend's house, and Spike is being babysat by Dee. I could have left them, but Jake's back in school on Monday morning, and I didn't know how long I was going to be.'

'Oh, no worries there. You wait till you see him. He's looking as fit as a flea.'

'And what about Jonathan? What's he doing now?'

'I spoke to him earlier. He's staying put in Cervia for another week. They'd got themselves a few days work helping to strike camp for one of the big firms down there.

'Strike camp?'

'It's end of season. They have to dismantle all the tents. Big job, by all accounts. Then he's going to come up and stay with us for a few days.'

I wonder at that, but then I remember I've forgotten that Rob already knows Jonathan quite well. He's been over with Seb on numerous occasions. It was Jonathan, in fact, who took the first photo that I ever clapped eyes on of Rob's second wife, Elise. She's half French and baguette thin and luminously pretty, and I've only ever spoken to her on the phone. She sold Rob his current house and her *tarte tatin* is legendary. That's pretty much the extent of my knowledge. Except also that both my boys

185

really, really like her, which is actually just fine by me. Because she came along way after Rob and I split, it's uncomplicated. Easy. Something about which (bar this Christmas and that's strictly my problem) I don't have to trail any baggage. Which is something about which to be relieved at this juncture, what with already having so much in residence at home.

'That's really nice of you,' I say. And I mean it.

Despite feeling it's really a bit off to be doing so, I then end up sleeping for almost the whole of the rest of the journey, and when I come to, we're coming off the motorway. By the time I'm fully with it, we're in the hospital car park, which, bar the lollipop trees and the cicada-filled air, could just as easily be situated in Bolton.

Likewise, the hospital – no, the much more pleasing *ospedale* – smells like hospitals do the world over. It's a comfortable smell, a smell that I'm used to. And it reminds me that in many ways I do miss my own.

Rob leads the way along a couple of corridors and we eventually arrive on the ward. Though his French is good these days, he speaks little more Italian than I do, but the nurse who comes to meet us obviously knows him already, and nods a greeting before waving us through. Only half the beds are occupied, by an assortment of swarthy male patients in various stages of slumber, and I scan anxiously, keen to get a first glimpse of Seb. Rob veers off then, towards a bed in which a young man is sitting, propped up against several generous white pillows, reading a book by the light of a lamp and idly scratching his beard.

It's only when Rob greets him that it finally dawns on me that this stranger, in fact, is my son.

I'm still gaping when his face widens into a smile. 'Mum!'

'Oh, God, Seb! I almost didn't recognise you!'

He looks confused, and then not. He touches his hand to his chin again. 'Oh, this,' he says, slightly self-conscious now. 'Well, I just figured it would be less hassle.'

He lets me touch it too. It's baby soft. Nothing like his dense wiry hair. I can't stop looking at him. It's been months since I last saw him and I simply can't stop staring. But when I hug him, albeit carefully, he feels just the same.

I sit down on the bed, while Rob takes the chair.

And I scrutinise. 'So,' I say. 'How *are* you?'

He closes up the book and shrugs his shoulders. 'I'm *fine*, Mum.'

I shake my head. 'No, you're not. You've just had your appendix out. How can you be fine?'

'I just am. A bit sore. A bit stiff. A bit bored. But all in all, not too bad at all.'

Oh, my sweet, brave, precious child.

Except he's not a child. All of a sudden he seems anything but. 'You look tired, Mum,' he observes. Which floors me still further. Children don't *do* that. Children don't notice. You tell *them* when you're tired and then they pat you. Or offer to make cups of tea. Or give you biscuits. Yet Sebastian has. And now he pats *me*. On the forearm. 'You know, you really didn't need to come all this way,' he says. Then, seeing my expression, his own changes tack. He holds his hands up as if to ward off an imminent blow. 'Okay, okay, okay, then! Yes, then. Point taken. You *did* need to come all this way.' And he laughs. 'How's Jakey?'

'Jake's absolutely fine. Still busy with his band. They have a gig coming up so he's permanently hyper. He sends his love. As does Nana, of course.'

'How is she?'

'Oh, same as ever. Almost mobile again, thank God.'

'Has she found somewhere to live yet?'

'Not *quite* yet. Though I've given her notice to quit your room, obviously. I told her she can bunk down with the drum kit for the moment.'

And hopefully she'll find that so unedifying an experience, that she'll raise a tad more enthusiasm for moving elsewhere. But I stop speaking at this point because Seb looks confused. He's shaking his head. And also glancing at Rob. Who is now looking at me. They're *both* looking at me. 'What?' I say, somewhat confused myself now. '*What*?'

Seb shakes his head. He looks a little like Jesus. 'Mum, I'm not coming *home*.'

'What d'you mean, you're not coming home? Of course you're coming home!'

He shakes his head. 'Whatever made you think that?' He glances at Rob again. 'I'm going to stay at Dad's.'

I look from one to the other, stupefied. 'Not coming *home*? But…but you *have* to. You have to recuperate. To rest. You need to –'

'Mum, I'm *fine*. I told you. I mean I know I've got to rest up a bit for a couple of weeks, obviously. But I can do that at Dad's, can't I?' Rob's nodding. 'And when I'm well enough, I'm going to rejoin the guys. They're going to come and spend a few days with me at Dad's once they've finished up at the campsite, and then we're going to head off to Croatia like we planned.'

So *that's* what Rob meant about Jonathan coming up. God, I'm so stupid. But this can't happen. *Surely*. 'Sebastian, you can't possibly go galumphing back off around Europe – particularly eastern Europe – when you've just had major surgery. It's not safe. Supposing something happens?'

He's unimpressed. 'Come on, Mum. What's going to happen?'

'Well, I don't know! But something might. You might get an infection. Your stitches might weep. You might –'

'Mum, it wasn't major surgery. It was just my appendix. Look.' He pushes back the sheet and tugs at his boxers. 'See? Almost nothing. Just two tiny holes. Honestly, Mum. Stop *fretting*!'

I round on Rob as soon as we're back in the hospital corridor. Bloody hospitals. I don't care how great a job they did on Seb, I am all at once sick of the places. Not least because I'm sure they are making *me* sick. I've had enough hospital dramas and the last few weeks to script a whole series worth of episodes of that bloody A and E.

What a difference an hour makes. 'Why didn't you tell me? Why didn't you *warn* me? Why didn't you say something on the drive down about this?'

He looks completely nonplussed. 'Hang on, Abbie. Why didn't *you*? How was I supposed to know you had some plan on the go to whisk him back to Wales? It never so much as occurred to me for an instant. Why on earth would he do that when I'm just around the corner?'

'Marseilles is hardly just around the corner,' I snap at him.

He doesn't rise to it. 'But still a good deal closer than Cardiff. Besides, he was due to be coming to me soon anyway. You knew that.'

'*Yes*, I knew *that*. But that's not till October. In the meantime he should be home. With me.'

'Why, exactly?'

'Because he needs looking after.'

'Which is something I'm perfectly capable of doing.'

'I know, but –'

'Abbie,' he interrupts me. 'Just you hold up a minute. There's no 'but' about it. You don't have a monopoly on looking after the children, you know.'

'But I'm his mother!'

'And I'm his father.'

'Yes, I know *that*, but –'

'But *nothing*, Abbie. It's entirely up to *him* what he does. He's almost nineteen now. He's an adult. You can't keep him wrapped up in cotton wool for ever.'

'I don't keep him wrapped up in cotton wool! That's a really unkind thing to say! And what the hell would you know about it anyway?'

'Rather less than I'd like to. As well you know. Jesus, give me a break, will you? Why *shouldn't* I take him home with me? Why shouldn't I have the opportunity to spend some time with him, huh?'

'I've never stopped you seeing him. Not once. Never.'

'No, I *know* that. I'm not saying you have. I'm just trying to point out that *I'm* here, too.' He has, I notice, adopted the look of a man who is all out of energy for taking things on. Taking *me* on. I know that look well. Perhaps it's just as well we live so far apart. 'Surely – *surely*, Abbie – we're not going to have a row about this?'

I blow my nose.

'No. No, we're not.' Much as I wish it weren't so, he's absolutely right in everything he says. Infuriating though that may be. Except the cotton wool bit. I take exception to that.

189

'Look,' I say, because once I give it a nanosecond's thought, I realise the whole taking exception to things thing is wearing a little thin, even for me. I'm tired. He's tired. We've both come a long way. 'I'm sorry, all right? It's just that I assumed he'd be coming home with me and now he isn't – and the two of you have obviously got things all sorted already between you – and you'll be tootling back off to France with him, and I'm hardly going to see anything of him, and, well, it's just been a bit upsetting. That's all. I know it's all exciting for him, and he's keen to come and stay with you and start his work experience and everything, and I wouldn't dream of making any sort of a fuss about it to *him*, but you can't *imagine* the state I've been in for the last forty-eight hours – not knowing where he was, what was going on, what had happened…and now I get here and all's well and the two of you have got everything organised already, and I feel utterly redundant and like he's not even that fussed that I came in the first place, and –'

'Come on. You know that's not true.'

I flap my hand at him. 'Well, whatever. That's what it *feels* like. And it's all a bit hard to swallow, okay? I'm his *mother*.' I crumple my tissue into a ball in my fist. 'You'd be exactly the same in my shoes.'

Rob puts his arm around me and squeezes my shoulder. 'Actually, Abbie, – and please don't take this the wrong way – you're finding out what it feels like to be in *mine*.'

The next morning dawns fine and clear and sunny and warm, and Sebastian is, or so Rob informs me once he's spoken to the nurse at the hospital, going to be discharged at tea-time as planned.

And I realise I'm not going to bother. I'm not going to bother being in a flap, a state, a mood, a huff, or any other permutation of self-centred nonsense, up to and including the taking of exceptions.

He might be right, in any case. Perhaps I *have* wrapped the boys in cotton wool. Perhaps I have been too doting. But then, realistically, it's very hard not to. When you parent alone for months and months at a stretch, you can't help but overcompensate, even if you don't mean to. Because all the time you're conscious that you have to make up. Make up for the parent that's not there. It's only natural.

So I'm not going to bother being cross with myself either. I can't have been that bad, when all's said and done, or else he'd be hot footing it back to the UK with *me*. Except he's not. He doesn't want to. He doesn't feel the need to. In the needy stakes, *I* am the champ.

And I'm not going to bother feeling cross about Rob either. He's quite right. I know last night I could have written an essay on the subject, but I really have no business being off with Rob. Much as it was his choice to go and live in France, up until the time that our marriage began expiring, it had been my choice as well.

Well, not strictly. I'd always been happy where I was. But I would have gone, wouldn't I? Yes. Of course I would.

So we breakfast companionably and check out some leaflets, whizz down to the hospital and spend an hour there with Seb, then we have lunch in a five hundred-year-old restaurant in the Piazza, while he sleeps, take a whistle-stop tour round the (okay, yes, impressive) Basilica San Vitale, see more mosaics than a person can usefully ingest in one lifetime, buy some ham, some parmesan and some plump tortellini, have an ice-cream and a very small argument about art, then we head back to the hospital in the warm sleepy sunshine, and find Sebastian, as promised, has been pronounced fit to leave.

Bar the hospital, and the fact that we're five years divorced, you could almost imagine this day to be a cine-film excerpt from the swish Venetian honeymoon we never actually had.

Almost, but not quite. But very pleasant, for all that.

The original plan (there were clearly a number of plans originated before I got here) was that if Seb was discharged before Monday, which he has been, then we'd spend a further night at the *Albergo Capello*, and then Rob – along with Seb – would drive me to the airport, and then the two of them would head off, in his car, back to France.

Except right now, that just seems plain daft.

It would have been perfectly sensible had I been able to get a flight home from Bologna, but as I can't (I have yet another flight

191

booked, tomorrow lunchtime, from Venice), it makes no sort of sense.

So I do something so terrifically sensible and grown-up and unselfish that I manage to astound even myself. 'Look,' I say to Rob while we sit and debate it. 'You have hundreds of miles to drive as it is. And there's really no point in you two hanging about here for another night just to keep me company, is there? I think the best thing would be if you two get going, and I hire a car to take me to the airport in the morning.'

Hark at me, the frequent flyer.

'Absolutely not,' says Rob.

'I'm quite capable, you know.'

'I wouldn't dream of suggesting otherwise.'

'Exactly. So where's the problem? If you set off now you can have half the journey done this evening, then you can stop off at a motel or something for the night and get some rest, and then finish the trip in the morning. Much more sensible than trying to do the whole thing in one go.'

'Mum's got a point, Dad,' says Seb, about which I can't help but have some issues. But they're tiny ones. I'm only his mother. Not his leg.

Rob ponders. 'Well…hmm. Ah. Hang on. You got your driving licence with you?'

'Of course I have my licence,' I say briskly.

Thus it is that I feel quite the independent woman when we finally (okay, and tearfully, in my case) part company. Though I have, if reluctantly, allowed Rob to sort my car out via his super speedy business person's magic car hire arrangement thingy, I am now a lone woman in a small Italian town. I can perhaps take my book and amble down to a trattoria. Sit at one of the little candlelit tables in the piazza, drink Chianti. People watch. Star gaze. Soak up the atmosphere. Even go and visit Dante's tomb, if I want to.

I could but I don't. I go back to my room. I write a long thank you letter to the man who saved my son's life, which I will ask Gabriel Ash to translate once I'm home. Then I lie on the bed with a packet of breadsticks and watch a subtitled episode of *Morse*.

At close to midnight, just as I'm dozing off, I get a text.

Hiya mum. How ya doing? We nr a place called Tortona. Txt me tmoz. Nite nite. Love u LOTS xxxxxxxxxxxxx

So then I howl and howl and howl. As you do.

# Chapter 21

IT'S GETTING ON FOR five when I pull up outside the house, the gentian sky that accompanied my drive back from Bristol fast disappearing under a low dove-grey duvet of heavy cloud, which the first scouts of a threatening-to-be keen autumn breeze are prodding around irritably. I feel irritable too. No, not so much irritable as deflated, disenfranchised and denuded of spirit. After the soft hues of a sleepy late summer Italy, autumn, with its lengthening nights and leaden skies, seems suddenly very much here. As am I. All alone. Without Seb.

Which is all so, so silly. Were it not for what had happened I wouldn't have been seeing him anyway, would I? Not till after Christmas. Months and months away. This was a bonus. That he's so well, even more so. This is what I must keep repeating to myself. Until such time as I start to believe it, at any rate. Which could be some time.

But at least Dee's car, a heartening splash of yellow in the gloom, is parked cheerfully just down the road.

Dee herself, with Spike in her arms, is already out on the doorstep by the time I've parked my own car in Mr Davidson's space. Her holdall's in the doorway. She's obviously in a hurry to be off.

'Oh, you shouldn't have waited,' I tell her. 'I told you not to worry. Spike would have been okay on his own.'

Tim's leaving for a conference in the States later this evening. I'm sure she's anxious to see him before he goes. 'I know,' she says, taking my airport shopping bag from me and leading the way through to the kitchen. 'But I couldn't go without seeing you, could I?'

But she does need to get a move on. I give her a hug. 'Well, I'm here now, so just you skedaddle, okay? Thanks so much for everything.'

'Seb's okay?'

'Remarkably so. They did the op laparoscopically. Pretty impressive stuff. He's well on the mend.'

'Obviously. They sure let him out pretty sharpish. I thought you'd be gone for the week!'

'So did I. Well, a few days at least. It's all been a bit of a blur, to be honest.'

'I don't doubt it.' She inspects me carefully. 'Anyway, how are *you*?'

'I'm fine,' I say. 'Why wouldn't I be?'

She looks at me through narrowed eyes. 'Hmm,' she says finally. 'You sure?'

Okay, so I'm not one hundred percent all right. Patently I'm not. He's hundreds of miles away again. How could I be? 'I'm *fine*,' I say again. 'But I wish I could have persuaded him to come home, Dee. It feels all wrong, him there and me here.'

'I know,' she says. 'But you know, I'm quite sure his dad is perfectly capable of looking after him. Besides, it doesn't sound like he needs much looking after anyway. He'll be back to his usual self in no time, I'm sure.'

'I know,' I say. 'I'm just being pathetic, aren't I? *I* want to look after him.'

Dee pats my forearm. 'Tell you what,' she says brightly, 'if it's a spot of looking after you're after, how about I call your sister and have her bring your mother back this evening?'

'Er, no thanks.'

'Precisely. You just enjoy some time to yourself. You must be shattered.'

'I'm not too bad, actually. I slept on the plane. Oh, and these are for you. I was going to bring you some parmesan but I wasn't sure about cheese in your condition.' I start to pull out my purchases. 'Though chocolate, is, of course, obligatory. So here's these. Oh, and I couldn't resist this.' I present her with a bottle of balsamic vinegar and she laughs. 'Oh, but this is mine, I'm afraid.'

She picks up the bottle. 'Amaretto. There's nice.'

'Present from Rob, would you believe?'

'Oh, bless. That's nice of him.' Then she grins wryly at me. 'This'll be Malcolm, then, five years down the line, will it?'

'Er…maybe not.'

'Anyway,' she says briskly. 'Now I really better had get on. You sure you're okay?'

195

'I'm absolutely fine.' I sound like a stuck record.

'There's half a roast chicken left in the fridge, if you're hungry. And I called Tom's mum to let her know you were on your way home.'

'I'd better scoot straight round and get Jake, I guess, hadn't I?'

Dee shakes her head. 'No need. He's going to sleep over again tonight and go to school with Tom tomorrow. She said she'd drop his stuff round after school, if that's okay.'

'So it's just me and Spike, then.'

'Uh-huh. Enjoy the rest. Oh, almost forgot to tell you. Gabriel Ash called yesterday. I told him you'd be back tonight so he'll probably call you later.'

And then she's off down the path with her daisy-patterned holdall. And it's just me and Spike and the Amaretto.

And the washing, of course. Having showered and unpacked my few things, I'm just coming back down the stairs with a basket full of Jake's stained T-shirts and crusty socks when the doorbell rings. I go to answer it, the basket still tucked under my arm.

I open it to find that Gabriel Ash, who seems to be carrying a small door, is standing on my front step. In pale jeans and shirt and yet another linen jacket, a pair of sunglasses hanging from the top pocket.

He clocks my washing, my wet hair and my shock-horror jeans. (Mother: Abigail, how could you? Those jeans are absolutely shocking. How can you wear such horrible clothes?) He looks embarrassed. Or shocked? Or horrified? No. Just self-conscious. Which ought really to be my job. 'Oh,' he says, fiddling with his key fob. 'Sorry. Is this a bad time?'

I don't know what other sort of time he imagines I'd be having with a kilo of fetid clothing under one armpit, for sure. I open the door a little wider, to be polite, and stuff a sprouting of boxer shorts a little further down the heap.

'No, no,' I say, both surprised at his arrival and perplexed by his parcel. 'Just pottering. Come on in.'

'I did call,' he says, stepping hesitantly with his flat pack over the threshold. 'But I couldn't get an answer. I assumed you must be en route. Anyway, I thought I'd look in on my way home, just in case. Um…you know. See if all's well.'

I'm touched. Really touched. 'That was thoughtful of you. Yes. Yes, everything's fine. My son's gone to stay with his father. He's –'

'Oh?' he says, surprised. 'He's not come home with you, then?'

I usher him into the kitchen, his comment threatening to make me feel newly bereft. Except now I have company. Which cheers me up lots. 'No.' I shake my head. 'He was due to be going to his dad's soon anyway – he's doing some work experience with him for a few months – so it seemed sensible for him to take him back with him. He lives in Marseilles. Er…' I gesture towards him at the bin-liner-covered package that's still standing to attention beside him. 'Is that something you need to get off your chest?'

He stands it carefully in front of him, grinning.

'Not at all,' he says. 'My turn to be the bearer of gifts, in fact.'

'Gifts? What gifts?'

'Don't get too excited. Nothing that thrilling. Well, it might well have been for someone at some point, I imagine. Think it belongs to your mum. Corinne found it while she was at the house re-homing the fish.'

He strips the bin-liners off to reveal not an item of furniture but a life-size cardboard cut-out of my own dear mother, standing on one leg with her arms held aloft, doing some sort of bastardised, disco-style *plie*. Much lycra, much mascara, much gnashing of choppers. It was a promotional tool for when the video of Dance With Diana hit the shops. An unsettling thing for a daughter to be confronted with when popping in to Smiths for a Kit Kat, some Polos and the current week's *Jackie*.

'Good Lord, I had no idea she still had that,' I say. 'Hey, Jane Fonda eat your heart out, or what?!'

It – rather, *she* – used to stand behind the door in the downstairs toilet when we were teenagers, to the terror of startled occasional guests and the enduring amusement of us girls.

He folds out the tabs at the back to stand it up properly. 'It was laid across the rafters in the garage, apparently. Corinne was going to chuck it, but it occurred to me that if your mum had kept

197

it for that long, then she might want it back. Or *you* might. You know, family heirloom?'

'I think one of her is quite enough to live with,' I say ruefully. 'Though I guess at least this one wouldn't get through so much sherry.' Which piece of nonsense reminds me that I have once again forgotten my manners. 'I'm sorry,' I say. 'Can I get you a drink of something? Tea? Coffee?' And in saying so, it occurs to me that I seem to spend all our encounters engaged in the preparation of unexciting beverages. 'Um…glass of Amaretto?' I point to the bottle on the kitchen table. 'From the airport. It's very nice.'

He consults his watch at this point, for some reason. Though it could of course be some other sort of wrist-wear. A blood sugar monitor? A portable temperance lecture?'

He hesitates, so possibly the latter. 'Go on, then,' he says eventually. 'Why not? Yes, I will.'

He pulls out a chair while I go and fetch another glass from the cupboard. I don't actually have two liqueur glasses that match. I did once have a set of sherry glasses I got with petrol station tokens, but they're all long since gone. In fact, I only have one glass that could be properly classed as a liqueur glass anyway. And I've only got that because Rob and I pinched it from a Plymouth-Roscoff ferry. We pinched a Guinness glass too. And an ashtray. Though in my defence it was only because our ferry had broken down and they'd billeted us on one that didn't have enough berths. If you have to spend the night on the floor of a saloon, then reparations need to be made. And I'm already using that one. So I plop his into a wine glass, add an ice cube and hand it to him.

'So,' he says, sipping it gingerly. 'More than enough dramas for one week, eh?'

I sip my own and eye my grinning mother. 'You're telling me.'

'Did you get to see anything of Venice while you were there?'

'I wish. No, tell a lie. I did catch a glimpse from the plane. And it looked, well, like it does in pictures, I guess.'

'You've never been?' I shake my head. He takes another sip. 'It's worth a visit.'

'Well, when I say I've never been, that's not strictly true. I was conceived there. While my mother was at some film festival or other. And then I was supposed to be going there on my honeymoon.'

'But you didn't.'

'I was scuppered by circumstance. Our car blew up. We decided to put it on hold. We went to Padstow instead.'

'So,' he says, twiddling his glass stem. 'When *is* your son coming home?'

'Oh, God, not till after Christmas now. He's due back mid February.'

'You must miss him.'

I nod. 'Pathetically so. I'm trying to get used to it. But do you ever?' A thought occurs to me. 'You must miss your daughter, too. How often do you get to see her?'

'Not often enough. About four times a year.'

I think guilty thoughts about Rob. 'That's a shame.'

'Yes,' he says, nodding. 'Yes, it is.'

He adds nothing more, and I reach to top my glass up, the silence edging its way out of the comfort zone. Little by little, I am beginning to get the distinct impression that, having come to my house entirely of his own volition, he is beginning to wish he had gone somewhere else. Either that or he is engaged in conversation with me while simultaneously trying to get to the bottom of an incredibly complex mathematical theorem, and can thus only commit one neurone in five to the task. Or that he's still wearing his earpiece from doing his last forecast and there's news coming in of a dust storm in Barry.

Or perhaps he's just got other stuff playing on his mind. His father? His fiancé? His far distant daughter? Something, at any rate. He looks awkward. I recall our last stilted encounter in my kitchen. That sense that if he was given half a chance, he'd sit down and tell me his life story. People do all the time. I think I'm that sort of type. Probably goes with the territory. Except he's not sure he should. It's a curious thing. Or perhaps I really am just plain boring. 'And how are the wedding preparations coming along?' I offer up. 'Any progress on the fur front at all?' This, too, however, fails to engage his full attention. He smiles and says 'hmm, hem,' then 'no, hmm, not really,' but he seems more taken with the chip in the base of his glass.

'I don't doubt it,' I say. 'In my experience, teenagers' principles are much more robust than they're given credit for. And quite rightly so.'

'That's about the size of it,' he agrees. He sips some more Amaretto, but in the manner of someone who's got something to get to and needs to get it down in a hurry. I don't think he likes it.

'But you'll work something out.'

'I intend *keeping* out.'

I sip some more of mine. It is a girl's drink, after all. And I wonder if I should press things a little. It's so difficult to judge him.

'How *is* Lucy?' I ask him.

'Oh, she's fine,' he says, nodding. 'Away filming right now.' He drinks some more Amaretto. Then he puts his glass down. Then he nods towards the effigy of Dancing Diana. 'Any progress on finding your mum somewhere to live?'

Clearly not, then. 'God,' I say, with feeling. 'Don't start me on that.'

'Like that, eh?'

'Precisely.'

'Right,' he says. 'I won't then.'

'Won't what?'

'Won't start you on that.'

I laugh. But it's a pathetic little excuse for a laugh, and is immediately swallowed by a much bigger silence. He seems lost for things to say. And now I am as well. Fancy! *Me!* 'Okay,' I say, trying not to sound desperate about it. 'So how about you start me on something else instead.'

'On what?'

I spread my palms. 'Some other conversational avenue. Something not involving my mother. Something that won't make me sound like a spiteful old baggage. "Have you read any good books lately?" Something like that.'

He blinks at me, confused and also, I think, a bit horrified. He doesn't know many physiotherapists, clearly. Banal conversation is our stock in trade. Then he clears his throat. 'Er...so have you?'

'Yes, I have, as it happens. I've just finished *Serious*. John McEnroe's autobiography. Been sitting on my pile for ages, but I've literally just finished it. On the plane. It's a thumping good read. You can borrow it if you like.'

'I've already read it.'

'Did you like it?'

'Yes, I did.'

'He's really good, isn't he?'

'At tennis?'

'I meant at writing. Though he's very good at both. How's your leg?'

He looks down at it as if he'd forgotten it existed. But then, perhaps he has. 'Actually, it's much better, thank you.'

'Are you going to book some more physio for it?'

'D'you think I should?'

'Yes.'

'Then I will.' He picks up his glass again and peers at the contents. Then peers at me. 'I'm sorry,' he says. 'But this is vile.'

Spike, at this point, having presumably noticed that our chat has limped to an absolute last straw of excruciating-ness, begins scratching at the back door in a point-making sort of way.

Now it's me that's checking the time. Poor Spike must be cross-eyed by now. I push my chair back and stand up. 'He's waiting for his walk,' I say.

'Oh,' says Gabriel Ash, pinging up from his own chair as if ejected via a slingshot. 'I'm sorry. I'm holding you up. I'd better get off and let you get on, hadn't I?'

Had he? He now doesn't seem at all sure. God, why are men so useless at communicating? His discomfort is becoming louder than my mother's purple lycra. And, like my mother, is just crying out to be noticed, it seems. 'There's no need,' I say, wondering quite why that should be. Is he just plain old lonely while Lucy's away? I must remember he's only recently been bereaved too. I get the impression he and his sister aren't close. Perhaps he's just in need of a friend. Like I am right now. I bend down and pick Spike up, decided. 'You know, you could always come with us. We'd like that, Spike, wouldn't we?'

He hovers by his chair, and once again I have a powerful sense that though he doesn't want to stay he doesn't want to go either. Then he leaves it and comes across to stroke the top of Spike's head. Nothing like a dog to help things along. 'He has interesting fur,' he says, leaning closer to inspect it. 'Kind of wavy. What breed is he, exactly?'

'We're not entirely sure. So we've decided he's the bastard love child of Hairy McClary from Donaldson's Dairy and Madame Fifi La Bucket, who escaped from the circus.'

'That so?'

'We like to think so. He does speak the most beautiful French. His mother was a *Bichon Frise*, you see. Used to ride a small bicycle round a big top in Fréjus. Go on. Come with us, why don't you? If you've nowhere else to be, that is. You can keep me company.'

'I thought you talked to the dog.'

'Don't be silly,' I say. 'I only speak English.'

A version of it, at any rate. Though not, perhaps, his.


We do the same route most days, if we've time, Spike and I. We walk to the end of my road, down the next and round the corner. Then up Cathedral Road and into Sophia Gardens. Where we mess around a bit with his little rubber bone.

The trees that line the river are becoming smudged with patches of banana and mustard, but it's still a green summer sward that greets us in the park. Gaggles of after school teenagers mess about with balls and eat crisps, while lone joggers weave their way around them.

Having to walk as well as talk seems to be good for Gabriel Ash. He's left his jacket in my kitchen and has rolled up his sleeves, and thus unbuttoned he looks altogether more, well, unbuttoned. Though only marginally, it seems; when I ask him about his father's stash of memorabilia and how he feels about it all, he tells me quick as you like that it doesn't change anything, and in tones that suggest that it isn't about to, either, so there seems little else to be said. So I move on to his daughter, about whom he's much more talkative, and ascertain that he wasn't ever married to her mother; they had a brief fling that wasn't ever going to be going anywhere, and she didn't know she was pregnant till after they split. But he supported her through it and has done so ever since. And when I comment that a lot of men would have made a bolt for the hills at that point, he seems genuinely shocked that I might assume he'd do likewise. How could he look himself in the eye if he abandoned his own flesh and blood?

'Plus,' he adds, ruefully. 'You haven't had the pleasure of meeting her terrifying Italian Grand *Mama*.'

Or the pleasure of having your own father abandon you, which I imagine is much more the point. 'So this is a first, then?' I ask him. 'Getting married?'

'Indeed,' he says, pushing a hand across his hair.

'Exciting.'

'If stressful.'

'Oh, they're always that, aren't they?' I pull Spike's bone from my pocket and reach down to unclip his lead.

'So I'm told,' he says quietly, watching me. 'So I'm told.'

Walking dogs, on the whole, is not a dangerous pastime. But even before it does, I can see, without a doubt, that on this occasion anyway, it's going to break with tradition. That it's an accident waiting to happen. I think people in my line of work do tend to have a bigger visual vocabulary about such things – all those years and years of listening to excitably recounted traumas. Or perhaps it's just because people who deal daily with the fall-out from injuries are more aware than most of how readily accidents *do* happen.

But I clearly don't see it soon enough. I throw the bone a few times, and Spike, legs like little pistons, races joyfully to catch it. And then, just as I lob the bone into the air again, out of the corner of my eye, I see him. An Airedale, *the* Airedale; the scourge of the park. He wears a heavy leather collar and he travels alone. I don't know who he belongs to because I've never seen his owner. I suspect they let him off the leash and then tootle off and go shopping.

Leaving him to terrorise the likes of *my* dog. 'That bloody Airedale!' I say, already now in motion, following the trajectory of the now airborne bone. There's no question that the Airedale's going to reach it before him, but possession is not always nine-tenths of the law. Not in the dog world, at any rate. But because Spike doesn't realise he's not an Alsatian, once the Airedale takes possession he's ready to do battle, and charges across the park in pursuit.

Gabriel, whose legs are much longer than mine, sees what's happening and starts running too, and soon – *quelle surprise* – overtakes me. But just as he's closing in on the rogue canine, Spike, clearly keen to go for safety in numbers, suddenly changes course and runs right across his path.

And I know, I just *know* someone's going to get hurt. I'd like to think it might be a some*thing* – that bloody Airedale, to be specific – but as he's already a good ten metres clear by this time, I know that it will be the some*one* today. And I'm absolutely right. Because three seconds after my premonition hits me, Gabriel, though vaulting Spike with the grace of an Olympian, makes a miscalculation by forgetting that he isn't one, and collapses heavily, awkwardly, down onto the grass.

The Airedale, by this time, is cantering away with Spike's bone, and Spike himself, all out of puff now, can do nothing more useful than yap out a tirade of doggy abuse. I reach Gabriel a scant five seconds or so later, by which time all the colour has drained from his face. He's lying on the ground in an embryonic crescent, rolling back and forth and clutching his knee. Were he playing for Liverpool, he'd be yellow card impressive. Except today there are no free kicks on offer and hence no dramatics; this is real. He's hurt, that much is obvious. I drop down to my knees beside him.

'Oh, Lord, Gabriel! Your knee! That *bloody* dog.'

'I'm okay,' he says. He's still short of breath as he speaks. And he patently isn't okay.

'No you're not. Where does it hurt, exactly? And did you feel anything? Did you feel a popping sound?'

He shakes his head. Manages a grim smile. 'No,' he says. 'No. Thank God. I've been there already. No. Just a medium sized dagger up the thigh. God, I'm so stupid.'

'No. I'm the stupid one. I don't know what I was thinking, letting you charge off after them like that.' I cast my eyes around. 'On this wet bloody grass. It's lethal.'

He pushes himself up into a sitting position and gingerly flexes and unflexes his leg. 'It'll be okay,' he says, exploring the area with his fingers. 'Don't worry.'

'Right,' I say, worrying anyway. 'We need to get you sorted out.' I swivel to look around me. 'That'll do,' I say, gesturing to the rank of benches that flank the path at the edge of the park. 'Let's get you up and over there, and then I can run back and fetch my car.'

He shakes his head. 'There's no need. I can walk.'

'You absolutely can't. If you've torn that ligament again – and I suspect you might well have – I'm certainly not going to allow you to walk back.'

'*Really*,' he persists. He's looking less pale now and his expression is determined. 'I walked a good deal further when I ruptured the thing in the first place, believe me. Come on. Give me a hand up and let's see how we're doing.'

I help haul him up and he grunts as I do so. 'Gabriel, it is really no bother whatsoever for me to go and fetch my car. It'll only take me five minutes, and –'

'No need,' he says firmly. 'Look, let's give it a go, eh? If I can lean on you, I can avoid putting too much weight on it. It'll be fine. Come on. If I can get as far as that bench, I can get back to yours. Come on.' He grins. 'And if it turns out I can't, then you can give me a piggyback, can't you?'

Spike, by now, has given up all hope of getting his bone back, and doesn't kick up his usual fuss when I clip his lead back on.

'Sorry, mate,' Gabriel says to him, having got the hang of including Spike in the conversation, which is sweet of him. 'I did my best.'

'Woof,' says Spike. 'Bloody Airedale.'

That bloody Airedale, I decide, has a great deal to answer for. Though, at that point, I have no idea *how* much.

# Chapter 22

'SO THIS IS HOW we do it, okay? You put your right arm around my shoulder, okay? That's it. And I'll put my left around your waist –'

'And then we do the hokey-cokey and we turn around, right?'

'Don't be silly. Concentrate. And then we walk in synchrony.'

'Dancing now, is it?' He took a step. 'Ow!'

'Right. This is no good, is it? I'm going to get the car.'

'No, no. Sorry. Sorry, miss. We walk in synchrony. Okay.'

'So go on, then. Take it more carefully this time. Put your weight on *me*. That's it. How does that feel?'

'Er. Like I've torn my anterior cruciate ligament. Again.'

'Yes, I think I knew that. But how does it feel? How much does it hurt? Can you actually put any weight on it at all?' We took a step. 'How was that?'

'Not too bad.' We took another. 'That's okay. No, that's fine. See? No problems. Mind you, you must get sick of doing this, don't you?'

'What?'

'Living on a perpetual busman's holiday. First your mother, and now me. What a pair.'

I laughed. 'There is zero comparison. You may be heavier on the back but believe me, Gabriel, you are infinitely lighter on the ears.'

'Like that, is it?'

'It tends to get that way, yes. When it's twenty-four / seven.'

'But hopefully not for too much longer, though. Yes?'

We had to stop then, so Spike could make the acquaintance of a slug that was slithering across the pavement and into the road. Where it would surely die a horrible death.

'In theory,' I said. 'But the trouble is that she has absolutely no interest in leaving.'

He squeezed my shoulder. 'Why would she when she's got the likes of you on tap, eh?'

Quite. *Quite.* 'Do you think it's morally reprehensible,' I asked him, 'not to want to have your mother to live with you?'

'Depends on the mother,' he said. 'Depends on the you. Depends on the circumstances, doesn't it?'

'Would you?'

'Have had my mother to live with me? I doubt it.'

'And you wouldn't feel guilty?'

'It never came up.'

'But you wouldn't? If it had done? Even if she'd asked you?'

'I don't imagine she would have.' I felt him shrug. 'But if she had...well...yes, still a 'no', probably.'

'On what grounds?'

'On the grounds that it wouldn't have worked.' He lifted his free hand and drew it across his jaw. And, Spike done, we resumed our slo-mo three-legged-race walking. 'But, you know, it's not even that. It was never an issue. She was too independent. I lived away lots. It just wasn't expected. She always made it clear that if she became ill or infirm we must promise to put her in a home.'

Much in the same way that I do with my boys. Much in the way most parents do. But my mother is not like most parents. 'But what if things changed?' I persisted. 'You know, when it came to it? What if she changed her mind? Wouldn't you feel guilty then?'

He shrugged again. 'I honestly don't know. That's the truth. How could I?' He shook his head. 'Hey, you know, morally reprehensible is a bit strong, don't you think? I don't think there's any *moral* obligation involved. Yes, you have a moral obligation to look after your children, but I'm not sure that holds true when it's the other way around. Do you?'

'I guess not.'

'I mean, people tend to do it because they want to. Because it feels right.'

'But what if it doesn't?'

He shrugged. 'Then you don't.'

'Just like that?'

We stopped for Spike again, and he turned around to face me. There was a blade of grass stuck in his hair. 'You know,' he said. 'You've just got to do what you think is best for *you*.'

'But what about what's best for her?'

'Abbie, I can't comment. I don't know either of you well enough. Look, all I know is that if it feels all wrong it probably *is* all wrong. Whatever the reason –'

'Oh, God, there are *so* many reasons.'

We continued walking. 'Then you mustn't feel you should.'

'I know that. *Rationally* I know that. But I just feel so *guilty*.'

He grinned then. Nudged me. 'Hey,' he said. 'So do I!'

'About your father?'

'God, no. I didn't mean that. About *you*. About the position we've put you in.'

'It's not your fault. This point could – probably would – have happened eventually.'

'But not now. Not so unexpectedly.'

I smiled. 'I guess five years in which to prepare would have been nice. To cram a life in. Have some fun. I just don't feel *ready* for all this stuff, you know? You're right. It has all been a little bit sudden.'

'I know. And I'm sorry.'

'You don't need to apologise.'

'But you know,' he said, stopping again of his own volition, causing me this time to backtrack two steps and turn around. 'About the house sale and everything? I know you must feel badly about it all, but, well, there's quite a bit more to it than you probably think.'

I began to shake my head. Shrugged. 'Well, that's…'

'With my sister. Corinne's in a bad place in her marriage right now.'

'I'm sorry.'

'Her husband… Well, in words of one syllable, he…well, he's been violent.'

'Oh, God, that's *awful*.'

And shocking. And completely unexpected. Though not to him, obviously. He nodded grimly. 'Not to the kids, thank God, but to her. And it's got worse this past year. She has to leave him. Get away. Take the children. And my father's death…the house and everything…well, it's obviously not the best way for it to happen, but at least it finally gives her the chance.'

'I'm so sorry,' I said again. 'I really had no idea.'

208

'Why would you? You don't know them. And in any case, who ever does?' He fell silent. We hobbled in silence a little further. Who indeed, I thought. She'd seemed so self-possessed, so confident. So in control. How easy, I thought, it is to misjudge people. How complex and unfathomable other lives could be.

We'd reached the junction of my road by this time. 'I'm glad you told me,' I said, as we carefully dismounted and then mounted the kerbs. 'I know it doesn't make any difference to anything, but, well, if nothing else, it makes me realise I don't have a whole lot to complain about, do I?'

'I don't know. You tell me. Mother notwithstanding, of course.'

'No,' I said firmly. 'I don't. I have two healthy sons, and a job that I love, and a nice home, and I'm pretty fit, and…well…er…my knees are both intact.' I grinned. He didn't.

'And what else?' he asked, voicing my very thoughts.

I shrugged. 'And nothing. Isn't that enough?'

'I don't know,' he said, turning. 'Is it? You tell me.'

I was just tussling with how best to answer that one, when it was answered for me anyway. Charlie, clutching a carrier bag, was walking up my garden path.

He'd already seen me. Seen us. *Was* seeing us. He raised an arm to wave. 'Who's that?' asked Gabriel.

'Ah,' I said, letting go of his hand to wave back. 'That's…um… Charlie. He…I…we used to work together. At the hospital. Before I joined the clinic.'

'Oh, right,' he said lightly. We continued our jerky progress up the road.

By the time we reached the house, Charlie had already deposited the carrier bag on the doorstep and was making his way back down the path.

'Just thought I'd drop your things off,' he said as he approached us. Then he gestured to Gabriel's leg. 'Hello?' he said. 'Have we got an injury here?'

I nodded. 'Torn ligament, we think. Nothing too dramatic.'

'Oh, dear,' he said, stooping to stroke a now belly-up Spike, while Gabriel and I manoeuvred our way around the gate. Then he straightened and stuck a hand out. 'Charles Scott-Downing,' he said.

'Gabriel Ash,' said Gabriel, removing his own hand from my shoulder to shake it.

Their eyes locked in masculine appraisal for a moment, very obviously and naturally attempting to calculate what part the other man played in my life. Which was novel, if uncomfortable, provoking unwelcome stirrings of the furtive nature of the life I'd lived these past months. 'I'm sorry,' said I, wishing he'd been a little more specific about my things. Things from work, perhaps. Things *for* work. *Some*thing at least. 'I should have introduced you,' I added, hastily. 'Gabriel is Hugo's son. You remember Hugo?' Charlie nodded. 'How are you, anyway?'

'I'm just fine,' he said. He looked it. Hale and hearty. Lightly suntanned. Much like the Charlie I'd first become infatuated with. Except not. Because that Charlie didn't really exist. He was a construct; a full-blown romantic ideal. A hero on which to hang the hook of a silly crush. But all things must pass. And this had. I felt gladdened. He smiled at me. 'You?'

'I'm fine too,' I said.

'Your mother?'

'Getting there. Almost stickless now.'

'Well, hurrah for that!' he said brightly.

I turned to Gabriel. 'Charlie replaced my mother's knee.'

'Oh, I see.' He nodded.

'Well,' said Charlie. 'Let's hope *yours* remains in one piece, at least. You're in capable hands, at any rate. Um. Well. Best be off, I guess.' He stepped around Spike and placed a kiss on my cheek.

'Thanks for bringing my things round,' I said.

'You're very welcome. Take care, now.'

We watched him cross the road and get into his car, and then headed up the path ourselves. I scooped up the carrier as I put the key in the front door, re-locating it and its incriminating contents to the third step up the stairs. Though there was really no reason for me to do so, I felt strangely uncomfortable with the notion that Gabriel might deduce what we'd been.

'Right,' I said, helping him over the doorstep and into the kitchen. 'Rice is what we need here. Come on. Let's get that leg up.'

He sat down heavily on the kitchen chair I pulled out for him. 'Rice?'

'Yes. Rice. R.I.C.E.' I pulled out a second chair and dragged it round to face the other. 'Haven't you heard that before? Rest, Ice, Compression and Elevation. Come on. I'll help you.' I reached to do so. 'Except…' I stopped. 'There's a thought. You're going to have to take your jeans off, aren't you?'

He winced as he straightened his leg out in front of him again. Then he smiled. 'Yes. I suppose I am, aren't I? My, you certainly know how to sweep a guy off his feet. What an afternoon this is turning out to be!' He pulled himself upright again. 'Er…'

'Tell you what,' I said, ingesting his comment and realising that perhaps having a man in his pants in my kitchen was not the most professional way to proceed. 'I'll pop up and get you Seb's bathrobe. Won't be long.'

'There's really no need,' he said, unbuckling his belt.

There absolutely was, of course, so I skipped off up the stairs to get it anyway. And the letter about Seb that I wanted him to translate. Take his mind off the throbbing while I bound his leg, perhaps. But by the time I got back downstairs with them both, the jeans were hanging over the back of a chair, and he (barelegged now, and with shirt tails covering said pants) was back on the chair again, grunting as he bent over to inspect his knee. There were coils of damp hair sticking to the back of his neck. It had been no small thing, him walking all that way. I should have insisted. Should have been firmer. I tried not to worry about the proximity of his pants.

'Here,' I said, coming around the table and shunting his shoes underneath it. 'Let me get that up on that chair for you.'

'It's okay. I can manage.'

'I'm quite sure you can, but I shall do it even so. It's me that got you in this state in the first place, after all.' I eased it up on to the chair seat and then grabbed another seat pad to give it a bit of extra height. That done, I fetched an ice pack from the freezer.

'No peas, then?' he asked, as I gently placed it across his knee.

'No peas. We have all mod cons round these parts.' I straightened. 'And two paracetamol, I think. And a cup of tea. A cup of tea, yes?'

'You know I can't think of a single thing I'd like more at this moment. Except perhaps another Amaretto.'

'Oh! Then –'

He winked. 'Only kidding.'

So I made a pot of tea and sorted some food out for Spike and rummaged for some biscuits in the cupboard. The light was beginning to fade now, and the kitchen was growing dusky. It was a pleasant enough gloom, but hardly useful right now. I went across and switched on the lights at the wall, and then, on an impulse, to cheer the place up, I lit my little row of scented tealights on the windowsill above the sink. They flickered gaily, dancing in the slight draught from the hall.

'Right, then,' I said when I was done. 'No football for you for a bit, I don't think.'

He grimaced. 'Right now I can't imagine for a moment that I'd want to kick a feather, much less a ball.'

'You know,' I said, coming round to join him at the table with two mugs. 'You really do have to be careful, though. You've obviously been left with some residual weakness. You've got to remember you're not so young any more.'

'Gee, thanks for that.'

'But you do. Contact sports are so risky. You wouldn't believe the number of horrific injuries I've seen over the years in men of a certain age who still think they're teenagers.'

'I hope you're not suggesting I take up golf.' He sipped his tea. 'You're painting a very gloomy picture here, you know.'

'Oh, it's not that bad. Not quite yet, anyway. But you do need to exercise those thigh muscles properly. It's really important that you do them regularly. You're coming in next week, aren't you? Remind me to show you how to do them properly. I'll give you a sheet to take home.'

'Yes, miss.'

'Right, then,' I said, getting up from my own chair and coming around the table. 'Let's take a look and see how we're doing.' I took the pad, now just coolish, from his knee, and made a gentle exploration of its contours. The swelling had got no worse, thankfully. If tear it was, it was hopefully quite minor. I ran my fingers over his skin, feeling the hard line of his original scar.

'You know, this doesn't look too bad now,' I said. 'How's it feeling?'

He leaned forward to inspect it himself. 'Not too bad. Not sitting here with you doing that, at any rate. A little stiff, that's all.' He sat back again, his mug cradled in both hands, while I pulled my chair around so I didn't have to bend. He wasn't the only one getting a bit creaky. I'd been too long in the car and on the plane. Yesterday suddenly seemed a long time ago. His arrival here at tea time only slightly less so.

'You have a very gentle touch,' he said. I looked up at him and smiled.

'When I'm not pummelling you mercilessly, you mean.'

'And soft hands. Like a surgeon.' His gaze moved beyond me, towards the window. 'You know, I hope you don't have nosy neighbours,' he observed. 'They'll think you're engaged in unnatural practices.'

'With a *knee*?'

'It's been known.' He sipped his tea while I went and put the ice pack back in the freezer. 'It's a very tactile sort of a profession, yours, isn't it?' he said.

I nodded. 'But then I'm a very tactile sort of a person.'

He smiled. 'I suppose you'd need to be, wouldn't you? I mean, it must be strange going to work every day and getting to grips with the intimate parts of absolute strangers. Don't you find it strange?'

I shook my head. 'I've been doing it so long I don't even think about it. It's just what I do.'

'You don't ever feel self-conscious?'

'Occasionally. I guess I do, a little, right now, with you sitting in my kitchen in your underwear.' He smiled at this. 'But, no. Not really. It's what I do. It's just work.'

'But *they* must. You know. Sometimes. Your patients.'

'Sometimes. When they're new. But never for long. Five minutes of my twittering at them and they soon forget to be.'

213

'But it's still very intimate, isn't it?'

I shrugged. 'I guess so. But like I say, I've always been a very huggy, touchy-feely sort of person, so it feels perfectly natural.'

He drained his mug. 'Runs in the family, then?' he observed.

But it was an observation that didn't immediately have resonance for me. 'I'm not sure about that,' I said.

'I was thinking of your mother.'

Which had even less resonance. 'My *mother*? God, no.'

'Really?' He looked surprised. 'She's always struck me that way.'

I shook my head. 'That's not my mother. That's Diana Garland.' I said the name with her customary flourish. 'Different animal altogether. The public persona and the actual person are not the same at all. Far from it. We were pretty light on cuddles and hugs in our house. After my dad died, in any rate.'

'That's sad.'

'I guess I didn't know any different. That's just the way she is. She finds intimacy difficult. Always has.' I laughed. 'And I don't doubt a psychologist might draw some conclusions from that about why I chose to go into the profession that I did.'

And leave home and go to college ( husband-to-be number three had already been installed by this time), and then rush off and get married and have my babies so young. Which *was* something I'd thought about. And very probably true.

'Anyway,' I said. 'It's actually very good for you to have another person touch you. You know, at least half of what makes physio work – for lots of people, anyway – is just that basic physical contact. You know, some of my patients – particularly now I'm working in the clinic – well, for some of them it's the only physical contact they have with another human being from one week to the next. Can you imagine that?'

'I don't think I've ever really thought about it. But now you mention it…' he gestured to my hands now, which had come to rest around his calf muscles. 'You know, you don't have to stop doing that on my account.'

Napping on the job, in fact. 'Oh.' I could feel myself blushing. 'Right. Sorry.'

'…I suppose that really is quite something to contemplate.'

'I seem to contemplate it all the time right now. You know, with my eldest being not here. You take it so much for granted when your children are small and then...' I tail off. 'Actually, I shouldn't have said that, should I? I suppose you never did take it for granted.'

He shook his head now. 'Er...no.'

Which left a melancholy flavour in the air once again. How transient, how quickly over, all the stages of life were. And how little you realised the fact while you lived them. He was right. How very quickly it was all over, and golf beckoned.

But not just yet. I got up and moved past him to go rummage in the cupboard. 'I'm going to strap it for you now. It's elastic bandaging so it won't restrict your freedom of movement too much. You'll need to keep it on overnight and... Ah. Here we are.'

When I turned around he was stretching his arms high above his head. 'God,' he said. 'I'm not sure sitting here is doing me any good after all. I'm stiffening up all over now.'

I started picking at the end of the roll of bandage. What an idiot I'd been letting him run after that bloody dog. He'd been so helpful, so thoughtful, and all he'd got in return was more damage to his knee. 'You will be,' I said wryly. 'That was quite a fall you had. You'll be stiff as a board by the morning.'

He put his arms back in his lap and began slowly rolling his head on his shoulders.

'Tell you what,' I said, leaning over and plopping the bandage in his lap. 'Grab that while I give your shoulders a quick once-over. Can't hurt, can it?'

'I'm not so sure. That sounds worryingly like a contact sport to me.'

'No, really,' I said briskly, splaying my fingers across his shoulder blades and smoothing my thumbs into the gullies either side of his spine. 'You forget, I'm a qualified sports masseuse.'

'I know,' he said. 'It says so on your business card. Ouch!'

'Relax. You're all hunched up where you've been tensing. Probably that walk back. I wish you'd let me get the car.'

I felt his shoulders begin to soften. 'I'm very glad you didn't,' he said. 'Because now you're here doing this.'

And even then I didn't fathom. I'm not even sure he had. 'Least I can do,' I said firmly. 'Do you good.'

Though I'm not sure the same could have been said about me. Because it was now fully dark outside, and I hadn't pulled the blind yet, I could see our reflections in the kitchen window, just as I could when he was here before. Him sitting, eyes closed now, a dreamy half smile on his lips. Me standing behind him. Bent slightly forwards with my elbows sticking out, my hair moving in rhythm with the action of my wrists, in swaying twin curtains either side of my face. My fringe was in my eyes, so I took a breath to blow it, and as I did so I saw that his eyes had now opened. They weren't all the way open. Just half-awake open. Trance-like. Relaxed. And were looking into mine.

'Feel nice?' I asked.

'Mmm,' he said, still gazing at me. Our reflections smiled at each other above the flicker of the candles.

'Good,' I mouthed at his now. 'I'm glad to be of service.' And I continued to work on the muscles of his shoulders, gloriously innocent. Gloriously unaware. Unaware, that was, until I did become aware. Aware that his eyes were now not just looking, but staring. And suddenly in a wholly discomfiting way.

And even as I thought that, I watched his hands leave his lap and his arms travel upwards, till all his fingers were resting on top of my own. I stopped moving, my expression in the window still politely enquiring. But he didn't provide an answer. Just sat perfectly still. We were like a painting in the window now. Or a Byzantine mosaic.

I raised my brows and met his eyes in the window. His hands were hot. 'What's the matter?' I said.

'You know, I really think you'd better stop doing that,' he replied.

When I was about eight, my parents took Pru and I to a bird sanctuary. A swan sanctuary, I think it was. We picnicked in a sunny field next to a farm. We had egg sandwiches, orange squash, crisps and pork pies, and I decided I would organise my feast inside the plastic tray that had held the pork pies. Picnic in hand, I took Pru off to have a potter in the field; there were some cows in an adjacent one, which she wanted to moo at. Except the two fields were separated by a low wire fence. I'd barely brushed it with the tip of my finger when, kapow! – a huge slug of electricity coursed through my body. Just four volts, but it might just as well have been a million. I'd never felt anything so powerful in my life. I leapt feet into the air and screamed my very lungs out. The pork pie was lost forever. The memory was not.

Which is why it came back to me now.

I whipped my hands from beneath his as if jet-propelled. And not knowing quite what to do after I'd done that, I walked across the kitchen and yanked down the roller blind. Not least to shut out the image in the window. My temples were thrumming. My cheeks were on fire. How on earth had I let something like *that* happen? How?

He said nothing. Just cleared his throat. Feigned utter insouciance. Whatever had passed between us wasn't up for debate. Best thing too. Only thing. *What* a thing, frankly. 'Right,' I said briskly, 'let's get this leg strapped then, shall we?'

Normally I'd pop the patient's leg up in my lap at this point, but for reasons that were becoming more insistent by the minute, I didn't. I bent over him instead, issuing a stream of stern entreaties about rest and recuperation and the importance of proper exercise. Anything to ensure that the ever threatening silence could not be left needing something to fill it.

And need there now was. It was growing, expanding. It was all at once as if there was a storm heading in. Right into the kitchen. 'There,' I said, finally. 'That'll do. You're all set. Keep this on overnight and see how you're doing in the morning.'

'Okay,' he said gruffly. 'Right then.' He lowered his leg to the floor and winced a little as he did so. I hardly dared look at him now.

'Not too tight, is it?' I said as I put away the roll of bandage.

'No,' came the answer. 'No. Not too tight.' He seemed almost as embarrassed as I was.

I took his jeans from the chair back. 'I'll…um…let you get back into these then, shall I?'

I turned away and busied myself at the sink while he did so. Wiping all the surfaces that didn't need wiping, fussily blowing out all the tea lights on the windowsill, then wiping down the surfaces all over again. God, how had I let this *happen*?

But happen it had. Still happening, it *was*. I could hear the swish of the fabric as he stepped back into his jeans. First one leg. The good leg. Swoosh. On it went. Then a huff as he balanced to attend to the other. The creak of the table as it took his hand's weight. I could see him in my mind's eye, if not in the window. See him tuck in his shirt. See him do up his fly. See the belt, even as I heard the metal jangle, being fed carefully back into buckle and fixed. And then silence. Then nothing. But it was such a powerful sort of a nothing that still I didn't dare turn around. What the hell had I been thinking, massaging his shoulders? This was not work. We were not in the clinic. How thoroughly stupid was *that*?

I was just trying to arrange my features into something breezy and work-a-day and businesslike and wondering quite how I was going to haul this situation back into some semblance of normality, when I felt his hand touch my hair, at the side of my face.

I spun around, startled. Wide-eyed. A little dizzy. Proper dizzy now in fact, because I'd forgotten to eat. Since the plane. That was it. I racked my brains. I'd had a muffin. Just a coffee and a muffin. Since then I'd had nothing. I was existing on air.

Which right now, we were sharing. He was standing so *close*.

'You have something caught,' he said slowly. 'Right here. In your hair. See?'

He lowered his hand and between his thumb and finger was a little fairy seed inside its gossamer star. It must have caught in my hair in the park. He sat it in his palm and we studied it together, like a pair of zealous biology students on a field trip. 'Thistledown,' he suggested.

'Um, no,' I answered. 'It's rose bay willow herb, isn't it? I think. I'm not sure. We always just called them fairies.'

'In that case,' he said, lifting his gaze to meet my own again. 'Now you have to make a wish.'

His voice was just a whisper. His eyes bored into mine.

'No, you do,' I heard myself say to him. 'You found it.'

He shook his head. 'No, no. You're wrong. It found *you*.'

He took my hand then and placed it over his upturned one. So the fairy in his palm wouldn't become skittish and fly away. 'There,' he said. 'Go on. What do you want to wish for?'

'Gabriel, I –'

'What? What's the matter?'

'You know, right now, I don't think I'm up for making any wishes.' I licked my dry lips. 'Besides, you're not supposed to tell anyone what you're wishing for or it doesn't come true.'

His hands were still cupping my own, between us. I felt his thumb trace a gentle yet deliberate arc ever so slowly across the back of my palm. 'Simple,' he said. 'Then I'll wish your wish for you. Sort of by proxy. Okay?'

'Er, okay,' I said, conscious even as I said it that there was something that was far from okay about all this.

'Close your eyes, then.'

My heart thumped. 'I don't think I dare to.'

We could almost rub noses now. He smiled. 'Why ever not?'

'Because if I close my eyes now, I think your wish might come true.'

'I told you, it's *your* wish.'

'You don't know what I'm wishing.'

'You want to know something, Abbie McFadden? I think I *do*.'

'So you lied, then.'

'Lied?' He looked amused now. 'About what?'

'About how confident you are about your skills of prediction.'

I felt the pressure of his hand on mine increase as he spoke. 'Well,' he whispered. 'There's only one way to find out.'

I don't know what happened to the fairy exactly. Though Dancing Diana might, of course.

# Chapter 23

'GABRIEL ASH,' SAYS CANDICE, drawing little spiral doodles on the appointments book. 'You know, it occurred to me just then. Isn't that the name of that character in that film?'

It's now Thursday and Gabriel Ash has just telephoned to cancel his appointment for physio next week. She hasn't said more and I can't bring myself to ask her, because I can't trust myself not to turn beetroot. Or weep.

'What film?' I ask her.

'You know. That one with Alan Bates in. In the Sixties. No, Seventies, probably. Come on, you *know*. And Julie Christie, wasn't it? Of the book by Thomas Hardy. God, I've even read the bloody thing. And she was called Bathsheba. Come on, you *do* know. Anyway, wasn't *he* called Gabriel Ash?'

Candice seems to think I know most things, which is flattering. And Candice knows much more than I give her credit for. Which is humbling. So easy to make assumptions about people. But I do know this, because I've read the book too. '*Far From the Madding Crowd*.' I tell her. 'That's the one you mean.' I think some more. Even thought it pains me to do so. 'But he was called Gabriel Oak.'

'That's it!' She looks pleased. 'That's the one. Gabriel Oak, Gabriel Ash. I knew it was something familiar. He was a shepherd, wasn't he?'

I suppose, I realise, that it was inevitable that he'd do that. And for the best. Yes, definitely for the best, all things considered. It won't work any more, him coming here. It can't. I really hope I never, ever see him again.

'Hellooo?' Candice flicks her fingers. 'You still there? He was a shepherd, wasn't he?'

'Yes. Yes, he was.'

'Hey, Gabriel Ash would make a good shepherd, don't you think? Because he'd be clued up on all that red sky at night stuff, wouldn't he?'

I turn the appointment book around to see how the rest of my day is going to shape up. 'I think it's the other way around, isn't it?' I say. 'Shepherds are generally good at forecasting the weather, yes. But I'm not sure being good at weather forecasting necessarily means you're also good with sheep.'

Or forecasting generally. I wish *I* could have forecast what's happened to me. Wish he had. And way before what happened in my kitchen. How could I have let it? How could I? 'Well,' says Candice, winking. 'I'll just have to ask him when he's next in, lovely, won't I?' Then her grin widens and she whoops and claps her hands. 'Hey, but he will be! He's Welsh, love 'im, isn't he?' Which pronouncement she finds so completely hilarious that her cheeks run with tears, she chokes on her coffee, and, still doubled with laughter, she has to retire to the loo.

Which he won't be, of course. Any more than I expected him to keep this appointment. Some things are for the best, after all.

When I was a teenager, I read a book by Malcolm Bradbury. It was called *Eating People is Wrong*. I don't recall the plot now; it's just the title that's stayed with me. Such a clever one. So gloriously self-evident a phrase.

Kissing people is wrong, too. There are lots of occasions when it's not wrong, obviously, but there is still a kernel of resonance between the one and the other. Yes, yes. You can kiss people on the cheek, kiss your babies all over, kiss your relatives, your friends, the more fragrant of your colleagues. But kissing – proper kissing – kissing of a sexual nature – has a very well defined code of conduct. You don't just kiss people. *Ad hoc. Per se.* Not without a clear invitation to do so. Because a kiss is almost always the answer to the question that our reproductive genes are continually asking us. Would you like to procreate us with this person? It is a statement of intent. Of bodily commitment. A statement that pre-supposes a mutual acknowledgement that the reproductive process is, at the very least, a distinct possibility. And if not now, then at some future time. Which is not something one tends to think about much. But that's what kissing is. That's what kissing's *for*. Which is why women tend to feel so uncomfortable when they wake up on the morning after the office Christmas party and think 'ohmyGod. *Him*! I *didn't*!'

Sometimes that's because you are frankly repulsed, but often – too often – it's not that at all. Sometimes it's because they are with someone else. Procreatively committed already.

None of which was going through my mind then. Far from it. Having thought the brace of thoughts I am biologically programmed to think (*oh! Gabriel's kissing me* and *he – no, we – shouldn't!*), I then stopped thinking rationally altogether. Utterly.

Which is, of course, why human biology works so very well, and by extension, why babies get made.

And so we kissed. We kissed hesitantly, lightly at first. A mere featherlight brushing of lips against lips; a tentative exploration of alien skin. But kisses are governed by forces of nature, so unless something crops up to call a halt to proceedings (getting snagged on a tongue stud, inability to breathe, discovering the kissee has breath that could fell a hippo), then they tend to gather pace. Because that's how they work.

And so this, had you joined the proceedings at that point, is how you'd have found us. Kissing one another with such terrible abandon that had the world seen fit then to slip off its axis and hurtle into the sun, we'd neither of have been any the wiser. All I knew was that where I'd begun this thinking 'Oh! Goodness! Gabriel!' my thoughts had long since changed both their tone and their timbre, and centred on thinking 'ohhh, *Gabriel*…' instead. And as so often happens when kisses reach that level of intensity (or, rather, that point where the kissing itself becomes mostly a metaphor for the carnal intentions you are attempting to pursue via the judicious and speedy shedding of clothing) Gabriel, similarly incoherent on the 'ohhh' front, had started to unbuckle his belt.

The very same belt he'd only buckled up minutes earlier.

Was it that that did it, perhaps? That necessary logistical break in the proceedings? Who knows. But pause it was. And into pauses fit thoughts. And not necessarily edifying ones.

'Oh my God,' he said suddenly. Presumably having thought some. Leaping away as if yanked by the hair. 'Oh, my *God*,

Abbie. I'm so sorry.' He was shaking his head now. Backing away from me. 'God, what am I doing? *No*.'

He was speaking mainly to himself as he said this, but even so, it hit home. Because the word 'no' is not the word one usually expects to be hearing from a man when he's speaking to a woman at such moments. Isn't it normally the other way around?

I don't know what it's like to be a man, obviously, but at that moment, now *sans* my T-shirt, very nearly *sans* more, standing like a window display mannequin by my dishwasher, blinking, appalled, under the way-too-bright strip light, I kind of felt I might have an insight or two. All those boys I'd beached up at rejection central as teenagers; no I don't want to dance. No you can't touch my bra. Don't do this. Don't do that. No I don't want to touch it. I've got a headache. You've got acne. Ugh. Put that away.

Yup. That was me now. Discarded by the dishwasher. By a man who had no business kissing me *anyway*. But more to the point, oh, *so* much more to the point, I had no business kissing *back*. What on earth had possessed me to *do* such a thing? And even more chilling, what might have happened next, had not Gabriel's conscience (and almost married status, presumably) kicked in? Sex on the floor with my mother looking on? In the absence of gonads and a stiff upper lip, I immediately burst into tears.

Gabriel, still grimacing and reeling as dramatically as if personally coached by my sainted dear mother, in fact, took a few more awkward steps backwards, fetching up eventually against the kitchen table, arms held up, palms forward, almost in supplication. As if at the behest of a bank robber with a sawn off shotgun.

With his shirt hanging out and all his buttons undone. I gaped. Had *I* done that? Yes. Every last one. I snatched my T-shirt from the floor and scrabbled my way back into it, to spare the blushes of my still heaving bosom.

He was breathing hard. He looked stricken. 'God, I'm so sorry,' he said. 'I am so, so sorry. I don't know what I was thinking. Oh, Abbie, I'm so sorry. I –'

'Stop saying sorry!' I snapped at him. I was shaking all over. Top to bottom. Head to toe. Nerve ending to nerve ending.

Erogenous zone to erogenous bloody zone. We had so very nearly...so *very* nearly... 'God, Gabriel. Why did you *do* that?'

I turned around and wrenched some kitchen roll from the holder. But I did it so hard that it just kept on coming, spooling round and around and spewing all over the draining board. Which brought on another wave of almost hysterical tears. I ripped off a wodge of the stuff and slapped it over my face. 'Why did *I* do that? God!' I sobbed into the kitchen roll for a good few seconds, and when I finally lowered it – tremulous, mortified – he was rattling through his shirt buttons as if competing in a school getting-dressed competition. Last one fully-clothed is a ninny!

'I'm sorry,' he said again, furiously stuffing his shirt back into his jeans (no buckle in play now, I noticed). 'I shouldn't have done that. I know I shouldn't. Oh, God –' His groan was both heartfelt and damningly impressive. 'Oh, God. But it just... Jesus.' He looked horrified. '*You* just –'

'Me??' I screeched. '*Me*?? So this is all *my* fault? Well thanks a lot, I don't think!'

He pushed both hands through his hair and then shook his head. 'God, *no*, Abbie. Mine *entirely*. I'm sorry. I'm *sorry*. I'm not trying to make excuses for myself. I had absolutely no...oh, *God*. I don't know what else to say to you. I just forgot where I was...what I was *doing*.'

'You forgot what you were *doing*? Well, there's a novel concept.'

'You know what I mean.'

'No, I don't know, as it happens. It seems to me –' I reached behind me and tried to do up my bra, '– that you knew *exactly* what you were doing. Every bit as much as I did, in fact.' Which reality hit me like a sledgehammer as I said it. I moved my fingers frenziedly, but I couldn't get it to fasten. My hands were shaking too much. I gave up. 'Seems to me, the only thing *you* forgot was exactly who you were doing it *with*.'

Which made me burst into tears again. So I abandoned the bra strap and went back to the draining board, to get a fresh pile of kitchen roll to staunch it. Then I rounded on him again. 'And then – pow! – you *did* remember, didn't you? Boy, you remembered and then some!' I gulped down a breath. 'Can you imagine?' I asked him, trying but failing to keep my voice level. 'Can you imagine how that makes me feel about *me*?'

He took a step towards me, his expression now morphing (if one wanted to be fanciful about it) into one of lovingly tender concern. 'Abbie,' he said gently. 'I really can't apologise enough. You're so lovely, really you are…and, and, well, you and I…well, it's always been…'

'Been what? Been on the cards that we'd start snogging at some point? Well, I'm sorry, Gabriel, but that's news to me!'

He hesitated at this, and I could see his mind whirring, presumably the better to fashion the delicate words that came next, which were, '…but it's just that…well, there's *Lucy*. I'm *engaged*.' He looked, in saying so, even more appalled now. 'It was just one of those things that happen in the heat of the moment, and –'

'*Whhaatt*!!!' I was so horrified at how entirely he had misunderstood what I had been trying to say that for a second or two I considered violence against him. Just to wipe the sorry slick of compassion from his face and replace it with something less sick-making. 'That's not what I *meant*! God, Gabriel! That is *so* not what I meant!'

He looked completely at a loss now. Which only served to fuel my horror even more. 'I *know* that,' I said. 'I know you're bloody engaged! That's precisely my point!' I yanked out a chair and sat down on it heavily, then put my face in my hands and groaned. I heard him approach and then felt his hand on my shoulder. I snapped my head up again and he jumped back as if stung.

'Abbie, I –'

I flapped my kitchen roll at him. 'This is not *about* you, okay? Neither is it about some mad, tin-pot scheme to lure you from her clutches. As if! God, Gabriel, don't flatter yourself!'

Stung twice, in fact. Still stinging, even. I blew my nose and glared at him. 'Look, Gabriel, just forget it, okay. Just forget it and go home. I feel bad enough about myself as it is without you cluttering up my kitchen looking tragic, okay?'

He didn't. 'Please don't feel bad about yourself, Abbie. This wasn't your fault. It was mine.'

I sometimes think men are irredeemably thick. Some men, at any rate. This one, for sure. I sat back in my chair and considered him. Which hurt.

And in ways I was only now coming to terms with. Don't flatter yourself? Who the hell was I kidding? How powerful, I realised, my denial had been. How overwhelmingly intense was my desire for this man now. Where did that *come* from? How did it happen? Candice was right. Life bloody well *was* a bitch. I shook my head. To clear all such nonsense away. 'No, Gabriel. You're wrong,' I said. 'The kissing bit, yes. That was absolutely your fault. You started it, after all.'

'*Exactly*. So –'

'But the next bit…' I felt my voice wobble. 'The next bit was not. The next bit I did of my own volition entirely. Would perhaps *still* be doing, if *you* hadn't stopped it. So you can apologise all you like but it won't make any difference. Yes, you made it happen – you're a man, after all – but I *let* it happen, which is much more important.'

He tried to smile. 'How very post-feminist of you.'

I didn't smile back. 'You can call it what you like, but the truth is that I knew what I was doing and I shouldn't have done it. Gabriel, we are not in any sort of relationship, you and me. Never have been and never will be. And, yes, you did what you did, and I dare say you're regretting it. But it's different for me. Can't you *see* that? I behaved like a slapper and I hate myself for it, so if you'll excuse me –' I got up from the table again, now. '– I've got to take a shower and you've got to go home.'

Gabriel stood up too now. Extra straight, I think, on purpose. His mouth was hanging open. 'That's an outrageous thing to say!'

But then he would say that, I thought. Because he didn't know the half of it. Didn't know how I'd felt that way already in my life. Didn't know what it felt like to *be* me. I'm wasn't even sure I did. All I knew was that right now I felt dirty and ashamed and appalled with myself.

I shrugged. 'Even so, Gabriel, that's how I feel.'

'But, Abbie, it wasn't *like* that. You shouldn't *think* that. It just happened. I'm a man and you're a woman, and well, we've both been…' Been what? But he didn't seem to know how to begin to explain. 'Abbie,' he finished. 'It just *happened*, okay?'

Which I would, I knew, now have to repent at my leisure. Ad nauseam. But this was pointless. 'In which case,' I said stiffly. 'Let's *forget* it happened then, shall we?'

'We can't leave things like this.'

'What other way would you have us leave things? Come on, please. Let's not drag this out any longer. Like you say, it was a moment of madness, and it's done now. We can't undo it, can we?'

I was already walking out into the hall at this point, and he followed me, reaching across me to collect his jacket from the newel post. 'Look,' he said, once he'd shrugged it over his shoulders. 'Abbie. Please don't hate yourself. You know, I really want you to know that even if anything *had* happened…well, I wouldn't have thought any less of you. Not one iota. *Ever*. You do know that, don't you?'

It was such a wild and ridiculous scenario – him standing there, etching out the cosy hypothetical emotional aftermath of a rash hypothetical coupling on my kitchen floor – that I almost couldn't stop myself from laughing out loud. Wasn't that the ploy most men used as *fore*play? Except he was really in earnest and it really did seem to matter. I wanted to touch him but I dared not. 'Gabriel, don't stress. It was *never* going to happen. You're way too nice a man.'

He looked sad. In disgrace. Ashamed of himself. 'I'm not that.'

'You just *proved* it. And I'm sure Lucy knows it too. She's a lucky woman. Hey, you take care of that knee, now.'

He negotiated the front step and started limping down the path. Then he turned. 'So I'll see you in clinic next week, then.'

I was already closing the front door, so I didn't answer. No point. I already knew he wouldn't.

When I got back into the kitchen, I saw the letter about Seb still sitting on the table. I put it in an envelope, wrote out the address, affixed first class stamps, added 'Airmail' and double underlined it, then walked Spike to the letterbox and slipped the thing in. I'd just have to hope he had a friend who spoke some English. Because I no longer had one who spoke Italian.

*     *     *

Which just goes to show that weathermen, however impressively tooled-up with education and intelligence and complex statistics, do not have a monopoly in predicting the future. Us mere mortals, with our reliance upon instinct and feelings, can be almost – no, probably *are* – as good.

Which insight did nothing to make the day any less depressing. It only led me down avenues I didn't much want to travel. Because all of them led to exactly the same place. My shame. My guilt. My disgust with myself. My utter conviction, once I'd dissected things properly, that this was not Gabriel's fault. It was mine. That, entirely without meaning to, I had, in fact, seduced him. Like he'd said – oh, cruel irony – swept him off his feet.

It wasn't his fault. He was a man. He couldn't help it. I, on the other hand, *could*. The most ridiculous piece of nineteenth-century garbage ever thought up. I *knew* that. It didn't matter. That's still how I felt. And they say we women are emancipated. I wish. Oh, I *wish*.

Which was a shame because this day had already been made depressing enough, what with being bookended by Welsh men-and-sheep jokes at one end and the prospect of my mother's return at the other.

In fact, Pru and my mother have already arrived by the time I get in from work. They've made themselves tea and bought a bag of Welsh cakes, which they are chomping as I enter the kitchen. Dancing Diana is still in the hall where I left her, parked up and gurning beside the dining room door. Oh, the sorry tales she could tell.

Pru gets up to pour a mug of tea for me too.

'I hope you're going to move that thing,' my mother says irritably, nodding towards the open kitchen doorway. 'I nearly had forty fits when I saw it. Wherever did you get it from?'

'Gabriel Ash dropped it round,' I say, feigning a workaday lightness when I mention his name that's feeling ever more difficult to do. 'Corinne found it in the garage. She thought you might want it.'

228

'*Want* it? Abigail, when you get to my time of life, you will come to appreciate that looking at pictures of oneself in the full flush of beauty is about as horrendous a torture that has ever been devised.'

I can think of worse. Far worse. But this *is* from a woman who would only countenance mirror sunglasses if the mirrors were on the inside. Not that I'd know, in any case. I never did have what you might call a 'full flush' of beauty in my youth. It wasn't a given. It always felt like a privilege if any one thought I was pretty. Just pockets here and there when the lighting fell right and I conceded I would basically *do*.

A long and deep pocket in the case of Charlie, admittedly. But that was just a blip. And a damaging one, too. My experience with Gabriel confirms it. Overall (and how much I'd like to return to that state), I've not been used to feeling like that. Not been used to that sort of attention on a regular basis. With Rob, yes, but he was a notable exception. And it was quite possibly why I loved him so much. Because he didn't fancy my mother. What I mostly remember was the dropped jaws of boyfriends when they called round to take me to the pictures.

And I do concede that for my mother the passage of time must hang heavier than for most people. If your self-esteem is so closely connected with your beauty, then its fading must be difficult to bear.

'Why d'you hang on to it, then?' I ask her.

She shakes her head. 'I didn't. That was Hugo. He had a bit of a thing about lurex.' She mimes quote marks around 'thing' and accompanies them with the sort of face that's best not enquired into. So we don't. Not her sex life with Hugo, pur-lease. 'Anyway,' she says. 'How is my poor precious grandson?'

Pru puts tea in front of me. 'He's just fine,' I tell them both, happy to move on to less difficult ground now. 'Quite happy to abort the grand tour for a while, to be honest. He's looking way too skinny. Oh, and he's grown a beard, would you believe? Hang on. I've got a picture in my mobile.' I pull it from my bag and find it.

Pru shrieks when she sees it. 'God, you'd hardly recognise him!'

'I almost didn't. I tell you, Pru, there is nothing that makes you face up to your terrible age than seeing your child with a beard.'

Or indeed, contemplating your ageing mother as a housemate.

'She said anything to you?' I ask Pru while she tootles off upstairs for her reading glasses, the better to do the clutch of Su Dokus that have stockpiled while we've both been away.

Pru glances towards the stairs. 'Actually, I don't want to worry you, Sis, but, yes. She was asking Doug about loft conversions last night.'

'Loft conversions? But you've already got a loft conversion–'

'Er, wakey-wakey. Hello? Engage brain. Not as in my place. As in *here*.'

She moves her eyes heavenwards again, and this time, so do I. '*What*?' I squeak. 'As in here? As in *my* house?'

Pru nods. 'Well, she didn't actually admit as much, of course. She wouldn't risk it. Just told him she was investigating possibilities. She was grilling him about how much it would cost and everything – you know she's had the cheque through, don't you? No, actually. You probably don't. Anyway, she has. And she's clearly got her own ideas about what she wants to do with it.'

'Oh, gawd.' I groan. 'Has she said anything to you about it?'

Pru shakes her head. 'But I've been doing my bit, promise. I spent half the journey here today banging on about how much you're looking forward to having a bit of independence in a couple of years or so – you know, after spending so many years devotedly and slavishly looking after the boys, and what with the divorce, and Rob always having been away so much anyway, and how you really deserve to have some time to yourself, a chance to do all the things you've never been able to, to travel and see the world and have fun blah blah blah.'

'God, you make me sound like I've been Mother Theresa.'

'Well, I thought I'd lay it on a bit. Make her think. Make her see things from where *you* stand. Clear the way a bit.'

'And what did she say?'

Pru tips her head back and snorts at me. 'She said she'd always known that you married the wrong man.'

*     *     *

Pru leaves a little after six, having had a promise extracted that she will, if at all possible, come to see One Black Lung play (from Jake), and another that she'll persist with project Mother (from me).

Mum and I go out on to the doorstep to see her off, and in doing so, the very first thing that catches my eye is the loft conversion the Thomases across the road had done last year, evidenced by two Velux windows amid the roof slates, both with gay yellow roller blinds, at present half closed, to shut out the glare of the low late September sun. I've been up there. It's nice. I think they call it their den. At one time, I might have considered one too. Early on, it was. My post-partum post-impressionist period. When the boys were both small and I only worked part-time and still nursed vague dreams of Doing a Bit of Art.

But now I look across the road and I fashion a bleak (and wholly artless) future, a sort of Jane Eyre/Mrs Danvers in Rebecca type amalgam, in which mother sits in the attic, jotting car registrations, and periodically rapping on the floor with a stick. I'm down in the kitchen, of course, boiling bones to make broth and harbouring unspeakable thoughts.

'Now,' she says, stepping back inside. 'Time I had my lie down, I think. I've promised to be at Kenneth's by seven.'

I follow her indoors. 'Kenneth? Kenneth who?'

'Kenneth, your neighbour?'

'What, you mean Mr Davidson?'

She looks at herself coquettishly in the hall mirror. 'Correct. I'm going round to help him with some postures.'

'Mr Davidson? Postures? What sort of postures?' The mind seriously boggles.

She looks at me via the mirror and rolls her eyes. 'Well, *yoga* postures, obviously.'

'You're teaching him *yoga*?'

She narrows her eyes. 'I don't know why you find that concept so funny, Abigail. You know, you'd do well to be altogether less judgemental generally, in my opinion. He's a very pleasant man.'

'Yeah, right, Mum.' And then I have a thought. 'You don't – I mean, you and him…'

'Oh, for pity's sake! *No*. Honestly, Abigail, the way your mind works is beyond me.'

Still, it does occur to me that Mum working the Garland charms next door will be no bad thing in the short-term at least, as Jake's gig is less than a fortnight away now and they'll be rehearsing their play list with a vengeance. With any luck she'll put Mr Davidson in a deep yogic trance, from which he won't emerge until November.

# Chapter 24

Late Sunday afternoon, and against all predictions, expectations and forecasts, an air of almost palpable excitement is growing in the McFadden household.

Which is something of a relief. It's been almost three weeks since my last brush with Gabriel Ash. But however deeply he's burrowed his way under my skin, I'm relieved to find I'm made of stern enough stuff that I can just about manage to itch without scratching. Compartmentalise, even. Put the whole sorry charade to one side. Just as headaches can be healed by putting pins in one's buttocks, so the dull ache of unrequited romantic yearnings can be to some extent soothed by a robust concentration on all the wonderful things that one has in one's life.

And I do. And it works. For the moment at least. And it seems to be cumulative too. Jake is excited, thus I am excited. Even

Spike is excited because he's very intelligent and knows excitement invariably means extra choc drops and hugs. Sadly, however, there is an air of an entirely different flavour emanating from the phone. Ten past six and I pick up the receiver in my bedroom to find Dee hissing at me in a most un-Dee-like way.

'Abbie?'

'Dee? What is it? What's the matter?'

Her voice is so low as to be barely audible. Not good. 'I need a favour. Can you come round? As in *now*? Can you come round and get me?'

Double not good. 'Get you? Where are you?'

'At home. In the en suite. And Malcolm's…' She takes a breath. 'Malcolm's taken my handbag and my car keys and everything, and I don't have any money and I don't know what to do. And if I don't get out of here soon something bad is going to happen, and I can't get hold of Tim, and –'

Oh, God. 'Dee, what's happening? What's going on?'

'I told him.'

'What, everything?'

'Yes, everything. God, I'm so *stupid*, Abs. What possessed me? Why didn't I do it somewhere public? Abs, I'm scared.'

As well she might be. 'Okay, so just *leave*. Just get out of there. *Go*. Start walking and I'll leave now and I can…'

'I *can't*. I daren't even go downstairs! He's smashed. He's gone ballistic. He's bolted the front door and he's thrown stuff and… God, Abbie, you've *got* to –'

'Okay, okay. I'm coming! I'll –'

Click. A new voice. 'Hello?'

Oh, typical. 'Mum,' I say. 'I'm on the line right now.'

'Oh, I see. I do beg your pardon.' Another click.

'Dee?'

'I'm still here.'

'Are you calling from your mobile?'

'Yes. Thank God. It was on the charger in the bedroom.'

'Good. Right. Stay put. I'm on my way.'

I negotiate the stair treads two at a time. My mother is standing at the foot of them.

'Something the matter?' she enquires over the top of her reading glasses.

Should I call the police, perhaps? Now? Before I leave? 'Yes, actually,' I answer, pulling my jacket from the newel post. 'I have to go round to Dee's house.'

'Only I wanted to know if you might be able to give Celeste and I a lift to Wilfred's on your way to the show.'

'Um…er…I don't know, Mum. It depends on –'

'*Gig*, Nan,' says Jake, emerging from the kitchen with some drumsticks. 'It's not called a show. It's called a gig.'

'Ah, Jake,' I say, turning to him while I pull on my jacket and start looking for my bag. 'I've got to pop over to Dee's. What time do we have to leave here to set up?' My heart, I realise, has already started thumping. Yes, police? No, police? No, police, I decide. It cannot be that bad. Bad but not *that* bad, surely. Can it?

'Like, in half an *hour*, Mum!' says Jake, following me back into the kitchen. 'How long are you going to be?'

'…for Brian's birthday,' continues my mother. 'Only we can't go to Brian's because he's had a flood in his kitchen…it's not too much further. It's only in –'

'Nan,' Jake explains, 'we can't fit you in. Not with the drum kit. There isn't enough room. Mum, you've *got* to be back, okay?'

'Yes I know. And I will. Don't worry,' I tell him, grabbing my mobile from its charger. 'Straight there, straight back. No need to fret.'

And perhaps I'm right, at that. Because when I get to Dee's road there's certainly no sign that anything bad has happened. No flashing lights. No gaggle of concerned neighbours at the gate. No pressmen or riot vans or packs of sniffer dogs or cordons. The house stands, in the watery remnants of a low October sun, as still and serene as any one of its fellows. As houses do. From the outside. Like marriages, I guess.

Which is precisely why I ignore the evidence of my eyes and park the car expecting the worst. This day, I think, as I clamber out and stride purposefully across the road towards their house, has been too long in coming. Dee must be – I calculate – some eighteen or nineteen weeks pregnant. Almost beyond the point that even an idiot could fail to notice. She's been putting it off, I know, and I understand her reasons. There was never going to be a right time to do this. I unlatch the gate and push it open. I don't know where Malcolm is, of course, but if he's in there, there's at least some chance he's watching me do so, and I want him to know I mean business.

Malcolm, who works at the sort of impenetrable job of being something in procurement services for the council (beats me), is quite a big man. Six foot-ish, fairly beefy, good at hefting and digging and also, or so I am informed by Dee, currently drunk. Nothing new there, then. He very often is. Which presents a somewhat worrisome picture. But though I am only five foot five inches tall, slight-to-average of build and not particularly tough, there is one thing that both of us know. That I am not frightened of Malcolm.

This certainty (and the action I'm taking as a consequence) might, of course, prove to be my bloody undoing very shortly, but somehow I think not. I have known Malcolm for over a decade; known him jolly, known him cross, known him drunk and known him sober. I have known him be aggressive to Dee on numerous occasions, known him scare her with words if not actually with deeds. But I have never known him raise so much as an eyebrow at anyone else, and he's certainly never behaved badly towards me. Not in public and not in private. Not ever. He wouldn't dare.

In fact, sometimes I wonder if the opposite is true. And that Malcolm's just a little scared of me. It's a comforting thought, even if it's fiction. I walk up the path and press my finger on the doorbell for a full and reassuringly sonorous ten seconds – I hope she's heard it – and step back as I wait for him to answer the door.

Which is precisely what he does, and in double quick time, sliding back the bolts and smiling easily and readily as he swings the front door back to greet me.

Malcolm, who is dressed now in lichen-coloured cords and a loose black sweatshirt, is what I think experts usually call a 'well-preserved' alcoholic. He goes off to work, he functions when he gets there, he is socially competent among his friends (at least till he's downed the first six or so, by which time everyone else is generally too merry themselves to notice that he's two pints ahead at-all-times), and his outburst in the pasta place and the vinegar aside, anyone who didn't know either of them well wouldn't know that in private he lives a parallel life in which he mostly enjoys the company of his good friend Mr Daniels and his busty and Teutonic pal, Stella. Most important, however, for my purposes right now at least, is that he's well aware that I *do*. And also that the consequences of me broadcasting the fact are potentially the end of the whole sorry charade.

Though now we're where we are (Dee pregnant. Dee divorcing him), it suddenly occurs to me that everything's changed. He's already lost much of what he was so anxious not to lose. Which means he has less to lose now. Perhaps I should be frightened after all.

Except my best friend needs me not to be. I swallow and then I smile. 'Hi, Malcolm,' I say nicely. 'Is Dee there?'

'I'm sorry,' he says, looking for all the world like he means it. Looking perfectly personable and almost sober, in fact. The only evidence that he isn't is pretty hard to spot. He keeps his trembling hands fixed; one in pocket, one on door jamb. He shakes his head instead. 'She's gone out.'

'Oh?' I say, glancing at her car parked in the road. I gesture towards it. 'Are you sure?'

He glances, then. Past me. Then nods. 'Yes, I'm sure.'

I take a deep breath, happily conscious as I do so that there is a woman walking past the house right about now. I have to hope she'd see if I was yanked inside by my hair. 'That's strange,' I say, scratching my head. 'She just rang me. Ten minutes back. We're supposed to be going out. Er... Jake's gig?' He looks at me blankly.

I look straight on back. 'She didn't mention?' I go on, brow now furrowed. 'I said I'd be straight here. Are you *absolutely* sure?'

Where is she? Where *is* she? I can see his brain whirring. She's called me. He's cornered. He knows full well now that I'm fully aware. But thankfully, we don't have to take things any further, because Dee now appears at the head of the stairs, holding her mobile in one hand and her stomach in the other.

237

'Ah! There you are!' I say, smiling nicely at Malcolm. 'Are you ready? Come on.' I make a big show of consulting my watch. 'It's getting late.'

Dee starts down the stairs, pale-faced but managing to get sufficiently with the programme. 'I'll just grab my coat,' she says.

'And your bag,' I remind her.

'Ah,' she says, casting about. 'I think I left it in the kitchen. Hang on. Won't be long.' She heads down the hallway.

'Lounge,' Malcolm growls at her. 'You left it in the lounge.'

We hear Malcolm shut the front door almost as soon as we turn to walk back down the path. He's said nothing more to either of us and I'm mightily glad of it. In fact I'm really quite astounded that it all went so smoothly. That we got her out with so little confrontation.

'Bloody *hell*,' says Dee, rummaging feverishly in her handbag as she climbs into my passenger seat. 'They're not here.'

'What aren't?'

'My car keys. The sod's taken them. What the hell am I going to do now?'

I start the engine. 'What's going on, Dee?'

She jangles her key ring in my face. 'He's taken them off. Look! The bloody sod!' She thrusts them back into her bag and dumps it angrily down into the footwell. 'That's it. That's the absolute last straw. I'm not going back, you know. Not tonight. Not *ever*. Oh, God, Abs. I so need this to be over.'

'You're telling me!' I release the handbrake and flip down the indicator. 'Never mind. We'll get you back to mine and then you can –'

'Oh, Lord!' she cries suddenly. 'Oh, I don't *believe* it!'

'What?' I dip my head and strain to see out, beyond her. So much for it being so unbelievably simple. Malcolm, who clearly has a fine nose for farce, is lobbing clothes – Dee's clothes – out of the bedroom window.

It takes a good ten minutes to gather up all Dee's possessions. Not just her clothes, but all her make-up, her books, a bunch of magazines, shoes. Everything, in short, that he can readily lay hands on. And all of which, being without bags in which to put it, we have no choice but to dump, in a muddle, in the boot.

It's now ten to seven. And I am seriously stressed.

'Right,' I say, starting the engine once more. 'Home. And we'd better get our skates on or I'm for the chop.'

Dee swivels. Checks her watch. 'Can't you drop me at Tim's?'

'I thought you said you couldn't get hold of him?'

'I couldn't. I can't. His phone's off. I think he's working on an installation or something. But he'll be back soon enough, I'm sure. Please? It won't take long.'

'Dee, I *can't* take you to Tim's. I have to get back to take Jake to his gig.'

She chews her lip. Checks the time. 'It's not far.'

'Dee, I know that. But far enough. And besides, if he's not in – and you have no reason to suppose he will be, have you? – I can't just leave you sitting on his doorstep, can I? Supposing he has to work late? Suppose he's been held up somewhere? Come on – let's get you back to mine, okay? I'm sure he won't mind collecting you from there, will he? Besides, I really do have to get back, Dee. I have to get Jake's drum kit down to the club or there's going to be all sorts of trouble.'

As if a telepathic prompt, my own mobile starts ringing at this point. Dee answers it and listens. 'It's Jake,' she says, finally. 'Look, Mum's driving, Jake. Can I take a...yes. Yes, okay...Right...okay, then...yup...okay, I'll tell her.'

She disconnects. 'He's okay. His friend's dad is going to pick him up and take the kit down there. He said he'd see you there.'

So I take her to Tim's house, which is out towards Radyr. But Tim, as predicted, is still not at home.

'Dee, I can't leave you here. No. I *won't* leave you here. It's dark and it's cold and it's beginning to rain and there's absolutely nowhere to shelter. I'm going to take you back to my house, and as soon as you get hold of him, you can have him come and pick you up from there.'

'But what about Malcolm?'

'What *about* Malcolm?'

'Isn't that just where he'll expect me to be? Supposing he turns up there?'

She does have a point. But I shake my head firmly. 'I'm quite sure he won't.'

She looks unconvinced. As I guess she well might. I'm pretty unconvinced myself. Anything could happen.

'Look,' I say, trying to quell my ever-rising anxiety about the time. 'I really do have to get down to town, Dee. If I don't get there I know Jake will never forgive me. You'll be quite safe at mine. Just bolt the front door. Spike will look after you.'

'I think it will take more than Spike to do that, Abs, don't you?'

But I can't, can't, *can't* spend so much as a minute more worrying about it. It takes another precious ten minutes to relocate all Dee's belongings from car boot to hallway – something I almost forget to, but have to get done, as I need the car empty to bring the drum kit back home.

Dee's calmer, at least, once she's safely inside. So I leave her with Mum, who's still waiting for Wilfred to collect her, and rattle off back in the car, reflecting that acupuncture's all very useful, but not half such a good way of dealing with pain as having a resident mother, an important gig with a deadline, and other people's marital crises to deal with. Time to mope is a luxury I simply don't have.

By the time I get to the club it's teeming with rain, and because it's right in the middle of the main drag, I have to park some distance away and sprint back.

I can hear before I see, but I'm much relieved to realise that I don't recognise what's being played.

When I actually get inside it's difficult to make out what's going on at all. Every inch of the floor space is one amorphous, pulsating mass of bodies. But my ears didn't deceive me, because I manage to establish that the frenzied quartet currently occupying the left side of the stage are not Jake and his pals, but some other band. Though Jake's kit is, I notice, already pretty much set up. Thank God for Tom's dad. I can breathe out again.

The club consists of a large stage and a vast central dance floor, which forms a well between two opposing areas with bars, only one of which is open tonight. I thread my way behind the crush of people lining the railings, and pick out Charlie and Claire, with Oliver's brother and stepsister, huddled with Tom's parents beside the bar at the far end. Because it's a teenagers' night, there's no alcohol available, and they are all of them swigging from bottles of juice.

I make my way down to them, waving as I do so, and have almost reached them when I think I hear my name called out from behind me.

'Thought so! Hello, you!' says a voice. I turn around to see Lucy Whittall.

Lucy Whittall Of All People. 'Goodness!' I say, shocked and completely appalled. Is *he* here, then? Oh please, no. I rearrange my expression by sheer force of will. 'What a surprise!' I say gaily. 'What are *you* doing here?'

She looks surprised that I'm surprised. 'Oh?' she says. 'Didn't Jake mention?'

Mention? My brain fails to compute. 'Well, he did tell me they mentioned the gig to you when you were at our house in the summer...but I never imagined...well, um...' oh *gawd,* Abbie. 'Well, how lovely that you found the time to come along. Does he know you're here? I'm sure he'll be thrilled to –'

She nods enthusiastically. 'Oh, God, yes. We just watched the last band together. Don't worry,' she adds. 'Not a patch on your boys.' She has a slight sheen of moisture across the tops of her cheekbones. Which on her manages to look like it was gently deposited from the wings of a tropical butterfly, en route to Paradise Island.

'Well that's really sweet of you,' I reply. 'I'm sure it's really made his day that you came.'

She shakes her head. 'I was in town anyway. Been to some God-awful ad premiere. And later on I have to go to some God-awful aftershow party as well. So I thought, I know! I'll nip down and check out how your lovely boys are getting on. This is so much more my sort of thing than poncing around with my arse of a publicist and a bunch of self-satisfied gonks, I can tell you –' she lifts her bottle of juice. '– lack of vino notwithstanding, of course!' she tips her mane of glossy hair back and laughs.

So perhaps he's not here, then. I feel the tension ebb slightly. 'So,' I say. 'D'you want to come and join us?'

'You're all right,' she says, winking, and gesturing back to the dance floor... 'I'd rather be down there, if it's all the same to you. Anyway –' She leans towards me and brushes her fragrant cheek against my own. 'Good to see you, Annie!'

And then she's gone. Tripping down the steps, and then sucked once again into the welcoming throng.

I move further down the bar. Jake's there now too, I see, his forehead shiny and his fingers rat-a-tat-tatting against the bar.

'Yo, Mum! You made it!' he shouts as I approach. 'Just in time, too. We're up next.' He looks past me. 'Yo, Hamish! Come on! Where you *been*?'

Charlie's deep in conversation with Tom's dad close by, having the sort of comedy exchange that you can't help but do in these sort of decibel levels; making seeming close inspections of one another's ear hair.

His wife, Claire, pushes past them to get to me.

'Isn't this exciting?' she says. She looks animated. Happier. Entirely different to the way she did last time I met her. Out of role, I suppose. And not so very different from me, after all. She grins, revealing dimples. 'I've never been to anything like this before. Have you?' I shake my head. 'I think it's wonderful that they lay this sort of thing on for young people, don't you?' She bends her mouth closer to me and gestures to her drink. 'Have to say, I wouldn't mind a G and T, though!'

Just the G would do for me, I think, as I nod and smile and agree.

The boys play their set – their whole seven precious, much practised songs – with barely a pause to draw breath. While I (much like Charlie and Tom's dad as well), have been charged with the business of capturing the action, on the video camera his father sweetly bought him for the purpose; an awesome responsibility for a woman who finds herself quite unable to breathe either. And I do. Because almost as soon as they've begun, I find myself locked in the grip of an appalling and completely unexpected anxiety. I have listened to them play these songs so many times now. I know every word, every beat, every bridge, every chord change, and my heart thumps in anticipation of every single next note. I know they're note perfect. *Absolutely* note perfect. But it doesn't seem to matter. This is live. This is real. This is (like, Mum, you know), *really* important. I barely respire from the first to the last.

By the time they're done, therefore, and the crowd are clamouring for pictures and autographs, mobiles and programmes and beer mats held aloft, I'm so overcome with pride and relief and, yes, oxygen depletion, that I'm almost too tearful to speak. I want to march right on up there and shout from the rooftops. I'm not sure what it is that I want to shout, exactly, but something. Just some sort of primeval noise. But I'm also aware that the height of uncool would be a mother with the vapours in the picture right now. Time for that soon enough. So instead I slip away to get a handful of loo roll to mop my eyes with.

The toilets, as is so often the case in these types of venue, are located not on the premises, but in an underground, and possibly uncharted region at least five shop fronts down and on the other side of the road. It doesn't seem in the least fanciful to assume that I might come upon a slumped female skeleton, clutching a Bacardi Breezer and a clutch bag, who had given up trying to find a way out of the labyrinth and simply expired where she sat. I pass a kitchen, a stock room full of Brobdingnagian bean cans, and several doors sternly marked 'private'. Private, I assume to refer to privation. What species of troll would want to work in such a place? When I eventually light upon the door marked *Senhoritas!*, I have almost forgotten why I came. They do, however, have some loo roll, at least – in fact, several great spools of the stuff. Here be giants also, it seems.

I look a mess, but a proud one. So I don't linger long. And on my way back up, I almost collide with Charlie, himself groping his way out through the gloom.

'This sure takes me back,' he says, jovially. We fall into step and head back up the sticky stairs. 'Trouble is, it also reminds me how terrifically ancient I am. He glances at me. 'How are you, anyway? Still working at the clinic?'

'Still working at the clinic.' Another bright shaft of sunshine in what's been a mainly cloudy sort of day, is to find I can be here and have chats with Charlie and that everything – almost – is back how it was.

'And still enjoying it?'

'Yes,' I nod, 'yes, I am. Very much.'

He frowns. 'That's a shame.'

'Why?'

'I was rather hoping you'd be bored by now.'

'Bored?'

'Well, it's not quite the same, is it? You must find it lacking in challenge compared to the work you used to do at the hospital, surely?

'Not really. It's just different.'

'But you must miss the acute stuff.'

There's all sorts of acute stuff I do miss, for sure. But lots that I absolutely don't. I shake my head. 'Well, obviously it's not as–'

'Not as challenging. Can't be. '

'No, but –' I turn to face him as we mount the final steps. 'Charlie, what's with the interrogation?'

He shoves a hand in his pocket. 'Well, you know, I've been thinking.'

'Oh, dear. That sounds worrying.'

'No, seriously. You should never have left in the first place. We both know that. And, well, you could always come back. They've still not managed to find a replacement for you. And you must admit you're wasted on that kind of –'

'Charlie, I really don't think that would be a terrifically good idea.'

'No, I'm serious. I'm talking work here. No games.'

I shake my head. 'No, I *know* that.'

He stops. 'Do you?'

I stop too. And smile at him. 'Yes, I do. And I'm glad.' I gesture towards the bar. 'Claire seems nice. I'm glad you and she…well…whatever…'

He smiles broadly and claps me on the back. 'So I guess I just keep on with the guilt trip, then, do I? Anyway, speaking of which,' he says. 'How's your friend's knee?'

He raises his brows as he say this. I stiffen. 'Oh, improving I think. I haven't actually seen him since then.'

'Oh?' His brows change direction and converge at the bridge of his nose now. 'I got the impression you and he were, well…'

'Then you got entirely the wrong one, Charlie. I told you, he's just my mother's dead fourth husband's long-lost son.'

He looks at me hard. 'And that's a lot of things to be. Quite enough to be going on with, I imagine.' Then he grins. 'For the moment, at least.'

'Look, I need to get back and help dismantle Jake's drum kit.'

'And we need to be off.' He pecks me on the cheek. 'So it's farewell, then, my lovely,' he says.

By the time we return to the stage itself, the last gaggles of teenagers have said their farewells also, and the bar manager, much tattooed and with a back-to-front baseball cap, is already attacking the floor with a broom. Guitars are nestled back into cases and amp leads wound back into their liquorice roll coils. That done, and refusing further offers of help, we wave off Charlie and Claire and Oliver and Oliver's brother and stepsister, and Ben and Ben's auntie, and I have a sudden sense of just how very precious all this is. And how much I'm looking forward to getting Jake home, and the two of us sitting, over toast, in the kitchen, watching the video I've recorded of their set, and deconstructing every single moment before bed. And also a sudden rush of complete understanding about why I should never feel resentful of Rob about the boys. He doesn't have this. I'm very lucky.

But it seems I'm wrong about everyone else having left. Jake and Tom – whose dad has gone to fetch his car from the multistorey – are just setting to work with the drum keys, when I hear a clatter of spiked heels coming towards us from across the now empty hall.

It's Lucy Whittall, who's obviously collected her coat now; she's lusciously encased in a long shaggy sheepskin, which dips in places to the floor and which I fear for in the rain. Lucy Whittall who I thought had left some time ago. But no, it seems, for she's come back to say goodbye.

'Ah!' she says as she approaches. She's bright-eyed. Looks as if the night is still young. As it is for her, I guess. 'The superstar lifestyle, eh, lads?' she calls gaily. I think, from my depressingly sober perspective, that's she's more than a little well-oiled.

But then why shouldn't she be? I shake my head. 'I sincerely hope not. I'm hoping they'll be superstars with sufficient cash to employ someone else to do all the donkey work for them. '

'Tsk! What am I like?' she says in response. 'Standing here watching you guys work.' She shrugs off her coat and flings it down, without a backward glance, amongst the massed amps and leads and other muso paraphernalia, and then pushes up the sleeves of her slinky red top. And once again I'm struck by how much I like her. For everything I've read about her, everything I've heard, there is something so warm and engaging about her. She even, though I'm not sure why I should consider it a plus point exactly, reminds me of my mother at her age. Grabbing life by the lapels and giving it a good shaking, while people like me skirt cautiously around the hem.

I'm just thinking, in fact, that she *is* so like my mother must have been at her age, when I hear her name called from the back of the hall. She swings around to see. Then she waves. 'Over here!

I hear the voice again. 'Are you coming?' It's *his* voice. It's Gabriel. I feel cold.

She shields her eyes from the glare of the still burning stage spots. 'Won't be a mo. I'm just lending a hand.'

She turns to me. 'Like, what's the big rush anyway? If I know Gabe, no sooner will we get there than he'll be whining on about leaving again.' She rolls her eyes at me, then turns round once again. 'Gabe?' she calls. 'Come and help out here a minute will you, angel?'

Oh, *God.* 'There's no need –' I begin.

'Nonsense,' she says firmly. 'Didn't your mother always tell you? Many hands make light work.'

And too many cooks make the kitchen too hot. Or something like that. 'Er,' I hear him mutter as he emerges from the shadows. 'Er. Okay, yes…sure.'

Angel. Angel Gabriel. Archangel Gabriel. With his hair-back lit by the spots as he approaches the stage, he could almost cut the mustard, celestially speaking. Except not. He's fully mortal. As I've had occasion to find out. Flustered at the thought even as I'm cross with myself for my pathetic inability to stop it happening in the first place, I fish in my bag for my car keys and then point to a couple of stands that are lying closest to me.

'Right. These ready to go now, Jake?'

246

He looks up from where he's unscrewing the bolts on the cymbals. 'Yep. And you can take the snare too. And the toms.'

'Okay,' I say, picking up a couple of stands. 'Why don't you guys bring everything as far as the back door while I go and get the car. I'll try to park it just outside so we don't get everything soaked.'

'Will do,' says Jake brightly. He's still running with perspiration. I remind myself not say anything mumsy about putting on his hoodie so he doesn't catch a chill.

'Shall I grab these, then?' asks Gabriel, gesturing to the drums at the side of the stage.

'Sure,' I say levelly. 'Thanks. You're very kind.'

The rain is being kind too. It's eased up, at any rate, and is now only visible as sparkles around the street lights and in the steady drip and gurgle from the gutters and drains.

I jog across to the car and drive it back to as near to the back entrance as I can. When I get out, I see Gabriel leave the step by the back door and lope across with a small tower of drums in his hand. He's got the collar of his jacket pulled up around his ears, and he grimaces when he sees me.

It could be just because of the rain on his face, but I know better. It's because he's very much in I'd-rather-be-elsewhere mode. And he's not the only one. My insides are churning. How unutterably tenacious this feeling has become. I really wish Lucy hadn't suggested he help. I wish they'd just gone. He obviously wanted to.

*Wants* to. I feel exactly as I did when I was almost fifteen, and had, in the woefully misjudged belief that he liked me as-a-person, let Owen from the lower sixth inside my bra while we stood outside some sorry school disco. Owen then went out with a girl from the fifth form and I was advised (by a well meaning bitch-friend called Emma) that his triumph – because triumph it had been, apparently – earned him the coveted title of Primus. For his enviable ability to heat up cold stuff. As in rather stiff, rather swotty, dreary lab-rat-type pupils. As in *me*. He never spoke to me again.

Still, now we're here, and I'll just have to lump it. Lump this whole sorry *dénouement* to our whole sorry moment. The whole

247

sorry away-with-the-bloody-fairies encounter. Fifteen or forty. It still feels the same.

I haul open the boot to get the first of the kit in. 'How's your knee?' I ask him, because I have to say something. I ask it in what I hope is a light-hearted and friendly manner, but his gruff answering 'okay,' is anything but.

He's not looking at me either. I take the toms from off of the top of the snare so he can put the latter in the boot first. I feel mortified. Quite unable to think what to say. The silence lengthens. 'Well, have you had any treatment for it?' I ask eventually. 'You know, done some physio? It's –'

'No,' he says, cutting through my brisk attempts at small talk. He puts the snare in and carefully slides it to the back. Then he takes the toms from me again and bends down to put them in too. Then, less harshly now. 'I haven't had a chance.'

I'm conversing with his back now. 'You didn't need to do that,' I say. 'You know, cancel your appointment and everything.'

He rises again now and turns to face me. He's looking at me properly for the first time at last. Which is no good thing for my health, I decide. Or his, clearly. He's still frowning. Because I obviously remind him of his pre-nup transgression. His dalliance with the idea of succumbing to his loins and of having a quick bit on the side. The thought doesn't do him justice, but I know that's what he's thinking. It's so plain on his face. He shakes his head. 'I think I did.'

I don't know what to say to that. He's probably right. Probably thinking he doesn't want to upset me. Embarrass me. Which it would have, but even so, I really don't want him to think that. I don't want to be cast in the role he's assigned for me. Don't want to be the cause of his discomfort most of all. 'Well,' I scrabble together finally. Briskly. 'Whatever. It's up to you. But you shouldn't just leave it.'

'Look, Abbie, it's fine now. Okay?'

I swallow the frost in his words and wish a freak tornado would happen along and spare me this torture. And him too. For torture it certainly seems to be. This is as ridiculous as it is painful. 'Gabriel,' I say, in as matter of fact and dignified a tone as I can muster. 'You know, you really don't need to be like this with me.'

He doesn't answer. Just turns back then, to where the rest of the kit is beginning to pile up in the doorway. 'Look,' I say as I follow him. 'You know, you don't even need to *be* here. I'm perfectly capable of doing this myself. I've done it enough times before, believe me. *Really*. And you have to be somewhere, don't you? I don't want to hold you up.'

Jake's just placed some more kit in the doorway, and I watch his retreating torso as he goes back inside for more. It's pitch dark until we approach the building and then the security light blazes into being again. Just short of the doorway Gabriel stops and turns around.

'I know that,' he says, pushing up the sleeves of his jacket. The halogen lights up the golden fuzz on his forearms. 'But I'm here now, aren't I? Bass drum. Where does that need to go? Does it fit in the boot too? I'm not sure it'll go.'

'It...um. No, it doesn't...it goes on the back seat.' I feel so agitated now that I almost want to punch him. I cross my arms across my chest. 'Gabriel,' I say. 'Will you please just stop this?'

He blinks at me. 'Stop what?'

'Being so bloody poker-faced, that's what!'

We're still standing in the halo, the back door to the club now sighing closed ahead of us. I can hear sounds of car doors slamming, engines firing, and bubbles of laughter, all mingling and floating as one back across the car park. His shoulders drop visibly. His breath makes a cloud in front of his face. He picks up the bass drum and as he leans to do so I breathe in the coconut.

He takes a breath too.

'I knew this was a bad idea,' he says finally, almost under his breath, to himself.

But as I hear it too, I feel I have every right to answer. I'm feeling crosser by the moment. 'You're telling me,' I say, as I pick up the two remaining stands. 'I'm beginning to feel like I've got a communicable disease.'

He frowns. 'Oh, Abbie. It's not that. It's just...well...' He glances back inside.

I follow his gaze. Oh, I *get* it. Of course. *Lucy's* in there. 'Gabriel, for God's sake, stop looking at me like that! Just get

249

over yourself will you? Is that what this is about? That you're worried I'll *tell* her?' I glare at him. 'I told you already. Don't flatter yourself!'

He starts back towards the car, shaking his head as he does so. Then he turns back to me suddenly and looks me square in the eye. A whole handful of seconds thump by before he speaks to me. 'I'm not,' he says quietly. 'Believe me, I'm not. Don't worry. You've made that abundantly clear.'

I don't know how to respond because I'm not even sure which bit of my question he's answering. Only that there is something in his expression that makes my heart thump all the more. But, tough. His precious ego is really the least of my worries. 'Well, good,' I say anyway. Firmly. Like I mean it. 'And you really needn't worry in any case.' I spread my palms and dredge up an air of insouciance from somewhere. 'I mean, it's not as if we're even likely to see each other again, is it?'

*Ever* again, I think. 'No,' he says. 'No. I suppose not.'

He walks on, then, holding the bass drum out in front of him. He could almost be a stray from a minstrel marching band. He's certainly marching right now. I watch him get to the car, place the drum gently on the ground, then open the passenger door and manhandle it inside. The rain's getting heavier again now. Visible even in the darkness. We need to get a move on. Quite apart from anything else, Jake has school in the morning. And I have work, and he has work, and mother has any number of social engagements to be ferried to, and normal service must resume next week. As it does every week. As it will every week after that. I grab the bag of cymbals and the bass pedal and follow him back to the car.

I let him take them all from me and slot them in turn into the well in front of the back seat. I can think of nothing else useful to say to him. Nor him me, it would seem. His jaw is now rigid as he goes back to the door and returns with the last of Jake's kit. Two more drums and another stand, all of which he busies himself with fitting in as well, the rain rat-a-tatting onto the back of his jacket. It's getting so heavy now it's clumping his lashes. He straightens and runs the back of one hand across his brow. Then, just as I think he's about to say something else, an explosion of noise pours out from behind us. I turn around. Jake and Tom, laughing, are emerging with Tom's amp, Lucy Whittall and Tom's father behind them.

Gabriel turns too, and lifts a hand in greeting.

'Is that it, lads?' he calls out to them. Jake lifts a thumb.

'Well, goodbye, then,' he says softly, closing the car door with a clunk. He leans forward, and brushes his lips against my cheek. 'You have a nice life, Abbie, okay?'

Our eyes meet momentarily, sealing his words. Then we go and join the others, job done.

# Chapter 25

IT'S HARD WORK, REFRAINING from crying. Hard on the throat, hard on the tear ducts, super hard on the nerves. And yet, somehow, by some miracle, I manage to do so. All the way back inside the club. All the way back outside again. Throughout the hearty farewells. The well dones, the see you laters, the mutual appreciation society back-slapping and the urging of the manager to come again, soon.

Even when the last image that is burned on my retina is of the two of them, her stooping to climb into the back of a taxi, his hand gently guiding, on the small of her back.

Once we get into the car, Jake, to my relief, is soon plugged once again into his iPod. Yet even that – grateful though I am for the absence of the need to make words – only adds further to my misery. It's been thoroughly spoilt now, this precious red-letter evening. Invaded and soured by horrible emotions that, however intently I don't want to be feeling them, I seem powerless to make go away.

When we finally get back, I have to park the car six houses down, ironically just behind Hugo's Nissan, which sits, stubbornly still refusing to attract any buyers, under the horse chestnut outside the Thomases' house. Mr Thomas doesn't mind us like Mr Davidson minds us, because he's six houses down, and also deaf.

I'm so preoccupied with my fragile state – my need for some sort of oblivion from my wretched post-morteming – that it's only as I put my key in the lock that I realise something's not right. Not because of anything immediately visible, but rather because the action's accompanied by the sort of ear splitting squawk a cat tends to make when you inadvertently step on its tail.

Except I don't have a cat.

Just a dog. I push the door open. There's a thought, I think. Where *is* my dog? My dog who loves me. Who is *always* there to greet me. My mind moves seamlessly from thoughts of my heartache, to other, more insistent, less self-indulgent ones. Now I'm thinking Dee, who I left here three hours back, and, by logical extension, to Malcolm. To Malcolm, to Tim, to sharp kitchen implements, to cuckolded husbands and to murder most foul. Thus I step into the hall, expecting the worst. What I find, however, is no sign of either Dee or her belongings, but a woman of about sixty, in a peppermint-hued sweater and wearing glasses on a chain, emerging from my downstairs loo.

I say see, but in fact that's a loose-ish description. For the hall seems to be wreathed in a soft autumnal mist.

A soft yet undeniably acrid autumnal mist. And there's not been smog in Cardiff in decades. 'Oh, hello!' she says pleasantly, smoothing down her skirt front. 'I'm Pamela. And you must be Abbie.'

At least I assume that's what she's attempting to convey, because what she actually says is 'air hell air! M Pamla. Anchew musby Ab-hic.' I pull the key from the door and put the cymbal bag down on the hall floor.

'Er, yes,' I say back, because what else is there to say? 'Hello.' I put the bass pedal beside it.

She sways minutely, then smiles, and then returns to the living room, shutting the door promptly behind her. Jake, by this time, is hard up behind me with his drum stands. I step aside to let him in.

'Blimey, what a stink!' is his considered opinion as he props the stands carefully up against the lower stairs. 'Is someone having a party, or what?'

'I'm not entirely sure,' I say. I am now, if belatedly, gathering momentum. 'But I certainly intend to find out.'

I am still, at this juncture, loosely working on the Malcolm/Dee/Tim bloody domestic conflict scenario and wondering where M Pamla slots into the equation. Is she Malcolm's AA counsellor? Tim's mother? What? *My* mother's not in. My mother is at Wilfred's. Because Brian's had a flood. It's all coming back. Wilfred was coming to pick her up. I remember.

Another gale of laughter blasts through from the living room. Seems I've remembered all wrong about that. Seems someone is indeed having a party.

And in my living room, too. 'Ah,' I say, opening the door again. 'Hello.' Heads turn. Hands flap. Greetings various are proffered. Cigars are wafted. Glasses are raised.

'Hello, dear,' says my mother, sitting regally at the head of what I suddenly realise is my kitchen table, clutching a small fan of playing cards in one hand and a half-finished sherry in the other. 'I've had a few friends round. I do hope you don't mind.'

'Er, right,' I say, through the noisome, head-level fug . 'Fine. Um – right. Okay, then.' I don't know what else to say, to be honest. I look around. Still no dog. 'Mum, where's Spike?'

'Oh, we had to pop him into the dining room, darling. Poor Brian's allergic, you see.'

'Just as well,' I tell Spike, once I've released him from purdah. 'You'd probably asphyxiate with that lot.' They haven't even bothered to take his bed in there for him. Just marooned him on the laminate. How cruel. I press my nose into his fur and let him rootle in my ear. 'C'mon, honey. Let's get you to bed.'

By the time I get back into the kitchen my mother is in there. With the person called Brian, and an empty glass bowl. Which she is currently filling with crisps.

'Ah, Mum,' I say as lightly as I can. 'What's going on?'

She shrugs. 'I told you. I've had a few friends round.'

No. Wrong answer. Not had. *Have*. I look at my watch. 'Well, fine,' I say, continuing, as I must, in the polite and measured tones of a person for whom, irritatingly, there is a stray Brian present in the equation, denying me the opportunity to rant in my own kitchen. As they're denying me the opportunity to *sit* in my own kitchen. 'But it's almost eleven-thirty and it's Sunday night. I have work in the morning, Jake has school in the morning. So do you think you could start to wrap things up reasonably soon?'

Which I think, even as I'm saying it, is pretty damned *reasonable* of me. In fact, were my arms long enough I'd be patting myself on the back.

Just as Brian is patting my mother on the back now. I wonder if Brian is shaping up to become the next Hugo. But then I recall that he's already married to someone. Isn't everyone *always* already married to someone? Or, and how it's hurting now, if not, then about to be. Which is almost just as bad.

No. It's worse. In any case, the substance of her answering 'Oh, don't worry about us. You get off to bed and leave us to it. We won't disturb you,' is somewhat diluted by another bone-shaking shriek from the living room, and I wonder if Macbeth's going to join us as well. I feel suddenly angry. Proper throwing things angry. The sort of angry that cannot be easily discharged. The sort of angry my mother used to be with me on the rare – oh so rare – occasions when I got home late.

'Well, I'd be grateful if you'd try to keep it down, please,' I say levelly, gathering mugs from the drainer. 'Jake's got school, as I said. And please, Mum, would you at least open a window or two?'

They leave the kitchen with their crisps just as Jake himself enters. His reflection's in the window. His tall shaggy silhouette approaching my smaller one. And I feel myself welling up all over again. 'All inside,' he says. 'Give us the keys and I'll lock the car up.'

'Thanks, darling,' I say, ferreting in my bag for them and wiping my eyes on the back of my hand. 'You know, you guys were brilliant tonight. Absolutely brilliant. I'm so proud of you, you know that?'

He takes the keys from me, grinning sheepishly. 'Yeah, whatever, Mum,' he says. Then he looks at me harder. 'Mum, what are you *like*? You're not supposed to cry when you're *happy*!'

'Oh, don't mind me. You know what I'm like. I'm just…oh, Come over here and let me give you a hug.'

Which he submits to. His hair smells all sweaty and boyish.

'Tea and toast?' I say.

'Nah,' he says. 'You're alright, Mum.' Then he grins. 'I'm going to go to bed, if that's okay with you. Way too many wrinklies down here.'

I kiss him a reluctant goodnight, and am just thinking I ought to call Dee and see how she is, when Mr Davidson appears in the doorway. A wrinkly in waiting. He's making good progress.

'Er,' he says. 'Hello. Um…d'you have a cloth?'

\*     \*     \*

'Ah, Abbie, dear!' booms Celeste as I follow him back into the living room. 'Are you going to come and join us? I think there's some champagne left. Can I pour you a glass?'

'Er…no, thanks,' I tell her. 'I'm going to have a bath and get to bed. Busy day. Busy night.'

'Of course! How'd it go, lovely?'

'Fine,' I say. 'Just fine.'

Till right about now, that is. There's a stain the size of a dinner plate beside the leg of the table. Red wine, by the look of it. Fabulous. On my white wine-coloured carpet. A stupid choice in the first place, all things considered. But it was on special offer. I liked it. I thought it would look chic.

Mr Davidson's knees click as he gropes down to try and mop it. The Pamla woman proffers a handful of pink tissues. Okay, I tell myself. Nothing to stress about. It's just a carpet. An old carpet. An inexpensive carpet. A stain on a ropey old inexpensive carpet is no way – no *way*, Abbie – the end of the world.

It's just that everything feels like the end of the world right now. 'Salt,' someone's saying. 'You need salt to soak it up. Leave it a while and it'll hoover up a dream. Kitchen, Di? Shall I go? What cupboard is it in?'

Then the someone, who could possibly be Wilfred – how would I know? – pushes his own chair back to go run his errand. And in doing so, manages to knock over the dish of nibbles at his elbow, sending peanuts and cashews and silverskin onions to go forth and populate the further reaches of the room.

I decide that in the interests of the NHS budget (it's not cheap, calling doctors out to section people on a Sunday), that I will – that I must – simply take myself upstairs. If I stay down here a moment more I might feel the need to kill someone. Ms Garland in the Kitchen with the Kenwood Chef most probably. Wouldn't want to add to the stain count in the lounge.

'Please don't worry,' I entreat them, as nicely as I can. 'I can sort things in the morning. Good night all,' with which I exit the room.

I hover a few seconds in front of the hall mirror, seeing terrifying traces of the woman I'm becoming. Which is the kind of woman that old ladies would cross the street to avoid. My hair, which up to now, I haven't given much thought to, has danced its merry rain dance and now looks like linguini. I have gobs of mascara in twin stripes across my eyelids, and a cherry tomato for a nose. I have the face of a woman whose heart has been broken and who finds herself all out of plasters.

My ears are still intact, though, about which I have mixed feelings. Because just as I stand and address the sorry state of my visage, Celeste's words come floating forth to greet me from the lounge. That's the thing with being merry. No volume control.

'She okay, Di? Your Abbie? She seems a bit raddled. D'you think we ought to call it a night?'

There's a pause and a grunt – Mr Davidson rising? – then my own dear mother's voice wafts out, load and oh-so very clear.

I can't *see* her roll her eyes, but I know that's what she's doing.

'Oh, don't worry,' I hear her say. 'Ongoing mid-life crisis situation, that's all.' She's lowered her voice now, but not quite sufficiently. Not if I edge a bit closer to the door. 'Man problems,' she adds. 'Take no notice.'

Take no notice. Yup, she's right. That's me, that is. The sort of person whose occasional vagaries of temperament are of so little importance, of so little note that, just like warts and growing pains, they are best dealt with by taking no notice.

I remain in the hallway for a further half minute. Fashioning a scene in which I burst into the living room, brandishing something – the bread knife? The kettle? A brace of Jake's cymbals? – with which I hysterically commence the dispatching of her houseguests, like a serial killer on speed.

Except I'm not the serial-killing type. I'm the go off and absolutely seethe instead type. So, seethe duly building, I trudge up the stairs. I shall call Dee, whose safety is still a cause for some concern, and then, assuming she's okay, I shall seethe in the bath.

And she is, as it turns out. Tucked up in bed with Tim. And going to worry about tomorrow, tomorrow, she tells me, before instructing me to get to bed myself. Which takes a bit of the edge off my fury. How ridiculous to get in such a state about my mother when real problems, *bad* ones, feel so very close to home.

And, of course, there's nothing like a long hot bath to soothe away your cares. Or so the ads would imply. Or so my own bloody mother would imply, as it happens. Nineteen seventy-six, or thereabouts. An ad for some bath foam or other that smelt of eggs.

But despite my hopeful mindset, some cares are too entrenched to be amenable to soothing, whatever the unguents and potions in which you're sloshing around. Because though the protracted contemplation of one's navel can often be relied upon to banish the day's tensions, the contemplation of one's previously unacknowledged status as someone who is apparently gripped in the charmless embrace of a middle years crisis situation is not. But perhaps there's a kernel of truth in what she said. *Am* I having a mid-life crisis after all? Could that be it? After all, presumably one doesn't *know* that one is having a mid-life crisis until such time as some well-meaning person points it out for you, does one? And unless you've had a mid-life crisis of your own, you're probably not in the best position to recognise the symptoms, are you?

I spend forty-five minutes in the bath, wallowing, a further two in Jake's bedroom, stroking his sleeping cheek, and a good fifteen sitting on my dressing-table stool, frowning, and wondering quite how I have become the sort of woman who needs it pointing out – and by *him,* and in so breathtakingly patronising a way – that she should go off and Have A Nice Life.

None of which, bar stroking my son's cheek (without which morphia I would be catatonic by now), serves to make me feel any less incendiary about it. And specifically (and in tandem with feeling so bloody strung-out about Gabriel), incendiary about my Dear Mother. Thus when I do finally venture downstairs – a good fifteen minutes after the last shrieking harpy and phlegmatic old codger has departed (and yes, I do include Mr Davidson in that – though am obviously cheered by the new balance of relations as a consequence of the wine stain debacle) – and find the spiny anthill that is my mother's bottom glaring defiantly up at me from the living room carpet, it is all I can do not to pull back my best foot and then propel her, with force, into the grate.

But I don't do that. Because that would be illegal. So I plant both feet on the living room threshold and consider her instead. I think, momentarily, that she is engaged in some sort of yoga posture; the Swan, perhaps, for it has that sort of look, or maybe the Recently Beached Sea Cow. But then I realise she is not in fact posturing but scrubbing. At the carpet. With the new Landmarks of Venice tea towel I bought at the Airport.

'You shouldn't be kneeling,' I say, automatically. She ignores me. I try again. 'Mum, you know you shouldn't be kneeling. Will you please *leave* that?'

She scrubs a bit harder. I walk around her and go and open all three of the top living room windows, causing billows of icy air to mushroom into the room. At which point she stops scrubbing and goes 'tsk' instead.

My mother could 'tsk' for Britain. My mother being, lest we forget, a dancer *and* an actress, has a variety of 'tsk' available for almost any situation, much as Inuit peoples have lots of words for snow. This 'tsk', this passive-aggressive little nugget, is a 'tsk' that means 'bog off and leave me alone.'

So that's exactly what I do. I go into the kitchen instead, where the table has been returned to its rightful position in the corner of the kitchen and Spike, order having been restored and the roof returned to his sleepy hole, is flat out and dreaming about whatever it is he dreams about. Not rabbits, I fancy. Has he ever seen a rabbit, even? No, perhaps he dreams dreams in which he vanquishes Airedales. I really must get him a new rubber bone.

And while I'm at it, a new rubber heart for myself. Something sturdy and unbreakable, ideally. I leave Spike to his slumbers and survey the chaos on the other side of the room. The worktop by the sink is now a sea of plates and glasses. Some of them empty, but some still playing host: to beer and whisky. Wine. Sandwich curls. Pringles. Cigarette ends. Cigar butts. Gherkins. Smears of pickle. I take it all in and I pull open the dishwasher. Which is still full from lunchtime. I click it back shut.

At which point my mother enters. In her slippy-sloppy slippers. I turn around. 'Quite a party,' I say.

She puts a foot on the pedal bin and empties the dustpan into it. It closes with a snap and Spike starts. 'It wasn't a party, Abigail. It was just a few friends round, for goodness' sake!'

She turns on the hot tap and fires a stream of water into the washing-up bowl. Except there's a plate sitting in there and the water bounces back, showering her skirt front instead.

'Mum, can you just leave that? Please? I'd really like to get to bed and I –'

'So *go* to bed, then!' she snaps, slapping at her clothing. 'Go to bed and leave me to it. I'm quite capable of washing a few glasses, you know.'

'I'm well aware of that, Mum. I'd just rather you didn't. They can go in the dishwasher in the morning.'

She carries on regardless, while I stand there and scowl. Then she turns around, clearly with something else to say. Which she does. Oh, and then some. 'Honestly,' she snaps, orange dish-brush in hand. 'Why do you have to be such a shrew about everything?'

I gape at her. '*What*?'

She exhales. 'Well, for goodness' sake, take a look at yourself, Abigail! You are becoming so joyless and shrill! Why are you always in such a bad mood all the time? So I had a few friends round. Is that such a crime?'

Because I'm still stung on the joyless and shrewish bit, it takes me a couple of seconds to absorb the rest. No, it's not a crime. And yes, I *am* in a bad mood. A very bad mood now, in fact.

'No. Not a crime,' I say, trying to keep my voice calm and measured. 'But pretty off of you, even so. Tonight of all nights, Mum. With Jake's gig and everything. And what on earth did you think you were doing, letting people smoke cigars in my house?' I know I sound petty, but that's just how I feel. 'Why couldn't they smoke in the garden, for God's sake? I don't want to be a kill-joy, but the whole place stinks!'

She tsks again. Which is getting *really* irritating. 'Abigail, I cannot *believe* you are making such an enormous fuss about a few perfectly civilised human beings sitting in your living room playing cards. "Oh, *no*! End of the *world*! People are *smoking* in my *house*!"' She grabs the washing-up liquid bottle and wafts it towards me. 'What is this place anyway, Colditz?'

'That's not the point. It's the principle.'

'Oh, and we mustn't upset your precious principles, must we? Dear me, no.' She fires washing-up liquid into the bowl and then slams the bottle back down onto the drainer. Three little rainbow bubbles float up and away. Much like fairies do. Sometimes. Not always. I want to cry.

'And Jake has *asthma*. Or did you forget that?' She says nothing. So, yes, clearly. *Yes*. Why does that not surprise me? 'Mum, just leave this, will you? I want to go to bed.'

'Oh, no,' she says. 'Oh, no. Not likely. I'm not having you tutting your way about the place in the morning with *that* look on your face.'

I fold my arms. 'Oh, right. Of course. And which face would that be? My mid-life crisis situation face, perhaps?' She looks at me sharply. I glare right on back. 'How *dare* you say that! I am not having a mid-life crisis, okay? Just a crisis, which is different.' She continues to fill the sink with dishes and glasses, each one entering the water with a point making bang. I half hope she breaks one. Serve her right. 'And it may have escaped your notice but if you had so much a shred of intelligence you might have realised the crisis might have something to do with *you*.'

Now she turns. 'I beg your pardon?'

'You heard what I said, Mum. How *dare* you patronise me like that!'

'I was not being patronising. I –'

'Not being patronising? Yeah, right. Sitting in my living room discussing me with all your friends? "Oh, *poor* Abigail! Man problems. Oh, *bless*." How dare you! Did you fill them in on all the details, too?'

'I most certainly did not.'

'I should bloody well hope so.'

She lifts her hands from the suds and scrutinises me for a moment. 'Hmm,' she says then. 'So it *is* still going on, then.'

I could weep. I really could. I'm too tired for all this. 'I don't believe it,' I say. 'You really have *no* idea, do you? No. '*It*' is *not* 'still going on', as you put it. This has *nothing* to do with bloody man problems, okay? This is all about me. *My* life. That thing that happens to *me* everyday! You may not have actually noticed, of course, but I have one too! I get up. I go to work. I come home again. I shop. I cook. I clean. I wash. I run around after everyone.

261

I run around after *you*. And then I collapse into bed. And then, you know what? I get up and do it all again. Every single day, Mum. Ad nauseam. *Endlessly*. My life is just one big round of attending to other people's needs!' I stab myself in the chest now. 'Well, *I* have needs too. And it would be nice, now and then, if you'd appreciate that fact and not turn my home into a bloody bordello. But no. The only person you ever think about is *you*. So, yes, you're right, Mum. I *am* feeling joyless.' I cast an arm about me. 'Can you *blame* me?'

She stops banging about at the sink and dries her hands on a tea towel. Then she sniffs. 'There's no point in talking to you when you're in this sort of state, Abigail. I think you should get yourself off to bed.'

Something in me snaps as she says this. And she's lucky it isn't her neck in my hands. 'That's exactly what I'd planned to do when I got home two hours back! Except you'd taken it upon yourself to invite all your bloody luvvie friends round for a knees-up!'

'That's uncalled for, young lady.'

'Don't you 'young lady' me! I am not a child any more. I'm an adult. And this is *my* house, okay? *Mine*. Not yours!'

She puts the tea towel, still in a ball, on the table. 'I think you've made that much clear.' She sniffs again. 'Still, I'll know to go elsewhere next time, won't I? Somewhere a little more hospitable.' She sniffs a third time, obviously going for the hat-trick. 'You could at least have *tried* to be civil!'

I snatch the cloth up and hang it from the hook, where it belongs. Civil, indeed. Yeah, right. As in civil bloody servant. And then I think some more and I find myself seething anew. Because I *was* civil. I have been civil throughout. Yet, despite that, I realise that at no point since I got home tonight has it occurred to my mother to say sorry. Or if not that (one mustn't push the bounds of probability too far), at least made some sort of enquiry about how *I* feel. Which is strung-out, strung-up, heartsick and lonely, and very much in need of a hug. 'And you could have been less thoughtless!' I bark back at her. 'God, you are *so* selfish.' I can feel tears welling up now. 'You don't care a jot about anyone else, do you? All you care about is whether *you're* having a good time. Just the same as you always did. Me, me, me.'

'I resent that.'

'Well, resent all you like. It's still true.' I start to gather up the detritus that litters the kitchen table. She stands and watches, hands on hips now.

'It most certainly isn't!'

I slap the papers that I'd collected up back down on the table.

'Yes it *is*, Mum!' I look at her now and all of a sudden I'm fourteen again. Waiting for her to come home from some rave-up or something. Making Pru's packed lunch for the morning. Worrying. Fretting. Wondering when she'll get home. Frightened that I can't actually bolt the back door because she won't be able to get in. Night after night. So many wretched nights. And then coming down in the morning to find her gone again. Just a note. Always a note, on the hall stand. With bus money, but not always. Scrawled in haste. Always. 'Byee, girls! Have a nice day!'

Then as now. Nothing's changed. Nothing. 'God, I don't even know why I should expect any different!' I rail at her. 'It's not like you've ever *been* any different, is it? You've never ever worried about *anyone* but you, and I'm sick of it, okay? I'm just sick of it!'

She removes her hands from her hips and stabs a finger in my direction. 'That's *not* true.' Her voice is cold. Each word tipped with its very own icicle. 'You really have no idea, do you? You have absolutely no idea what I went through when your father died. Oh, you can be as misty-eyed as you like about *him*, but who do you think it was that kept things together? Who put the food on the table? Who was it that paid for all your fancy clothes, your school trips, your riding lessons? Me! Don't you *dare* talk to me about selfishness, Abigail! You haven't the first clue about the sacrifices I made!'

'But I didn't *want* that. *We* didn't want that. We didn't want riding bloody lessons – we wanted *you*!' I sound plaintive, I know. Fourteen again. Wretched. I spread my hands. Swallow. Feel the crack in my voice. 'But you were never *there*, Mum, were you?'

263

I flee the room, altogether too choked-up to speak now. She goes back to doing the washing-up.

Symmetry. I've always rather liked symmetry. Especially the symmetry that is everywhere in nature. In a spider's web, a crystal, a butterfly, a leaf. The human body, for which I've also always had a fondness, is symmetrical in so many useful regards. Almost everything in it has its own mirror image. Two hands to engage with, two legs for walking. Two kidneys. Two lungs. Two each of everything, from eyes, ears and nostrils to thumbs.

But crucially, just the one liver to take care of. And also, more crucially, just the one heart. Which is why it so needs taking care of.

And if it stops, so do you.

My heart feels so full tonight that as I lie in bed I am actively aware of it. The shuntings and whooshing and general activity; the doppelganger effect of each lub and each dub. And beneath that, the steady and insistent sensation that it's working on go-slow: not up to full throttle, as so much of its energy is channelled elsewhere.

On Gabriel Ash. My mother's fourth dead husband's son. Who I very much wish I'd never met.

But try as I might – and I do try, because it's such a pointless occupation – I can't *stop* thinking about Gabriel – I just can't. How could I *ever* have imagined that what I felt for Charlie was anything even remotely connected with this? It's a feeling so powerful, so exquisitely painful, that I'm quite at a loss to know what to do. Where does it hurt? Everywhere.

It's almost two. My mother has finally ceased crashing about, and the house, similarly, has long since ceased all its wheezings and mutterings and sunk slowly back into silence. And now I do sleep, fitfully, though not for very long, because the silence is almost as distracting as the noise was. And then, through it, I now realise why it is I've woken. Because there *is* noise. Soft, indistinct, but still insistent. Cutting through brickwork and plasterboard and paint. Faint and yet keening. Impossible to ignore. And then, suddenly, I realise that what I can hear is the sound of my mother. Who is crying.

I feel just like I did when my babies were tiny. I listen for a minute or two, anxious and fretful. Hoping it will stop so I can go back to sleep. But you never can, can you? It's a sound that won't let you. A siren-call, tractor beam, noose of a sound. I kick back my duvet, get out of bed, then I pad along the landing to see her.

I push open the door to Seb's room and look in. Despite all the announcements stuck on there to declare it (keep out, radioactive, enter at your own risk) it isn't Seb's room any more. It is in the process of being reclaimed by nature. My mother's nature, which, little by little, is imposing its practices and rituals and ethos on to the organised, creative and exuberant chaos that it was before its real owner left.

Only temporarily left, I remind myself. I cross the carpet and sit down beside her on the bed. 'Look, Mum,' I say softly. 'I'm sorry. Okay?'

She's curled up foetally, facing the wall. Such a small shape in the bed. She doesn't respond.

'I'm sorry for what I said. I didn't really mean it. I was just het-up and tired and irritable and unhappy, and...'

Now she rolls over. Her face is streaked dark where she's been crying. Runnels of make-up having coalesced into train tracks that fan obliquely across her cheeks to her temples. She looks old and tired and sad.

'Why are you unhappy?'

I smile wanly at her. 'Oh, no reason. Just, you know, everything.'

She pushes herself up into a sitting position. 'That certainly sounds like reason enough to me.'

'Life's like that sometimes. I'll get over it, I'm sure.'

She pulls tissues from the cube beside the bed. 'I wish you'd tell me. Is it *honestly* not about this man friend of yours?'

Who was a friend. And then a lover. And is now a friend again. So much so that even *he* knows my heart is elsewhere. Irredeemably, hopelessly, achingly so. How *ever* could I have believed I had fallen for Charlie? I shake my head. 'I told you, that's history. Long over. It's not that.' I swallow. Perhaps this is not the best time. But will there ever be a good time? A better time, even? Perhaps now – this rare time of soul-searching – *is* the best time after all.

I shift a little on the bed. 'Mum, you know. Well, look…'

She blows hard on her nose and speaks to me through the clump of tissue. 'Well look what?'

'Mum, we have to find you somewhere to live. You can't live with us. Not permanently. I'm sorry, but you can't. It won't work. It's just that –'

'I know.' Her voice is quiet. Almost mouse-like. 'I realise that, Abigail. I *know*.'

'It's not about tonight. That was just me being silly. It's just that it's not going to work.'

'I know.'

'And I'm sorry –'

'So am I. But there's no need to apologise, Abigail.'

'Yes there is. I should have told you before. We should have discussed this ages ago, Mum. I shouldn't have let you build your hopes up. Let you think…'

'No, Abigail. The fault is entirely mine. I built my hopes up all by myself. And I shouldn't have. I shouldn't have assumed.'

She's staring past me now. Not at anything in particular. Just at whatever thought is suspended in front of her. Then she puts her hands into her lap and sighs.

'Funny, isn't it? How things come around?' I wait. She sighs. 'You know, I never thought my life would end up like this. I didn't *plan* for it to be like this. You do know that, don't you?' A remnant of a smile crosses her features. 'My perpetual folly, you see. No sense of reality. Always assuming…' She pulls out another tissue and dabs at the corner of her eyes. 'But you know what, Abbie? You know why I did? Why I *do*? Because I'm scared.'

'Scared of what?'

'Scared of *everything*. Scared of living on my own. Scared of *being* on my own. Scared of dying. Scared of *not* dying. Scared of ending up drooling and incontinent and bereft. Just scared.'

'But Mum, you have nothing to be scared of. You have so many friends. And Pru and I. And your grandchildren and everything. And okay, so you've had some problems with your knee, but you're fit as anything apart from that. God, You'll still be dancing on tables when Pru and I are in our dotage!'

She smiles properly then, but it's a strange sort of smile. One I've never seen before. And then she slowly shakes her head. 'You're so young, Abbie. So very young still. You think I want that? You really think that's what I want for myself?' She sighs. 'You know, I look into the future and all I can see is this great grey gaping void. An endless procession of days that need filling. But you can't, you know. You can try all you like but it's all so much desperate window dressing. Every morning you wake up and you have to consider. How shall I fill today? What can I do with this period of time that will give it an iota of meaning?'

'Mum, don't talk like this. You're just tired and over-emotional. You'll feel a hundred percent better in the morning –'

'No, Abbie.' Her voice is sterner now. 'You're wrong. I will feel a hundred and one percent the same.'

I don't know how to respond to that, because I realise it's true. A truth that I've never really thought about before. 'You're missing Hugo,' I suggest hopefully. Slightly desperately even. 'Aren't you? After all, it's been less than six months. You can't expect to –'

'Abbie, this is not about Hugo. This is entirely about me.' She takes my hand in both of hers and strokes it absently. 'You know,' she says, 'people don't change. Not really. Look at you. My little mum.'

I don't know what she means and she can see it in my face. 'That's what you always were, you know. My strong one. My big girl. My proper little mum. That's what we always used to call you. A proper little mum. Taking charge. Taking care. Looking after your little sister for me.'

'It didn't feel like that to me.'

'Because it came so naturally to you. And you know, you *are* right.'

'About what?'

'About me. About how selfish I was. How selfish I still *am*.'

'Oh, Mum, I didn't *mean* that –'

She pats my hand now. 'Oh, no need for platitudes, Abbie. I've long since come to terms with myself. Let myself off, even, because that's what I'm like. Oh, I can give you countless speeches about all the sacrifices I've made – Lord, I've rehearsed them often enough – but the truth is that none of it *is* true. I *was* a bad mother. I *am* a bad mother. How could I ever have been anything else?' She looks at me earnestly. 'You see, the thing is, Abbie, I never really knew *how* to be a mother. I didn't have a clue. I loved my career. I loved my life. I loved success and fame and adulation and everything else that I took so much for granted. And the truth is that when your father died I was mortified. Grieving, of course. But mainly mortified. I simply didn't know what to do next. Yes, I loved you girls – and more than you can possibly imagine – but not enough to give up everything I'd worked for. Not enough to give up on *my* life for yours.'

'But you *had* to work, Mum. To provide for us. We knew that –'

'Don't pretend, Abbie. There's no need to spare me. I know what I'm like. What I *am*. Always something or someone and moving on and moving on… Except in the end you reach a point where you realise that moving is no longer an option. That there is nothing else to move on *to*. The best years of my life are behind me, you see. So all I can do is look backwards. Revel in the glories – oh, I've done lots of that – but also to survey the detritus. Wallow in regrets. Torture myself with all the right things that I never seemed to find time to do.' Her eyes are bright with fresh tears. 'It's a lot to come to terms with.'

'Mum, you don't know that.'

'Of *course* I know that, Abbie. I may be lots of things but I'm not stupid. I know there's a price to pay.'

'For what?'

'For not paying *my* dues.'

'That's ridiculous.'

'Not at all.' She dabs the tears away irritably. 'I'm just reaping what I've sowed. It was always coming. It's just happened rather sooner than I'd anticipated, let's say.'

'Oh, Mum. It's not like that.'

'Yes it *is*.' She squeezes my hand with sudden strength. Almost seems to pull herself together physically. 'And you look shattered. Come on, now. Get yourself off to bed.'

'Are you sure you're okay?'

'*Yes*. Now skedaddle.'

I get up off the bed. 'Can I get you anything?'

268

She shakes her head. 'Nothing. I need nothing. Go on. Off you go now.'

Just as I'm about to close the bedroom door behind me, she speaks again.

'Abigail?'

I put my head back round the door again. 'Yes?'

'I knew, you know. About the house.' She clears her throat. 'I should have told you.'

'What, Hugo's house?'

She nods. 'Well, not as in *knew*. We never actually discussed it. But I always knew there was something not right.' She looks past me for a moment. Then back. 'There were lots of things not right with us, Abbie. I knew he was a scoundrel.'

'So why on earth did you marry him? Sell your flat and everything? Give up all your independence? *Why*?'

She looks at me tenderly. 'You really *don't* understand, do you? To *be* with him, Abbie. Because that's what I *do*.' She smiles then. 'Yes, he was a scoundrel, but a very charming scoundrel. And because, well,' she shrugs. 'You know me. *Que Sera.*'

I go to leave then, because even though my head is still full of questions, I'm absolutely dead on my feet. But as I step back through the doorway, though, I have a sudden thought.

'And Gabriel? Gabriel Ash? Did you know about him too?'

She shakes her head. 'No.' Then she muses for a moment. 'Now, that really *is* tragic. Don't you think?'

'That you didn't know?'

'No. That Hugo paid such a high price for *his* failings. Terrible to die without coming to terms.' She settles back against the pillows and folds her hands in her lap. 'I'm a very lucky woman, I think.'

Her eyes are still shining. I pad back to the bed. Then I take her in my arms and I tell her I love her, which is something I haven't done in decades.

For three-quarters of my life, in fact. A very long time. And, poignantly, I realise, neither has she.

# Chapter 26

It, it, it. Such a little word for such a big embracing meaning. And to my shame it takes me a full five seconds to work out which 'it' Sebastian means. Mother 'it'? Me 'it'? Generalised life 'it'?

That and the fact that I'm trudging through the day as if via a filter of porridge, because I have had precisely two hours of sleep.

'Hey, hey, hey!' announces Candice with her usual vigour. It is, I remind myself, the first Monday morning of my newly prescribed Nice Life, and I really must get with the programme. Except every time I think about having a nice life, I also think who it was who told me to do so. Which means my progress is scuppered before it's even begun.

'Hey!' she says again. 'Doesn't it just make you *sick*?'

Candice has got this week's *Depth* open on the reception desk in front of her, so it's at least clear which species of 'it' she is referring to.

'What does?'

'Listen.' She points to a heading. It says 'Angel to Demon?' in big cerise letters. But it's nothing to do with Dan Brown. '"*Lucy Whittall*,"' reads Candice, '"*is to swap her scrubs for a Cat suit and an AK47. The 32-year-old actress and darling of the tabloids has just landed the part of a lifetime. Beating off some pretty well-upholstered competition, she's just been announced as having landed a plum role in the latest Bond outing, playing bad girl Comtessa Therese von blah blah, opposite the divine Daniel Craig. Shooting, which is due to start late November, is taking place mostly on location in the Caribbean. 'It's the most thrilling thing that's ever happened in my life,' Whittall gushed, when we caught up with her outside London's Ivy restaurant last week. THE most? Whatever happened to romance, Lucy love? But fear not, the Whittall nuptials are still very much on track. Reported to be costing a cool thirty grand —"* thirty grand! "*— the much-hyped* *union of the angel and her BBC weatherman was due to be taking place over Christmas. But we can exclusively reveal that the happy couple are going to rush everything through for a November 5th bash, before their Caribbean honeymoon beckons... We forecast fireworks aplenty! Ding dong!'"*

She plops the paper in front of me. 'Ding bloody dong, indeed. Lucky cow,' she says. 'Why isn't my life one big round of thirty grand weddings and Caribbean holidays and getting parts in Bond movies? Eh?'

I look at the photo. Lucy beams back at me. 'More to the point, who would spend thirty thousand pounds on a wedding? That can't be true.'

'Oh, it can, sweet,' says Brendan, coming up to join us. 'Friend of mine spent close on that and all she had to show for it was a marquee, a chimney sweep and a fork buffet supper. You two are *so* out of touch. These things *cost*.'

I don't know why, but it's Brendan's words that depress me the most. Caribbean honeymoons, parts in James Bond films. These are things that mean nothing to the likes of me. But the concept of weddings – his wedding – *their* wedding – is the absolute last thing I want to think about right now. Particularly in conjunction with Nice Life directive. Were it not for the slightly inconvenient fact that I never, ever want to see him again, *ever*, I'd be straight round the television studios to confront him. Let him know what an ill-advised, stupid, thoughtless, banal, and yes, damned patronising thing that was to say. Him with his TV career and his movie-star fiancée and his Caribbean honeymoon and his posh linen jackets *and* his poncey selection of Liberty silk ties.

No wonder, I think, that Lucy Whittall was so jolly when she saw me. And no wonder Gabriel wasn't. I close the magazine and sniff at nothing in particular. Well, he can keep it. *All* of it.

If he does. 'Waste of money,' Says Candice, plopping the magazine back on the pile. 'I'll give it six months, tops. Once she's out there schmoozing with all those Hollywood hunks, he'll be for the chop, for certain sure. History before you can say biscuits. Don't you think?' She glances at me. 'Hmm,' she observes. 'You look like you've dropped Owen Wilson and picked up Danny De Vito. Heavy weekend?'

I smile, albeit wanly. You absolutely *have* to keep smiling. 'Hmm,' I say. 'Something like that.'

I then make a manful stab at giving her the highlights of Jake's gig, while editing out all the rest. Candice knows Club One. She went to a hen night there three years back, in which the bride to be, gobbling brufen after a hockey injury earlier in the day, was mistaken for a drug dealer, and was thrown out on to the street.

And then arrested by the policeman who had come to her aid, for assaulting him bodily with her comedy penis.

'Seven the next morning, they let her out. They kept the penis for evidence, of course.'

I'm even managing to find a nugget of amusement in all this – I *am* trying – when Mr Dobson comes in for his appointment.

But even Mr Dobson, who is unfailingly gallant at all times, passes comment on the state of my face.

'You're looking tired, dear.'

'But all the better for seeing you,' I tell him. Which is true. 'How are you?' I add, as I take him through and pull the curtains round the cubicle. 'It seems like an age since I saw you. I was beginning to wonder if I'd been a bit brutal and you'd decided to take your business elsewhere!'

Mr Dobson, ever the gent, assures me that he would do no such thing. That he's been really looking forward to coming in today. And that he's missed our little chats. He's so sweet.

'So,' I say, once he's gowned-up and ready on the couch. 'Have you been away on holiday, or something?'

He's face down, of course, so I can't see his expression. He doesn't move a muscle as I begin pummelling his back. 'No,' he says. 'Sadly, my wife passed away.'

I stop pummelling. Come around to the top end of the couch. Squat down in front of him. Take his hand in my own. 'Oh, Mr Dobson. I'm so sorry. I'm so *sorry*.'

He looks a little embarrassed. 'Please don't be, dear. Really.'

'But that's so sad, Mr Dobson. Oh, I'm so sorry.'

'Don't be,' he says again. 'She'd been so, so poorly. Really. It was a blessing.'

'But even so…'

'Believe me, young Abbie, it was. She really couldn't bear to suffer any longer. See *me* suffer. It was a very courageous decision.'

I blink at him. Swallow. 'You mean she –'

'Yes,' he says simply. 'She did.' I don't know what to say. And as I'm still crouched in front of him, clutching his hand, he presumably feels he needs to move things along, or he might well be stuck there all day. 'Please don't be upset,' he says, with such gentle kindness. Such care. 'She'd had a good life,' he says firmly. 'The best. And there's not very many that can say that, are there?' He eases his hand from beneath mine now, and pats it. 'I consider myself very blessed.'

I feel really teary when Mr Dobson leaves. I know his wife was elderly and had had lots of problems in the last year or so, and, yes, by all accounts, she *had* had a good life. And yes, one must be thankful. But it's still shocking – heartbreaking – even so. So when Brendan declares that I look fit for nothing, I can do nothing but tell him he's right. And as he generously insists on seeing my last patient, I head home early to catch up on some sleep.

I like sleep, I decide. Sleep equals unconsciousness and unconscious equals oblivion, and a spot of oblivion is just what I need. On my way home I pass the grey bulk of the hospital and I wonder at all the bracing, resolute, optimistic thoughts I'd been thinking when I made the decision to leave it. It all seems such a very long time ago now.

But very present in my thoughts, as I turn into our road, is that not only has a lot of time passed since that day, but also that an equally large number of words passed between my mother and I last night. It feels like a weight pressing down on my shoulders. What to do next. How best to proceed. Whether all the decisions I felt so secure in are, in fact, entirely the wrong ones.

It's only when I pull the key from the ignition that I realise quite how much I've been dreading having to face her. Having to see her in this new incarnation. With all that's been said, and all that's been admitted, I really don't know what to do. How, in all conscience, can I move her out now? How will I cope with the guilt? Yet if I don't follow through it will have all been for

273

nothing. Worse than nothing, in fact, if the mother who always kept up such a good front is now so in touch with her innermost regrets that I spend the rest of her life trying to make her feel better, when the bottom line is that I *can't*.

Jake's in the kitchen with Ben, eating crumpets, when I get in, and I'm all at once struck by how precious this all is. This time. This chunk of life that I can load up and always carry with me. No matter what happens next I've already got it in the bank. And in thinking that thought, I also think I realise what my mother was trying to articulate last night. She's right. She doesn't have this. She may have her trophies and awards and her precious stacks of rave reviews. But where family's concerned, where what *matters* is concerned, I realise she has nothing but guilt and regrets.

Which is a lot worse than nothing. Yes, she had her glittering career. But everything comes at a price. 'Where's Nana?' I ask Jake, dipping to kiss his head.

He shrugs. 'I dunno. She wasn't here when I got in from school.'

I fill the kettle. It's cold. Jake and Ben are swigging Sprite. And the teapot, when I look for it, isn't in its space on the worktop. It's still empty and rinsed and sitting upside down on the drainer. Exactly as it was when I left it this morning. All day without tea? My mother? Surely not. I put it down on the drainer and cast my eyes around the kitchen. Bar the packet of crumpets and tub of butter on the worktop, everything is much as I left it this morning. My coffee mug still sits upside down on the draining board. The paper lies unread with the post on the table.

And then something hits me. 'Thank you,' she'd said. I'd told her I loved her and she'd thanked me for doing so. And that she didn't deserve it. As if you even have a choice. And something else. She mentioned Hugo as well. About how sad that he'd died without coming to terms. Is that what we did last night? A coming to terms? I feel cold. Even colder when I recall something else. That I didn't actually even *see* her this morning. Her bedroom door was shut and I'd left without waking her. Imagining she'd sleep till mid morning, at least. It must have been four when we finally turned in. So I'd left her to sleep; padding around quietly so as not to disturb her. I hadn't actually checked on her at all. OhmyGod. Ohmy*God*. What on earth has she *done*? I sprint from the kitchen and fly up the stairs.

There are twenty-nine of them on our stair case. Twenty-two and then a dog leg and a little half-landing. And then a further seven. It's a high-ceilinged house. Negotiating our staircase takes a good twenty seconds, which is just about long enough for me to fashion the sort of scenario that makes my heart thump in my ribcage and my blood run cold. By the time I reach Sebastian's bedroom, therefore, I have it all worked out. She has killed herself, plainly. She has taken on board all the things we discussed, and decided there's nothing left to live for.

But when I enter the room I do not find such horrors. Merely silence and order and a neatly made bed.

I don't realise Jake's followed me up here until I hear his voice behind me. 'Mum?' he asks. 'Is everything, you know, okay?'

I turn around and switch on a breezy smile. He has Spike in his arms and is scratching his ears. 'Oh, I'm sure it is. It just suddenly occurred to me that Nana might be up here. You know, had a fall or something.' He looks stricken. 'Or a nap. Jake *ignore* me. You know how I worry.'

He looks unconvinced by my lightness of tone. Looks past me into Seb's room and frowns. 'It's just that I, like, heard you last night. You know, arguing and everything. Is everything all right?'

Oh, God. How I wish now that I'd spoken to him this morning. Spent altogether less time with my head in a bucket and a great deal more being a bloody grown-up. I grab his upper arms and squeeze them. 'Jake, everything's *fine*. Really it is. We just had a bit of an argument, that's all. Like everyone does. Like *we* do sometimes.'

'What about?'

'About, well, about living here, really. I was a bit over-tired; a bit cross about her party, and, well, we just did a bit of straight talking. That's all. It was nothing. We made up. Don't *worry*.'

I'm noticing more now, even as I speak. That her slippers are absent. That her bathrobe has gone. That her little zip lock bag full of pills has gone from the bedside table.

That she's left. With her pills. Where's she *gone*?

'Perhaps she's gone on a sleepover,' decides Jake. He has Seb's wardrobe open. Her fur coat is gone, but the rest of her clothes seem to be all there. I'm not sure if that's a good thing or a bad thing, however. I walk across and pull out the top drawer of Seb's dresser. The drawer I emptied for her to keep all her underwear in. It's similarly bulging. Jake looks in too. He looks anxious. 'Do you think?'

'Yes, you're probably right. Don't fret. You know Nana.'

But he looks like he doesn't any more. He looks even more anxious.

'But she'd say. She always says. She just doesn't *go*.'

'Well, perhaps she was in a hurry.' But he's right. She does always say. In some fashion or other. Mostly voicemail; 'Abbie, dear? I've run out of Rennies. Will you pick me up a box on your way home from work?' Or a note in the kitchen: 'Have gone with Wilf to Brian's. Will need collecting at 8 p.m. Thank you.' Something. *Always*. She doesn't just *disappear*. Four months my mother's been living in my house now, and in that time she has never gone anywhere or done anything, without somebody else being involved in the equation in some way. Never. Not once. This is not good to know.

I usher Jake from her room. 'Oh, you know what she's like,' I reassure him anyway. 'I'll call Auntie Pru and see if she knows.'

Hearts, patently, are of a certain sort of size. They don't vary a great deal from person to person, as far as I'm aware, and if I had to find a suitable size-related analogy I suppose I would plump for a potato. The sort of potato you'd use for a jacket potato. And no one, at least of my acquaintance, anyway, has a mouth that is remotely roomy enough to fit a jacket potato in all in one go. Which is probably why I am so very weary of having my heart in my mouth all the time.

Even so, that's exactly where it has decided to lodge and I'm just going to have to work around it. There's no answer at Pru's, but I get her on her mobile. She's standing at the edge of a football pitch in Bristol, and hasn't heard from or spoken to Mum all this week. And she doesn't like my tone.

'Abbie, what's *happened*?'

'We had words. Last night.'

'What sort of words?'

'Bad words. And it was just – well, you know – some of the things she said to me.'

'*What* did she say to you?'

'Things that…well, just things I've never heard her say before. You know, real things. Like how she's so frightened of the future. That the best part of her life is over. Like every day is like a black hole. Or something.'

'A black hole? Oh, dear. But you know how melodramatic she can be when she wants to.'

'But that's just it. This wasn't like that.' I hear a thud above my head. 'Look, I can't really go into it now. Jake's coming down the stairs. I just thought she might have called you, that's all.'

'Have you tried Celeste? Perhaps they've gone off on one of their outings or something.'

'No. I don't have her number.'

'I'm sure I do. Damn. But not here. Tell you what. We'll be finished up here in twenty minutes or so. I'll try her as soon as I get home and call you back.'

'Thanks. But now I think about it, I might just as well drive over there when I've dropped Jake at his drum lesson.'

'And you'll call me, yes?'

'I'll call you.'

'And if I hear, I'll do likewise. Oh, bloody, *bloody* hell,' she says. 'This is all we need, isn't it?'

'Oh, God, Pru. I hope she hasn't done something stupid.'

'It wouldn't be the first time,' she says drily.

Jake's still quiet as I take him off to his lesson. Quiet yet not even plugged in. and I silently curse myself that I've been so busy worrying about me, that I've never found a second to discuss this with *him*.

And that, now, clearly, is not the right time. Or so I think, anyway. Jake's obviously got his own ideas about that.

'Perhaps she's run away,' he suggests, his tone difficult to read. 'You know. Like to pay you back for last night.'

I wonder how much he's heard. I wonder what he's thinking. I wonder at my imbecility in having got to this point in the first place. I attempt levity. 'I was a bit of an old bag last night, wasn't I?'

Now he does turn. And he's shaking his head. 'No you weren't, Mum,' he says. 'Nan was bang out of order. She shouldn't take advantage of you like that. It's not fair.'

'Well, it's all over now,' I say, stunned by his frankness, and anxious to reassure him.

'Good,' he says firmly. 'Because…well, I mean I know I love her and everything, but sometimes, Mum, you know…the way she treats you…'

'Like a child.' I pat his knee. 'I *know*. And I shouldn't let her, should I?'

He turns towards me. 'I was going to say like a servant. She does, Mum. You shouldn't let her. You should tell her. It's *skank*, Mum. You should make her do things for herself.'

This from my son? My son who's so young still?

But he's absolutely right. He's heard that from *me* often enough. I should have sorted this stuff at least thirty *years* back. Oh, I could weep. I really could.

But I don't weep. I rally. I'm a mother. I *must* rally. With Jake's sage words still making ripples in my head, I turn the car around and head off to Celeste's. But my mission there proves equally fruitless, and without any sort of coherent plan in my head, I head back for home. Perhaps Pru's had some luck.

I'm just parking the car when Mr Davidson appears, and for a moment I think salvation's at hand and that she's been in there helping with his Triangle stand.

But no, he hasn't seen her. Has just come out to give me money. He presses a ten pound note into my hand.

'What's this?' I ask, completely at a loss to understand it.

He looks sheepish. 'It's to pay for some carpet shampoo. I'm most terribly sorry.'

I try to give it back. 'Mr Davidson, please don't be. Mum managed to get most of it out already, last night.'

He looks unconvinced, and he won't take the tenner. 'Then buy yourself some flowers,' he says.

Flowers. At a time like this. I don't think so. Though I'm very touched by the gesture, I still can't help but think that flowers are what you use to make wreaths.

I'm still thinking that – well, thinking how utterly ridiculous it is to *be* thinking things like that – when my progress through my own front door is arrested mid door-swing. And by, it turns out as I ease myself around it, the two suitcases that are standing to attention in the hallway. My mother's two suitcases, in fact. I walk around them and into the kitchen.

Where my mother is sitting, at the table, with Wilfred, who is pouring from a pot of freshly-brewed tea.

Not dead. Not departed. Sitting in the kitchen. As if absolutely nothing is wrong. 'Hello, dear,' she says brightly. 'Can we pour you a cuppa? Did you have a good day at work?'

I am so relieved to see her I do what almost everyone does when they have a bucketful of adrenalin coursing through their arteries and suddenly nowhere for it to go. I explode. 'Mum, where the *hell* have you *been*?'

She looks perfectly astonished. 'To see *Pride and Prejudice*, since you ask.'

'*What?*'

'At the pictures. Goodness me, Abigail. Calm *down*.'

'Calm down? Calm *down*?' I slump down, none the calmer, on one of the kitchen chairs. I can't cope with this level of hormone production. Neither can I cope with this level of disingenuousness. I know her far too well to be fooled for an instant by her affectation of surprise at my tone. Amazing, I think, even in the midst of my ranting, how quickly we all revert to type. Behind our masks. 'Typical,' I say. 'You can't even do that, can you? You can't even take yourself off in a huff without causing a bloody drama about it. Have you any idea what's been going through my head? *Have* you?'

Mother blinks and turns to Wilfred, who looks up at me with the expression of a man who's been round the block in the woman department and who certainly knows a mid-life crisis when he sees one. Though his powers of observation are pretty academic, I remember. He's already been told. By my mother.

Which makes me even more furious. I pull my bag from my shoulder and dump my keys on the table. 'Mum, I have spent the

279

past hour and a half in a state of complete and utter panic, thanks to you.'

'Why?' she looks indignant.

'*Why*? Think about it! I get home. There's no sign of you. Jake doesn't know where you are. No note. No message. No nothing. Your nightie's gone missing. Your pills are all gone. Pru hasn't seen you. Mr Davidson hasn't seen you. And after last night and everything…' I glare at her. 'Think about it. What the hell do *you* think I've been thinking?'

She looks at me as if I've gone quite, quite insane. And then, the penny dropping, a touch guilty.

But only a touch. 'Goodness,' she says, with a reedy little laugh that I assume is entirely for Wilfred's benefit. 'You make all this fuss about me being under your feet and then the very moment I leave you in peace you're flapping about like a headless chicken. Abigail, calm down. I'm here *now*, aren't I?'

I gesture towards the hallway. 'And also packed, by the look of it.'

'Well, yes, of *course* I'm packed. That's why Wilfred's *here*. I was going to collect the rest of my belongings in the morning, but he's kindly offered to bring them for me now.' She sips her tea daintily. 'Bar my cheval mirror, of course. It won't fit in his Micra.'

I look from one to the other. 'To go *where* exactly?'

'To Celeste's, of course.'

'I've just come from Celeste's. She's not home.'

'Yes, I *know*, dear. She's at her salsa class till seven. Besides, we were waiting for *you*.'

I get up and go across to open a window. I feel too strung-up to sit down. 'But why didn't you tell me earlier? Discuss it with me? Why didn't you phone me at work? Or leave a note, even? Or tell Pru? *Anything?* We've been frantic!'

She gets up as well and fetches me a mug. 'Let me pour you a cup of tea,' she says. I don't want a cup of tea but I let her pour it anyway. 'Abigail, I'm telling you *now*. I didn't call you because there's really nothing to discuss. And besides, I didn't want to bother you at work. And why on earth would I leave a note? How was I to know you were going to finish work early?'

Which is a fair point, I guess. I sit down at the table again. There's a box of chocolates on it. Wilfred shunts them towards me with a concerned air about him. 'For you,' he says, gently. As if talking through bars to a dangerous beast. 'Just a little thank you for last night.'

Chapter 27

OH, BALM ON MY wounds. An email from my much-missed son.

Ye mum!

Yeah, I'm fine. And yes I did get the sweatshirt and I did get the CD and I did get the photos. J looks beast! All well this end. Am off to Cannes with Dad tomorrow to see a man about a marina. I tell you, mum. This is the life! xxx

PS can you send my ski gear? Plz? xxx

Memo to self: I don't care who said it. I am going to have a nice life. I AM going to have a nice life. I am going to have a NICE LIFE.

'At EXO' I read carefully. 'You, the customer, is paramount. Mind. Body. Spirit. The essential triumvirate of the human condition…'

'The rule of three,' says Dee, equally carefully. 'The holy trinity…'

Because much of what takes place at Exo involves the client in being either prostrate or supine, much of their philosophy of personal wellbeing is written on the ceiling and the floor. Written lavishly, with lots of curlicues and flourishes, in gentle earthy tones that match their gentle earthy sentiments about how best to achieve personal nirvana

Not that it's working. We have been here almost an hour, but I can still feel twangs and creaks of stress and irritation infiltrate my personally prescribed de-stressing mask. It is so thick and so hard now that my frown lines have been disabled. My lips are dry from breathing through the small fixed aperture that is my mouth. I cannot breath through my nose because a small gob of face mask hangs from my left nostril like a small avocado-scented bogie, and vibrates if I try to inhale through my nose, which tickles and makes me want to sneeze.

I have the impression that I am neither in a place or a situation where the violent expulsion of the contents of my bronchii would be considered an appropriate happening. I am, I muse, with no small degree of bitter irony, engaged, as is my ambition, in the pursuit of a nice life. And everyone knows that people with nice lives only have them by virtue of a rigorous commitment to de-stress and de-tox.

Even if it is all utter crap.

'It is, you know,' I tell Dee. 'De-toxing. It's all phoney pseudo-science. Assuming you have a functioning liver and a pair of kidneys, there is absolutely nothing you can buy in Boots or from Carol Vorderman that will do the job of de-toxing better than your own body will, left to its own devices.' I point. 'And what's with 'triumvirate' when it's at home? What a load of pretentious twaddle.'

Dee has a different face mask on to me. Hers is the colour of a Chinese chicken curry and was specially mixed for her to address the unique skincare concerns that a woman must attend to when she's 'with child'. Or presumably face the consequences. Which have been spelled out in terrifying detail by Brandi, our nice Exo therapist-for-the-day. Dee moves her face carefully towards me.

'Still. It's nice this, isn't it? You know. As a way to spend the day. A bit of quality time. We do deserve it.'

'You do. I'm not sure that's quite how I feel.'

'Oh, piffle. My God, Abs, you've been through it too.'

'Not like *you* have.'

And I'll brook no argument on that score. The fall-out after the fall out was short but fairly bloody. Having made such a public statement of intent via their bedroom window, Malcolm has since consolidated his position. By putting the house on the market, counter-petitioning for divorce – for adultery, naturally – and also by selling Dee's car. Which wasn't Dee's car, as it turns out, but his. Though in practice she drove it (he had a company van), it was Malcolm that owned it. His name on the documents, his finance agreement, his right (till the divorce settlement's sorted, at any rate) to dispose of it as he saw fit. Dee's been staying with Carolyn and her three Persian cats and getting the bus into work.

'That's as maybe,' she says. 'But when they're handing out the medals, they can certainly leave me out. If I'd a bit less time being such an utter wimp, we wouldn't have come to this.'

'But you wouldn't have met Tim either, don't forget.'

And thank God she has. Thank every deity in the firmament. And she does. Despite the mask, I can see it in her face. 'And now we need to find you one.'

'One of what?'

'A *Tim*, stupid.'

I grimace. With difficulty. 'Blimey, give me a chance, Dee. I've only just uninstalled Mother, don't forget. I think I could do with an emotional break. Besides, everyone knows that there's nothing less sexy than a woman on a mission to find a man.'

And I'm not on one anyway. Because I simply can't imagine that there's another man on the planet I'd so much as glance at right now. These things take time. Too much time, frankly. But then I suppose I've got plenty of that.

'So she's gone, then? Like, properly?'

I nod carefully. 'As of last Monday. She's moved in with her friend. I'm popping over later to take her some things. Fingers crossed the two of them are still speaking.'

She chuckles. 'And this is permanent?'

'I think so. I *hope* so. To be honest, with hindsight, I'm surprised this didn't come up as an option months ago. I mean Celeste's been on her own for quite a few years now. And she certainly has the space. And they've been friends for, like, decades.'

'And how's Jake with it all? He okay?'

'He's just fine. Which is such a relief I can't tell you. I was so sure he'd hate me.'

She laughs again. 'As if.'

'No, I *was*. They're so close. And I felt awful. We'd never even discussed it. Not properly.'

'But he understood.'

'He didn't see there was much to understand. What he'd said, well that was just a spur of the moment thing really. He never actually assumed that was what was going to happen. Didn't want it. He said we'd drive one another mad.'

'There you are then. All that fretting for nothing. And now you can put it all behind you.'

And have a nice life. And move on. And spend my days off coming to places like this where there is silence and serenity and Indian head massages on tap. All the better to concentrate the mind. But when your mind is so chock full of demons and goblins, is concentrating it in any sense *helpful*? 'Yeah, I guess.' I say. 'Trouble is, I still feel so awful about it.'

'Oh, you shouldn't!'

'I know. But I do, even so. You know, the thing that really gets to me is that I never really thought about it properly.'

'About what?'

'About Mum. Why she's the way she is. I've been pretty hard on her, Dee.'

'No, you haven't! You've been an angel!'

'Only on the surface. Up here –' I touch my finger to my temple. Carefully. 'Up here I've been furious. Resentful and furious. But she's right, you know. She never really *did* know how to be a mother. And how would she? She was only four when hers left her...'

Dee touches her stomach. 'God, so *young*.'

'Which must leave some pretty big scars, don't you think?'

She mimes quote marks. 'Issues.'

'Exactly. Issues.' I raise a hand. 'Don't worry. I'm not planning to write a dissertation about it. Just endeavour to think a little harder, that's all.'

'But you've got to quit the guilt trip.'

'I shall try to quit the guilt trip. Anyway. Enough. How's Carolyn?'

'Oh, bearing up under the strain of living with a bag lady, I think. Still,' she says. 'Not for too much longer. I'm on the move too, as of next week.'

'To where?'

She looks surprised. 'I'm going to move in with Tim, of course.'

'Are you sure? I mean I know things are great between you, but are you sure you don't want to give yourself a bit of space before making such a big commitment? It's not as you've known each other *that* long.'

Dee pats her stomach and snorts. 'I think it's a bit late for that, don't you? Commitments don't come much bigger, in my book. And you know what? I'm glad. Because if it wasn't for this baby, who knows how long I'd still be limping along with Malcolm? Trying to do the right thing. Trying to make it work. You know, before I found out I was pregnant I was seriously – and I *mean* seriously – contemplating ending things with Tim. Can you *believe* that? You know, that thought scares me more than anything. That I might have done that. Despite everything I feel about him, I actually might have let him go.

'So thank God for this baby, is what I say. Thank God that I didn't have to make that decision.' She turns and smiles. 'You know, I don't *need* space, Abs. Really I don't. I've been living in a vacuum for so long. I've had enough space to last anyone's lifetime. What I need is exactly what I've got. I know I haven't known him long. I know it could all go wrong at any point –'

'I'm sure it won't.'

'But it still *might*. I'm not so naïve I haven't considered the possibility. But I'm going to go for it. I'm going to give it my best shot.' She smiles. 'Become a bit more like you, in fact. Stop being such a *victim*. I've spent way, way too long not daring to dream about having any sort of happy future; walking around with a cloud over my head, not expecting things to get any better. Well now I have to *make* them better, don't I? Get back in the driving seat and run my *own* life.'

Whereas conversely, I'm beginning to feel that, bar Charlie, of course, I've been travelling solo for way, way too long. Which reminds me of something. 'By the way,' I say. 'I had a thought when I woke up this morning. How d'you feel about fostering a beige Nissan Sunny? Just the one careful owner, full service history, and only smells very slightly of mice.'

Celeste lives in a house with a novelty doorbell, which played *Tie a Yellow Ribbon* when I called round last week, and is now playing *Strangers in the Night*.

Which seems fitting. Because that's what he was. What he *is*. Except the rest of the lyrics don't fit.

Still, it does feel nice to be visiting my mother. With special emphasis on the word visit. Dee's right. This is best. This is progress. This is right. It won't feel exactly comfortable till I banish the demon guilt from my psyche, but I think I can live with it. Just.

'Ah, Abbie, dear!' coos Celeste as she answers the door. 'What perfect timing, too. I've just cut the cake.'

'Cake? Is it somebody's birthday?'

'Oh, no, dear. We don't tend to celebrate those these days. No, no. We've just been up to Lidl and they had some on offer. Anyway, do come on in. Mind the boxes as you go.'

'Pru's been round, then?'

'Yes, bless her. With some of it, anyway. I don't for the life of me know where we're going to put everything. But we'll muddle through together. As we do.'

My mother is coming down the stairs as I enter. As ever, I'm amazed at her astounding resilience. Were it not for the scar, you wouldn't know about the knee op. Won't be long, I surmise, before she's back at the dance club. And back with another Hugo. Despite what she's said.

'I brought your cheval mirror,' I tell her, as she gives me the two perfunctory Garland air kisses. 'Oh, and here's your post.'

She takes it. Riffles through it. Re-sorts it. Pulls one to the top. 'Well, well, this looks exciting. I'll just get my glasses.' Then she's rattling back off up the stairs.

Celeste, in the meantime, takes me through to the living room, while she goes off to pour me a nice cup of tea. It's a warm, fuggy room with much sat-upon sofas, that have crisp embroidered caps on the backs and the arms. There's a brace of little plates and, as promised, a sponge cake, which is sitting on a cake stand atop a silver doily, as if beamed here from the pages of an Enid Blyton book.

There are photographs everywhere. Of Celeste's children and grandchildren. Soon to be augmented, no doubt, by my own mother's extensive collection. Of my mother, my mother, my mother. I think once again about existing on memories, and I hope she will find some that bring her some peace.

'So,' says Celeste, handing me a cup and saucer and then perching herself at the other end of the sofa. 'How *are* you?'

Don't you just hate it when people ask that? Well, not so much ask that, but ask it *like* that. How *are* you, with special reference to the word in the middle. As in shorthand for saying that they're very well aware that things are not all that they might be. Well, not so much aware that *things* are not all they might be, but that one specific thing, which they are too polite to mention, is at the nub of the question they're asking. Well, not so much asking, but politely implying. Which is all well and good, if you know what they're on about, but altogether less good if you don't. What on earth does she mean? Is my wretchedness really that obvious? Or has Mum been banging on some more with her mid-life-Charlie crisis? Celeste pats my hand and says, 'hmm?'

I pull a blank face. 'I'm fine.'

'Oh, my *dear*,' she says, turning the pat into a squeeze. 'I am so, so glad to hear you say that.'

'Er. Um,' I say. 'Great.'

She gives me my hand back. 'Your Mum did say, of course.'

'Say what?'

'Well, you *know*. This and that.'

I sip my tea and try to fathom where all this is leading. This and that? I must be looking fairly nonplussed, because she then grabs my hand again. 'Abbie, you're *sure* you're not cross about all this?'

'About what?'

She puts her cup and saucer down on the coffee table. 'About your mum moving in here. With *me*. I mean, I would hate to think you were. I know what a help she's been to you these past months.' *What?* 'And I know you feel her place is with you – and why wouldn't you? She is your mum, after all – but it's just that your mother feels, well, that now she's back on her feet again that it's important that you have a little time for yourself. Oh, I know what it's like when your children start to fly the nest – believe me, I've lived through it – and I know it's difficult to adjust to the thought of being on your own –' *Whhaatt*? '– but you're still a young woman and the last thing you want is your cronky old mother under your feet.' She looks tenderly at me. 'You know, sometimes, being on your own is the best way forward. The best way to *grow*. To make a life for yourself. Particularly given, well, your situ*ation*, of course.' *Whhhaaattt*? 'I don't know what she's said to you, but I know she's been ever so worried about you, dear. Which is why she feels it's for the best that you have a little time and space to yourself without having to run around looking after her. And I absolutely agree with her. I'd just be mortified if I thought you felt I was stealing her away from you, that's all.'

I put my tea down and pick up my slice of raspberry sponge. I have a fancy that she's actually reading from a script. 'That's very thoughtful of you, Celeste,' I manage to muster through the cake. 'And, really, I'm absolutely fine. About everything.'

She beams at me. '*Good*. I'm glad we've got that sorted.' She pats me again. Should I wag my tail as well now, perhaps?

It takes me several bites of cake to digest the salient points of Celeste's speech. And I find myself quite at a loss as to whether to feel relieved it's all sorted, upset at Mum's chutzpah, or just plain-old in a huff that the most salient point is that because of what Mum's said to her, and she's obviously been doing so, Celeste seems to think I need patting. Just what has she told her? And why? But then it occurs to me that there are many, many ways of getting through endless grey voids, and re-inventing yourself as a post-modern martyr is actually probably quite a sound one. My mother is an actress. Fiction is her business. So facts get blurred too. What of it?

So I'm glum and fed-up. That's a fact, for sure. And does it really matter now whether I'm glum because of her? *Am* I even, in fact? When I think about it hard? Yes, I *was*. That's a given. That's always been a given. But things have moved on since that momentous day in June. Now I'm glum big-time; cinemascope glum. And that really has nothing to do with my mother, and everything to do with the weather.

I'm just thinking that, when my mother reappears in the living room with her glasses on her nose. And brandishing the post I gave her. Amongst which, it seems, on this occasion anyway, there is something more thrilling than personalised offers of unsecured loans at Extremely Competitive Rates. 'Saints alive!' she cries. 'There is a God after all!'

We both blink up at her, startled. She's flapping a letter in front of her. 'What, Diana?' says Celeste. 'Tell us! What's happened?'

'Salvation!' she declares. 'Oh, pinch me, Cel. I can't believe it!'

'Believe what?'

She pauses to inspect herself in the nearest mirror. 'That I've got a job!'

'A job?' says Celeste. 'What sort of job exactly?'

'Well, an *acting* job, of course. What do you think?'

I'm certainly not thinking she's been invited to appear on Strictly Come Dancing, that's for sure. I reach for the letter she's handing to me. And scan it. And, coo, she's right. She does have a job, too.

She claps her hands together. 'And there was me thinking he was dead!'

Celeste shakes her head. '*Who* was dead? Diana, you are making no sense.'

'Her agent,' I tell her. 'The letter's from Mum's agent. She's been asked if she'd like to make a TV commercial.'

'And how flattering!' She whips off her reading glasses and primps her hair in the mirror. 'Me! I mean I know June Whitfield's knocking on a bit too, but haven't I seen one of those with Linda Bellingham in it?'

Celeste spreads her hands. 'Linda Bellingham in *what*?'

'Oh, you know, Cel. They're *always* on the television. Those ads for insurance policies you can buy to pay your funeral expenses.'

'Charming!' says Celeste.

Mum laughs. 'Who cares? They're damned lucrative too, believe me.'

'Speaking of ads,' I say, the mention of funerals having caused me to remember. 'Hugo's car. I was speaking to Dee earlier. And I wondered if perhaps she could borrow it. She doesn't have the money to buy one at the moment, but it occurred to me that as it's just sitting there rusting, and no one seems interested in buying it, she could use it until she gets back on her feet, and then maybe Jake could still have it after all.'

My mother claps her hands together again, all at once alight with good cheer and bonhomie, and I marvel. That a simple request to do a couple of days work could make such a huge difference to her life. But then I realise that has *always* been her life, more or less.

'Oh, of course she can!' she says expansively. 'What an excellent idea. Yes, yes. Of course. Do whatever you will with it, darling.' She pops her glasses back on and picks the letter up again. 'Do not go gentle into that goodnight! Rage! Rage! Against the dying of the light!'

'Beg pardon, dear?' says Celeste, somewhat startled.

'Dylan Thomas,' I tell her.

'In*deed*!' cries my mother. 'And now I must get on to Lance about this lovely, lovely, lovely, *lovely* news!'

And I have to get on with life as well. I still have to take all Seb's ski gear to the post office and walk Spike and do Jake's washing and...and...well, and.

I go out to the car and manhandle the mirror from the back, then carry it back up the front garden path.

Mum's standing in the doorway, holding it open for me. Beaming. Her default expression for a while now, I guess. Which is, I decide, no bad thing.

Oh,' she says, just as I'm carrying it inside. 'What with all this excitement, I almost forgot!'

'Forgot what?'

'Forgot about the watch!'

'What watch?'

'Hugo's, of course! Hang on there. I'll have to go up and fetch it from my bedroom.'

She ascends the stairs once again, as if propelled on faerie feet, and returns moments later with a small cloth pouch, from which she tips a fob watch into my hand.

The metal is cold. 'What's this?'

'It was Hugo's. I found it earlier in the week, when I was sorting out some of the things Pru bought over. In the bottom of my old jewellery box. I had entirely forgotten it existed. Go on, open it. See what it says.'

It's very old, obviously. And very gold. And somewhat heavy. I prise open the cover, and Mum points. 'There. See?'

It's inscribed. Inside the lid it says *Gabriel Ash. With gratitude*. And underneath, *1952*. I feel a lump form in my throat. How ridiculous *am* I? I swallow it. 'Well, I never,' I say.

'It belonged to Hugo's father. I imagine it was presented to him when he left some job or other. Anyway, there it is. I thought Gabriel would like it.'

'I'm sure he would.' I close it up, and Mum passes me the pouch. I slip it back inside and hand it back to her. But she shakes her head.

'No, no,' she says. 'You take it.'

'Me?'

'That's why I brought it down, silly. For you to give to him.'

'Me?' I say again.

'Yes, of course you. I told the girl you'd give it to him when he came to the clinic.'

'What girl?'

'The girl I spoke to at the BBC. He wasn't in when I called so she said she'd pass on the message.'

'But he doesn't come to the clinic any more.'

'Doesn't he? Oh, well, no matter. He can pop round for it or something. Anyway, I dare say he'll be in touch. It's rather splendid, isn't it?' She presses it into my palm once again. 'And you know, dear, here's the funny thing. As soon as I saw it, it all came back to me.'

'What did?'

'The business with the watch. Oh, it was years ago, now. Before I married him even. But I remember saying at the time what a shame it was that he didn't have a son or a grandson to pass it on to. And you know what he said?'

'No, I don't know what he said.'

'It was the strangest conversation. He said – and I remember it now, clear as yesterday. He said, 'Oh, I dare say it'll find it's way home.' Such an odd thing to say, when you think about it, wasn't it? But what with the name and everything, it makes perfect sense now.' She pats the hand with the watch in and opens the door for me. 'Poor Hugo.'

'Poor Hugo.'

'God rest the old bugger.' She mwah-mwahs my cheeks. Order is restored. 'Do remember to send Gabriel my love.'

# Chapter 28

LOTS OF THINGS MAKE sense. Umbrellas make sense. Non-stick frying pans make sense. Even fiendish Su Dokus make sense once you've licked them. What does not make sense, however, is the fact that now my mother has gone from my house, it suddenly seems so much smaller.

As if the walls are closing in on me. As if, without the constant white noise of her presence, I have nothing to buffer me from the thoughts in my head.

And I wish I could whistle up some better ones, frankly. This lot must have been a bunch of Friday afternoon ones. They're all completely substandard and of no use at all. And worse, they're all of a mind, too. It wouldn't be so bad if I could lay hands on a nice one. That it's the weekend, perhaps. That I have a nice job. That my boys are such a joy. That I'm healthy (if not wealthy), that I have all my teeth. That there's nothing so bad that it can't be made better. That life's a bloody minestrone. *Anything*.

But I can't seem to find one. They've all flown the nest.

And I am doubly bereft on this bright and frosty late October morning, because I am standing outside Jake's high school and waving him off on a coach. He's going on a geography field trip for four days, where he will, or so he tells me, be standing thigh deep in water for the most part, apparently measuring stones. All part of the business of quantifying the fact that in the fast-flowing environment that is your average river, the rocks that fall in, having sheared off whatever mountain they were originally a part of, are progressively tumbled and whittled and blasted, all the way on their long, long journey to the river mouth, thus when they reach the coast they are much reduced in size. Which is why you get sand at the seaside.

It's called weathering. Which to my mind is a word that has no business invading my brain, being altogether too much the same as weather. And the weather round these parts is as bleak as can be. Oh, I wish I was going with him. I wish I was going to the seaside. I wish…

'What *do* I wish, Spike, eh?' I ask him once we've got home, parked the car and transferred instead to Hugo's. Which is mildly unpleasant on account of having to sit on his revolting discoloured plastic seat covers. 'That's just the trouble with making wishes, isn't it? That it's a complete and utter waste of *anyone's* time. And sometimes dangerous to boot. Mark my words.' I turn the engine over and it hacks at me twice, before finally, reluctantly, convulsing into life. It coughs a bit more, obviously indignant about being pressed into service once again.

'That was me, that was,' I tell Spike as we pull out into the road. 'Out of practice. Caught napping. All this time I've spent up on blocks, romantically speaking, and then – bam – I get a boot up the carburettor by Charlie, and as a consequence everything's working again. Which is no good thing, let me tell you, my little munchkin. Not for nothing do people put plastic covers on their car seats.' I squint into the mirror. He's sitting on the parcel shelf. And doesn't have a clue what I'm on about, clearly. 'They do it,' I explain, 'to stop them getting dirty. Keep them pristine and protected and safe. Whereas…' I brake, to let a squirrel cross the road. 'Whereas once you expose them to the elements, to people, it takes no time at all for them to spoil. Tell you what, mate, you may not have liked it at the time but believe me you are *so* much better without your reproductive equipment. God, let me tell you, affairs of the heart are appallingly painful. You know? I really don't know which is worse. The thought that Gabriel Ash might want to come and get his watch back or the thought that he might decide not to.'

When I get to Tim's place, which, now I see it in daylight, is a modern two-bed terrace on the edge of a pretty and well tended estate, Dee is out in the immaculate little front garden wearing gardening gloves and a sleeveless puffa jacket and attacking a flowerbed with gusto. Her cheeks are pink. Her stomach is swelling. She looks like Demeter, the goddess of the harvest.

And now she has a Nissan Sunny too.

'Oh, this is brilliant!' she says, having made her inspection. She is clearly more grown-up than I am about cars, and altogether less fond of looking gift horses in the gasket. 'And it is just *so* sweet of your mum. You must give me her address so I can send her some money. Something, at least. I'm so grateful.'

I follow her back into the house, where something rich and autumnal and parsnippy is cooking, filling the hallway with sweetness and warmth.

'I told you,' I say. 'She won't hear of it. She reckons that with the repeat fees she'll get from this advert she's making, she'll be rich enough to take taxis everywhere anyway. And she's probably right. They run to thousands. And Jake's completely beside himself, of course. He's already ticking off the days till his seventeenth. So everybody's happy.'

'Except you,' she says, now giving *me* the once over. 'You look glum.'

'It's just the botox.'

'Yeah, right. As if. Look. Tell you what. Why don't you come over to us for dinner tonight? Be nice for you to have a chance to get to know Tim properly. And Hattie, too. That's his daughter. She's staying over tonight. We're going to have a bit of a Halloween thing going on. Nothing major. Just a pumpkin and a couple of skeletons and so on.'

I don't know about pumpkins but I rather think I'm up to here with skeletons, really. Particularly the one that was holed up in Hugo's closet. Everything would have been so much better if he'd stayed there. I shake my head.

'That's really sweet of you,' I say. I look out into the back garden, which is a jungle of truly Amazonian proportions, and am tickled that, away from the eyes of the world, there's a different side to life round these parts. 'But, oh, I don't know, Dee. Now Jake's gone off I'd kind of earmarked this evening for a spot of self-indulgent moping about in front of the telly, to be honest. You know, get in a bit of practice for when I really do have an empty nest on my hands.'

She looks appalled. 'Gracious, Abs! this is *so* not like you! No. I won't hear of it. I absolutely insist. I will *not* have you sitting in the doldrums.'

I know about the doldrums. The doldrums are not a state of mind, but a place. A region somewhere in some part of the South

Atlantic Ocean, where the weather conspires to be petulant and wicked and causes sailing ships to have, well, no means of transportation, because there isn't any wind to blow them on their way. So they sit (or so they sat; I imagine these days, they'd fire the motor) completely without the tools, and thus the impetus, to leave. I don't know where I learned that and I could be wrong about the ocean, but I remember it now, because that's just how I feel.

Tim drives Spike and me back in his prehistoric jeep, which is every bit as jolly and dishevelled as he is, and a part of what he does when he's not inventing software. He works for a charity in his spare time, planting trees. I think I'm going to like Tim. He's sweet and quite shy and he's nothing like Malcolm, and I think he'll make Dee very happy. He tells me a joke on the way home that makes me laugh. I know I'll forget the punchline in twenty-seven seconds, but I'm grateful to have done so, for all that.

He also talks to me a little about his brother, the alcoholic, and how meeting Dee – the silver lining in that black cloud, he tells me – has so comprehensively transformed his life. And also just a little – he seems not at all the sort for whining – about how difficult his own has been since his divorce.

'But isn't that just the great thing about life?' he says as he drops us. 'You slog along miserably, thinking things will never get better. But you never know what's around the corner.'

And even though I come away with the distinct impression that I've just been given a bit of a pep talk – *God*, now Dee's at it as well – it seems Tim might be right, even so. Because when I let Spike and me in, still thinking dark thoughts about all the corners I've been round in the last six months and how most of them have involved me in crashing headlong into something I'd rather have avoided, the first thing I see is a small piece of card on the doormat. I pick it up. It's a Cardiff County Council parking voucher, which, or so the scratched off panels tell me, was used at 10.45 on the 8th September. Which has absolutely no relevance to anything that I can think of. I turn it over, nonplussed. And then am altogether *too* plussed. Because there's something of unequivocal relevance scribbled in ballpen on the back.

*Sorry I missed you. Tried to call but no luck. On way to Exeter
for a few days to escape the paparazzi...Was hoping to catch you.
Call me sometime? G xx*

I take it into the kitchen and put it on the worktop while I wonder
at the mysteries of the endocrine system and whether I should ask
for a refund. Mine's now a shambles. A complete and utter
shambles. I pick up my mobile. Which is also in cahoots. Two
missed calls. I check them. Both from *G xx* too. I put it down. I
consider. I feel sick.

Proper sick. Sick, as they say, to the stomach. And as I don't
much like feeling sick at the best of times, I decide on an
immediate salt water gargle. It's just a simple transaction. Just the
giving of a watch. Make the call. Get it over with. That's the best
thing.

I pick my phone up again. I press reply. And then I wait.

'Abbie!'

The sound of his voice leaves me, somewhat frustratingly,
utterly unable to speak. Which takes me completely unawares as
well as firmly by the larynx. So by the time I do manage to get
any words out, they all come at once, like the bubbles from a
bottle of shaken-up Coke. 'Gabriel? I'm sorry I missed you. I'd
popped out and my mobile was at home on the charger and, well,
I got your note through the door and saw you'd called and
everything and, well, sorry. Um. Anyway, yes. Fine. Pop round
when you get back from wherever it is you're going...er...'

I imagine their flight from the rabid photographers. How
curious and alien a life they must lead. 'Look,' he says, his voice
straining above the roar of the traffic. 'I can't talk right now. I'm
driving down the M5 and we're going through some road works.
I don't want to get arrested. Can I call you right back?'

'Oh, I'm sorry. Of course. Absolutely. No problem.
I'll...um...well. No need to call, really. I'll see you whenever I
see you.'

'No, no. I'll get back to you. Soon as I can.'

When Seb was small – two or three – he had a thing about
balloons. A real full-on phobia, in fact. He loved them – what
tiny child doesn't? – but he was petrified about anyone popping

them. So balloons didn't get popped in the McFadden household. Just became retired. Put out to grass. Parked away in corners, under beds, into cupboards, or left to waft, abandoned, round the garden.

That's just how I feel right now, I decide. Like an aged balloon that never got popped. Just quietly deflating back into itself, till it's nothing but a sad wrinkled shadow of its former self. Yup. That's exactly how I feel. Damn, but I wish I hadn't phoned him.

I hang about near the phone for some time, even so. Stupid, really. Because Gabriel doesn't ring back, of course. Not that I really expected him to. He's on his way to…where was it he said he was going? I can't remember. Well, whatever. No matter. I shouldn't have rung him. Speaking to him is bad for my health.

Cheesecakes, on the other hand, if taken in moderation, are unquestionably good for you. The making of them even more so, as it involves nothing more emotionally draining than the prospect of a less than tight seal on your tin. Which, in the scheme of things, just ain't that tragic.

So Spike and I compile our short list of ingredients and then we head off to the Spar. I could have hopped in the car and driven to the supermarket, of course, but the idea is distinctly unappealing. It will be too full of families, piloting huge trolleys. Filling them with giant-sized packs of comestibles, gallons of pop, packets of washing powder the size of small tractors and three-for-two flagons of liquid soap and shampoo. Reminding me that many of the things that must pass in this life have, for me, already done so. That I'm a lone woman (okay, only for four days, but I'm in a self-indulgent mood), with no one to shop for, no one to cook for, no one to look after except a middle-aged dog.

Perhaps, I decide, I should get a cat too. Go the whole hog and start buying products that come in individually wrapped packets – 'for freshness!' – and those peculiar full-height-but-half loaves of bread.

In short, I feel lonely, so the Spar suits us best. We can go there together. And shop with all the others who have no pressing need to buy twenty-seven loo rolls at once.

And it does make me feel better. Better, that is, until I assemble my cache of ingredients in the kitchen and realise I've forgotten to buy biscuits.

Thus it is that I'm in the hall, clipping on Spike's lead for our second Spar sortie, when I become aware of a shadow in the glass in the door. And then movement, and shortly after, the bing-bong of the doorbell.

So I open it. Expecting Mr Davidson, maybe. Or little Sam from the house on other side, who's six, and often kicks his Bob the Builder ball into our garden. Or the man who sells onions. Or double-glazing. Or dusters. Or, well, *someone*. Not him. Not *him*.

Yet that's who it is. It can't be, but it is. And he's still got his finger on the button.

'Good God – Gabriel! What are *you* doing here?'

'Oh, dear,' he says, lowering his finger and frowning. 'Have I come at a bad time again?'

My mouth is hanging open. I close it with a snap. 'No, no. Not at all. It's just that I thought you were on your way somewhere.'

He nods now. 'I was.'

'But now you're here instead.'

He has his serious face on. 'I said I'd get back to you, didn't I?'

'Yes, but –'

'So, here I am.' He takes in my coat, my woolly mittens, Spike's lead. 'Except you're off out somewhere, are you?'

I peer out, past him, to scan the road for his car. Where's Lucy? I can't see her. They were escaping the paparazzi. That's what the note said. She should be here. But she isn't. Unless he's bundled her up under a blanket in the boot, she's absolutely not in his car.

Perhaps he's dropped her off somewhere else. I try to gather myself. 'Only to take Spike for a walk down to the shops. I have to get digestive biscuits. I'm making a blood and guts cheesecake. I'm off to a Halloween soirée tonight. Have to make an effort. You know how it is.' I don't know why I'm telling him all this rubbish. No that's not true. I know exactly why I'm telling him all this rubbish. It's because I cannot right now think of a single thing to say. So rubbish it is, then. 'And, er…well, goodness!' I say, opening the door wider to wave him inside and behaving for all the world like a functioning mortal. 'When you said you'd get back to me I thought you were going to phone. I didn't think you were actually going to *come* back.'

'Well, to be scrupulously honest, neither did I. My initial plan of action *was* to ring you.' He carefully wipes his feet on the doormat and steps into the hall. He doesn't smell of coconut today. He smells of leather and crisp autumn air. 'So I came off at the next junction and pulled over in a lay-by, and then I thought, what the hell. This is absolute madness. So I thought I might just as well get straight back on the motorway again and drive here instead. So that's what I did.'

I wonder what kind of a dictionary it is that he uses to define the word 'madness'. I don't think Dr Johnson had anything to do with it, for sure. But then I'm all out of trying to fathom Gabriel Ash any more. Plus I mustn't. I must remember that it's bad for my health. I pull off my gloves. 'Well, you're in the nick of time,' I say, still trying to gather up the facts and assemble them into something I can usefully work with. Except I can't. I'm at a loss. And my heart's in my mouth again. 'Five more minutes and you'd have missed me a second time!'

He seems to find this intelligence difficult to digest. Either that or he's got a heart in his mouth too. 'Look, I'm sorry,' he says, frowning again. 'I wasn't thinking. Do you want to get off?'

'No, no. It's fine.' I shrug my coat from my shoulders and slip it over the newel post. 'Hardly life and death, is it? A packet of biscuits. Come on. Come in. D'you want a coffee or something?'

He shakes his head. 'No. No, not really.'

And he says it in such a way that I'm immediately transported straight back to the last time we stood there. For someone so reticent when it comes to making words, he's incredibly verbose on the body language front. He's looking awkward. Uncomfortable. Even a bit shifty. He's come all the way back here on God knows what whim, and now he's here he plainly wants to be gone again. I feel silly that I've taken my coat off. 'Well, then,' I say, crisply. 'In that case, hang on there. I'll go upstairs and get the watch for you. I won't be a tick.'

I turn to mount the stairs, but am only two steps up them when his voice makes me stop. 'Watch?' he asks. 'What watch?'

I turn around again. He looks confused now. He's spreading his palms. '*The* watch,' I tell him. 'Isn't that what you're here for? I assumed you'd called because you'd got my mother's message.'

He shakes his head at me. 'Message? What message?'

'The one she left you last week.'

He shakes his head again. 'I didn't get any message. Mind you, I haven't been there for a few days, so perhaps that's why. What watch?'

'Your grandfather's watch. My mum had it. She found it when she moved.'

'She's gone?'

'Yes.' I nod. 'Yes, she's living with her friend now. And she found it in her jewellery box. She thought you ought to have it. Hang on there and I'll bring it straight down for you now. It's very nice,' I add. 'And it has your name on it, too.'

With which I turn around once more and head off up to my bedroom, where the watch, in its pouch still, sits on my dressing table. Which means I catch my reflection as I go in to get it. Which means I see my face, which is very lightly flushed. And also my expression, which is trying to tell me something. It's all of a fluster. It's looking at me strangely. It's saying, 'Wake up, you silly woman. Get with the programme! Gabriel Ash *has not come here for the watch*.'

And if not for the watch, then why *is* he here? I'd quite like to ask Spike but he's still downstairs. As is Gabriel Ash. In my hallway, and waiting. But not waiting for the watch. *Not waiting for the watch*.

I pick it up anyway and head back out on to the landing, every single bit of me that isn't nailed to another bit, trying to make a bid for kinetic supremacy and in so doing causing the sort of physiological chaos that renders me a wibble of jelly. Thus it's with no small difficulty that I make my way back, step by shaky step, down the stairs.

He's looking at me strangely. I lick my lips. 'Did you escape, then?'

'From what?'

'The paparazzi. Your note. You said you were going to somewhere –'

'To Exeter.'

'That's it. To escape the paparazzi.' I'm back at the bottom of the stairs now. 'What's at Exeter?'

'The Met Office.'

'Oh, yes. Of course.'

Of course nothing. 'I'm going away for a fortnight. Some research I'm involved in there.'

'Oh, I see. Anyway, *did* they catch you?'

He shakes his head. 'No. I told you. I gave them the slip. I doubled back at Tiverton and came here.'

I, I, I. Not we. *I.* My temples are thrumming. 'Tiverton? But that's *miles* away. You drove all the way back here from *Tiverton*?'

He looks like I've accused him of the worst kind of felony. 'Er...yes.'

He manages the smallest, most fleeting of smiles.

'But that's such a...'

Suddenly I stall. I'm about to say that it's such a long way. Except I don't manage to get any further because something else bursts into my poor beleaguered brain. A fortnight? Did he just say a fortnight? In *Exeter*? 'Hang on,' I say. 'Aren't you...well, I thought. I mean...I mean, aren't you and Lucy supposed to be getting *married* next week?' What smile that remained now disappears from his features. 'I read it in *Depth*,' I finish lamely.

I think he's probably about to chide me, as he's already done before. About not believing what I read in the papers. Except he doesn't. He nods. 'I know,' he says. 'We were.'

'But now you're not?'

'But now we're not.'

'Oh. I see...'

'She's already flown out to Antigua. Went on Wednesday.'

'Oh, I see,' I say again. But in truth I see nothing. Suddenly I'm a vole scrabbling round in a storm drain. 'So,' I say. 'You decided to postpone after all, then?' The watch, in its pouch, is growing warm in my hand. 'I must admit, it did seem as if it would be a terrible rush. What with all those politics to sort.' I pull a sympathetic face. 'And so on.' He doesn't join in. And I can't bear the silence. So on I go. 'I guess it makes much more sense to postpone it till after. Though whether fur will still be *de rigueur* next year, I don't know.'

He doesn't laugh. In fact, he looks as if this is actually no laughing matter. 'No,' he says. 'No, Abbie. We haven't postponed it. We're not *getting* married. Not now. Not at all.'

# Chapter 29

MY HAND FLIES TO my mouth at this point, because that's the kind of thing hands do in situations like this. All by itself. Whump. And there it stays. Stays long enough for me to allow all this to sink in. And, boy, it sinks quick. Like a stone. Then bobs back to the surface and brings a friend with it. Why didn't it occur to me before? No wonder he's looking so stressed. So *unhappy*. No wonder. It's *happened*. Candice was *right*.

And here's me twittering on at him like a mad woman and cracking jokes. What an idiot I am. 'Oh, my God, Gabriel,' I say. 'I am so, so sorry.' And then I'm all out of ideas of what to say next. Because what *do* you say when someone says something like that to you? You think you can, but when it happens, you actually *can't*. You can hardly quip 'plenty more fish in the sea'. Or 'all for the best', or 'everything happens for a reason'. Platitudes, all of them. Useless bloody platitudes. The very last things he's going to want to hear right now. And I can't even offer him a bracing cup of tea, because I've already offered him a coffee. All I can do is stand here and say sorry.

So I say it again. At which he points to the watch. Clearly he doesn't wish to dwell. Shut *up*, Abbie.

'Can I see that?'

I'm all flustered. 'Um…yes. Yes, of course.' I pass it to him and he slides it into his palm. Then he opens it, reads the inscription inside, and another small smile comes to visit his features. Then he snaps it back shut and slips it back into the pouch. What on earth's going on inside that beautiful head? All I know is that he's here. And that I don't know what to say.

But I have to say something. So I haul out my standard physiotherapy default. I touch his arm. 'D'you want to talk about it?' I say.

He considers for a moment then he shakes his head slightly. 'Not right now,' he says. 'Later. Yes, later. Not now.'

Later? What later? *When* later, exactly? I take a good gulp of air. Fair enough. O*kay*. But if not that, what *now*? What *does* he want from me? Sympathy? Marriage guidance? A hug? He's come here for *something*. And it's not for the watch. I gesture to it. In for a penny and all that. 'Gabriel,' I ask him. My head is now reeling. 'If you didn't come to get this, then why *did* you come here?'

His frown burrows deeper. Making waves on his forehead. He seems to be finding this question somewhat of a poser all of a sudden. He shifts his weight from one foot to the other, and then chews on his lip for a bit. As so often before, I'm immediately struck by the sense that he's fishing around in that muddled male brain of his, and failing to find anything useful.

And then he does something completely unexpected. He plunges a hand into a pocket in his coat and pulls out a small rubber bone. It's not quite like the one that was purloined by the Airedale. But similar. He stoops down to give it to Spike. Then he speaks to him too. I am now quite at a loss.

'There you are, mate,' he says softly. And he ruffles Spike's fur.

'Thank you,' I say, stunned. 'That was...um...really thoughtful. But you really didn't need to go to all that trouble, you know.'

Not when you've got so much else on your mind. Not when... Oh, God, Abs. Just *not.*

He rises. A touch stiffly. 'No trouble,' he says. 'I was in a pet shop with my niece and I saw it. So I bought it.'

And looks almost embarrassed to be admitting that he's done so. Or maybe just embarrassed full stop. I fold my arms tightly across my chest and observe him. I can barely breathe anyway, so it won't make much difference. 'Gabriel,' I say. 'Are you honestly trying to tell me you drove all the way back here from Tiverton just –' I gesture, '– to give that toy to my *dog*?'

Now he shakes his head slowly. 'No, Abbie,' he says. As if only just having made his mind up. 'I'm not.'

I unfold my arms again. 'Then why *are* you here?'

'You really need to ask that?'

'Yes, I really need to ask that.'

'To tell you I love you,' he says.

\*       \*       \*

There's probably a protocol. There must be. It's like Dear Sir and Yours Faithfully. Rhubarb and custard. Thank you and you're welcome. There *must* be.

I must have seen countless films, read countless books, heard countless stories, any and all of which could readily supply me with an appropriate response to what he's just said, but for the life of me, I can't think of one that feels right.

There's the obvious one, of course. And, to be fair, it's the one that came right into my mind. As it would. Didn't have to travel far, after all. Except my heart's in my mouth and it's getting in the way. I am dumbstruck. Astounded. Can this *be*?

Gabriel is still standing in the middle of my hall, still frowning, still filling the whole space with his increasingly agitated presence. And looking like he's just had a communication down his earpiece that a low pressure system is due in any time.

Which might squash him. 'I'm sorry,' he says. He looks, if anything, even more uncomfortable than at any time I've seen him before. And quite possibly as pole-axed as I am. Bar Charlie, who doesn't count because he says it to everyone, I haven't had a grown man declare that he loves me for something approaching twelve years. He clears his throat. 'I'm sorry,' he says again, searching my dumbstruck expression. 'I shouldn't have sprung that on you, should I?'

Questions, questions. I don't know. Should he? Is there ever a wrong time to tell a woman that you love her?

'No! I mean…well, *yes*, but, *God*, Gabriel. You can't *mean* that!'

He looks astonished himself now. 'Of course I mean it. I *love* you.'

Again. A second time. I *love* you. He *loves* me. 'But –'

He grips both my hands now. 'But nothing. I *do*.'

'But *Lucy* –'

His face clouds again. And then he exhales. And it's a veritable Mount St Helens of a blow. Then he lets go my hands, and brings one of his own up to my face.

'Abbie,' he says, and his voice is very soft now. 'This has been the most appalling and wretched week of my entire life, and

I'd have given anything for it not to have happened. Not to have hurt her. Not to have done such a terrible thing. But it *had* to happen. Because much as I care for her, she isn't *you*.' He moves his thumb across the contour of my cheek. 'Why else do you think I cancelled my wedding?'

'I didn't realise,' I say, feeling the warmth of his palm suffuse my skin. 'I thought *she* had. I thought…oh, God, Gabriel, I don't know what I thought. I don't know what *to* think. This is all just…well. It's just such a lot to take *in*.'

He lowers his hand now, for which I'm really most grateful. It's affecting my balance. It's affecting my brain.

And his too, it seems. He's looking angsty again. Frowning. The hands go back into the pockets and then he's off down the hall. Four strides to the dining room door and then back, Spike looking on, lead in mouth, from halfway up the stairs.

'Oh, God,' he says, as if he'd just whipped Him out for the purpose. 'I've got this all wrong, haven't I?'

I grab the newel post, for support. 'Got what wrong?'

He exhales heavily again. 'About you. About *us*. I thought you knew. I thought you felt the same…I thought…' He's close in front of me again. 'Abbie, are you really trying to tell me that you had no *idea*?'

I shake my head. '*No*. I thought you loved Lucy! Why would I think otherwise?'

'Because…because, God, Abbie, isn't it *obvious*?'

'Yes, *now*.' Gawd, and then some. It's dizzyingly obvious. 'But before – I mean the last time I saw you and everything –'

He grabs my hand again. 'I can't believe what I'm hearing. I honestly can't believe you didn't know.'

'Gabriel, I *didn't*. I thought she…I mean, you looked so *unhappy*. I –'

His face is pale. He grips my hands tighter. 'That's because I *have* been. It's been hell. To have to *do* that to someone…'

'I know, Gabriel. I *know*.' Which is not strictly true. I can't even begin to imagine. Such a terrible decision to have to make. Such a big, big decision. To have to break someone's heart.

And for *me*. Even now, I can barely take it in. He did it because of me. Because he loves me. And no matter how much I would wish things to be otherwise for her sake, for myself, for *my* happiness… 'Oh, Gabriel, this is so *difficult*.' I grab some air. It feels thin. As if I'm beached up at the summit of some mountain as well. Or up in the stratosphere. Up in the clouds. Above the clouds, even. He'd know. Yes, there.

'All right,' I say, because there seems little point now in doing otherwise, really. I've already bared more than my soul to this man. 'Okay, yes,' I say. 'Yes, I thought, Gabriel. I thought lots. I thought all sorts of things I had no business to be thinking. I thought things I didn't even *dare* to be thinking. Because however incredulous you are at the thought, I never thought for so much as a microsecond of an instant that someone like you would fall in love with someone like me. And you were *with* someone, weren't you? You were engaged to Lucy. And so I unthought them quick. Because thinking them *hurt* me. So yes, you're quite right. I had no idea. *Really*. I mean I did but I didn't and I couldn't have wished it because that wouldn't have been right, and I so, so don't want to be someone like my mother, lurching from one pointless infatuation to the next one, but now it *is* right, because you're here and you did that for me and now I'm all in a state and I think I may need to sit down fairly soon. There. Will that do you?'

I thought he'd be relieved. But he's not. Now he's frowning. He lets go one hand and inspects me through narrowed eyes. 'Can you quantify an instant?'

I blink at him. *What*? Can I? yes, I can. 'It's the same as a moment.'

He lifts an index finger. 'Ah, but can you quantify a moment? You know, in temporal terms?'

I am utterly at sea. 'I don't *know*. You tell me. You're the scientist round here, after all.'

He waggles his finger. 'No, you can't. It's too imprecise a term.' He brings his arm down. 'But it'll still do very well for my purpose.'

'*What* purpose?' I ask him. 'You'd better hurry up and tell me, Gabriel, because I think I'm about to keel over at any moment.'

He looks around him. Considers. Then he takes my left hand, and he leads the way through to the living room. And then sits me on my sofa and then sits down beside me. And then gathers up all my wispy overgrown bits of fringe and coils them gently, oh-so-gently, behind my ears.

'The purpose,' he says finally, 'of explaining, *precisely*, just how very little time it took for someone like *me* to fall in love with someone like *you*.'

Time stops for, oh, about twenty-seven years. And when it starts up again, he's still there, just the same. But now he's moving towards me and caressing my face with his fingertips, and his image is blurring because of the tears in my eyes. I brush them away because I want so much to keep it. Crystal-clear in my mind, with the words he's just spoken. Because I really can't believe that something so wonderful will ever be said to me again.

'Or, more precisely,' he murmurs, as he folds his arms around me, 'not someone *like* you. Just you, Abbie. *You*.'

I never thought it was possible to think such utter twaddle, but right now, as our lips meet, it doesn't feel silly. I really *could* drown in his eyes. Swim around a bit first. Feel their charcoal caress. And then just drift into the depths and die happy.

But I'm a level-headed girl and besides, Spike is watching. With his lead still in his mouth and a face on.

Gabriel sees too. 'I think he's feeling left out. Do you think we should take him for his walk?'

*We*. For his walk. Should *we* take him for his walk. Yes, we must, and we will. And we'll do lots of talking. About us. About him. About the watch. About my mother, and his father. About the terrible thing he's had no choice but to do, and about how I shall make him feel better. About all the things – so *many* things – that I don't yet know about him. But we won't buy any biscuits, and Dee really won't mind.

I stand up. I pick Spike up. I take him to the kitchen. I give him some choc drops and I plump up his bed. And when I go back into the living room, Gabriel's standing by the window. Scanning the pink remnants of the low October sunshine, his hands clasped together in his thicketty gold hair.

He turns as I enter and spreads both his arms. 'Spike's tired,' I tell him. 'So he's gone to have a lie down.'

He enfolds me between them. 'Is that so?' he says.

I'm in heaven. I must be. 'Just a short one,' I tell him. 'A power nap. Half an hour, tops.'

He smiles then, and dips his handsome face to meet mine. But then he stops. 'Abbie,' he says, glancing behind me and smiling. 'Why is there an artificial leg on your mantelpiece?'

I turn to look. 'Oh, that. Don't worry. It's not related or anything. It was given to me when I left my job at the hospital. It was our mascot. It was supposed to bring me luck '

His kiss meets my words just as my hands reach his hair. As gloriously golden as an archangel's should be. Celestial. Perfect. He moves his lips softly against my cheek as he speaks. 'And has it been lucky for you, Abbie McFadden?

I kiss him again. Just to be sure I'm not dreaming. 'You know what, Gabriel Ash?' I answer. 'I think it has.'


End

# Epilogue

NOEL, NOEL! A FESTIVE Email from Seb!

Hiyah, Mum. How's it going? Merry Christmas and all that!

Actually, I just thought I'd check in before we head off for the Alps. Jake says Hi. Dad says Hi. Elise says thanks for the chocolates and the cake. Can she have the recipe, plz?

So. What's new? Are you packed yet? We're all over the moon to hear the news about the New Year gig. Think I am going to have one famous little brother! I shall make sure he comes back in one piece...

Oh, by the way, didn't have Nana's new address so have sent her card and stuff in the envelope with yours. That okay? Pass it on when you see her? Hey, and you must tell me when the ad is going to be on. We can pick it up on satellite. LOL!!!!!!

We're leaving for Courcheval sometime tomorrow. 30 cms on the lower slopes already. Hurrah! J and I have a bet on with Dad that we can get down from Saulire back to 1850 before he does. There's beer riding on this so I'm well in training. You'll be missed, of course (natch!) but I guess you won't mind (!!!!)

Can't tell you how pleased J and I are about your trip. We were worried about you being stuck at home on your own over Christmas ☹. (Ahhhh...) You will have such an ACE time. Don't bother about trailing round the Murano factory. They'll only make you buy some awful vase or something. But you must go and have a Bellini in Harry's bar (tho v.v. expensive!). Gabriel sounds cool. (Note from J – NOTHING

311

like H!!!) But amazing how things turn out, huh?! You're having almost as hectic a gap year as me!

Anyway, better dash. Have to go pick up Jon from the station. Off on the piste (again! U can tell, non?) tonite ☺ !!!! (don't worry 'bout J – I will take care of him, promise...) Love to one and all. Give Spike a big hug.

Take care.

Love you Mum.

   Seb xxxxxxx (and Jake!)

PS Oh, and if you spot my sunglasses anywhere in St Mark's Square, grab them for me, ok?!!!!!!!

# About the author...

Lynne Barrett-Lee is the author of five novels and has also been selected to be part of the new Quick Reads initiative with her book, *Secrets.*
Lynne lives in Cardiff with her husband and three children.


For more information please visit
**www.lynnebarrett-lee.com**

# Also by Lynne Barrett-Lee...

## A modern twist on Cinderella

Radio Wales DJ Jack Valentine finds a lost trainer on a station platform. With echoes of Cinderella, he appeals on his show for its owner, Hope Shepherd, to come forward.

Hope handles publicity for a Cardiff based charity, Heartbeat. Encouraged by colleagues to secure Jack Valentine to raise the profile of an upcoming fun run, she reluctantly heads for the studios.

The attraction between Hope and Jack is immediate but, bruised and battered by their recent divorces, they are reluctant to risk romance again

*Barefoot In The Dark* is a bitter-sweet novel about taking the first steps towards trusting again. But when love at first sight is the last thing you're after, is a fairytale ending an impossible dream?

ISBN 9781905170371 price £6.99

A witty and romantic thirty-something novel
about a woman who thinks she may have found
her soulmate - via e-mail.

Fed up, frustrated and fast approaching forty, Charlie Simpson
hasn't had many high points in her life just lately. The only
peak on the horizon is her ambition to climb Everest, if she
could only get organized and save up the cash.
However, via her newly acquired laptop, she stumbles upon a
stranger who's a like-minded soul. Like-minded, perhaps, but
no fantasy dream date. Though virtual, he's of the real-life
variety - he may be a hero, but he has a wife.
Charlie hasn't a husband, but she certainly has principles, and
they're about to be hauled up a mountain themselves. And, of
course, her mum's always said she shouldn't talk to strangers.
The question is, is now the time to start breaking the rules?

ISBN 9781905170166 price £6.99

If you have enjoyed this book
please visit our website at
www.accentpress.co.uk
to discover more great authors like
Grace Wynne-Jones, Jane Wenham-Jones
and Della Galton.

Thank you!